# OUT OF LOVE

*Victoria Clayton*

**ORION**

Copyright © 1997 Victoria Clayton Ltd

*All rights reserved*

The right of Victoria Clayton to be identified as the author of this
work has been asserted by her in accordance with the
Copyright, Designs and Patents Act 1988.

This edition published in Great Britain in 1997 by
Orion
An imprint of Orion Books Ltd
Orion House, 5 Upper St Martin's Lane, London WC2H 9EA

A CIP catalogue record for this book is available
from the British Library

ISBN 0 7528 0728 5

Typeset at The Spartan Press Ltd,
Lymington, Hampshire

Printed in Great Britain by
Clays Ltd, St Ives Plc

# CHAPTER ONE

'Of course you remember the quarrel,' Min said as she looked down at the glass of wine she held and then at me.

Of course, I did. Even now, after so many years, to hear it mentioned made me shiver a little, inwardly. The quarrel was one of those milestones in my past which divided the years sharply into before and after, as firmly embedded in retrospection as leaving school, the death of my father and getting a junior fellowship. I think my hands trembled but I tried hard to keep my expression impassive as I looked at the face of the very best friend I had ever had and remembered it as I had last seen it, fifteen years ago, pale with pain and anger, and in her eyes a look of hatred that had cut me to the heart.

Min put her hand on my arm and I saw, with amazement, that she was smiling.

'Darling Daisy. I can't believe how good it is to see you! Oh God, remember Hugh Anstey? What an ass! What fools we were!'

She began to laugh, causing the earnest young women around us to stare rather wistfully. They were finding conversation with former tutors and deans uphill work. The common room at St Hilary's, Oxford, was gloomy with afternoon light. It was strikingly cold but the fireplace was bare except for a pot of tattered Chinese lanterns. A glass of South African sherry, rather sweet and warm, or a white wine, pistachio green and acidic, was not enough to take the chill from the meeting between dons and alumni. A combination of factors, and prolonged absence of the latter and the social incompetence of many of the former, unhappily mingled in an atmosphere of sombre refrigeration, made many of us wonder why we had been silly enough to come.

Min continued to laugh until her eyes began to water and she had to clutch at my arm for support. I steadied her glass and began to laugh myself. I could not quite match her in abandon. The quarrel had been my fault, and the consciousness that I had behaved very badly made me wince to recall it, like pressing on a painful bruise. When I had seen Min, quite unexpectedly, walk into the common room five minutes before, I had felt such a flood of emotion that my eyes had filled with tears.

By now Min's face was flushed and she was beginning to snort. I led her off to a hard, liver-coloured sofa and sat her down.

'He was rather amusing,' I said. 'And terribly handsome.'

A student approached us with a plate of sausage rolls. 'Do have one of these,' she urged with a zeal which stopped Min in her tracks for a moment. Min looked at the girl's encouraging expression and at the sausage rolls, which lay, greasily deliquescent, within a fringe of yellowing mustard-and-cress, and broke out again into tremendous shouts of laughter. The girl blushed and I took one of the sausage rolls quickly, deploring Min's utter lack of tact and at the same time loving her for it. How could I have allowed fifteen years of my life to go by without Min? I watched her fondly as she searched for, and found, a grubby handkerchief, with which she dried her eyes.

'Min Bartholomew!' The Principal, a fat woman in grey tweeds and a pink botany wool jersey which contrasted oddly with her long, wolfish face, approached us. Min got up, which was the least she could do, but didn't bother to look pleased. 'How many years is it? Dear me – and how is that excellent piece of work going on – who was it? Lamartine?'

No attempt was made to bring me into the conversation but I was too well acquainted with academic manners to feel ruffled. Instead I remained where I was on the sofa, holding the sausage roll between finger and thumb, and thought about Hugh Anstey.

I remembered him as he stood in the drawing room of Foxcombe Manor, holding my hand in his as Mrs Studley-Headlam introduced us. I had thought, lucky, lucky Min, as I ran my eye over his dark curly hair, brown eyes and white teeth. He was tall and lean with pale, unblemished skin. There was a shading of beard about the jaw-bone which was very attractive. Even his hands were well-shaped, with long fingers and unbitten fingernails. I could scarcely fault him except that he had an air of being rather pleased with himself, for which one could hardly blame him.

Min had written to me about him in the gasping, telegraphic style we affected in those days which made us feel sophisticated and Nancy Mitford-ish.

Darling Daze [short for Daisy, which was in turn short for Diana]
Essential you attend Soppy Johnson's dance as too, too heart-breakingly beautiful Hugh is coming and we're madly in love. Profondissimo!! Have made Soppy ask you too – invitation enclosed – and you and Hugh are staying with Mrs Studley-Headlam – American – divine house. I've got to stay with Soppy, groan! but can't be helped. If you come it will be the most perfect evening EVER. Bound to be other dishes. Met Hugh at one of Ma's parties!!! Tell you *everything* when I see you. This is IT.
Deliriously yours,
    Min.
PS You are to arrive at Mrs S-H's at four.

Of course it was not altogether pleasant to find that Sophie Johnson's hand had been forced with regard to my invitation. But as the next few weeks stretched out rather drearily without much happening, I decided to accept. Min's mother (she was a widow) was much grander than mine (divorced). Although Lady Bartholomew's income had shrunk to what was considered penury in her circle, she had kept all her friends and did the rounds of large, cold, country houses and warm, smart London ones, thereby saving herself considerable expense. That she kept her friends was attributable to her intelligence and her loyalty. Though she was witty she was never unkind and this rare quality made her very much liked. Although she had once met my mother and clearly been quite astonished, she had nevertheless continued to ask me to stay and always treated me as one of her own sort. A lot of very good invitations, and some excoriatingly awful ones, had come my way through Min. In fact, to be truthful, any social pretensions I might have had I owed entirely to her.

My mother was the daughter of a composer. At least that is what I said when anyone asked me. In fact my grandfather had written tunes for dance bands, one or two of them winning a brief popularity and enabling my mother to go to art school. She had discovered a minimal talent there and also a violent and abiding love for artists. Paris had followed and, according to her, sublime, smoky, spirituous existence in ateliers, draining life's cup. Certainly there seemed to have been plenty of dregs, mostly in the shape of my mother's lovers. They had been fat, thin, bearded, bald, rich, poor, sadistic, masochistic, Rabelaisian, poetic, alike only in their devotion to art and, briefly, to my mother. For a woman basically plain, (eyes rather too close together . . . fortunately I look like my father) it was remarkable how attractive she was to men. It was something to do with her constant excited involvement with whatever was going on. She could find diversion anywhere. Even a Parents' Day at my snobbish little boarding school in Sussex was transformed by her presence into something full of potential for amusement. On one occasion she astounded my headmistress and the Domestic Bursar by claiming to have met the latter at Cannes.

'It was that wonderful party given by Lambert – such a charmer – what a rake – you were wearing something rather delicious with feathers!'

'I can assure you . . .' Miss Dill, a waspish spinster of fifty, began.

'Nonsense! I remember you distinctly. Of course I was surprised. But my goodness, you've earned a little fun! Who could grudge it!'

'Mrs Fairfax!' Miss Dill drew her thin frame up stiffly, seeing the expression on the Headmistress's face. 'I must contradict you, I am afraid. I have never been to Cannes in my life!'

'I seem to have put my foot in it,' said my mother, winking conspiratorially at her. 'Not another word to anyone about it. Oh look, Lady Wilton! I must speak to her. So good to see you again.'

It was one of the few times when I distinctly felt, as she turned away with another wink especially for me, that I loved my mother after all.

The trouble was that there were too few of these times. In

4

general you could guarantee that wherever or whenever she had told you to expect her, she would fail to turn up. I tried to train myself not to expect her so as to avoid disappointment. But however hard I tried there was always an irrepressible fraction of hope that she might come. Like most children I was agonisingly superstitious and I jumped pavement cracks, counted cherry stones, went up stairs two at a time holding my collar, and made up complicated penances to be done in order to invoke her presence. When the magic failed to have the wished-for effect I felt enough misery and guilt to give me a real stomach-ache.

I was less than a year old when my parents divorced. According to my mother, they had met at a party and my mother had been very much attracted by my father's hand-some face and aristocratic hauteur. They had had a brief liaison during which I had been conceived. My mother often said that it was a mistake to have told him as there was a discreet doctor she knew of who could have dealt with the problem at a very reasonable charge. As it was, my father insisted on marrying her. Perhaps he was even in love with her at this stage. And she, no doubt, dreamed of a little painting and very much more partying, comfortably sheltered by money and a handsome, complaisant husband. But by the time I was born things had gone badly wrong between them. My father retired to an ugly stone house in Kircudbrightshire to nurse his two passions, the iconography of Romanesque reliquaries and his hatred of my mother.

I was five when Hitler invaded Poland. The *carpe diem* attitude which prevailed generally in England after this suited my mother's temperament exactly. But a child was an encumbrance in this reckless enjoyment. I was sent to Kircud-brightshire but I was wretchedly lonely and frightened of everything . . . the cold, dark house, the housekeeper who, I think from the bits of strange behaviour I recall, must have been a drunk, and, most of all, of my father. I remember nothing of him from that time except that he was very tall and very thin and that when I was taken to his room on my arrival he offered to shake hands with me. His hand was very cold and bony. That night I woke the house with my screams, dreaming about a picked-clean corpse who was trying to get into bed with me. Its ribs were as sharp as blades, opalescent and gleaming as though just stripped of flesh. The dream returned nearly every night and after a few weeks I was returned to my mother in disgrace. In those days the only people who had 'nerves' were veterans of the Great War and charwomen.

My mother sent me to boarding school in the country, ostensibly to shelter me from the Blitz. The bills were met by my father and at the beginning of each term I received an envelope containing a five-pound note. This was very generous but I understood from the absence of any message that I was not forgiven. I did not see my father again for thirteen years.

For two years I scarcely saw my mother either. Holidays were spent with my housemistress. It was during this period that the elaborate rituals for conjuring up my mother were formulated. The most exacting consisted of stealing the housemistress's penknife from her desk, a frightening enough thing to do in itself, and then cutting the palms of my hands with it. I was inspired by the wooden carving of Christ on the rood screen in the school chapel. The first time I did it the pain was so bad that I fainted in class and had to be taken to the sanatorium. Sister seemed satisfied with my story, that I had picked up a piece of glass from the greenhouse. She was beginning a lecture on disobedience, for we were forbidden to play there, when she was called away to the telephone. It was the headmistress, with a message from my mother to say that she was coming to visit that afternoon. I almost fainted again with the shock. I felt delirious with power. Now, I thought, I had control of my mother and could summon her whenever I wished.

Of course, to my anguish and frustration, the trick never worked again. I tried repeating it exactly, then I tried variations, saying a 'Hail Mary' while I pushed the blade in, and so forth. There was almost pleasure in the pain and I loved the beads of blood that trembled on my skin, like rubies. But all that happened was that my hands became infected and the doctor was sent for. Sister told him that I was absurdly careless and naughty. The doctor's half-moon spectacles frightened me very much but he was an intelligent man and the father of four girls. He coaxed the truth out of me and then explained that the stratagem would not work again because no one could really have control over someone else in that way. It would be dangerous and wrong and God would not allow it. I made the decision pretty much on the spot to abandon God since he was clearly not only incomprehensible but also very unco-operative. The doctor gave me a prescription for M&B and then asked me to come to his house to tea the next day to meet his daughters. They were pretty and kind and quite a lot older. They treated me like a baby sister, which I adored. After that I often went to visit them and some of the grief I felt for my absent mother was assuaged.

The following term Min arrived at school. I first saw her standing in the entrance hall, in a uniform which was several sizes too large, looking bewildered while Miss Lewin berated her for her slovenly appearance. There was a large ink stain on the front of her tunic and her hem hung down at the back.

'You need not think, Minerva Bartholomew, that because your mother is a friend of the Chairman of the Governors, I shall tolerate slipshod ways.' Miss Lewin was a small, stout bully with a pigeon chest and an angry mauve face. Her suspicion that Min would be favoured by the headmistress, with whom Miss Lewin was passionately and unrequitedly in love, made her Min's enemy from the start. She beckoned to me.

'Diana, Minerva is in your dormitory this term. Show her where to go and make sure that she is presentable by the tea-bell.'

Min, having been looked after by the nannies and governesses of rich relations, was perfectly helpless in every practical sense. It was her first experience of school and she might have been a purblind kitten for all the sense she made of it. She explained to me that she had got the ink-stain from having tried to fill her fountain pen in the train. She had only ever used a dip pen and had not realised that squeezing the bladder of the fountain pen twice instead of once would have a catastrophic effect. She had caught her heel in the hem of her tunic when getting off the train.

'Nanny Porson stitched it up as it's hopelessly too long. Mummy must have bought quite the wrong size for me. She ordered it by telephone from Scotland and the line's very bad. Nanny Porson's only put about ten stitches in it all the way round. It's never going to stay up unless perhaps you've got some glue?'

She looked at me despairingly, a smut from the train

blackening her nose, and sniffed. I could see that she was on the edge of tears. Life at a girls' boarding school was brutal. It was a sign of unforgivable weakness to be seen on friendly terms with any girl who was in the smallest degree vulnerable. There existed an inner circle, a hegemony of bold, good-looking girls who were powerful and very much feared. Then there was an assemblage, much larger, of lesser beings, spiteful, unimaginative and orthodox. Roaming miserably on the outside were the pariahs, girls who looked odd, fat or ugly or who lacked self-confidence. Sometimes they were eccentric on arrival, usually they became so after several terms of the severest isolation and unkindness. The loneliness was unremitting for it would never have occurred to the staff, who were all themselves grown-up pariahs, to treat any of the girls with friendliness. I could never understand why the outcasts didn't befriend each other, if only for companionship, but they hardly ever did.

I had fought hard for a position commanding respect and had had to overcome the considerable obstacle of my mother. I had gained the high ground solely because of my looks and a certain sharpness of tongue for I was not good at games nor did I have money or connections, which were the easy routes to position and popularity. It was obvious at a glance that Min was quite unlike the other girls. She was candid and unaffected, naive in fact. She was unsophisticated and unfashionable. One word of disapproval from me to the other girls and she would be condemned to years of unrelieved loneliness.

I scrubbed at the ink-stain until the surface of the cloth was sodden and snagged but more or less clean. Then I began to sew the hem of her tunic with neat stitches. Needlework was the obligatory occupation of wet weekends when the others had gone home so I was very good at it.

'Gosh, how clever!' said Min, watching me. 'I can't ever keep my needle threaded. You must let me do something for you in return.'

She looked about desperately at my tidy cubicle, with its green and white cotton counterpane and ugly yellow-varnished furniture, seeking inspiration. Then she said, 'Would you like to come home with me next weekend? Our cook makes the best apple crumble and our cat's had kittens. There are four of them, one ginger, two black and one tabby.

They're more beautiful than anything you've ever seen in your whole life!'

Her eyes filled with tears again and my heart, generally so well defended, was touched. Usually if I went to stay with the other girls they felt obliged to put on a good show for me so that I should report back on their enviable, fashionable home lives. It was a terrible strain for everyone, not least me, and there was always a wretched sense of effort about it. The idea of apple crumble and kittens as an inducement was novel and, to me, immensely attractive. I helped Min unpack her things and while I was re-plaiting one of her braids which had come unfastened during the journey, explained as many shibboleths as there was time for before the bell rang for tea. Most of them struck Min as quite ridiculous and, seen through her eyes, I realised that they were pretty absurd. By the time I had told her about bending the knee to the portion of St Sexburgha's little finger which was housed in the chapel, we were both giggling.

I spent a good deal of time that term rescuing Min from disaster and shielding her from the acid tongue of Miss Lewin. To my astonishment I found that looking after her acted as a balm to my secret feelings of pain at my mother's neglect of me. My attempts to mother Min and her gratitude and reliance gave me confidence. I realised, with great surprise, that I did not like my mother, nor did I want to be like her in any way. The expansion of feelings and ideas that followed was bewildering and intoxicating.

Min cared nothing for the opinion of the other girls and was generally oblivious to the barbs and slights by which we retained our power. This resilience and her tendency to find things funny, especially the things that had been held sacred by the rest of us, won her a wary respect and after a while they left her alone. Naturally I had not seen myself as absurdly solemn, over-dramatic and over-sensitive. I had, until that point, been wholly lacking in self-awareness. Min's sharp eye for the pretentious, ridiculous and comical fundamentally changed my own view. She felt grateful to me for my protection but I know now, looking back, that my debt to her was immeasurably greater. By the end of the term we were fast friends, helped, most probably, by all these things but in the main due to the unfathomable chemistry which ferments all human relationships.

As for the weekends of kittens and puddings which rapidly became a part of my life, they were undoubtedly the happiest times of my childhood. As soon as Lady Bartholomew understood that my mother rarely visited me, and my father never, a standing invitation was given. Lady Bart, as everyone called her, received many invitations. As she explained to us, though she hated not to see Min for a single minute when she was home, she needed to accept some invitations or else fall out of society altogether. In which case, when Min was grown up, she would have a lonely mother as a dreadful burden on her hands. So on Saturday evenings she would go out, looking very elegant and pretty, to the lavish parties or smart little dinners of her friends while Min and I would go down to the kitchen of the tiny London house and play with the kittens and eat apple crumble, jam roly-poly, meringues, gooseberry tart, or any of the wonderful things produced by Gina, Lady Bart's Italian maid.

Gina was everything that a cook in a private household should have been and so rarely was. For a start she could actually cook very well, both English and Italian food. For us she made the simple things we preferred but on the occasions when Lady Bart had a supper party at home, we would watch with admiration as Gina flipped a turbot out of its diamond-shaped pan, dressed game or decorated pies. On one magnificent occasion she assembled a *croque-en-bouche* encased in a spun-sugar cage of finest glassy, amber threads. As we grew older she was delighted to find that we liked *torta sabbiosa*, *bomboloni* and all the sweetmeats of her childhood.

It was Gina who taught me to appreciate food and to respect the art of cooking. I spent many happy hours at her side, learning how to roll pastry and beat egg-whites while Min, who wasn't interested in cooking, read aloud to us the romantic novels that Gina loved. Gina was wonderfully good-tempered and never minded that Min would sometimes mock the story or the characters. She laughed with us, happy in our company, happy that we both loved her. Sometimes we lay with the cats on the rag rug in front of the range and listened to Gina's stories of life in the great palazzo where she had worked as a maid when she was young and pretty. The kittens grew up and were found homes but others were born and were idolised, kissed and played with in their turn. As substitutes for my own parents Lady Bart and Gina could hardly have been bettered.

The only period when my mother was almost regular in her appearances at school was during the six years when she had as her lover a man called Poppy. He was Greek, with a polysyllabic name unpronounceable by English tongues so he was called Poppy by everyone. He was dark and plump with a black pencil moustache and oiled black hair. His eyes were large and moist and protuberant, either melancholy or weeping with laughter. He was a man of extremes. He was the only one of my mother's lovers who took any real interest in me. The others occasionally bought me presents but it was Poppy who took me out for ice-creams and to the cinema. He was a great crier and we sat through all the Disney films in various states of unhappiness, from mild to extreme. Poor Poppy was made as wretched as I was by the maternal divestments of Dumbo and Bambi and we both cried all the way home on the bus after seeing the soldiers and horses falling through the ice in *Alexander Nevsky*. Poppy's shirt-front was stiff with salt after *Anna Karenina* though I liked the snow and the fur-trimmed clothes. When poor Moby Dick was harpooned by Captain Ahab, Poppy let out a howl of rage and sorrow and the usherette told him he would have to leave if he couldn't be quiet.

He read to me a great deal, his bulging, dark eyes welling and his voice thickened with emotion at the rejection of the Ugly Duckling and the death of the little Match-girl. We never got to the end of *Black Beauty* as my mother threw the book on the fire. She said it was like living with two alcoholics, intolerably maudlin and full of self-pity. She wanted to be able to enjoy half an hour without someone grizzling about Poor Ginger. Actually, I think that both Poppy and I were secretly relieved not to have to go on with it.

It was Poppy who remembered my birthday and, more importantly, reminded my mother of it. On my seventh birthday he gave a party for me in his studio. He made a cake covered with blue icing and we drank blue lemonade and smoked pretend cigarettes of marigold petals. He made crowns out of sweets and gold paper for each of the prim little girls I had invited, and we played wonderful games with paint and glue and sequins and tissue paper. Then we made a painting by jumping and rolling over a huge canvas in our vests and knickers. Though he made us take off our party dresses it was remarkable how much paint managed to get on to them. He gave each child, now very dishevelled and overexcited, a live rabbit to take home. No doubt there was endless trouble later over ruined party frocks and probably everyone came out in spots from too much food-colouring. I shudder to think what became of the rabbits. But at the time I thought it had been the most wonderful party ever dreamed of and for a while I enjoyed an immense popularity with my friends.

Once, when I had a high fever, Poppy sat up with me all night, giving me aspirin, clearing up sick, pouring drinks, sponging my face, and finally taking me to the hospital in a taxi when the doctor diagnosed appendicitis. My mother came the next day with chocolates and a guilty conscience and spent the visiting hour charming the nurses with tales of her Bohemian past. But it was Poppy who took to us Brighton for a week so that I could get better and who sat with me on the pebbles making crinoline ladies out of shells while my mother went shopping.

Almost the last time I saw Poppy was when he came to my boarding school when I was twelve. It was the school play and we were doing *Selections from Shakespeare*. I was Hamlet, more because I was tall and could remember my lines than because of my acting ability. I thought I looked rather good in black doublet and hose and I felt very pleased with myself until I saw Mother and Poppy. Mother looked almost reasonable with her hair streaked red and gunmetal and wearing a black dress. Poppy was wearing a suit he had had made out of dress fabric . . . a white background with flaming scarlet poppies all over it. Among the dark-suited, conventional fathers he looked fat and ridiculous. I saw Valerie de la Mare and Susan Dartford sniggering behind their hands, which gave me a sick feeling of shame.

Poppy held out his arms when he saw me. I knew everyone was looking at me. I would have given ten . . . twenty years of my life to be able to vanish on the spot. I gave him a burning cheek to kiss and kept my head turned away when he spoke to me. Despite his efforts to improve the atmosphere and make me laugh I looked more and more sullen. As soon as I could I pleaded a headache. I went to bed and wept tears of rage and embarrassment. I cursed them both and I prayed that they might have a car accident on the way home and be killed. At the time I really thought I meant it.

The following day I started to attend in class and to take my work seriously. It seemed to me that the only way of ridding myself for ever of this impossible couple was to be clever and successful. I slogged away all that term, reading like mad and concentrating on what I was doing. I was fired by the idea of myself as a heroine, driven by external circumstances to solitary, grinding struggle. Soon I improved my class position from somewhere in the middle to the top. Min, though ignorant of my reasons, realised that something serious was going on and decided to join in.

Curiously, the intense competition that developed hardly threatened our friendship at all. Our strengths lay in different subjects and I was willing to help Min with her maths, knowing that she would never overtake me, while she undertook the same service in French. We saw ourselves as united against the other girls and competed jointly for the first two places. Gradually other aspects of school life lost interest for us. We gave up lacrosse, cut our favourite art classes, abandoned sunbathing behind the gym. All that mattered were the positions in the weekly assessments and the end-of-term exams. We became the school's star pupils and better still we actually began to see the point of it all and to enjoy some of the work for its own sake. No one was surprised when after five years Min and I both won places at Oxford, she to read Modern Languages and I to read English.

I only saw Poppy once more after the débâcle of the school play. Mother took me to his studio the next holidays. I was bewildered by the alteration in his apperance. His skin was a horrible colour, muddy with spots of crimson, and though his stomach was fatter than ever, there was a shrunken look about his limbs and cheeks. The whites of his eyes were very bloodshot and their lustrous beauty had gone. His unhappiness was patent though he made an effort to be cheerful. With the egotism of the young I thought he was sad because of our last disastrous meeting and I tried, half-heartedly, to be nicer to him. He held my hand and seemed pleased about my improved school report. When I left he gave me a signet ring which he had always worn on his little finger. I thought it very ugly and lost it almost at once.

He died in the middle of the following term. I went to the funeral. I couldn't understand what it meant or what I ought to be feeling. It was impossible to imagine his body inside the coffin. I kept my eyes fixed on the rain which dripped on to the brass plate and trickled off the hideous varnished wood because I didn't want to catch the eye of any of the grown-ups, whose excesses of grief seemed like showing off. The nasty, green, artificial grass which lined the hole, just like the stuff at the greengrocer's, was slipping off at one corner to expose lumps of yellow clay and stones. Mother was wearing crumpled black chiffon with mud-splashed suede shoes. She cried loudly and dramatically. My hands and feet were very cold.

Afterwards, as we walked from the graveside to the waiting taxi, Mother was angry that I hadn't cried. She told me, hiccupping with grief, her mascara in little dots over her cheeks and brow-bone from the sharp black spikes of her eyelashes, that she had been jealous of me. She had suspected that Poppy only stayed with her because of me. But he had clearly wasted his affection on a cold-hearted, selfish little girl. An ungrateful, callous little brute. I stood there letting her words break over me, feeling worse and worse inside and trying to keep my face from registering any expression. Finally we drove back to school in silence, she still weeping, I too terrified to speak.

'I suppose, now Poppy's dead, you will see more of your father,' she said as the taxi drove in at the school gates.

'Will it make any difference?' I replied, puzzled. Did she mean that she had less desire to see me herself? I wondered.

She turned to me with such fury that I thought she was going to hit me. Instead she pushed me out of the taxi and slammed the door without saying goodbye. I walked into the dormitory, feeling stiff and cold and sick. The other girls gave me sympathetic glances and avoided speaking to me. Death was something unimaginable, alarming and awkward. Min, who had been sitting on my bed waiting for me, saw my face.

'Oh Daze,' she said. 'He was such a very nice man. Just a dear.'

Then she put her arms around me while the terrible wrenching misery came somehow out from my chest into my mouth and I cried until my head sang and my face burned with heat and salt. Then Min soaked my flannel for me and I lay on my bed with it over my face to bring the swelling down and we talked about our history essays until the bell rang for supper. We didn't speak of him again. But as I grew older I found myself thinking of him often and I grew more ashamed of myself and more sorry with every year that passed.

## Chapter Two

Sophie Johnson's dance was held in the Easter holidays during our second year at Oxford. It was 1954. Though the war had been over for nine years, expectation and imagination were still frozen by years of going without and making do. Walking into Foxcombe Manor was like opening a door into Arcadia. To begin with, the house was warm, a wonderful all-over warmth which met you at the front door and made taking off coat, scarf, hat and gloves a pleasure. For another thing, the house was beautiful, inside as well as out. There was not an inch of the horrible dark green or ginger-brown paint which made England so ugly during the war years. I wanted to prowl about on my own and look at everything but a young and handsome butler showed me into the drawing room at once.

'Ah, here she is!' cried Mrs Studley-Headlam.

There was impatience in her tone as though they had been awaiting my arrival for hours and been put to considerable inconvenience, though in fact the train had been on time and the enormous, expensive car that had met me at the station had swept through the narrow lanes dangerously fast, as if gliding on oil.

'Miss Fairfax. This is Caroline Protheroe – Michael Protheroe – Hugh Anstey.'

'Diana,' I murmured, shaking hands with each of them in turn. Caroline was flat-chested and toothy, with a nervous manner as though she felt apologetic for being unattractive. She was carefully and expensively dressed and her hair, which was her only good point, was a beautiful red and very well cut.

Her husband was a good-looking man in an uninteresting way. His face was smooth and brown with neat, conventional features. He had sharp, white teeth which made him look predatory when he smiled. He was a little too short and held himself very upright. I speculated that he was probably Army and perhaps had married Caroline for her money. Certainly her eyes rested on him nearly all the time with a look of puzzled devotion as though she could not believe her luck in having got him. He, on the other hand, looked me up and down with an expression akin to a dog wagging its tail. His smooth cheeks darkened to ruddiness and he stroked back his hair with the palm of his hand, with the general air of someone who finds that what he had expected to be a dead bore has unaccountably looked up.

'We shall be a small party for dinner,' said Mrs Studley-Headlam, handing me a cup of tea, china, weak, with a shaving of lemon, without asking me if that was how I liked it. 'Leo will be late back . . . such a nuisance. We shall have to make our own fun.'

She looked as she said it as though fun was something she never usually allowed herself, but as hostess it was a tiresome necessity. She was tremendously slender and gave the impression of painstaking maintenance. Her hair was very short and soft and fair, her tweeds were a misty green and her pearl-grey jersey was undoubtedly cashmere. Even her stockings had a soft sheen to them. It was a carefully understated country look, a fine imitation of a pre-war English gentlewoman. Her eyes were hard and blue and impatient.

'You were at shool with Sophie Johnson, Diana?' asked Mrs Studley-Headlam, examining my shoes, my skirt, my pearls, and then returning her eyes to my face.

'Yes.'

We had been taught at school that it was poor style to limit one's part in conversation to 'yes' and 'no' so I added, 'But I don't know her very well. We were in different houses and different classes.'

'I'm sure you were,' replied Mrs S-H. 'Lady Bartholomew tells me that you are at Oxford with her daughter. I would not expect Sophie, charming though she is, to be able to keep up with that.'

She laughed, rather unpleasantly, in a way that seemed

unkind in mocking Soppy who existed in a twilight of incomprehension, and yet at the same time accused me of showing off.

'And what subject are you studying at Oxford?'

'I'm reading English. Chaucer and Middle English this term.'

I felt myself blushing at the schoolgirl quality of this contribution. Mrs S-H raised her eyebrows and then looked away to Michael, with a slight shrug of her shoulders as though, her social duty being done, she required him to lift her from the slough of boredom into which I had plunged her. He responded at once while I continued to feel hot and awkward.

'Salacious fellow, wasn't he, Chaucer?' winking and raising his eyebrows.

'Not particularly. Perhaps you are thinking of Boccacio.' Embarrassment made me sound more scornful than I had intended.

Mrs S-H laughed contemptuously, though it was unclear which of us was the object of her derision. 'You'd better not play the intellectual, Michael. Diana will take us all to task for having forgotten our lessons.'

Having branded me gauche and bluestocking, she turned to Hugh. 'You must tell us about your flying. Lady Bartholomew mentioned something about solo flights for charity.'

'Well, any excuse, you know,' smiled Hugh, leaning forward eagerly. 'Do you mind if I smoke? The trouble with flying is that it's expensive and the Pater kicks up sometimes about stumping up the readies.'

I could hardly believe my ears when I heard this frank *Boy's Own* paper stuff. Surely Min would never fall for this, however attractive the wrapping. Mrs S-H was simply loving it, I noticed. This was evidently her idea of the perfect young Englishman . . . boyishly modest and enthusiastic. It occurred to me then that Hugh was simply giving her what he thought she wanted.

Mrs S-H encouraged Hugh to talk and questioned him about his various trips, parading an ignorance with regard to geography that was winsome and irritating. There was more than a touch of the older-woman temptress in the way she teased and flattered. Hugh's response was an excited confusion which I thought overplayed. Michael Protheroe threw in a few remarks and questions but began to grow sulky as he felt himself left out of it. Caroline uttered little expressions of amazement which everyone else ignored. I had no part to play in any of this so I was free to look about the room, which I enjoyed doing immensely.

Clearly a very expensive interior decorator had been given *carte blanche*. It was beautiful, the very essence of the English country-house look. It should perhaps have been a little shabbier to be quite perfect: there was no fraying of silk or damask, no ring-marks on the eighteenth-century walnut, no dog hairs on the Aubusson. And the room smelt of something artificial: not wet animals, garden flowers, mice or damp, but of essence of something expensive which betrayed its foreign mistress. I liked the room so much, despite these minor criticisms, that I decided any amount of Mrs S-H was worth enduring and looked forward to seeing the rest of the house.

I did not have long to wait. Although Hugh was in full spate about his adventures when forced to crash-land in the Australian bush, Mrs S-H suddenly got up, saying, 'Caroline, how tired you look! Definitely dark circles, darling. Quite fagged. You must have a rest before dinner or you'll be a hag by midnight. I'm going to my room for an hour or so. Hugh, you and Diana might take Leo's hounds for a walk if you've nothing better to do. If Diana can be persuaded to do anything so frivolous.' She turned away from us and lifted a peremptory finger. 'Michael, I must have a word with you. Leo leaves everything to me and there is some mistake in the farm accounts I simply don't understand.'

She left the room arm-in-arm with a depressed-looking Caroline. Hugh looked at me, smiling, trying not to show that he was a little crushed by Mrs S-H's cutting him short so off-handedly.

'Would you like to come for a walk? There's half an hour before it gets dark.'

I would much rather have had a leisurely bath but he looked at me with such entreaty that I nodded. A very plain maid showed me to my room. Was Leo not to be trusted, I wondered? I had been put on the top floor in what had undoubtedly once been a servant's bedroom. But as soon as I saw it I was enchanted. The ceiling sloped charmingly and was

'Can we let Trissy and Issy off the lead, do you think?'

'I can't see anything they could hurt. What about the sheep, though?'

'They won't cross the ha-ha,' said Hugh, so authoritatively that I believed him.

Naturally, within fifteen bounds they had dropped down into the ha-ha, leapt with ease the fence that ran along the bottom of it and were up the other side among the sheep.

'Fuck!' said Hugh.

'Exactly!' I said crossly, thinking of the effect on my hair of a chase after the dogs.

'It's my fault. You stay here. I won't be a jiff.'

Hugh cantered elegantly over the grass, disappeared into the ha-ha for a second and then re-emerged amongst the sheep. I turned to admire the façade of Foxcombe. It seemed that Fate was indeed blind when she handed out such an architectural jewel to someone as toxic as Mrs S-H. The sky was darkening to grape behind the pedimented roof and from most of the perfectly proportioned windows a lambent maizey light threw shadows of architraves and pilasters against the handsome stone. Suddenly there were footfalls on the grass behind me and I turned to see Hugh running up with both dogs.

'Heavens, how did you manage it?'

'It wasn't difficult. I used an old Eskimo trick for training polar bears. No, not really,' he added, seeing my eyes widen, 'actually they're already very well-trained and they come when you call them.'

Hugh grinned, and I thought again, Lucky Min. His dark hair flopped in curls on his white forehead and his eyes, black in the twilight, gleamed with health and exercise. Most men would have sulked or been bad-tempered about having to run after the dogs. His good humour was irresistible.

'Come along.' He tucked my hand into his arm. 'A brisk walk to the summerhouse and back and then we can go and find a drink. Hope Emma didn't see all that from the house.'

'Emma?'

'Mrs Studley-Headlam.'

'I think she was otherwise occupied.'

I told Hugh what I had overheard on my way downstairs. I wondered whether he would take a tolerant view of such goings-on. He looked quite amused.

'Rather him than me. I should think she'd be quite hard work. The bitch. Poor Studley-Headlam.'

'Poor Caroline,' I said.

'Perhaps Leo and Caroline . . .? One can only hope.'

'You seem very different now from how you were earlier, in the drawing room. It's confusing.'

Hugh laughed, something he did well. Voice pitched low, a glimpse of strong, white teeth.

'You mean the schoolboyish charm with Emma? Always goes down a treat with Americans. I'm going to be an actor, you see. So I practise various characters when I think I can get away with it. Actually it's something I've always done, even before I had the idea of becoming an actor. All those tedious social occasions. I've made up the most tremendous stories. People always fall for it. You have to be just improbable enough to keep yourself interested and invention flowing but not so much that people realise you're fooling them.'

'You mean all that stuff about the plane crash in Australia – ?'

'Boloney from beginning to end. Never been there in my life.'

'But you do fly planes?'

'Nope. Never so much as touched a pair of goggles or flappy boots. Told Lady Bartholomew all that stuff last time I had lunch with her. Went for it like a terrier spotting a rabbit-hole.'

'But it must get you into difficulties sometimes?'

'Not really. I just invent something else to get myself out of it. For example, if someone asked me to do a flight for a real charity, I'd accept and then ring up saying I'd broken my leg and couldn't do it. And then I'd have all the fun of staggering about with a stick . . . a plaster cast would be necessary . . . I've got lots of friends training to be doctors so that wouldn't be hard to arrange . . . and I could have everyone rushing round looking after me.'

'It sounds like a great deal of trouble.'

'It can be slightly hard work but at least it isn't boring. How often do you sit next to someone at lunch or dinner who really interests you? Mostly it's an effort, isn't it, to find something you both want to talk about. I'm always placed next to women who want to talk about their children, gardens or golf if they're over thirty-five, or horses, clothes or sex if they're under thirty-five. Deadly. Well, not the last perhaps, but I find it a great mistake to discuss sex with a girl with whom you haven't been to bed. It seems to prevent getting her there yourself. Kills the spontaneity, I suppose.'

'I suppose you don't want to go to bed with every girl you sit next to who's under thirty-five?' I asked with a touch of asperity in my voice.

'Why not?'

I could think of no answer to this that did not sound priggish so I took another angle.

'When someone is rather decent, agreeable . . . oh, nice, you know, Lady Bartholomew, for example . . . don't you feel a heel deceiving them?'

'I think I'm doing them a good turn. What could I tell them about my real self that would be half as interesting? I'm twenty-three, I read engineering at Birmingham, never open a book now, went to a boarding school in the middle of a moor, had the dullest childhood imaginable. I haven't had time to do anything very interesting. Why should I inflict my half-formed opinions or limited experience on other people?'

I really could think of no objection to this, except that it was lying. What did truthfulness have to do with the art of conversation? I wondered. Nothing, I answered myself.

'I think we'd better go back. It's getting quite dark.'

'And your hands are cold,' said Hugh, rubbing the one which held his arm with a degree of solicitude which I would have found utterly charming if I did not now believe him to be wholly insincere.

'Look, headlights,' I pointed towards the drive. 'I hope it isn't Leo back early.'

'The fat would certainly be in the fire,' said Hugh, sounding quite pleased at the idea. 'She deserves it, the faithless hussy!'

'You seem very certain it's all her fault. What about Michael's infidelity?'

'It's always the woman who's responsible in these things. What man could refuse Emma Studley-Headlam if she was set on having him? If it's just sex with no strings, it's irresistible for men. But not, if I'm informed correctly, for a woman.'

'You mean that men can go about behaving as selfishly and carelessly as they like, taking no responsibility?' I felt myself getting angry.

'Now we're talking about IT,' said Hugh, squeezing my hand. 'Remember, Diana, it's not a good idea.'

We had stepped into the light of the front-door lantern before I had time to think of a suitable reply and the appearance of a servant to take the dogs from Hugh prevented any further talk.

'Is that Mr Studley-Headlam's car?' I asked as a Daimler crunched to a standstill behind us.

'No, madam, it is one of the guests for dinner. The gentleman is early as he has just arrived on the train from Edinburgh and has to change.'

'I must change, too, Hugh. See you later.'

I was glad to see that Mrs S-H's door was closed as I went up to my room and I rushed past as quickly as possible so as not to hear so much as a gasp. The bath was heavenly, deep and hot. I helped myself to a generous quantity of expensive bath essence. The towels were large and soft. There was an armchair by a table on which were flowers and the latest *Vogue*. I began to wonder whether I wouldn't prefer to spend the evening in the bathroom.

But there was my dress to be shown off. I had had it copied from a photograph of the Duchess of Windsor. I'd found the silver lace, wrapped in acid-free tissue paper, in a drawer in my mother's bedroom. She seemed entirely indifferent as to whether I took it or not, being at that time in her ethnic phase and wearing only caftans and djellabahs in blood-curdling orange-and-black stripes. My dressmaker was very cheap. She had made it beautifully and I thought it looked better on me than on the Duchess who was, despite her smartness, essentially a plain woman, perhaps even ugly. I put on the dress and examined myself in the mirror. It was tight-fitting, with a low neck and tiny scalloped sleeves, the skirt narrow and falling straight to the ground, very different from the strapless, full-skirted evening dresses most girls would be wearing. I made up my face carefully and put on my paternal grandmother's pearl choker. My silver glacé kid slippers were shabby but the dress was full-length so no one would see them. My confidence rose. I felt suddenly excited by the evening's possibilities.

Min and I always had much less to spend on our clothes than the other girls. In my case this meant careful planning, extensive window-shopping and much ingenuity. In Min's case it meant that she usually looked a mess. I hated to see her badly dressed because she was really something of a beauty. She had wonderful eyes, deep blue, large and soft, with the unfocused, romantic gaze typical of the very short-sighted. Her nose was slightly beaky but it gave distinction to her face and stopped it being merely pretty. Her skin was good, except for the occasional outbreak of spots when she forgot to wash. As a child she had looked rabbity but now, after long years of brace-wearing, her teeth were very good. Her hair was straight and brown and pretty. Often it hung in greasy tails but when she remembered to wash it, it gleamed like animal fur. Her chief defects were her eyebrows, which were heavy and met in the middle unless I plucked them for her, and her slightly dumpy figure. Her hands were, despite the grubby fingernails, white and beautiful. As I spat on my mascara brush and scrubbed it up and down the rectangle of black I worried about Min's eyebrows. I hadn't seen her for some weeks. Would she have remembered to pluck them? Would she even have a pair of tweezers? I put mine in my evening bag just in case. Perhaps love and Hugh would have brought about a new concern for appearance. Folding my green-velvet evening cloak (second-hand and one of my favourite possessions) over my arm, I went downstairs.

Michael and Caroline Protheroe were already in the drawing room, together with four other people I didn't know. The butler offered me a glass of champagne from a tray and then Caroline came over, with a nervous, high-stepping gait rather like a dressage horse and the evident, kind intention of drawing me into the group. She was wearing a very elegant dress of black-and-white moiré which sat oddly on her thin freckled chest, throwing what should have been her cleavage into deep shadow. I felt a sudden pang as I looked at her anxious, gentle face and remembered her recent betrayal.

'You look quite stunning, Diana,' she said, grinning toothily at me. 'Where did you get that wonderful dress?'

'Oh, a little shop in Beauchamp Place. Closed down now, I'm afraid. And yours, Caroline – couldn't be more elegant!'

It was difficult not to gush in the effort to reassure someone so painfully unhappy about herself.

'Mummy always buys my clothes for me,' said Caroline,

with a little grimace. 'Even though I'm a married woman and have been for five years. She has the most marvellous taste.'

'Don't you resent your mother choosing your things?' I asked, smiling. 'I should hate it. Besides my mother's taste is grim . . . fake leopard-fur skirts with white boots, that sort of thing.'

Caroline let out a really genuine laugh at this, which pleased me.

'How I envy people who can be mean about their parents and not mind. Whenever I'm critical of Mummy I suffer such agonies of conscience afterwards that it just isn't worth it.'

'But is it being mean to say that my mother has ghastly taste? Isn't it just truthful?'

Caroline looked thoughtful for a moment, an expression which did not suit her as it made her face look long and bony. Her skin was very white with pronounced blue veining, like craquelure, under the skin, giving her an unhealthy, exhausted look.

'I suppose if you would make the remark to a person's face, then I don't count it as mean,' she replied with a great air of seriousness. There was something childlike about her, held in this state of immaturity by a dreadful, dominating mother and an insensitive, unfaithful husband. I began to feel very sorry for her.

'I've often told my mother that her taste and mine are not the same. Will that do?'

She smiled at me with an air of sadness. 'I envy you your certainty,' was her surprising answer.

'I'm not certain about anything!' I was startled into truthfulness. 'It all seems . . . messy. Chaotic. Life, I mean. I'm not at all certain with people. I like the beauty and constancy of things.'

Just in time I remembered that it was instant social death in Lady Bart's world to be intense. I assumed my cool and amused face.

'Wasn't it Benjamin Franklin who said that nothing is certain but death and taxes?'

'I'm afraid I'm awfully stupid,' said Caroline. 'I missed so much school through being ill. But I'm trying to catch up now. I wish you'd tell me what I ought to read.'

There are few things I like better than being asked for advice.

I know that once given it will be as chaff thrown upon the wind. But the sensation of tidying, shaping, moulding and reforming I find profoundly satisfying. I was just about to suggest beginning with *Jane Eyre* when Hugh and Mrs S-H came in and dinner was announced at the same time.

## CHAPTER THREE

Mrs S-H took the head of the table and waved Michael Protheroe to the other end. I was seated between a young man called Ninian Reed Mather, who had tiny, blinking eyes and a plump, petulant lower lip, and a man whose name I couldn't read on his place card – something like Bothersome. He had a face like a brick . . . terracotta-coloured and pitted, perhaps the scars of teenage acne. Above it strands of grizzled hair clung in tendrils to his large, red ears. A silk cummerbund the colour of dark plums strained across a tumid gut. Hugh was seated opposite me. I began with Ninian over the lobster cocktail.

Ninian had strong views which generally is something of an asset in conversation. It wasn't long, though, before I began to feel that he was a great deal too opinionated. He told me at once how he was in the middle of a row with his bishop . . . a man, according to Ninian, of heretical Low-Church inclinations, who was criminally dishonest with funds and was certainly a bare-faced liar, a dog-beater, child abuser and seducer of nuns.

'Surely,' I murmured, when I could get a word in, 'if this is so it will be a simple matter to expose him to the authorities?'

'Ah!' cried Ninian, causing everyone at the table to stop talking and listen to him. 'But there is the man's fearful cunning!'

And he was off again. As no one present knew the bishop we were soon, all of us, in agonies of boredom. Separate conversations broke out again. Ninian was egocentric to the point of mania yet I found myself unable to put a stop to his monologue. The flowers were admirable . . . tight little pink rosebuds, apricot ranunculus with green centres, Rembrandt tulips striped in darkest crimson and ivory. Ninian's voice faltered as he pushed a piece of coral lobster-flesh between his pouting lips.

'What's the name of the man on my other side?' I asked in a low but determined voice.

Ninian looked annoyed at the interruption. 'That's Bollingbrook. Made a lord in the New Year's honours list. Something in steel. Parvenu. Of course the bloody old Bish is as lower-middle-class as they come. His wife's probably decorated the Palace in teak dining suites and wrought-iron plant stands.'

'How old is the bloody old Bish?' I asked as Ninian paused for breath.

He gave the matter long and serious thought. 'About fifty-five I should say.'

'There's no help for it then. You must either move to another diocese or change your creed. You could go over to Rome. Or what about Shin Buddhism? That can't be anything to do with legs, can it? What do you think Homo-ousians get up to? They must be a very small, selective sect, I should think.'

I had intended to develop the discussion into something more general so as to have a chance to talk myself. Ninian looked at me aghast, as though I had spat in his eye. Then he stared at the table before him where the lobster cocktail had been seconds before. He did not alter his gaze as a plate of duck was slipped under his nose. His lips moved silently and slowly as though he were praying. I had no idea whether he was seriously considering apostasy or merely reviewing with indignation my heartless frivolity. Anyway it was a relief that he had stopped talking. I turned to Lord Bollingbrook. He eyed me speculatively.

'Are you looking after Emma's horses?' he said at last.

'What?' I did not conceal my astonishment.

'Just wondering what a pretty little thing like you is doing here, that's all. Too young for Emma's set. Shouldn't say that, I suppose,' he chortled, looking waggish, a fleck of mayonnaise on his chin. 'The last pretty girl I met here was Emma's groom. No brain, of course . . . didn't need one. Almond eyes and mouth like a cushion. Moved like a racehorse.'

'Bunny, I hope you're not flirting with Diana,' called Mrs S-H, who I could not bring myself to think of as Emma, having once had a kitten of that name of which I was very fond. 'Diana is fearfully clever, you know. A student at Oxford.'

Lord Bollingbrook (Bunny was a misnomer as he was the reverse of something sweet and soft) turned to me with a look of mistrust.

'I don't know anything about horses myself,' I said quickly. 'But my great-aunt was the suffragette Emily Davison who threw herself under the King's horse at the Derby. I expect you've seen the newsreel. My grandmother always said that the horrors of force-feeding and imprisonment must have driven her insane.'

I caught Hugh's eye and gave him the very slightest of smiles. My heart was beating very fast. Although like everyone else I constantly tell small lies of one kind or another, such a bold piece of fabrication made me nervous.

'Really?' Lord Bollingbrook, who had been on the point of turning his back on me for good, twisted in his chair to look at me. 'Good Lord, how interesting! Ridiculous thing to do. Can't think why a pretty woman should kill herself simply in order to be allowed to vote. We men are putty in your hands, my dear. You ladies have all the power.'

He lifted his upper lip, exposing long, yellow teeth, in a way which I supposed was intended to be flirtatious.

'Rather hard on the horse,' put in Hugh, returning my look.

'Oh, the horse was all right,' I said airily. 'My great-aunt was exceptionally small and thin. I except it was just like running over dead branches.'

'Good Lord!' said Bollingbrook, again. 'And are you a young lady of strong conviction?'

'Oh, I don't believe my great-aunt was really so passionate about female suffrage. I think people who do that sort of thing are always in the grip of some dreadful despair, don't you? A melancholy . . . *taedium vitae*, you know. Surely if you really believed passionately in something, getting the vote for example, it would make you want to live to see something accomplished, wouldn't it?'

I was rather enjoying this actressy way of talking. Opening my eyes very wide and shrugging my shoulders exaggeratedly, I almost began to convince myself.

'Do you think it a brave or a cowardly thing to do?' asked Hugh.

'To kill yourself? Both those things, I suppose.'

'Nonsense!' said Bunny, his bony nose and jaw nodding emphatically, like a horse over a stable door. 'It has to be a coward's way out. A decent person would face the music, no matter what. I except your great-aunt, my dear, since you say she was potty.'

Lord Bollingbrook's mental grasp was evidently neither sensitive nor subtle. I began to enjoy hoodwinking him. I went on, 'Supposing they didn't consider the music worth it? Suppose it wasn't fear but distaste . . . a feeling that it was all no longer relevant?'

'I think it's an immensely brave thing to do,' said Hugh.

'Imagine Anna Karenina crouching down and choosing the exact moment to jump between the wheels of the railway carriage.' I was warming to my theme. 'Tolstoy describes her feeling of astonishment in the very second that she throws herself forward. She wants to draw back . . . as though she never really meant to do it at all. It was only a fantasy, a spiteful game to hurt Vronsky. Perhaps it's essential to get oneself into that dreamlike state of utter irresponsibility, of make-believe, so that it's possible to override the instinct to survive.'

'Who is this Anna person?' demanded Bunny Bollingbrook, querulously.

'Just a girl in a book,' I muttered.

'Fellow I knew in the Army shot himself,' said Bunny reflectively. 'Damn silly. Fiancée was raped. By a black. Damn silly to shoot himself over it. Never understood myself why he did it. Shoot the black, yes, one could understand that. But himself, no. Plenty of fish in the sea after all.'

Bunny was, if anything, more unpleasant than Ninian. Luckily the pudding arrived at this point . . . a syllabub with a glass of Château d'Yquem to go with it. I knew that was what it was because one of the guests, a man with a nose not unlike the tulips in colouring, that is to say, a very streaky purple, made a great fuss about it and he and Bunny had a long and tedious exchange about great wines. Hugh, by this time, was getting on pretty well with a woman on his right who was giving him blatantly lascivious glances. I made a mental note to papered, like the walls, in red-and-white *toile de jouy*. The bed had an eiderdown of palest pink silk and there was a bowl of white hyacinths beside the bed. But the most marvellous thing about the room was the window, a long oval, a beautiful Georgian *oeil-de-boeuf*. A cushion ran the length of the window-seat. It was irresistible. I stretched myself along it and propped my head on my elbow. The garden was park-like, with magnificent trees coming quite close to the window. I could see the dew dropping through the shivering air on which lay a bloom of dusk. Across the ha-ha sheep were grazing. The rippling of the old glass gave them a ghostly evanescence. '"My . . . something . . . are shaded with trees, and my hills are white over with sheep,"' I muttered to myself. 'Grottoes – "My grottoes are shaded –"'

Suddenly I remembered Hugh who would be waiting for me in the drive with two dogs, possibly frisky and hard to control. I flung on my coat and wound a scarf about my hair. I wanted to look my best for the party. I was walking along the first-floor landing, my footsteps muffled by deep carpeting in the fashionable shade of *caca du Dauphin* when I heard my name mentioned. I did what anyone else would have done. I stopped to listen. Mrs S-H's voice, with its hard timbre, rang out and as the door to her room was fractionally open I had no trouble in hearing.

'The Fairfax girl has gone for a walk with Hugh. I told him to give them a good long run so they won't be back for at least thirty minutes. What a bore the young are! So self-absorbed.' Then she gave a little, excited laugh. 'You don't like young girls, do you? You prefer women who know how to do it.'

Michael made a noise which reminded me of a donkey braying. Someone, Mrs S-H I supposed, moaned. I moved on swiftly, resisting the temptation to close the door. I found Hugh standing patiently on the gravel before the front door, two dalmations on leads lying calmy at his feet.

'Ah, here you are.' He looked very glad to see me. 'Let me introduce Acne and Pox.'

'Not really!' I said, aghast.

'No. Actually Tristan and Isolde. Shall we go this way?'

The beauty of the park made me feel suddenly very happy, despite the cold. 'Look, a summerhouse or folly or something. Let's go and see.'

remember how ridiculous she looked, so that when I reached middle-age myself I would not be tempted to play flirtatious tricks on handsome young men.

'Of course my great-uncle, Commander Fairfax, was largely responsible for the sinking of the *Lusitania*, you know,' I remarked conversationally to Bunny when I could get his attention. 'Under orders from above, of course. But it was he who organised it.'

Bunny's eyes, rather bloodshot by this time, seemed to oscillate in their sockets.

'The *Lusitania*! Good heavens, what do you know of that business? Forgive me, my dear young lady, but you can't know what you are talking about! It's a damned lie, whatever anyone says. Churchill would never have played such a trick! Anyway it's all been turned inside out a score of times. No proof whatsoever.'

'You remember the second explosion,' I said, very solemnly. 'My uncle left a letter about it with his solicitor. Obviously his conscience was deeply troubled. It all came out by mistake when his will was read.'

'No! My God!' Bunny ran his hands through his grey crinkly hair. Perspiration stood out on his lip. 'My dear young lady, you cannot possibly realise . . . extraordinarily careless . . . I hardly know what to . . . you must say nothing more of this to anyone.'

I was sorry Hugh was too engrossed elsewhere to appreciate the success I was having with his stratagem. I was really enjoying myself now and the lying began to seem effortless. I took a large swig of Château d'Yquem, my fourth glass of the evening counting the champagne before dinner. It was more than I usually drank and it made me careless enough to wink at Hugh who was looking at me across the table. Bunny turned his head towards me at the same moment and saw us grinning at each other. He looked terribly angry suddenly and I felt a little alarmed. Then his eyes narrowed and he began to smile in a most sinister way. He put his face close to mine so that I could feel his mouth brushing my hair.

'I'd like to put you over my knee, you wicked girl. You've enjoyed making a fool of me, haven't you? You think I'm just a silly old man. But I'll show you something.'

Then to my disgust I felt his hand on my thigh and he gave

me such a hard pinch that I jumped. Bunny was smiling at me, his face very close to mine with the kind of soppy, swimming look in his eyes that men get when they are excited. I hadn't bargained for this at all. He was breathing very hard, almost whistling through his nose, and I felt his hand fluttering unpleasantly over my knee.

Fortunately Mrs S-H chose that moment to get up and take the women back to the drawing room for coffee. I stood up quickly and followed her without another word to Bunny or Ninian. I saw Mrs S-H exchange a look with Michael Protheroe as he held the door for us. The expression on her face was so blatant in its desire that I was quite startled. Then I saw that Caroline, who was standing beside me, was staring at Michael. Her face was very red and her eyes were filled with tears.

I hate scenes. My mother adored provoking storms and squalls. I would become silent while she stamped about me, flashing her eyes and gnashing her teeth. Of course my silence enraged her further. Sometimes she would slap my face and then break down in paroxysms of remorse. I never believed any of it.

I took Caroline's arm and drew her past Michael into the hall. A log fire was burning there and we went to stand in front of it. I pointed to the painting which hung above. It was a portrait in the style of Gainsborough.

'I noticed it when I arrived this afternoon,' I said. 'It's a painting of Mrs Studley-Headlam, isn't it? Despite the powdered hair and the clothes, the face is absolutely her. It's a good likeness. But what made me look at it first was a bogus quality about it, colours too pretty, brushwork too smooth, something wooden about the figure. I find it strangely heartening that genius is so hard to imitate. This painting's been varnished and darkened to age it but I bet it was done in the last ten years. What I wonder is . . . is it just a charming conceit or are we meant to think that it's an ancestor?'

Caroline pushed her bottom lip beneath her protruding front teeth and stared at the painting.

'You're right. It is her. She's very attractive, isn't she?' She gave a small, unconvincing laugh. 'You might say that she is someone who has everything.'

'I hardly know her. What's her husband like?'

'Oh, Leo. Poor man.' Caroline sighed. 'He's really quite a dear.'

This sounded interesting but I forbore to question Caroline further as we were expected in the drawing room. Caroline seemed more composed. She accepted a cup of coffee from her hostess and we sat together on the sofa talking about books and what she should read.

As soon as we had finished our coffee Mrs S-H organised us into cars for the journey to the Johnsons' house, some ten or so miles distant. The men came out into the hall as we were getting into our coats. Bunny was smoking a cigar but with his free hand he held my cloak for me with, I thought, an unpleasantly proprietorial air. I hadn't noticed before that he was very tall, well over six feet. It made him seem more than a little threatening. I began seriously to regret my conversation with him.

Just as we were about to go, a smallish man with a large, hooked nose and horn-rimmed spectacles came in. He seemed very tired and responded to the various greetings impassively, merely allowing himself a faint smile at the room in general. This, then, was Leo. Mrs S-H introduced me and he took my hand without even glancing towards my face. He smelt very strongly of whisky.

I was to travel in the same car as Bunny, Caroline and the woman who had sat next to Hugh at dinner. Fortunately Bunny had to sit in front next to the driver. He was obviously furious about it but Mrs S-H was adamant. He sat in silence and sulked, blowing his cigar smoke into the driver's face all the way, ignoring the poor man's coughing.

I hadn't seen Sophie's house before but it was very much what one might have predicted. It was huge, mid-Victorian and built in the architectural style of a railway station. It was hardly more comfortable. The Johnsons were a hardy breed and saw no need of a servant to open and close the front door. It stood wide and the hall was so cold that our breath made clouds of mist about our heads. With extreme reluctance I took off my cloak and exposed my bare arms. We all trooped, shivering and chattering, down a long passageway.

There are few sounds that strike more hideously than the sound of a party within when one is without. A roar of sound, voices and music, broke upon us. My face, particularly my mouth, felt distressingly quivery. I would have nothing to say. I would be neglected, ignored, humiliated. Then we were through the door and the terror began to recede.

## CHAPTER FOUR

My hand still shook as I took the glass offered me but my mouth was back under my control and the moment I saw Min, standing with Hugh, on the opposite side of the room I forgot my fears. Colonel Johnson, who was standing with his wife, the Honourable Daphne, and Sophie, shaking hands with the guests, was a military man of the terrier type, wiry and aggressive. Sophie had her father's narrow face and long nose but her mother's pale eyes which drooped at the outer corners. Her hair was fastened into a wispy sort of bun and the effect was of unrelieved plainness. Her frock of white and French navy with puffed sleeves and a full skirt added to the depressing, governessy look.

This would have been sad but for the fact that Sophie was entirely lacking in self-consciousness and it had never occurred to her that she lacked wit and intellect, or even that they were desirable. Her only interests were hunting, 'picking up' for her father's shoots, and running stalls for her mother's charities. At school she had been snobbish and something of a bully. She assumed that Min was a friend because their parents moved in the same circles. She despised me because of my mother. There her interest in either of us ended. We kissed each other briskly and said how lovely it was to see each other. Her rather fat arms were very hot and there was the faintest smell of the stables about her, a compound of hay and urine. She turned to the next guest and I went over to Min.

She was looking very attractive in a black dress, with clean hair and dark red lipstick. There was a suggestion of shadow over the bridge of her nose but the sophisticated gamine character of the dress made it somehow less noticeable. Even her fingernails were painted red, a sign that Min had devoted extraordinary effort to the occasion.

'Daze! Wow! You look amazing! You've met Hugh, of course, at Foxcombe. What did you think of La Belle Dame Sans Merci?'

'You could whet knives on her. Purest viridian over the house though. A diamond!'

'The cat's pyjamas,' agreed Min. We embraced delicately so as not to disturb our make-up. I noticed that there was a powdery white rim to her dress beneath her arms where sweat and deodorant had dried. 'Hope this evening's going to look up a bit. The band's awful.'

I looked over to the bandstand which was hedged about with moth-eaten hydrangeas. The musicians were dejectedly strumming their way through something Latin American. A few middle-aged couples were steering each other determinedly about the floor.

'I'll fix this,' said Hugh and went over to the band leader.

'What do you think?' asked Min, looking after him. 'Isn't he absolute heaven?'

'Positively empyrean.'

'Isn't he Darcy, Will Ladislaw, Mr Rochester and Daniel Deronda all rolled into one?'

'You've forgotten Heathcliffe. And Mr Rochester wasn't handsome, was he?'

'No, I suppose not. Just terribly, terribly sexy. Yum!'

'I think you might throw in a touch of Sir Felix Carbury. A lily of the field – just a bit?'

'Could be. But who cares with a dial like that.'

'I thought you were always telling me that I attach too much importance to looks. What's he like in bed?'

We asked each other this question about every man who took us out. I always lied myself black in the face for I was, in fact, still a virgin.

'I can't tell you how wonderful. Very tender to start with and then, when his passion gets too much, an utter brute.'

Hugh returned at that moment after a long discussion with the band and I looked at him with something of a flutter in my heart. It did sound pretty exciting. Very different from what I had experienced so far. A lot of rather boring fondling and fumbling, the unpleasantness of a pimply tongue in one's mouth tasting of cigarettes. Then pleading or accusation, anger or sulking, which was the last straw. I was tired of being told that I had led them on.

Now as I stared at Hugh, so deliciously framed by his dinner-jacket, I actually felt the very first intimations of what it might be all about. What a pity that Min had bagged him. Suddenly the band broke into a loud and racy rendering of 'Sock It to Me, Baby'.

'That's more like it,' cried Min. 'Come on, let's dance.'

She grabbed Hugh's hand and pulled him on to the dance floor. The middle-aged couples tried to bounce harder and faster to the new rhythm but spectacles, straining trousers and arthritic hips militated against it. A young man, red-haired with pale lashes, a large Adam's apple and spots like pebble-dashing, asked me to dance. He tried to make conversation while we danced which was a nuisance as we had to yell 'What?' at each other all the time as the band was thumping out the tune with maximum decibels. By now I was thoroughly warm and beginning to hope that I was about to enjoy myself.

Suddenly the music came to an abrupt end and as we paused to catch our breaths, I saw Colonel Johnson speaking to the band leader and then marching away, looking very cross. The band began to play a slow rumba. All the young people sloped disgruntledly off the dance floor and the previous generation took over again.

'This is a bloody ghastly party,' bellowed a man who was standing equidistant between myself and Sophie. He was slightly drunk and I looked at him with a new respect for the wine cup we were drinking seemed to be composed entirely of lemonade, flabby segments of browning apple and unidentifiable stalks. Sophie must have heard him for she went very red. Hugh went over to the band and spoke to its leader. They broke out at once with 'Honey, Love those Lips' at a cracking pace but before they had played more than ten bars, the Colonel was there again.

'Who's for a spot of debagging?' roared the drunk man.

Luckily the Honourable Daphne appeared and took her husband firmly by the hand. She escorted him, ignoring his protests, out of the room. That was the last any of us saw of him. The band got into full swing and someone extinguished the mock Georgian chandeliers. It became an evening of possibilities except for one crucial ingredient lacking . . .

tolerable men. Ginger talked never-endingly. I only heard snatches but I gathered that he was very keen on motor-racing. He was eager to explain to me the advantages of the Silverstone circuit over Brands Hatch. I wondered what the female equivalent of this conversation was . . . perhaps the superiority of Marshall and Snelgrove over Swan and Edgar. The difficulty of finding common ground between two sexes who had been reared apart from the age of eight was felt by both sides. I knew nothing about anything except Eng. Lit. and there was hardly a soul in the room who read anything thicker than *The Field*. So we all danced frantically and I, for one, began to despair.

The drunk man seemed to have fastened on Sophie and was throwing her about energetically in a very eccentric kind of rock and roll. She appeared not to mind that he was plastered. In fact I would never have guessed that she could be so agile. Her bra-straps hung down from her beefy shoulders and her hair was drifting down from its bun. She looked almost attractive in a pagan way, like a fat kelpie. I saw him grab her large breasts as she rolled towards him. She gave him a playful biff on the chin. I envied profoundly her ability to abandon herself to play. The harder I tried to escape myself the more I found myself theorising about my own incapacity to fuse with my fellows. I felt more lonely by the minute.

Ginger, whose name I still didn't know, was beginning to clutch me tighter to him, though still bellowing about intake manifolds, and I foresaw a struggle to come. I would have to get rid of him. There wasn't a decent man in the room apart from Hugh and he was strictly out of bounds. Ginger ran a damp hand over my back and began to blink excitedly. He was panting . . . from the exertion of dancing, I hoped. The band stopped playing and the leader announced that there would be a supper interval.

'Back in a minute,' I told Ginger.

I found the ladies' cloakroom but it was cold and uncongenial, packed with women queuing for use of the lavatory. I combed my hair and renewed my lipstick while wondering what to do. I shrank from straightforward rejection. Poor Ginger couldn't help being overwhelmingly dull much more than he could help having less sex appeal than a boiled egg. I opened a door to the left of the ballroom. It was foggy with cigar-smoke and several fat middle-aged men were playing billiards. I closed it quickly, for one of them was Bunny. Another door revealed a sitting room in which was an assorted crowd of men and women, including Sophie's mother and Mrs S-H, playing cards and talking by a good fire, and drinking what looked like champagne. Gloomily I wandered back to what was clearly the hoi polloi.

At least there was no sign of Ginger in the room which had been set aside for supper. I wasn't hungry, having been so well fed beforehand, so I took only a few grapes over to the table where Min and Hugh were sitting.

'Hello, Diana. I was wondering where you were. My God! This rice salad is drier than a washerwoman's knickers,' said Hugh, prodding his food around with his fork.

'Shh, Sophie'll hear you,' admonished Min.

'I doubt it,' I muttered. 'She seems to have both ears stuffed with that man's dress-shirt. I wouldn't risk it myself. He looks drunk to the point of chucking up.'

'And how has he managed it?' asked Hugh resentfully. 'I've had pints of this vegetable-ridden ichor and I feel as sober as a baby after its evening bottle.'

'Probably got his own supply,' I said, eating a grape. 'Mm, these are good anyway. It looks as though these grapes are going to be the high point of my evening. Talking of private supplies, they're drinking champagne through there.'

'No! The impudence! Which room did you say?' Hugh stood up, looking very determined.

'The one to the left of that door. The Honourable Daphne's in there mounting guard over it, though. You won't get any.'

'We shall see.' Hugh wove his way between the tables and left the room.

'You don't seem to be having a particularly good time,' said Min, with what seemed to me a marked lack of sympathy.

'No, I can't say I am. And the rest of it doesn't look too promising. There's a gingery-looking boy I've got to avoid at all costs. If he comes in I'm going to hide under the table.'

'Dull?'

'Stuporific!'

'Poor Daze. There just aren't many men around like Hugh. I'm having a marvellous evening!'

I could have done without the gloating tone in her voice at that moment. Happiness spilled out of her like a beam from a searchlight. Min could be insensitive to other people's moods, I reflected.

'Get that swill out of your glasses,' said Hugh, peeling the gold paper off a bottle of Bollinger.

'Hugh! Darling! How did you do it? You may kiss me as you're so clever.'

Min put up her face to be kissed and I noticed that he gave her the most perfunctory peck before returning to the opening of the bottle. He is not in love with her, I thought. He poured us each a glass and then stood the bottle in a clump of hydrangeas behind us.

'No telling, you girls. We don't want any other proboscis having a dip in our nectar.'

'I adore champagne!' said Min, taking a sip and widening her eyes at Hugh. It was the first I'd heard of it. 'It makes me feel adventurous.'

'That sounds promising,' said Hugh, very calmly.

'I tell you what,' said Min, and then whispered something into his ear.

As I was the only other person sitting at the table I began to feel distinctly *de trop*. I understood it all. Usually I had better luck with men than Min. I'd never really thought about it before but now I recognised that she'd resented it and was thoroughly enjoying her moment of triumph. I emptied my glass and was on the point of making a dignified retreat to the ballroom when I felt a hand on my arm. A cold, strong grip. I looked up. It was Bunny.

'I've been looking for you.'

He sounded annoyed, quite as though we'd had some arrangement to meet. He was looking very purposeful, quite unsmiling and even more intimidating than I'd remembered.

'Come and dance,' he said, pulling me up. 'I've got to catch an early train back to Edinburgh tomorrow morning so we haven't much time.'

Time for what? I wondered, searching for my evening bag which I must have kicked under the table.

'Is that Ginger?' murmured Min to me, with a look of amusement that I could have murdered her for. I shook my head.

'What the bloody hell are you doing?' said Bunny, stubbing out his cigar in my beautiful grapes.

'Looking for my bag!' I retorted, getting cross myself.

'Leave it alone, can't you. I'll buy you another.'

Then he took me by the wrist and led me off to the dance floor. The music was slower and quieter now and he pulled me into his arms and held me so tightly that I could feel his pearl dress-studs digging into my breast-bone. He smelt like distilled essence of man. Not actually unpleasant . . . a compound of eau de cologne, heated wool, hair oil, smoke and whisky . . . but foreign. Male. He put his mouth next to my ear and spoke buzzingly into it.

'Now, Diana. All that nonsense at dinner . . . you're a clever little girl and more interesting than most. Were you trying to make a fool of me?'

'It was a game to amuse myself. Why should I want to make a fool of you? I don't know you.'

'So you were hoping to get me interested, eh? Well, it worked. And you're going to know me rather better before very long. I want you.'

At this point he held me even tighter and I felt something hard pressing against my pubic bone.

'You're holding me too tight!' I protested. 'Do let go! You're taking much too much for granted! I'm not in the habit of making love to perfect strangers.'

Bunny laughed and pushed his thigh between mine. It was profoundly disagreeable and I began to detest him. I saw Ginger standing in a corner talking to a lanky, bespectacled girl and almost envied her. Then I saw Min and Hugh circling stylishly near us. Hugh looked at me over Min's shoulder and raised his eyebrows at me. I made a grimace of horror and raised two fingers to my temple in imitation of a pistol. Bunny ran his right hand down my back and let it rest on my bottom.

'For God's sake,' I said, trying to push myself away. 'I'm going to get very angry if you don't stop mauling me. I really can't stand it. Let me go!'

He suddenly let me go and held me by both wrists so tightly that my eyes filled with tears of pain.

'You're a little tease, aren't you, Diana. You want to be subdued, eh? I love women when they're angry. Why don't you start swearing? I bet you know some filthy language, don't you?'

He laughed, very excited, and I began tó wonder if he was quite sane.

'Excuse me, sir. Colonel Johnson's looking for you.' Hugh's hand was on my shoulder as he looked apologetically at Bunny. 'There's a telephone call for you. Scotland, I think.'

'Damn!' said Bunny, gripping my elbow and making me yelp. He looked furious.

'Come on, Diana. This one's ours.'

Hugh peeled me out of Bunny's arms and we swept away.

'Hugh! God! Talk of relief flooding . . . I could easily drown!'

'I thought you were looking unhappy.'

'Look at my wrists! They're going to be dreadfully bruised.'

'We must keep you away from that horrible old lord at all costs. Any minute he'll find out that there wasn't a telephone call and he'll come charging back like an elephant in must. Let's ring for a taxi and go home. I'm fed up with this dance anyway. And Min's finished off the champagne.'

'It's a bit early to leave, isn't it? What will Min say?'

'It's nearly midnight. We'll say you've got a headache.'

He didn't answer my second question. I reflected that our departure was perhaps only an hour or so earlier than might have been expected. Min was sitting on a sofa with Sophie and her drunken swain, who had his eyes closed and seemed deeply asleep. Min and Sophie were laughing together.

'Come on, be quick. He'll be back any minute.'

'We must say goodbye to Min,' I insisted.

'No time for that,' Hugh protested but I ran over to Min and explained, rather incoherently, about Bunny.

'Well, I don't see why Hugh's got to go too. Can't you take a taxi on your own?' Min definitely looked annoyed.

'Yes. Of course I can. I wasn't thinking. That man got me into a panic. Of course I'll go on my own.'

'I can't let Daisy do that,' said Hugh, coming up behind me. 'That fellow's dangerous. Anyway I'm tired. I want to go now. I'll telephone you in the morning. You can come over to Foxcombe perhaps.'

'All right.' Min lit a cigarette with every appearance of unconcern but I could tell she was furious, also rather drunk. 'I might come over or I might not. Perhaps I'll dance with Hamish. I think I will as you're going. Poor Hamish, he's always been nuts about me. Perhaps I'll be too tired to come over in the morning. Let's make it lunch. Goodnight, Daisy.'

She attempted to get up and flounce off but Sophie's partner was sitting, fast asleep, on her skirt. Hugh laughed and patted her on the head.

'Don't drink any more, Min, or you'll be too sick to eat any lunch. We must go.'

''Bye, Min darling,' I said, anxious and placatory.

Min gave me a look compounded of anger and wretchedness. I thought she was making rather a fuss. Hugh was certainly safe with me. I intended to bolt my door, take a pill and get fast asleep as soon as possible.

We made our way through the house to the front door without being spotted by Bunny. Mrs Studley-Headlam was coming downstairs, a cigarette in one hand and a glass of champagne in the other.

'You two going? Rather early, isn't it?'

'Diana has a rotten headache,' said Hugh, looking at once very boy-scoutish. 'I'm going to ring for a taxi and take her home.'

'Get Briggs to drive you. He can come back for me.'

I attempted to thank her but she just waved her cigarette at me and wandered off. As Hugh was helping me into my cloak Michael Protheroe came downstairs, straightening his bow-tie and smoothing down his coat. He waggled an eyebrow at us and followed Mrs S-H.

'No prizes for guessing what they were doing,' said Hugh as we went out into the cold.

The journey home was warm and fast. There was a glass partition between Briggs and us. It was lovely to feel safe and enclosed and comfortable, with the smell of leather from the seats and wool from the rug which Hugh put over my knees. The headlights picked out silvery hedgerows and grass verges only to lose them again in swallowing blackness. Hugh smoked a cigarette and for a while we were silent, thoroughly happy.

'I'm sorry we left Min cross,' I said, at last, speaking languorously as though struggling from a dream.

'Why should she be cross?'

41

'Because she thought it was my fault that you were leaving early.'

'So it was. Your fault, I mean.'

'No! You said you were tired and fed-up. I could have gone by myself.'

'I wanted to leave because you were going. I wanted to be with you. And now I am.'

'Don't be ridiculous, Hugh. You're playing games again.'

'I've known all evening I wanted to be with you. You're beautiful, Daisy. You're the girl I want.'

'But what about Min? Oh, this is absurd. I refuse to take you seriously.'

'What about Min? What has she to do with it?'

'Well . . . you know . . . there's something between you, isn't there? Don't be obtuse. You know perfectly well what I mean. In the vulgar phrase, you're "going out" together.'

'Not as far as I know. Just because I've taken Min to a few parties it doesn't mean that I've taken vows. There are at least three women in my life who are more important to me than Min. I like her. She's pretty and amusing but I'm not in love with her and I've never said I was.'

I was silent for a while, thinking. Poor Min, she'd got it bad and it didn't look as if it would turn out well. As far as I was concerned he was still her property, whatever he said, but of course such a good-looking man was bound to be pursued by desperate women, all breaking their hearts for him. The problem with handsome men was their rarity.

'The trouble with you intellectual girls is that you're all so intense. You're always trying to categorise. I don't belong to anyone. Nor, as far as I know, do you. Of course, if you don't find me attractive, that's another matter. Do you?'

'I don't know you . . . we only met a few hours ago . . . it isn't just a question of spontaneous lust.'

'That's all you know. Anyway, enough talk. You're the most beautiful girl I've met for quite a long time and I've been thinking about you all evening until I've worked myself into a lather of desire. If you want to read me your poems or discuss George Eliot, I don't mind, but it isn't what interests me about you.'

At that moment the car drove through the gates of Foxcombe Manor and we were passing beneath the trees which lined the avenue. The only thought which I held on to was that Min was in love with this man. The moral imperative to forbid even a kiss lay heavily upon me.

The house seemed very bright after the womb-like interior of the car. We went into the drawing room where the remnants of the fire lay in mountainous, pearly ashes. Hugh helped himself to a brandy and soda and took a sandwich from the tray. I knew I should go upstairs straight away but I was excited. I had never before felt so attracted to anyone as I did to Hugh.

'Lord Bollingbrook has this moment telephoned, madam,' said the butler, sliding gracefully round the door. 'He wished to know if you had returned. I told him that you had arrived five minutes ago. He then said that he would be returning himself, at once.'

'That's it. I'm going to bed,' I said as soon as the butler had gone. 'Alone. With my door bolted. That man terrifies me.'

'All right,' said Hugh, his good humour for the first time disturbed. 'Goodnight, Daisy.'

He turned his back on me and went to the window. Pulling aside the curtain he stared out at the moonlit park. I went up to my room, feeling suddenly tired and, it must be confessed, disappointed. But a good conscience is a continual feast, I told myself as I threw my cloak and bag on to a chair and kicked off my shoes. I went to the door to fasten it. There was nothing but a keyhole, minus a key.

Damn, blast, bloody hell! I began to undress quickly. I felt that I would be safer in bed, asleep, with the light out so I washed my face and cleaned my teeth with less than my usual thoroughness, got into my nightdress and found my sleeping pills. I didn't have trouble sleeping but my dreams were generally of the nightmarish kind. My mother, who always had bottles of drugs of various kinds about her, had recommended these as 'happy' pills and had given me at least two hundred. The little pink pills gave me the most glorious nights of rapturous contentment and I was probably already addicted. I swigged down four, double the usual dose, with a glass of Malvern water, so thoughtfully provided. I was safe up on the second floor, I told myself, as a delicious sensation of peacefulness began to steal over me. Bunny could hardly break into every room in the house. And the servants would surely be awake to the impropriety of telling him which was my room.

I began to dream that I was walking by a lake on which the sun was splintering into brilliant sparks. A swan slid smoothly along beside me. Then I was the swan, the water soft and cool against my feathered breast, the sun warm on my back. Suddenly the heavens shattered with a searing light and the water whipped into a snowy foam which dissolved into white sheets. I was sitting up in bed and Bunny was standing in the doorway, a black shape against the light from the corridor.

'Diana? Where the hell are you? God, this is a bore having to hunt through the damned house. You can push a man too far, you know.'

'Good evening, sir,' said Hugh politely, emerging from my bathroom, wearing only a pair of underpants. 'If you're looking for a housemaid, their rooms are further down the corridor, I think. Move over, Daisy.'

He slid his warm body into bed and took me in his arms.

'Just close the door, sir, if you wouldn't mind. I'm susceptible to draughts.'

The door banged so hard that I felt the bed shake. Or perhaps it was just our laughter. I suppose it was the effect of the pills but I found myself unable to stop giggling. Of course it was infectious, and Hugh and I laughed until we cried.

'What were you doing in my bathroom?' I asked as soon as I could control myself.

'I heard the old bastard banging about through the rooms on the floor below. I didn't fancy playing the hero and confronting him as guardian of your virtue. He's bigger than I am. But I guessed that if he found me in situ he'd give up. Rather humiliating for him.'

'Thank you,' I said, yawning as the pills began to take over. 'Eternally grateful – goodnight.'

'What about expressing a little of this gratitude?' said Hugh, nuzzling my neck.

'Can't – pills, sleep – night.'

'Daisy! Wake up!'

'Night.'

'Hell!'

I felt him fumbling with my nightdress. I was too comfortable and happy to care. He became a Jersey cow, blowing grassy breath in my face and licking me with a dark, wet tongue. I was just admiring the cow's eyelashes when there was a burrowing sensation between my legs and he became a blind, black mole with big white hands scrabbling under the earth. There was a short, sharp pain and then all was comfortable again. We were at a fair rocking ourselves in swing-boats, each holding a fat, tasselled rope in our hands and flying higher and faster until I flew out of my seat and found myself resting beneath a beautiful tree with a large black labrador, panting hotly, lying beside me.

When I awoke the room was filled with daylight. Fragments of dream floated aimlessly in and out of my mind and I stretched my limbs to find a cool part of the bed. I was not alone. Then I remembered ... rather dimly ... Hugh. I opened my eyes and looked at him. He was sleeping on his side, turned towards me, his face calm, his breathing quiet and even.

I groaned aloud. What had I done? I would swear Hugh to absolute secrecy. Bunny was unlikely to tell anyone for fear of looking ridiculous. No one would ever know. I would make myself forget about it. It would be as though it had never happened. I turned my head to look at the window. It must be quite late for the sun shone glaringly through the *oeil-de-boeuf* window and hurt my eyes. I shut them again and the spider-shape of its glazing bars burned red inside my eyelids against the livid viridian of the sky-filled pieces between. But there was a red blob, quite large, that was not formed by the glazing bars against the light. I frowned and tried to focus on it as the image began to fade. I opened my eyes.

Min was sitting on the window-seat, her legs crossed at the knee, one hand holding a cigarette, its smoke blown into feather-shapes by the draught.

# CHAPTER FIVE

The train emerged from beneath the canopy of Euston Station to a snow-laden sky, striated and yellow like old piano keys. The weather, even for January, was harsh and before we had left the suburbs of North London the carriage windows were streaked with soot and melting snowflakes. It was one week after the Oxford reunion and fifteen years after Min had found me in bed with Hugh. I was on my way to the village of Dunston Abchurch in Lancashire, to spend a long weekend with Min.

My spirits were high despite, or perhaps because of, the number of unknown elements in prospect. I knew that Min was married to Robert Weston. I still had the photograph of their wedding, cut out from the society section of a magazine thirteen years ago. It was a bad photograph. It showed him to be tallish, fairish and unsmiling. Min had looked utterly unlike herself with her hair drawn into a tight knot on the top of her head and a crumpled, ballooning dress and veil. She was grinning idiotically and squinting as though the sun were in her eyes. At the time, although we had not seen or spoken to each other for two years, I had felt a stab of anxiety that she had done this important thing without me there, to pluck her eyebrows, iron her dress and supervise the packing of her clothes. Then the anxiety was swiftly blotted out by the realisation that now she was gone from me for ever. Now she had someone with a legal obligation to look after her, someone to whom she was bound in mutual love, one hoped, and who would probably make a far better protector than I had proved to be. This realisation had brought about a feeling of desolation which had stayed with me as a sort of basso ostinato running through my daily life for about a year.

Of course I forgot about it in time. My academic career required hard work and meticulous planning. The ground has always been thick with Eng. Lit. graduates who are proficient at disembowelling prose and poetry and who don't want to get inky and chalky in a dreary school smelling of gym shoes and stew. After graduating from Oxford I had decided to go to Cambridge to do my Ph.D. I stuck at it, produced a publishable thesis on a very minor aspect of *The Faerie Queen*, wrote a few articles for the *Times Literary Supplement* and the *Spectator* and kept my name in the view of those who mattered. I had more or less cornered the market in the writings of Thomas Love Peacock, largely because most people found him too mannered to read with anything approaching pleasure. Then my college offered me a research fellowship and I accepted it.

I liked Cambridge from the first. I bought a small house in Orchard Street with the money my father left me and decorated it with as much French furniture and as many English eighteenth-century drawings as I could afford. In the late fifties the public imagination was captivated by contemporary Scandinavian furniture . . . long, low sofas in blond wood upholstered in tweedy fabrics . . . and by such whimsicalities as egg-shaped wicker chairs hanging from the ceiling by chains. My house was, in this context, striking and original. I shed the last traces of studenthood in my appearance, bought expensive French clothes, 'few but good' as Lady Bart's generation always advised, and courted a chic sexiness by wearing my hair very long and applying plenty of dark lipstick. I smoked Turkish cigarettes and drank only champagne. I drove an old two-seater Talbot-Lago. It was a style that was rather obvious and very affected, but as a substitute for self-confidence it was quite successful. Some people were put off by the arrogance of it all. I thought, in my ignorance, that it was as good a way of selecting friends as any other.

There were certainly plenty of men. Cambridge, in those days, suffered from such a preponderance of males that any female, knock-kneed, snaggle-toothed or pebble-lensed, was worth at least the softener of an eclair at the Dorothy café before beginning the relentless campaign to get her to bed. As my legs and teeth were straight and I had twenty-twenty vision I was taken to Covent Garden, Stratford and the Mirabelle. Instead of the éclair there was *raie au beurre noir* and crêpe suzette but the campaign was in all essentials the same. It was hard to say why some were successful with me and others weren't. It wasn't money, nor was it class. They all had brains to some degree. Good looks were important, which narrowed the field dramatically. Occasionally, it was sheer persistence. Rarely it was charm. But to speak of success here refers only to the campaigner gaining his objective. I can't remember one occasion of love-making which wasn't begun in extreme apprehension and ended in utter despair. Though the Pill existed in those days it was not generally available. The spectre of pregnancy lay between the sheets with us and stalked me for weeks afterwards. Even now I find the smell of French chalk disturbing, reminding me as it does of the treacherous and unlovely diaphragm which accompanied me on all my sexual adventures.

Daily newspapers and women's magazines did not write much, then, of sex and the skills of love-making. I was too ignorant myself to identify lack of expertise. I only felt, as I lay more or less immobile while some man laboured grimly above me, that this attractive and amusing creature, who had made me laugh at dinner and wept with me at *Madame Butterfly*, had become with terrifying abruptness a stranger, an enemy, secret and separate within his alien skin, his eyes opaque, his feelings unintelligible.

Some men were not put off by my frigidity. I had many declarations of love and several proposals of marriage. But independence suited me. I enjoyed teaching, liked most of my students and many of my colleagues, had society and solitude when I wanted it. I went to Bayreuth for Wagner and La Scala for Verdi. A girlfriend, who liked shopping as much as I did, had a flat in Paris. We spent heavenly days together buying clothes, eating and walking about the city and dining and dancing at night with her rich, intellectual friends. And, of course, at home, I spent a great deal of time reading and writing. My father was dead. My mother, by now, was best friends with the vodka bottle. She was married, for the fourth time, to a drunk called Ezra Pascoe. He used to try to kiss me and push his hand down my shirt. My mother, though moving in a fog-bank of alcohol, noticed Ezra's stepfatherly attentions. I saw her rarely and usually when Ezra was away. The only constraints in my life were of my own choosing and I considered myself extremely fortunate. I was thirty-four, single, moderately successful and genuinely happy.

The train pulled into open country. The dark ploughed furrows were filling with white as the snow fell more wildly. I was reminded of Keats's 'flaw-blown sleet' and the 'iced gusts that raved and beat'. Before long it was blizzarding and the train seemed to be running through a howling corridor of activity and commotion while everything above and beyond was frozen in hard white light, no sky, no earth, no trees or gates or hedges, no beginning or end.

At Hampstoke the train was delayed while the line was cleared. We were told that there would be a wait of half an hour or so but that the station buffet was open. Hampstoke was a Victorian station and there was a good old-fashioned fire of glowing coals which provoked a rush for the tables nearest it. I drank bitter, stewed tea and ate a liver-pâté sandwich which was the only kind they had. Anthony Trollope wrote of the railway-station sandwich as being like 'a whited sepulchre' which was witty but failed to capture quite the horror of it. I opened a packet of custard creams which I had chosen in preference to the doughnuts which blushed with cheap, fluorescent jam beneath a glass dome, and eavesdropped shamelessly on the couple at the next table.

It was 1969, two years after the summer of the social and sexual revolution. Accountants, stockbrokers, librarians, bank tellers and office clerks had grown their hair down to their shoulders and put on cheesecloth shirts, jeans, goat's hair socks and embroidered coats from the Far East. A boy and girl in their early twenties were dressed in just this way, she wearing in addition a browband which sat low over her protruding ear-tips. He wore a black felt hat on the brim of which was written in beads, 'Love and Peace'.

They were quarrelling ferociously in whispers and the girl was stabbing miserably at her doughnut with a penknife while the young man hissed at her through stubble-bound lips. I heard enough to understand that he was accusing her of sleeping with his friend. 'A bitch on heat' and 'common little tart' were two of the expressions which I caught, uttered with a most savage disgust. Finally the girl said sullenly that she thought he believed in free love. Wasn't he always going on about it until he bored the pants off her and everyone else? I found myself leaning sideways, the better to hear the reply. Instead the young man suddenly glared at me and got up and walked out. A goatish whiff trailed behind him like brimstone. Two tears slid down the girl's grubby cheeks and the doughnut bled a little squirt of jam in sympathy.

I reminded myself that she was not one of my students and would hardly welcome my interference. I was glad to return to my compartment which was cold but peaceful as I had had it to myself all the way from London. I spread my coat over my knees and looked at my luggage on the rack opposite with a feeling of smugness. Besides a new and very pretty dress and some jerseys, it contained a great deal of warm, silk underwear from Paris, a beautiful quilted dressing-gown and even a pair

49

of soft white bed-socks. I was prepared for every eventuality. In my bag I had a small silver flask of Rémy-Martin which would make an admirable *digestif* for the sandwich. I drank a thimbleful and opened my book with a sensation of pleasure.

But the argument in the station buffet, as well as the knowledge that I would shortly be seeing Min, brought the old scenes once more, for the hundredth . . . for the thousandth time . . . before my eyes. Again I lived through the moment of waking at Foxcombe and finding myself in bed with Hugh Anstey. I stared at an excruciatingly bad print of Lake Windermere above the seat opposite and, instead of freakishly vivid blobs of ultramarine heather, I saw Min's face as she sat on the window-seat, looking at me. I remembered just the tone of her voice, cold and hard, as she exhaled cigarette smoke through her nose and then said, 'It's rather late. Hadn't you better wake Hugh? If he wants any breakfast he'll have to hurry up. It's past ten o'clock.'

I sat up in bed. I wished I could remember clearly what had happened the night before. The happy pills had quite worn off and I felt only a sensation of strong foreboding. Had Hugh made love to me? I had a horrible feeling that he had.

'Min,' I said nervously. 'Please don't look like that. Whatever happened was absolutely unimportant. Hugh was trying to protect me from that lunatic. He actually came to my room. Luckily Hugh guessed that he would. Then he went to sleep. I took a double dose of my pills. I can't remember a thing . . .'

I was interrupted by a groan from Hugh as he turned on the pillow and stretched an arm over me. I pushed it away and he opened his eyes.

'Not very friendly this morning, my darling Daisy,' he mumbled reproachfully. 'How unmannerly. And you were so welcoming last night. So capricious, you clever girls. A simple little fuck isn't enough for you. You've got to be courted and flattered and wooed like Elizabeth the First . . .'

'Hugh! For God's sake! Shut up!' I shook him hard and he opened his eyes properly and sat up.

'Hello, Hugh,' said Min, looking admirably cool. It certainly didn't fool me but it seemed to convince Hugh.

'Min. This is a surprise, as Mary said to the Archangel Gabriel. Is it lunch-time already?'

He leaned over to look at his watch on the bedside table. I saw, with an irrational feeling of guilt for noticing it, that his back was very muscular, smooth and pale, like marble.

'Twenty past ten. Well, who's going to join me for coddled eggs and devilled kidneys? Nothing quite like sex for promoting an appetite.'

'Hugh! For heaven's sake!' I said despairingly. 'You're being deliberately insensitive.'

'Don't worry, Daisy,' said Min, in such a sweet voice that for a moment I wondered if things were going to be all right after all. 'I know Hugh's sense of humour. I want to talk to Daisy alone, Hugh, so do go and get something to eat. You're just in the way here.'

'All right, but don't bully me. A bloke doesn't like to be toyed with wantonly, drained of his vital essences and then flung aside like a used handkerchief.'

Min smiled thinly. Hugh got out of bed and I saw with a sense of shock, which was ridiculous in the circumstances, that he was naked. I had never seen a man naked before and, from the way Min was staring, I was suddenly convinced that she hadn't either. This was nothing like the collection of softly-rounded objects, reminiscent of a modest portion of mixed grill, which had adorned the fronts of all the male statues Min and I had examined in our childhood. It was altogether larger and frankly alarming. He saw our faces and laughed.

'Well, you would insist on my getting up at once. If you'd let me wait a bit . . . now, where are my pants? . . . it would have been more decorous.'

He burrowed between the sheets and gave my thigh a gentle squeeze with his hand before hauling his underpants out and putting them on. I had turned my eyes embarrassedly away but Min was staring at him as though about to sit an examination in anatomy. Hugh went into the bathroom and could be heard crashing about, presumably getting dressed. Min looked around vaguely for an ashtray and I held out the one by my bed, a charming piece of faience with a shepherdess painted on it. Min took it and ground out her cigarette, savagely. Then she lit another one immediately and smoked it with short, urgent sucks, never once looking in my direction. When Hugh emerged from the bathroom, wearing his evening clothes but with his dress-shirt open, water dripping from the ends of his hair and looking wonderfully tousled, I was on the point of begging him to stay.

'Isn't it rather early for this public-house atmosphere?' he said, waving his hands about in front of his face. 'You'll never make old bones, Min, with a habit like yours. I suppose we should be grateful you haven't taken to a pipe and fisherman's shag.'

He laughed and strapped on his watch. I realised then that he knew there was going to be a row and wanted no part of it. I couldn't really blame him. I watched him as he turned in the doorway and blew first me and then Min a kiss. The door closed behind him. I saw that Min, for almost the first time that morning, was looking straight at me.

'I suppose you imagine that you've proved beyond all possible doubt that I can't hope to compete with you when it comes to men.'

Her voice was very calm but there was a slight tremor which betrayed the tension in her throat.

'Oh Min, I'm sorry! I can't tell you how sorry I am! I'd give anything for it not to have happened . . .'

'Oh, don't give me that! I suppose you want me to believe that he raped you and you were unwilling!'

'Well, not quite but I had taken . . .'

'Oh, shut up!' she said with a real, hard anger in her voice and now I knew that it was definitely not going to be all right. 'I don't want to hear about how fantastic and sexy you are and how you can't help men falling for you. I trusted you. I told you what I felt about him. What a fool I was! You probably decided even before you saw him that you were going to have him for yourself. You absolute bloody bitch!'

'Oh, Min. Please! Of course I didn't. You know I don't have any self-confidence with men. Of course I didn't mean to do anything to hurt you. You can't possibly think that after all the years we've been friends . . .'

My voice tailed away feebly. The trouble was that the whole thing suddenly felt hopelessly unreal. I could see Min and hear her and imagine what she must be feeling. But I felt as though I were looking in through a window, watching someone unconnected with me, as though I myself had no part in it. This had so often happened at crises in my life, as though I couldn't face up to the outpouring of emotion. Instead of reacting to it I always withdrew to an unhelpful and unfeeling remoteness. I struggled to reach her, to say the words which might comfort or explain but my mind was blank, my feelings stupefied. I couldn't concentrate and with every second I felt myself going further away. Min pushed her hair out of her eyes and lit another cigarette.

'I suppose if I hadn't come up here this morning I wouldn't have known anything about it. I thought I'd been a bit grumpy last night and I was going to apologise. I wanted . . .' here her voice went up several tones higher and her eyes filled with tears ' . . . to talk about him. You see,' she laughed in a manner which struck me as theatrical and I hated myself the moment I thought this, 'I loved him and you've ruined it. I'll never love anyone else.'

'Of course you'll love other people!' I said, angry in my turn. 'You're only twenty. There'll be lots of others . . . hundreds. There will be for both of us. I didn't want to sleep with him. And I'm dreadfully sorry to have made you unhappy. But it wasn't going to be any good, anyway.'

I regretted this almost before the words were said.

'What do you mean?' Min got up and walked to the centre of the room, her jaw set. I was reminded of the sort of films Min and I loved, really awful feature films in period costume with mean, devastatingly attractive villains and defiant heroines. Again the proper feelings wouldn't come and a dreamlike sense of helplessness overtook me.

'I only meant that he isn't the type to take anyone seriously. Any girl interests him to a point . . . bed, I mean . . . but no further.'

'You discussed me with him, didn't you?' said Min, with inconvenient percipience. 'Go on, what did he say? Tell me. I want to know.'

'Well . . . he said . . . let me think . . . what was it exactly?' I was playing for time. 'How amusing he found you. And attractive. Definitely attractive.'

'Go on. I want to know everything he said.'

'He thinks you're very witty.'

'So you said. What else did he say?'

'Well, only that there were other women in his life and he didn't feel ready to commit himself to anyone in particular.'

'In other words I wasn't particularly important to him?'

'Oh . . . well . . . no, not that exactly . . . he's very fond of you . . .'

'I see.'

I didn't like the way she said that. There was something so like ugly contempt in her eyes. I hadn't made things any better. I tried again.

'Min, I honestly didn't intend to sleep with him. And I'm sure I don't mean a thing to him. He's very good-looking and all that but he isn't worth quarrelling over. Please say you forgive me. I really am sorry.'

I half got out of bed and put my hand to touch her arm but she struck it away and her face became scarlet. The action was so violent that I felt my skin prickle with shock.

'He may not be worth it to you but he is to me! I'm in love with him! Go on, laugh or triumph or whatever you did it for! He wasn't important to you but anyway you went ahead, knowing what I felt about him. You vain, selfish, narcissistic bitch! God how it hurts . . . his face asleep . . . I can't forget it. I shan't ever forgive you! I don't ever . . . ever want to speak to you again in all my life!'

She was panting now as though her chest hurt her and tears were spilling from her eyes. I felt sick and frozen.

'Min!' I said feebly. 'Let's be calm. Let's . . . please . . . talk about it. You're my very best friend. You're much more important to me than any man. Please.'

'Bugger off, Diana,' said Min, walking to the door. In a moment she was through it and had closed it behind her.

I got up and stared at myself in the cheval glass. My nightdress was spotted with blood. I looked at my face, bare of make-up, my hair sticking up at the back where it had been rubbed against the pillow while making love with Hugh. Was I narcissistic? The image in the glass was nothing if not thoroughly depressing. I had never loved myself less.

I went into the bathroom and ran a bath. I lay up to my neck in the steaming, scented water, which yesterday had given me such pleasure. I dried myself, dressed and began to make up my face, sitting on the window-seat with the sun dazzling in the concavity of my magnifying mirror. This made my eyes water painfully but still my thoughts were drifting and vague. I heard the sound of a car starting and looked down to the carriage circle in front of the house. I recognised Min's car, a blue

Hillman Imp, as it drew away from the front door and travelled, much too fast, down the drive. I began to apply mascara very carefully as the first small pinch of unhappiness made itself felt in the region below my ribcage. It was like the onset of physical illness, the first symptoms presenting themselves so insidiously that, despite the gradual accretion of abnormal sensations, the moment of conscious recognition that there is something wrong comes with a shock.

Now I identified a feeling of profound shame. The situation was detestable and the aspect that disgusted me most was that throughout I had behaved with complete passivity. Hugh had done what he intended and was, presumably, satisfied. Min was innocent, a victim, and had denounced me with all the consolation of righteous anger. No doubt she was very miserable now but she would get over it in time and she had the luxury of nothing to regret. But I had not meant to sleep with Hugh and the act had been without love or gratification. As far as I could remember there had not been a particle of pleasure in it and yet it had placed me absolutely in the wrong. I felt, like Lady Macbeth, that my hands would never be clean again.

There was a tap on the door and for one moment I stupidly thought that it was Min. Then I remembered that I had seen her drive away and the disappointment registered itself with a further sharp prick of misery.

'Diana?'

It was Caroline Protheroe's voice.

'Are you there, Diana? Can I come in? I need to talk to someone.'

The anguish in her voice was unmistakable. I sat very still, my mascara brush poised, hardly breathing. There was a silence during which I sternly charged myself to answer. But an overwhelming emotional fatigue prevented me. I could not, at that moment, throw myself imaginatively into someone else's feelings. I heard her utter a low sound, almost a sob, and then her footsteps went away. I finished my face and packed my suitcase. I put a pound note on the bedside table for the maids and took a last look through the window at the view across the park. It was a scene which should have delighted. Fat pigeons fluttered among the trees whose trunks were patched and stippled with sunlight. The sheep grazed contentedly in the meadow which was still glaucous with dew. A rook cawed somewhere in the glassy sky. I sighed deeply and went downstairs to breakfast.

Hugh was still in the dining room, an eggy plate pushed away from him, reading a newspaper. Michael Protheroe was there, too, cutting up a rasher of bacon with fierce concentration. Hugh just gave me a look over his newspaper and lifted his eyebrows before looking down again at the page. Michael leapt to his feet and pulled out a chair for me. Then he seized a plate from the side table and asked whether I wanted sausage, bacon, mushrooms, tomatoes, scrambled eggs or porridge. He was extraordinarily sleek and reminded me of a well-trained labrador, wet from fetching sticks in the river. His shoes, buttons, eyes, teeth and fingernails were lucid and shiny, his clothes smooth, expensive and well-fitting, his eyes fastened on me alertly, waiting for a command. He seemed profoundly disappointed when I wanted only a piece of toast. A maid brought me fresh coffee. It was a pity I was too dejected to enjoy this unusual comfort and affluence.

'Sleep well, Diana?' Michael asked, giving me the butter with an air of eager expectation as though he had dropped a soft, dead bird at my feet.

'Yes. Thank you. Very well.'

'One of the many good things about Diana,' said Hugh, not looking up from his newspaper, 'is that she doesn't snore.'

Michael's cheeks turned a dusky red. I was furious with Hugh. It was unforgivable. Mrs Studley-Headlam came in, with a gust of delicious and expensive scent. She looked cross.

'Good morning. I hope you slept well, Diana. Don't bother to get up, Hugh,' she said, as he lifted himself an inch or two from the seat of his chair, still holding the newspaper. 'What's the matter, Michael? You don't look at all well. I told you you were drinking too much. You look quite liverish this morning. Where is that girl? There is no marmalade. She forgets something every morning. These local girls are quite untrainable. She'll have to go. What is amusing you, Diana?' she asked sharply as she rang the little bell which stood on the table near her cup.

I suppose it was hysteria which made me suddenly want to laugh at the angry expression on Michael's face. Mrs S-H didn't wait for an answer but rang the bell again more vigorously.

'For heaven's sake, Emma!' snapped Michael. 'You'll damage our eardrums! I'll go and see where she is.'

But at that moment the maid came running in, looking frightened.

'Oh, madam! I'm ever so sorry. But Mrs Protheroe's cut herself! And Phyllis has fainted! She can't stomach the sight of blood and there's ever so much of it! Cook says she dursn't leave the poached eggs for Mr Studley-Headlam's breakfast and I can't find Janice anywhere.'

'My God!' said Michael, jumping up.

'Where is she?' demanded Mrs S-H, also getting up and looking rather pale.

'I don't know, madam. She was making up the fires . . .'

'Not Janice, you fool! Mrs Protheroe!'

'In the blue bathroom, madam. And Phyllis is stuck in the doorway, all crumpled up . . .'

'That'll do, Susan. Tell Mr Studley-Headlam what's happened and ask him to telephone straight away for an ambulance. He's in his study. Then come up to the blue bathroom at once.'

'Bit of an overreaction, isn't it?' said Hugh, when we were left alone. 'Everyone seems to be in a very bad mood this morning. Except me. I'm in an exceptionally good mood. But Min was crying fit to bust before breakfast. I told her her eyelids would be swollen like zeppelins if she went on and it seemed to make her cry more.'

'Are you absolutely heartless, Hugh?' I asked, severely.

'Certainly not. I'm quite prepared to go to bed with her if that's what she wants. I told her so. I said my loins were entirely at her disposal, but she merely screamed something at me . . . I couldn't hear what through all the gulping and sobbing . . . and zoomed off in her car.'

'Hugh! That was dreadful! You are an absolute bastard! But perhaps it'll make her fall out of love with you which would be a good thing.'

'Certainly it would. I didn't ask her to fall in love with me. I've been completely truthful throughout and yet I seem to have come in for a great deal of undeserved obloquy.'

Mrs S-H rushed in before I had time to think of a reply. She looked quite furious.

'Diana, go up and look after Caroline while Michael and

Leo move Phyllis out of the way. The girl weighs as much as a fattened bullock. Susan's having hysterics and that wretched Janice still hasn't appeared. Hugh, wait in the hall for the ambulance and tell them where to go.'

I went upstairs and found Michael and Leo in Caroline's bedroom, struggling with the unconscious body of poor Phyllis. Michael had taken hold of her shoulders while Leo had a large purple leg under each arm as they stumbled over to the bed and almost threw her on to it. Michael picked up the carafe of water from the bedside table and chucked it into her face. I didn't wait to see the result but pushed my way into the bathroom with great difficulty, the floor being covered with sodden, blood-soaked towels.

The sight was so shocking that suddenly I felt hot and sick. Caroline lay naked in the bath while swirls and clouds of bloody rust-red water gurgled slowly away down the waste-pipe. Her face and body were bone-white and there were mauve shadows beneath her eyes which were closed. I thought she must be dead. Absurd, irrelevant thoughts rushed through my brain. Mr Merdle cradled in a bath like a sarcophagus, his jugular vein severed by the tortoiseshell knife. Marat, murdered in his bath by Charlotte Corday. Agamemnon dying in his bath, murdered by Clytemnestra.

But Caroline had not been murdered. She had tried to kill herself. I remembered her voice, so dejected, outside my bedroom door. And my silence. I snatched a dry towel from the chair and began to wrap it round one of Caroline's wrists. The next minute Leo and Michael were beside me and together we lifted her out of the bath and carried her into the bedroom, laying her on the bed next to Phyllis who was beginning to come round. I pulled the eiderdown from beneath Phyllis and tucked it round Caroline's thin, blue-veined body and childish breasts. Briefly she opened her eyes and began to shudder as violently as though she had her finger in an electric socket. I wrapped the other wrist and pulled the rest of the blankets around her until nothing but the top half of her face was visible. Phyllis began to moan as she became conscious but was so abashed to find herself lying with her skirt about her waist and her knickers exposed to the full view of the two men that she was led away by a white-faced Susan without much more than a whimper.

'Should I get some brandy?' said Leo, looking down at Caroline. 'Poor little thing!'

'No. She mustn't have alcohol,' said Michael, who seemed perplexed and uncertain, all his swagger gone. 'Alcohol stops blood-clotting. She's a haemophiliac. My God, what a thing to do. She really meant to kill herself!'

He rubbed his hand over his face and looked so confused and wretched that it was impossible not to feel that he was a little to be pitied. Leo and I tried to rub some warmth into her while Michael went to find some proper bandages. He seemed eager to get out of the room. Mrs S-H met him outside the door. I heard her voice, loud and questioning. 'Her mother' and 'bloody fool thing to do' were two phrases which I caught before the door was closed. I stroked the wisps of hair from Caroline's blood-streaked cheek and her eyes opened again. I longed to say something comforting but felt inhibited in the presence of Leo. Then two ambulancemen and a doctor came in and I saw I could do nothing more to help. Hugh was alone, downstairs in the dining room, staring out of the window and jingling the change in his pockets. When he saw me he looked relieved.

'Shall we get out of here? I'll drive you back to Oxford if you like. I can't stand much more of this blood-boltered scene. Look at your shirt.'

I saw that there were dark red stains on my sleeves and cuffs. He didn't ask about Caroline and I was too shocked and too exhausted to speak about it myself. We drove back to Oxford in Hugh's two-seater Austin-Healey with the hood down and the cold wind blowing in my face, making my eyes run and whipping my hair over my forehead until it stung. It was too noisy to talk. By the time we reached St Hilary's I was stiff with cold but calm.

'Can I come in?' he asked, getting my luggage from the boot.

'No. Min would be bound to get to know if you did. The girls all gossip like mad.'

'Would that matter?'

'My only chance of making it up with Min lies in future good behaviour. That means never seeing you again.'

'Do you mean that she matters more than I do?' he asked, smiling but not able to conceal that his vanity was wounded. He had never looked more attractive.

'I'm sorry.'

'Is this moral blackmail? Do you want me to declare myself in love with you? Am I supposed to prostrate myself at your feet?'

'I'm afraid it wouldn't help at all. Thank you for the lift. Goodbye.'

I picked up my bags and walked into the college. I heard him call my name but I didn't look round. My room seemed very silent when I had unpacked my things, changed my shirt and thrown away the dead flowers from the vase on my desk. There were ten more days of the vacation to run and most of the rooms on my corridor were empty. I made myself some coffee and sat down to work. I was writing an essay on the Metaphysical Poets. I read some of Marvell's poems, sharpened my pencil and put a new file block into a binder. 'Society is all but rude, To this delicious solitude,' I read aloud in firm tones. Suddenly, overcome by anxiety and loneliness, I put my head on my arms and sobbed.

## Chapter Six

The brandy, and the warmth of the train, must have lulled me to sleep for I opened my eyes with a start and saw that we were standing in a small country station. Someone on the platform fumbled ineffectually at the carriage door. I pretended to work at it from my side and then made demonstrations of helplessness through the snow-speckled, weeping glass.

'Must be frozen,' I mouthed, while holding firmly on to the handle so that it couldn't be turned.

It was a little unkind, considering the clouts of snow which fell from the gutters of the station roof but I wanted to be able to fortify myself with brandy from time to time, and an audience would have made me feel like a disreputable drunk. Also I dislike very much the way strangers, encouraged by the intimacy of tête-à-tête within the carriage, use it as a confessional. Lacking the courage to be deliberately rude I have been forced to listen to a great many improbable confidences which

I seem cursed to revolve in my mind for hours afterwards, extending the tedium unendurably.

We drew jerkily away from the platform. I relaxed my grip on the handle and took another sip of brandy while my thoughts slid effortlessly back to that Easter vacation fifteen years before.

I had endured the remaining week and half after the Johnsons' dance and before the start of term with a painful impatience to see Min. She was not sulky by nature. I felt sure that if I could show her how desperately sorry I was and how humbly I longed to be forgiven, she was too generous to hold out against me. Perhaps she had already begun to see that Hugh was just as much to blame as I was.

But Min did not appear on the first day or the second. On the third day of term my tutor told me that Min had glandular fever and was on an open-ended leave of absence.

I wrote several letters to Min at her mother's house in London but I had no reply. Finally, in desperation, I wrote to Lady Bart, explaining that Min and I had quarrelled and though I wouldn't burden her with the substance of it, I was very anxious to make up the quarrel and would she very kindly intercede for me, tell Min how very, very sorry I was and ask her to write to me? I received a letter by return of post addressed in Lady Bart's familiar hand and the sight of the envelope was like food after famine. But the opening sentences were enough to make me wish that I had never applied for relief. She addressed me as 'Dear Diana' which she had never done before and which, from her pen, seemed to freeze me as I read.

> It was good of you to write, asking about Min. I am sorry to say that she is far from well and I am very worried about her. She is terribly tired, eats almost nothing and is a very bad colour. However she is being well looked after and Doctor Hallam assures me that it is a common complaint of girls of her age and that she will, given time, entirely recover her strength.
>
> I had gathered, before receiving your letter, that you two had quarrelled though Min has told me nothing of the reason why and it is none of my business. It certainly seems very sad after all that you and she have been to one another.

Despite my anxiety on Min's account, I received a letter a few days ago which almost put my concern for her out of my head, so shocked was I by its contents. As it was about you, I shall tell you exactly what it said as you should certainly know what others are saying about you.

Mrs Studley-Headlam, whom I have never met but with whom I believe you stayed during the weekend of the Johnsons' dance, was so 'disgusted and alarmed' (her words) by your behaviour that, after having spoken to Daphne Johnson, she felt herself compelled to write to me as she believed your own parents were either dead or living abroad. According to my correspondent, you flirted so outrageously with a very dear friend of hers, Lord Bollingbrook, that he called you a 'wanton coquette of the most dangerous kind' and Mrs Studley-Headlam had to give him an assurance that you would not in future be invited to her house if he was expected to be present.

She then said that you attempted to allure Hugh Anstey with secret assignations in the garden before dinner and that, according to her servants, Hugh spent the night in your bedroom. I had supposed, before that weekend, that Hugh was Min's boyfriend. I suppose this is the cause of the quarrel. As I said before, it is none of my business so I will not comment.

Distasteful as this all seems to me . . . and so out of character that at first I thought I must be reading about someone else altogether . . . Mrs Studley-Headlam then made an accusation so dreadful that I was unable to believe it. I quite thought the woman must be out of her mind. She says that you made such blatant attempts to fascinate a young man staying as a guest in her house that the following morning his wife tried to take her own life. I was so upset, Diana, that anyone should say such a dreadful thing of you, whom I have loved quite as my own daughter, that I made some inquiries. Imagine my distress when I telephoned the London Clinic and found that there existed a Mrs Protheroe and, as far as I have been able to ascertain from discreet questions amongst my own circle, Mrs Studley-Headlam was speaking the truth.

This is, of course, gossip and I know you young people are – perhaps rightly – scornful of its power to harm. But, you know, people will talk and reputations are made by what people say. You may feel yourself above such considerations. But I urge you, if these accusations are untrue, to make the attempt to clear your name. If you can assure me that you are innocent of these . . . what seem to my old-fashioned way of thinking . . . very serious charges, I shall do everything possible to put matters right.

I am most anxious to hear from you, and believe that I remain your friend.

Elizabeth Bartholomew

I read this letter once, then I read it again. I think I shouted aloud. I was so angry, more angry than I had ever been in my life, and with so many people, that for a while I could only pace the floor of my room holding my head in my hands and shout the worst swearwords I knew. A timid knocking on the wall reminded me that the college was full of girls trying to work. I sat down at my desk and read the letter a third time.

How could she? How could Lady Bart write me a letter such as this? I hated her. I wanted to hit her, to hurt her as she had hurt me. I couldn't think of anything bad enough to do to her. I stabbed my pen into the desk-top until its nib broke. I threw a bottle of ink through the open window into the quadrangle below and heard it smash on the cobbles. I took a Chinese plate, of which I was particularly fond, and broke it on the hearth. Then I flung myself on my bed and lay there for half an hour in a state of grief.

Lady Bart, who meant more to me than either of my parents, who had been the greatest grown-up source of comfort to me in my childhood, whom I really loved, had rejected me. It was clear from the phrasing, the cold tone of her letter, that she believed Mrs Studley-Headlam. Despite her assurance that she was still my friend, I felt that she had shut me out of her heart.

The little enamelled clock by my bed, which Lady Bart had given me one birthday, chimed one o'clock. It went through my mind to break the clock but then I dismissed the idea as melodramatic and silly. I was already regretting the Chinese plate. There were sounds of feet along the corridor going to Hall for lunch. I realised that I was cold and thirsty, though far from hungry. I shut my window, lit my gas fire and put on the kettle to make myself some coffee. Then I read the letter again.

My next impulse was to telephone Caroline Protheroe. I'd been to visit her in the London Clinic where she went to convalesce. I still felt guilty about her. If I'd answered when she knocked on my door at Foxcombe perhaps she wouldn't have tried to kill herself. At the Clinic we'd had a long talk about Michael and her life with him and I felt that we were on the way to becoming good friends. I could ask her to write to Lady Bart, refuting that part of the calumny. But Caroline's state of mind was fragile. Was it quite fair to ask her to expose intimate details of her life to a complete stranger? When I considered it, I felt such a request, if not actually selfish, lacked dignity. My pride was shipwrecked and its salvage must be carried out with circumspection. It was time for my tutorial. I would go to it, despite the beginnings of a headache. It would be salutary to have to concentrate on something else.

I spent five days going to lectures and seminars and wrote a reasonable essay on John Donne. I went to the cinema with a girlfriend to see *War and Peace*. There was a drinks party at Christ Church, and a poetry reading in the Sheldonian. I was taken to dinner at the Mitre by Peter Holdenby, who was the man I liked best in Oxford, or perhaps anywhere. He was a medieval historian, a fellow of Balliol and rather beautiful in a fair, faint sort of way, with large, blue, heavy-lidded eyes and curling hair. He was very thin, not very tall, and walked as though he were perpetually coming on to the stage as Siegfried in *Swan Lake*, with large strides, pointed toes turned outwards, his head very erect and his arms held out from his sides. He wore silk shirts and had his shoes made for him in London. He played the piano very well, and was passionate about gardens. As I had, at our first meeting, admitted my complete ignorance about them, he had taken it upon himself to educate me and we'd spent several afternoons the previous summer visiting Hidcote, Kiftsgate and all the other famous gardens within reach of Oxford. I always liked being with him. He made me laugh, he instructed me, he was kind and he loved beautiful things.

Twice he had taken me to stay for the weekend with his parents. His father was a bishop, a dull, sententious man whom one hardly ever saw and his mother was a woman who felt she had risen in the world by being the wife of a bishop and suspected everything and everyone of being in league to pull her down again. She was bossy and insensitive but it was just possible to see the lines of beauty that Peter had inherited – in her case eroded by age, fat and bad temper.

Peter took me there because he said that though his parents were dreadful, the palace in which they lived was worth enduring any amount of vulgar snobbery to see. It was seventeenth-century red-brick, very beautiful and perfectly untouched: electricity, one bathroom and two indoor lavatories being the only innovations for the last three hundred years. Also it stopped his mother asking questions. Peter's mother had not seemed to like me at all so I was very surprised when after dinner on my second visit she had confided in me that I was quite a relief after the last girl he had brought home who had said 'pardon' and 'phone' and talked about 'sweet' instead of 'pudding'. The possibility of Peter marrying this girl had given her sleepless nights and upset her digestion. I remembered the cod and packet trifle we had just eaten and wondered if it was altogether fair to blame the girl. Naturally I did not say this or that no one but she could imagine that Peter was of the marrying kind.

Over dinner at the Mitre I told Peter what had happened during the weekend of the Johnsons' dance and about Lady Bart's letter. I hadn't meant to tell him but the ease and pleasure of being in his company put me in a confiding mood. I left out the bit about Hugh staying in my room after sending Bunny off. Not that I was ashamed exactly but Peter and I had never discussed sex except in the most abstract way. As I talked about it the feelings which had been gradually fading with the passage of days returned with a renewal of anger and hurt. So I was astonished to see, suddenly, that he was having the greatest difficulty in not laughing aloud. I frowned.

'I *am* sorry, Diana,' he said, when he could no longer suppress a giggle. 'I do understand how dreadfully you've been traduced. But you must see that it is all just a teeny bit *drôle*. I admire the Studley-Headlam woman. *Quel toupet! Quelle effronterie*! I know the sort. She has married for money and she will do anything to maintain her position before the envious world. She has no finer feelings, no tender thoughts, no generous impulses. She cloaks her own misdoings at your expense without a qualm. Neither you nor I would have the courage to do such a thing. We would be certain that our sins would find us out. And the poor humiliated Bunny, all pride and bluster and spite!'

'I'm delighted that the defamation of my character has afforded you so much merriment,' I said haughtily, as Peter pressed his napkin to his lips in an effort to control his giggling.

'Yes . . . now look, Diana, my darling,' he leaned across the table and took my hand in his own soft, elegant one. 'If you have a fault . . . I only admit the possibility, for you are the best and loveliest of women . . . it is that you are inclined to take yourself too seriously. You must learn not to care about what the world thinks about you. Good or bad, its opinion will be worthless. The tiniest success will be inflated by toad-eaters and then the same inferior minds will be envious and want to see you brought down. The world wants to be shocked, entertained, distracted. It isn't interested in a scrupulous examination of facts.'

'Oh, you're right. Of course,' I said, sighing. 'But I find it rather hard not to mind what people say about me. Don't you really care?' I asked with some admiration.

'Oh, me. I'm as thin-skinned as a newly emerged damselfly, clinging to a stalk, shivering in the first chill morning breeze. But I know that it's absurd. I tell myself a thousand times a day that it is witless folly to give one jot of my time to other people's opinions. How profoundly I resent each pang that the beastliness of my fellow man causes me! But, listen Diana, this is important. I act as though I didn't care . . . and so must you. You must never betray yourself by behaving in a lackey-ish, ingratiating way nor must you be catty and vindictive because your pride is hurt. Only the opinions of the few people you love matter. Don't make a fuss about things that are trivial.'

This conversation was helpful. The fact that I was innocent of nearly every crime imputed to me absolved me from scrambling for proofs and justifications. This is what I said to myself with great loftiness. I could laugh myself, now, about Bunny and Mrs Studley-Headlam. But Lady Bart's good opinion had been important to me for so long. I could not disguise from myself the hurt I still felt. The most dignified thing I could do was to withdraw from the conflict. Accordingly I sent Lady Bart a letter which ran:

Dear Lady Bartholomew,
    Thank you for your letter. I am sorry that Min is so ill. I hope she will improve soon. As to the rest of your letter, Mrs Studley-Headlam is an unqualified liar. I don't give a damn what she says about me. Please don't trouble yourself on my behalf. My friends will know whom to believe,
    Yours sincerely,
    Diana

I posted this cold, hard little stone and hoped that it would stick in Lady Bart's throat and make her choke.

Min was absent all that term. The next academic year, my last at Oxford, Min went to France to spend her year abroad, obligatory when reading Modern Languages. Her clothes and books were packed up by the Domestic Bursar and despatched by Carter Paterson. After I had taken my finals, scraping a first, I decided to apply to do my Ph.D. at Cambridge, rather than endure the misery of being cut daily by Min when she returned for her final year at St Hilary's. Peter had gone to Rome for six months on sabbatical. It seemed time for a change, a chance to reinvent myself.

About a year after I left Oxford, when I'd almost managed to persuade myself that the dreadful weekend and its aftermath was nothing but a dimly remembered amusing episode, St Hilary's forwarded a letter from Lady Bart.

Dear Daisy [it read],
    I have just returned from Rome where I spent several weeks with friends. Among the party was a very charming and intelligent man called Leo Studley-Headlam. I remembered the name and I soon understood him to be the husband of my former correspondent. Chance threw us quite often together and after many conversations I ventured to bring you into our discussions. He was very open and forthright in his talk, much to the detriment of

his wife, I am sorry to say, from whom he is living apart. He also spoke warmly in praise of you.

I must now humbly ask your pardon, Daisy dear, for believing what that woman told me. I feel I have treated you very badly indeed. I was upset, you were (rightly) angry, I became (wrongly) angry in my turn. I take the whole blame on myself and I ask you to forgive me, if you can, for being very foolish and very much in error.

If you cannot, I quite understand. But it has been terrible to me to be on bitter terms with one who was so dear to me and would be again if I could have my way,

With love,
Elizabeth Bartholomew

It didn't take me long to make up my mind. The passage of time had softened my anger. I had salvaged my pride but at the expense of gratitude for so much former kindness. I allowed myself to review the wretched business with all the honesty of which I was capable. The result was a painful combination of love and shame. I sat down to write at once to Lady Bart but it was difficult to avoid sounding pompous and self-justifying. In the end I just said,

Do let's make it up. Of course I forgive you,
With love, Daisy

I waited to hear from her again with a sensation of lightness, of a burden put down. I longed to see her again, to be reconciled, to feel again the warmth of her approval and sympathy.

After ten days of waiting for her reply my disappointment was keen. I had so much feeling to expend that I found it hard to concentrate on my work. Then, while smoking a cigarette in the tea room at the University Library, I happened to glance at an open copy of *The Times* which was lying on my table and saw the reason for the silence.

Lady Bart's obituary was short but fulsome. Her childhood as the daughter of a brigadier-general, her brilliance as a diplomat's wife sadly cut short by the premature death of her husband, her volume of travels and reminiscences, her charity work, her wit and charm, her wonderful qualities as a friend, all were recorded. Her death had been sudden, according to the newspaper, and quite unexpected at the age of only fifty-eight.

I was astonished. How could I have been so cheated? I turned to the front page. Her funeral was to take place the following day at the Brompton Oratory. For a moment I contemplated going but my courage failed me. Instead I sent a bouquet of lilies of the valley and forget-me-nots, which had been Lady Bart's favourite flowers, with a card which said 'From Daisy with fondest love'. Min would probably see it. I would leave the thing in her hands. The sorrow I felt at Lady Bart's death seemed to take no account of the fact that we had not met during the last two years of her life. I remembered only the exemplary kindness and steadfastness of her character. From Min I heard not a word.

So it was that fifteen years passed without Min. I suppose weeks must have gone by without my once thinking of her. The wedding photograph grew dogeared in a desk drawer. When I did remember her it was with a fondness and regret so vague as to be almost indefinable. Certainly I imagined that the heat had gone out of the thing and that it was an old story of scarcely any importance.

I had driven to Oxford to hear a paper on Edmund Spenser. The author of the paper had suddenly gone down with flu and the paper was cancelled. I thought I might as well take up an invitation to my old college for the same evening which would give some purpose to my otherwise wasted journed.

When Min had walked in, I had been utterly unprepared for the storm of feeling which rushed through me, making my heart race and my eyes fill with tears. When she saw me she stopped and her eyes widened as though with shock. She came towards me through the crowd, taking a glass of wine from a proffered tray as she advanced. She looked quite unchanged, perhaps a little thinner, her hair an inch or two longer but still worn loose and straight. When she got close I noticed that there were some whiskers on her navy suit and that the collar of her white shirt was sticking up on one side.

'Hello, Daisy,' she said, looking at me very solemnly.

I wanted to fling my arms about her neck. Instead I said, 'Hello, Min,' hoping that she wouldn't notice that my eyes were wet.

It was then that Min spoke of the quarrel and began to laugh. As I looked at her I was stunned by the intensity of memory that flooded in. As Min laughed I recognised her with such force that I was amazed that I could ever have forgotten her so completely. Her soft, dark-blue eyes beneath the thick brows, the slight bump on the bridge of her nose, the short upper lip, the small white scar on her chin where she had cut herself on the sharp edge of the banister when we were running upstairs on our way to prep, the inflections of her voice, very quick and clear . . . all were as familiar to me as though I were looking in a mirror and seeing myself.

'It's quite hopeless,' said Min, after the Principal had left us alone, 'I want to know exactly what you've been doing every day of all the years we haven't seen each other and I've got to catch a train in half an hour. In fact I'd better go now and find a taxi. I only came on the spur of the moment. I've been looking things up in the Bodleian for my preface for Sisimondi's letters . . . the world's most painfully written opus, every page steeped in my heart's blood. If I don't finish it by March they're going to cancel the contract. I've been writing it for nearly two years and I can't get to the end of the bloody thing. If only I had six weeks without interruptions I might get somewhere with it but that's as likely as my being asked to substitute at the last minute for Maria Callas.'

I offered to drive her to the station and we went without bothering to say goodbye to anyone. All the way there we talked, almost gabbling in an effort to make up for lost time until Min said, 'Look, there's too much to say and no time to say it in. Promise me you'll come and stay. Come next weekend, come on Friday. Say you will!'

I thought quickly. A college drinks party on Friday evening. I could miss that. I should have to cancel an engagement for Saturday. Well, I would. I wanted to see Min more than anything.

'All right, I'd love to. I could leave on Monday morning.'

'Monday if you absolutely must. Stay as long as you can. There's so much to tell. And I want you to meet Robert and the children. Is there someone . . .' she hesitated, 'someone you'd like to bring?'

I shook my head with a smile.

'You look just the same, you know,' said Min, suddenly. 'I feel as if I've found a bit of me that was missing.'

She kissed me on the cheek and got out of the car, holding several books and papers, catching her bag on the handle of the door and dropping half her things.

'Look, that must be your train. You must hurry. Tell me where I'm to come.'

Min thrust her head in through the window. 'Car or train?'

'Train, I think. Lancashire's a long way.'

'Get off at Dunston Abchurch, then, and ring me from the station. I'll come and get you. We live at Weston Hall which is only two miles away. Family pile . . . only "pile" has a neat, orderly sound. Goodbye, darling Daisy. I'm going to sing all the way home, I'm so excited.'

She disappeared for a moment and then thrust her head back in. 'Bring warm clothes.'

Then I saw her back gilded by the station lamps and she was through the door and gone.

Now it was Friday and I had crossed the border between Cheshire and Lancashire. At Carnforth I had changed trains for a branch line. This time I had to share a compartment with several people for the train was only three carriages long and without a corridor. They had all stared at me with frank interest from the moment of leaving Carnforth until I began to wonder if I had come out in a rash or the tip of my nose had turned black.

'Tha's not from these parts then, lass?' said the woman opposite me, in a tone of gentle inquiry.

It was not difficult to imagine that I had slipped into a novel by Mrs Gaskell. I wondered if she was going to start crooning 'it's aw a muddle' as a piece of social commentary.

'No. I'm from Cambridge,' I said with a sigh for I knew that the inevitable train conversation was to be visited upon me and I would so much rather have looked out of the window into the darkening landscape. I had never been to Lancashire and I was keen to see what I could of it before nightfall. So far there were lots of trees and lots of cows and it all looked pretty much like any decent bit of England under snow. I interrupted a recital of Our Betty's travails in the South where people ate like sparrers and Our Betty was clemmed for want of a reasonable quantity of potato (more Mrs Gaskell), to ask how many stops there were until Dunston Abchurch. The occupants of the carriage took turns to give conflicting estimates, Our Betty's mother being firmly of the opinion that it didn't stop at Dunston Abchurch at all and that I was on the wrong train. They all advised me to get off at the next station and change to the down-line train back to Carnforth. I looked with some despair at my luggage, a large suitcase and a small holdall, and imagined myself struggling with it across a windy footbridge through the still falling snow.

'There'll be no porters at station,' said the woman with comfortable certainty.

I had begun to feel so depressed at the prospect of several freezing hours spent in pursuit of the right train that it was with as much indignation as joy that I saw that the station we were drawing into at that moment was none other than Dunston Abchurch. The woman peeled the paper from a packet of fruit gums and popped one in her mouth, rolling it about slowly, staring into space as though she were trying to guess the factory and year of manufacture. One of the men got my suitcase down from the rack and the next moment I was standing on the platform watching the lighted windows, framing the profiles of the passengers, chuff away into the darkness while snowflakes blew horizontally through the patch of lamplight and clung to my hair and clothing.

A porter came up to me and took my cases and I followed him into the damp little ticket hall.

'Taxi's just gone,' he told me with a mournful air. 'Takin' Mrs Taggart up to Morton Abchurch. It'll be a hour or so.'

'I'd like to use the telephone, please.'

He indicated the instrument. I had taken the precaution of ringing Directory Inquiries before I left home to get Min's number and I now congratulated myself on my foresight as there was only the empty cover of the directory hanging from a chain. My complacency was soon dashed, however, when the telephone produced nothing but a spluttering, hissing sound as though the life were being choked out of it.

'It doesn't seem to be working.'

'That'll be the snow. Lines is down. Tha's not from these parts, then?'

'No, I'm not,' I said, hastily. 'I want to go to Weston Hall.'

72

I half expected him to start, grow pale and roll his eyes in a terrified manner and urge me not to go 'up to Hall' if I valued my life and sanity. But he took the announcement calmly, merely saying that I'd best wait for taxi then. At that moment a man in a dog-collar came into the ticket hall with an elderly woman.

'Good evening, Vokins,' said the clergyman, with professional geniality. 'Just putting my sister on the five-twenty.'

'Evenin', sir. Would tha be goin' past Weston Hall? Young lady 'ere wants to go to Mrs Weston's.'

'Certainly, certainly.' He lifted his brown trilby in my direction. 'Delighted to drop you off. Just see my sister on to the train.'

This was a stroke of luck. In two minutes the five-twenty had arrived and departed, bearing the sister away and the clergyman, who introduced himself to me as Harold Liddell, was at my side. Vokins loaded my luggage into the dilapidated old Austin and after a minute's struggle with the starter button the engine got going and the sidelights and one headlight pointed feebly a few yards into the snowstorm. We bounced slowly along the road for some way, skidding and jerking very oddly until Mr Liddell had the idea of taking the handbrake off.

'We're only just in time,' he said, leaning forward to peer into the fan shapes cut by the windscreen wipers. 'This road will be blocked in another hour. Are you cold? I'll put the heater on.'

He pressed a switch and immediately there was a blast of icy air on my feet.

'It'll warm in a minute,' he said with a confidence that proved to be quite unfounded. 'Luckily the trees meet overhead in this part and they seem to be diverting the snow. Lammas Hill might be a bit tricky. More exposed, you know. It's fortunate that I've been travelling these roads for twenty years and I know them backwards.'

These words turned out to be prophetic for halfway up Lammas Hill we began to slide down it again.

'Sorry,' he said, crunching through the gears, 'I think I got into neutral there. Ah, this feels like first.'

With a roar and a spin of the wheels we leapt forward and I struck my forehead painfully on the edge of the sun visor. By the time we got to the top I felt as though I had driven the old

Austin up the hill by mental powers alone for my stomach muscles were locked in a scissors-hold and the relief was so great that I was perfectly calm as we swooshed down the other side at extraordinary speed into blackness.

At last the car beamed its single eye on to a pair of iron gates. Mr Liddell got out, despite my protests, and rattled manfully at the latch for at least a minute before he discovered the padlock. He rapped on my window which I wound down with a fearful shrieking, the window that is, though it might as well have been me for the next moment he stuck his head in through it and showered me with snow from the brim of his hat.

'It's no good, I'm afraid. Firmly locked. There's a side gate which is open. Perhaps you'll allow me to carry your luggage up to the house?'

I spoke very firmly against this plan and said that I was well able to manage for myself and wouldn't dream of putting him to any further trouble. He was round and in the car in a trice and who could blame him? I thanked him and waved as he lurched off into the swirling darkness with the window sucking in volumes of arctic air, having resisted all our attempts to wind it up again.

'Handbrake!' I shouted but the wind whipped the word heedlessly away.

I slung my bag around my neck and picked up my cases. The side gate was corroded and would only open halfway. I feared very much for the state of my coat, having been forced to act as a sort of human rust-remover to squeeze through the gap. Ahead of me, a dishearteningly long way off, were lights. I walked towards them, now and then stumbling into a drift, the cases rubbing and banging against my legs.

At last I reached the front door. A flight of steps ran up to the house beneath a grand, pillared portico. A line of light lay across the steps from the door, which was fractionally open. I pulled at the doorbell. It had the resistless feel of a bell that has not worked for some years and I was not surprised when no one came to answer it. I pushed open the door and went in.

# CHAPTER SEVEN

The hall was large and paved with Victorian encaustic tiles in peacock, terracotta and ochre which gleamed dully in the light from a great brass lantern swinging in the draught from the open door. I closed the door and put down my luggage.

Six fat columns of yellow scagliola rose up to a dome high above my head. I had a momentary impression of standing in an enchanted forest as the fog that had come in with me wove about the hall like gas from a swampy pond. My thighs and ankles were smarting from the bruising of the cases and I was very cold, very wet and very hungry. At that moment a pair of trousered legs emerged from the gloom at the top of the staircase ahead of me and came slowly down into the hall. The man was tall, fair-haired turning to grey, and I had no doubt that it was Robert.

He was clearly abstracted but the moment he noticed me his expression changed from preoccupation to anger.

'What the hell do you mean by barging in here like this?'

I stared at him. I couldn't think of anything to say.

'Daisy! How did you get here? I've been waiting all afternoon for the telephone to ring!'

Min rushed towards me from a door to the left of the stairs and flung her arms around me.

'I've been like a child looking forward to a party . . . imagining picking you up at the station . . . what we'd say . . . driving you home . . . I put masses of petrol in the car specially and a shovel in the boot and now here you are! Hello, darling,' looking at Robert. 'Isn't it your chess club night? I wasn't expecting you so early. Doesn't matter . . . there's plenty of shepherd's pie. Have you said hello to Diana?'

'The telephone lines are down,' I explained. 'I got a lift with the Vicar.'

'Oh, but the gates are locked. You'll have walked all the way up the drive. How wet you are, poor darling. Come into the kitchen where it's warm. Robert, take Daisy's things up to the green bedroom.'

I followed Min into the kitchen, a very big room, certainly two or perhaps even three degrees warmer than the hall. There was a four-oven Aga in the old fireplace and I ran to it gratefully but it was colder than a fishmonger's slab.

'It hasn't worked for ages,' said Min, seeing me press my chilled fingers to the glacial enamel. 'I keep meaning to get the man round. Come and sit by the stove. Give me your coat and I'll hang it up.'

I thrust my gloves and scarf into the pockets of my maltreated and rather beautiful taupe cashmere coat and watched Min sling it on to a hook. It would have a dreadful poke in the collar by morning and I made a mental note to move it discreetly when Min wasn't looking.

'Now let me get you a drink,' said Min, looking so pleased and happy that I found I couldn't care less about the dreadful smell the paraffin heater was giving off, though the chances were that an hour or two in an enclosed room with the thing would be fatal. I could see that its wick was burning red and I longed to trim it properly. Min looked tremendously attractive despite hair that needed washing, a scarlet jersey with holes in and the most deplorable pair of black ski trousers with straps under the instep which made her look like the Nutcracker Soldier.

'Here you are . . . white wine. All right?'

'Lovely,' I said, taking a large gulp though I could tell from the smell that it had been opened days ago. It was certainly warmer than I was. I drank it down bravely and smiled back at her.

'You're the only person I know,' she said happily, 'who could walk through a snowstorm and look marvellous. We're going out to dinner tomorrow night . . . you too . . . and you'll knock them for six.'

'Are you sure we'll be able to get there? The weather's pretty bad.'

I reviewed my wardrobe. Thank goodness I'd packed the dress. I'd almost left it out. It would need pressing, of course. I wondered about the chances of finding an iron without scorch-marks on the plate.

'We can always go in the Land Rover. That gets through anything. Like a glass of wine, darling?'

Robert had come in. He stood in front of me, a big man with the suggestion of a developing paunch. The collar of his Tattersall shirt showed more lining than fabric and his corduroy trousers were worn smooth over the knees. His navy jersey was darned, very badly, in several places. I thought he looked extremely arrogant though he was attempting a grudging smile.

'You must think me very rude,' he said, holding out his hand. 'I'm afraid I blasted you out. I thought you were a journalist. There's been some trouble at school and two newspapers rang up before I left to come home. I'd quite forgotten that Min said you were coming to stay. Welcome to Weston Hall.'

I shook his hand. His eyebrows went straight out to his temples where they curved up, giving him a puckish, almost diabolical look. He was probably a good ten years older than Min.

'What sort of trouble?' asked Min. 'Robert teaches at St Lawrence's in Winkleigh. Classics,' she added for my benefit. 'It's not Harrison's drinking again, is it?'

'No,' said Robert, gravely. 'It's worse than that. It's Gerald.' He hesitated, looked at me and then continued. 'He's been accused of seducing a fifth-form boy. Apparently the boy told his mother and there's been the devil of a row.'

'No! Poor Gerald! Which boy?'

'Dalrymple. He's a liar and a flirt and I don't believe a word of it. Someone's leaked the story to the local press, that's the worst thing.'

'Well,' said Min consideringly as she sipped her wine, 'don't bite my head off but I've always thought Gerald might be queer. He's sort of . . . over-sensitive, affected . . . prissy almost.'

'Of course Gerald's queer,' said Robert impatiently. 'I've know that for years. But that doesn't make him an unbridled ravisher of young boys. Really, Min! If you as an educated, intelligent woman think like that, what hope is there?'

He frowned and turned away, his arms folded across his chest and his shoulders hunched, expressive of extreme ill-temper. Then he sniffed and went over to the gas cooker where something was steaming vigorously.

'Oh God, another saucepan gone. Look, Min, the carrots have boiled dry. We ought to have shares in aluminium and get some benefit from the vast purchase of pots and pans in this household.'

'Sorry.' Min went over to peer into the pan. 'Oh, they'll be all right. I'll put some more water in.'

She put the pan under the running tap. There was a violent hissing and a horrid smell of burning filled the kitchen. She stuck it back over the flame and poured more wine into our glasses.

'Don't worry, darling,' she said to Robert who was leaning against the dresser, frowning. 'If Gerald's innocent, as you say, Harrison won't sack him. Gerald's too good a teacher.'

'It isn't just a question of being sacked . . .' began Robert. Then he rubbed his hand over his face and shook his head as though driving unpleasant thoughts away. 'This is all very boring for Diana. I'm sorry.'

He smiled at me rather bleakly and took a sip of wine, then sniffed it again.

'Is this wine all right? It tastes really filthy. Is it from that new case of Sauvignon I bought the other day? If so I'll have to take it back.'

'It's a bottle I found in the larder. There was only a glass out of it. I thought we'd better drink it up.'

'Oh Lord! I put that bottle there weeks ago for cooking. I won it in the school raffle. It's quite undrinkable. You are a fathead, Min.'

He laughed as he threw his wine down the sink and collected mine and Min's to throw away too. Then he disappeared through a door the other side of the Aga and reappeared a moment later with a bottle of red. It was certainly a great improvement though a bit cold. He was still laughing to himself as he got out knives and forks and laid them round the table. There were some coloured raffia mats already on the table and two red candles stuck in bottles, with a jar of mustard and a bottle of tomato sauce in between. The considerable size of the table meant that there were great bare expanses between the mats. The only lighting in the kitchen was from a single bulb, dangling from the middle of the ceiling and wearing a white ceramic coolie shade reminiscent of classrooms, which cast an unforgiving glare over the centre of the room and left the edges in brooding shadow.

'I think it's done.' Min bent down to pull a dish from the gas cooker. 'What a pity the top's got a bit too brown. This oven's simply hopeless. It either scorches everything or dries it into a state of mummification. It doesn't seem to know a happy medium. Where are the children? Ah, here they are . . . William, come and be introduced to Diana.'

My life had been remarkably untouched by children. I'd never known any since I stopped being one myself. Those friends of mine who had them also had au pairs or nannies and consequently I was under-exposed to the phenomenon. This made me feel rather nervous of Min's. William was a tall, fair boy, looking older than his reputed twelve years. He was flauntingly handsome with the best features of both parents. Looking at him I could see what Robert had looked like as a young man. William seemed absolutely composed, taking my hand and shaking it and smiling at me very politely. His dark blue eyes had enormous pupils and he blinked them very slowly which had a mesmeric effect.

Eleanor was nine, apparently, and had nothing to attract her. I couldn't see what colour her eyes were for they were hidden behind National Health spectacles, the rims of which were a virulent Elastoplast pink, presumably intended as camouflage but which made them emphatically evident. She was fat. No other word would do, not chubby, tubby or plump . . . certainly not well-built but, on the contrary, very ill-made with fat legs and a bulging midriff. That evening she had a painful-looking cold sore on her upper lip which did nothing to help. She was very shy and self-conscious and stood with her head down and her hands behind her back. I said 'Hello, Eleanor' in what I hoped were friendly tones. She mumbled something. It might have been 'Hello', and gave a juicy sniff.

'Have you washed your hands, children?' said Min vaguely as she brought plates to the table.

The children ignored her, sat down and began to fight over who should have the water jug.

'William, pour some water for Diana and then for your sister,' said Robert peremptorily.

William did so, spilling some on to my plate just as Min had given me a couple of spoonfuls of shepherd's pie. No one else saw and William simply gave me a slow smile. I decided to say nothing. There was a scraping at the door and in came the biggest dog I'd ever seen. Though I am never unkind to dogs, I don't know anything about them and I don't like them. This one had the sort of jaws that slaver and the kind of shaggy coat that sheds hairs with every breath. It was a black dog, something like a Newfoundland, and as soon as it saw me it gave a piercing bark.

'This is Ham,' said Min. 'Come here, Ham, and don't be so silly. Sit down and stop barking at Daisy. She won't like you if you bark at her.'

'That's an unusual name for a dog,' I said, in an attempt to curry favour with the children. 'Does he like ham very much?'

William laughed, rather patronisingly. 'Ham's short for Hamlet. And she's a girl.'

'She was already called Hamlet when we got her,' explained Min. 'Because of her black coat, I suppose. I don't think they knew she was a bitch. We didn't like to confuse her by changing her name. She's got the sweetest nature.'

Hamlet and I looked at each other. I was just thinking that she certainly didn't look very sweet-natured and that I didn't like the manner in which she was eyeing me with drooping, red, lower lids as though I were a rat lying in a dish marked DOG, when she came over to me and began to sniff my knees. There fell the pleased, expectant hush that comes over dog-owners when their pets behave in a conciliatory way towards their guests. I smiled as delightedly as I could and patted Ham's large, questing brow. She sat down heavily next to me, the hush was broken by expressions of great satisfaction and we were allowed to get on with our food.

The shepherd's pie was not an appetising colour but I was unprepared for the perfectly dreadful smell which hit my nostrils when I lifted the fork to my lips. What could Min have put into it? I was just imagining something in the last stages of decomposition when I happened to catch Ham's eye as she laid her head on my knee and then I understood that the shepherd's pie was not responsible. I tried to push her away discreetly with my leg but she merely leaned more heavily and lovingly against me. Suddenly Robert flung down his fork.

'That dog's flatulence is getting past all bearing. What have you been feeding her?'

'I forgot to buy her any meat,' said Min apologetically. 'I had to give her yesterday's potato and cabbage leftovers.'

The children were giggling hysterically and Robert looked

more and more annoyed. William was told to take Hamlet into the boot room and Eleanor to be quiet.

'I got a bad house-mark today,' said Eleanor, looking suddenly glum. 'Miss Pivot said I was taking the Lord's name in vein. Aren't veins what your blood goes through?' she asked, examining the inside of her wrist.

'Idiot!' said William who had returned to the table. 'Not that kind of vein. It means . . . what does it mean? It's a stupid thing to say, anyway.'

'It means using God's name improperly,' said Min. 'Miss Pivot is a tiresome old stick, I must say. What was it that you said?'

'I just wrote in my hymn-book "This book belongs to Eleanor Weston, Weston Hall, Dunston Abchurch, Lancashire, England, Great Britain, The World, The Universe, God." I couldn't think of anything else bigger than the universe. Katy Babbage always writes The Universe in all her books and she's the most popular girl in my class.'

'I bet you're the most unpopular girl in your class,' said William, with contempt. 'Probably in the whole school.'

'No,' said Eleanor, after serious thought. 'Anna Prink's more unpopular than I am. She smells of wee.'

'For heaven's sake,' said Robert, expelling a violent sigh as William went off into a fit of laughter. 'Is it quite impossible to have a sensible conversation in this house?'

'If the universe is endless there couldn't be anything bigger than it, could there?' said Min, who was trying not to laugh herself. 'And I want you to be specially nice to poor little Anna Prink from now on.'

'She hates me. No one can be nice to someone who hates them. Even God. He sent horrible plagues to his enemies . . . frogs and locusts and boils and things. I think it's very unfair of you to want me to be better even than God.'

'Supposing the universe isn't endless?' I said, in an attempt to improve the conversation and stop Robert frowning so magisterially. 'How can we know whether it goes on for ever?'

'Astrophysicists do,' said William. 'I've read about it. They're more certain about that than anyone has ever been certain of anything in the whole world.'

'Well, that seems pretty definite,' I said, after a small pause.

'I don't think that's quite right, William,' said Robert, in a kinder tone than any he had so far used, clearly warming to the masculine duty of righting someone else's misapprehensions. 'I think any scientist would be prepared to admit that every theory about the cosmos is just that . . . an idea with sound, logical reasoning behind it but in the end no more than a theory. Speculative, in fact. You see, matter is made up of three basic elements . . .'

But William was absorbed in tracing the shadow of the lampshade on the table with his spoon, no longer listening. Min and I went doggedly on with our eating though the meat was so chewy that twice I had to cough behind my hand, spit out the morsel and drop it on the floor where I was sure that the reluctantly vegetarian Ham would dispose of it with relish. After several minutes of patient explication, on which I concentrated with all the self-discipline of which I was capable, Robert paused to put in another forkful and I cast about for an intelligent question or two. I was startled when, before I could think of one, Min said, 'Do you know, Daisy, I think there must have been unseen forces at work which compelled us both to go, unpremeditatedly, to that reunion. I mean, have you ever been to a reunion of anything in your life before?'

It was so apparent that she hadn't been listening to Robert that for a moment I felt embarrassed. It was soon obvious that I was a complete novice as far as married life was concerned for Robert seemed little put out but continued to chew thoughtfully and examine the carrots, which did indeed taste burnt and nasty.

'Never in my life,' I said. 'What sort of unseen forces are you thinking of? The sort of spectre that hovers about in people's drawing rooms, hoping for a chance to deliver a pointless message via scraps of paper?'

'I don't know,' Min laughed. 'But the older I get the more some sort of pattern emerges. I mean, there does seem to be a pay-off, some kind of retribution if you like . . . for good behaviour, for example . . . which defies the notion of random, chaotic happenings.'

'Or you get better at finding patterns as you get older,' put in Robert, 'more expert at ignoring what doesn't fit. I don't suppose that any controlling entity is running things on the lines of a Sunday School prize . . . giving a nice new catechism to any child who can colour in a picture of Jesus in the Garden at Gesthemane without going over the lines. I'm sorry, but in the battle between Robert Weston and the gristle, the gristle wins. The fight was loaded in its favour. I think I'll just have some cheese.'

'There isn't any, darling,' said Min. 'I'm sorry I forgot to buy some. There's a tin of peaches.'

Nobody seemed keen on the idea of these.

'I suppose you forgot to get any coffee,' said Robert, with some bitterness.

Though I felt some sympathy with Robert's exasperation, I thought it was very mean of him to be rude about the food in front of Min's friends. It seemed to be a convention of their married life that he was critical and she was apologetic.

'I didn't forget, actually,' said Min, with disarming good humour. 'There's a new tin on the dresser.'

Robert made the coffee (instant, of course) and cleared away the plates, stacking them in the sink. I offered to do the washing-up but Min said she preferred to do it in the morning.

'Do you have help?' I asked, as I probed the tin of sugar with my spoon trying to find some grains that were not already stuck in a hard lump with damp. 'It seems to be an awfully big house.'

'We had someone until last year. She smoked all my cigarettes and started her first coffee break the moment she took her hat and coat off. She talked so much that I was more tired having to listen to her than if I'd done the work myself. I tried shutting myself in the morning room to write but she used to come in and stand in the doorway and talk and stub out her cigarettes on Robert's great-uncle's skull.'

'It's not as bad as you think,' said Robert, seeing my consternation. 'My great-uncle's been dead at least fifty years. He died out in India and my grandfather, who was touring the Punjab with him, brought his skull home. I think I'll go to bed now if you don't mind. It's been a trying day.'

He went away gloomily, having reminded Min to put the stove out before she went to bed, get Ham in (he having let her out for a last run), and to put out all the lights downstairs when she came up, as the last electricity bill had been large enough to pay for the consumption of the population of China.

'I don't suppose very many Chinese have electricity,' said Min to his unresponsive back. 'Poor Robert. I think he's upset about Gerald who's his best friend, really. Never mind, I don't want to spoil a minute of your stay thinking about it. It's a pity so much is happening this weekend because I really want you to myself. Vivien, Robert's mother, is coming to tea tomorrow. I long to know what you think of her. Now, give me a blow-by-blow account of what you've been doing since the morning after Soppy Johnson's dance.' She began to laugh again. 'I'm sorry, I can't help it. I behaved so stupidly. Now, go on.'

So I told her, as succinctly as I could, what my life had been like. I tried to be truthful but naturally I wanted to convince myself, as well as Min, that everything was going along swimmingly. It all sounded, anyway, pretty good and when I paused to draw breath Min said, with a sigh, 'Oh God, the glamour of it! Cambridge, London, Paris. And all those men. I'm not saying that I regret being married to Robert but I must admit I wouldn't mind knowing what it was like to make love with someone else. Oh yes,' she added, seeing my surprise, 'I was lying my head off when we used to talk about men in the old days. I never really went to bed with any of them, not even Hugh. I was scared stiff of getting pregnant. I was so impressed by your devil-may-care attitude. I was utterly terrified by the whole idea.'

'I was lying, too. Hugh was the first person I slept with. And,' I hesitated for a moment, 'I was so zonked by pills that I had absolutely no idea what happened. I might as well not have been there.'

'Oh Daisy. That's rather sad. Your first time.' Min was silent for a moment, contemplating. 'And did you sleep with him again after that?'

'I never saw him again after that morning at Foxcombe. He drove me back to Oxford. Then he telephoned me once and wrote to me once. But I wouldn't see him. I wanted you to forgive me and I knew there was no chance if I was still seeing him.'

'Goodness! And there was I, feeling so ghastly and torturing myself with envy. Glandular fever makes you feel horrible. First of all you feel as though you're going to choke to death. Then when that goes you feel more tired than anyone can possibly imagine. If you were standing in front of a herd of fleeing wildebeest you'd have to lie down and let them tread you into the savannah. But what made me feel much more terrible than anything was the conviction that you and Hugh were having the most marvellous time together. Candlelit dinners, moonlit walks, making passionate love, perhaps laughing together about me.' She looked down at her hands and picked at a cuticle. 'You see, I'd discovered by then that I was the most appallingly jealous person. Oh, I know everyone's jealous from time to time. But I had a sort of malevolent tapeworm within, a horrible, gnawing, organ-devouring beast, sucking all the nourishment I should have had, to make itself grow fat. I knew it, but I couldn't get free. My self-confidence was lower than the Marianas Trench . . . do you remember learning about that with Miss Bost? I felt hideous and hateful. I wasn't just jealous about Hugh. I saw my mother's letter to you and your reply to her. I was profoundly, savagely gratified. I'd been imagining that she preferred you to me, you see. I was always hearing about how wonderful you were, so clever, capable, organised, well-mannered, well-dressed. Poor Ma, she had no idea that instead of encouraging me to be all these things, she was feeding gobbets of flesh to my worm and turning me against you both. When you and she quarrelled I knew that I came first with her after all. She believed those things about you because you had hurt me by stealing Hugh (as she saw it) and her maternal instinct suppressed all reasonableness. Dear Ma, I still miss her.'

'So do I,' I said, 'I did love her, you know. More than my own mother, really.'

'Did you?' Min put out her hand and touched mine for a moment. 'I'm so sorry you didn't see her before she died. I found your letter after the funeral, when I was sorting through her things, the one about making it up. Ma was a good Catholic, you know, though she hated talking about it. I know it must have meant a lot to her to be reconciled. She was always so fond of you.'

'Did she . . . was it an easy death?'

'Couldn't have been better. She'd been having a bit of trouble with her heart. Her doctor thought it was because she'd had scarlet fever very badly as a child. There were plans for an operation. She died in her sleep, having been out to a very good dinner the evening before with her closest friends. I don't suppose she knew anything about it. Anyway she wasn't afraid to die, I don't think. It was such a shame, though. She was enjoying life and was only middle-aged, really. I saw the flowers you sent. I had my last little stab of jealousy then because they were so exactly what my mother would have liked. I'd forgotten that they were her favourite flowers. I was in such a state of misery and turmoil. I'd ordered a huge thing of lilies and carnations for the coffin. Then I saw your little bunch of lilies of the valley with forget-me-nots and mine looked like a large red-and-white scab, really ugly. After the funeral Robert took me away to Italy . . . we'd just met then and fallen pretty much in love straight away . . . and I went through a sort of catharsis of grief over my mother and tremendous love for Robert, a sort of purging. He was the most wonderful thing that had ever happened to me and it was the most perfect timing.'

'He certainly seems very . . . intelligent.'

'Oh yes. Of course he's wasted at St Lawrence's. He should have been a don. But his mother wanted to move to the Dower House and so we had to come here. The Dower House is much later than this. Red-brick Queen Anne with good central heating, only five bedrooms, plenty of hot water, tiny garden. It's on the edge of the park. I'll show it to you tomorrow. It's quite perfect. I hope I'll keep going long enough to go and live there myself. Imagine the warmth and comfort of it!'

Min lit a cigarette, one of mine as she had run out, and puffed at it with a dreamy look in her eyes.

'Do you have to live here?' I asked. 'Would it be heresy to think of selling it? Not that it isn't quite delightful,' I added hastily. 'How old is it, in fact? I thought it was Victorian.'

'All the front part is. Robert's great-grandfather had a rush of blood to the head and put on two enormous rooms, the staircase hall and the servants' quarters, plus the stable block and the walled garden. But the core of the house is Jacobean and much nicer. You'll see the back of it in the morning. It's really beautiful. Of course we have thought of selling it. Robert gets terribly fed up sometimes and says he's going to the estate agent the next day. But he never does. Robert's very indecisive. I suppose because of his mother. He wants to spend his life translating Thucydides, spraying his old apple trees in the orchard and listening to Wagner on his gramophone. Although he's so clever he's also a very simple man.'

And very bad-tempered, I thought, but naturally did not say so.

'Anyway when I married Robert, I began to feel much better about myself. Much more confident. We were so happy.'

'I suppose it's partly growing up, too, isn't it,' I said, looking about for an ashtray, not liking to put my cigarette out in the soil of a flowerpot on the windowsill beside us as Min had done, though the cyclamen in it looked as though it had been dead for weeks. 'If things go at all well, then accomplishment . . . achievement . . . makes you more confident. Before then self-confidence has to be callowness or ingenuousness . . . at best innocence.'

Min handed me the lid of an empty pickle jar for my cigarette-end and laughed.

'What a typically Daisy remark. And that serious look. I recognise it from when you were eight. What an anxious, solemn thing you were.'

I laughed with her while making a mental note to watch this tendency in myself. For though Min was astonishingly vague about practical matters she was acute about anything ridiculous in other people's behaviour and I didn't much like being laughed at.

'Of course one is consumed with self when young,' Min continued. 'I see it again in my own children and it's perfectly right and proper. It's all a question of survival. Though Ellie seems to be a bit short of it, actually. William is more selfish than I could have dared to hope. When he was born I was knocked out with gas-and-air but the moment I came round they put him into my arms and my first thought was "I wish Daisy could see him". It was extraordinary. I hadn't thought of you for ages but because I was still drowsy, only half-conscious, the thought rushed into my mind before I could prevent it. It was you I wanted, before Robert or any of the friends I saw all the time. I wanted you so badly that I cried. Everyone thought I was crying with happiness because of the baby but it was because I'd lost you.'

I was moved by this confession.

'Let's drink to the lecturer who got flu so that I went to the reunion after all,' I said, filling our glasses with the remains of the bottle of red wine from supper.

'And to my incompetence with train timétables, leaving me stranded for two hours after the closing of the Bodleian.'

'And to the rest of our lives.'

'The rest of our lives.' The clock chimed the half-hour after eleven as we drank. 'Bed, I think. Robert's got to invigilate tomorrow and he wants to leave by half past eight.'

We put everything in or out as instructed and I followed Min up the staircase. It was tremendously wide, separating into two after the first flight but so dimly lit that I had only the impression of a dado of chocolate anaglypta below plaster the colour and texture of marzipan. There were dark and sullen-looking portraits, presumably of dead Westons, but we mounted too fast for me to examine them.

'This is your room.' Min opened a door. 'I thought you'd like it because it's in the old part of the house and I know you were always spoony about anything old. Bathroom's next door but two that way. I put a bottle in your bed just before you arrived to air it. Have you got everything you need?'

She looked anxiously about the room.

'It looks perfect. Goodnight.'

We kissed cheeks and then she went off down the corridor while I closed the bedroom door. My luggage stood by the foot of the bed, looking rather lost and unbelievably clean and smart, like a child on its first day at school. It was partly the size of everything that made it look so diminutive. The bed was a four-poster but even *it* looked rather diminished by the proportions of the room. It was hung with heavy, dark-red damask curtains and as I looked at them I saw something small and black scuttle very fast up them and disappear into the pelmet at the top. There wasn't much furniture otherwise – a chest of drawers and a wardrobe, a rickety chair and a marble washstand, bare but for a hammer, a wire hook and a screwdriver, arranged neatly in a row. I looked at them, puzzled. They seemed strange ornaments. I wondered idly why it was called the green room. There wasn't, as far as I could see, a single green thing in it unless you counted the mildew on the wallpaper.

I opened my suitcase and took out my dress which was, of course, crumpled. I tried to open the wardrobe but there was only a bare patch in the veneer where the handle had once been. The solution came to me quite quickly. The screw-driver. With its help the door opened easily enough and I hung my dress and my tweed suit (just the thing for tea with Robert's mother) in its dark, mothball-smelling interior. It was easy to jam the door closed with a sharp push. The chest of drawers, a beautiful seventeenth-century piece, had drop-handles with no drops. I knew what I was about now. The piece of bent wire opened them in a trice. I threw in my jerseys and decided to give up unpacking the rest. I was dreadfully tired and longed to get to sleep.

I undressed very quickly for it was intensely cold. My breath steamed as I struggled to get my tights off without putting my bare feet on the floor. I had the mad notion that I would have liked slippers for my slippers as the carpet looked so grubby and stained. I ran along the corridor to the bathroom, which was just as I expected. There was a great deal of tiling, the colour of winter cabbage, and the bath had huge chips out of the enamel. There was a cupboard housing a malodorous lavatory and the end of a roll of Bronco lavatory paper as stiff and slippery as glass. I struggled with the tap of the basin and a stream of rusty water shot out quite suddenly, making the front of my dressing-gown very wet. I washed my face and then realised that I had no towel. I hadn't noticed one in the bedroom and had not thought to bring one with me. There was only a small rag, stiff with dried Harpic, in the bathroom. I patted my face dry with a sheet of Bronco and brushed my teeth, hoping that any lumps of rust would be a useful form of iron.

I was thankful to get back to my bedroom. I took off my dressing-gown and got into bed, cracking my toe painfully on a stone hot-water bottle. It was now a cold-water bottle so I slung it out and bravely pushed my feet down into the bed. The mattress and bedclothes were so damp that it felt like stepping into a pond. I remembered the bed-socks I'd had the foresight to bring. I put them on and after a moment's consideration pulled on a jersey and got back into my dres-sing-gown. I felt better at once though rather constricted. It was much too cold to read so I turned out the light and lay as though entombed, waiting for the temperature of the bed to rise to bearable levels.

There was a frightful shriek, suddenly, outside my bedroom window and my heart almost burst with fright. Another terrifying scream followed and I realised what it was. It had been so long since I had spent a night in the country that I was quite unused to the presence of wildlife. 'It was the owl that shriek'd, the fatal bellman, Which gives the stern'st good-night.' Shakespeare, of course, expressed everything in nature to perfection. I lay back on my pillow and smiled at my own foolishness as my heart-rate returned to normal. What could be more romantic and lovely than an owl calling to its mate through the sable night across a snowy garden?

After listening for twenty minutes to low, owlish mutterings broken by regular blood-curdling screams, I could willingly have picked up the hammer and dealt the fatal bellman a fatal blow. Instead I rapped sharply on the window until a pale shape separated itself from a branch some eighteen inches away and took off into the darkness.

Just as I was drifting into sleep, I became aware of a distinct, regular knocking. I sat up. It wasn't coming from the door. I put on the light. A thick, cobwebby pipe ran down the wall next to the bed and disappeared through a crudely-cut circle in the floor. As I looked at it the knocking rose to a crescendo and I could see the pipe reverberating. I turned out the light. All old houses had tricky plumbing. If one were lucky enough to stay in a Jacobean house one must expect these inconveniences. The knocking stopped. I was definitely feeling just a little warmer. My lids were heavy. I began to relax. At the very same moment that the knocking began again there came the sound of scratching. I wondered if the hammer was for guests to stun themselves into sleep. The scratching went on after the knocking ceased for the second time. I got out of the bed and opened the door. Ham sat panting on the threshold.

There was a door opposite. I opened it and switched on the light. It was a very small room, painted white, with a single iron bedstead and it was empty.

'Good girl. Come on now,' I said encouragingly to Ham and she followed me in, wagging her tail.

Quick as a wink I shot out and shut the door. I had only got one socked foot in the bed when a phantasmal howling started up. Before she could wake the rest of the house, I released Ham and we stood staring at each other in the gloom of the landing.

'Oh God, come on then,' I said, with none of the sweet nature for which Ham was celebrated.

I settled myself between the sheets, which had regained their marble chill, and Ham lay down beside the bed with a grunt of satisfaction. She went on grunting for some time before starting a general, all-over wash and a satisfying scratch, with much rattling of claws against the wooden frame of my bed. Gradually the absolute necessity for sleep overtook us and we dosed and mumbled, fretted and sighed through the dark hours until morning.

## CHAPTER EIGHT

I awoke from a distressing dream that I was being covered with tar preparatory to being used as a human torch. I was uncomfortably hot. Ham was lying stretched out on the bed beside me, breathing cabbage-smelling breath into my face. It wasn't the first time in my life that I have woken with feelings of strong antagonism for the partner of my sleep, but thoughts of fleas had me up and out of bed without the usual dreamy review of the day past and the day to come.

I braved the bath, the bottom of which had the texture of granulated sugar, and exchanged the dirt of travel for specks of rust. I had found a very small towel in a drawer in my bedroom. I put on my tweed suit, of which I was very fond, with a white cashmere jersey underneath and went down to the kitchen. Min was there, struggling at the stove with a smoking frying pan. I could see at once that the flame beneath it was too high but it was too early in the morning for anyone to take advice or criticism so I watched quietly as the eggs were frizzled to something resembling yellow kid gloves.

'Did you sleep well?' asked Min. 'I forgot to tell you that if the heating pipes bother you at all you only have to hit them with the hammer and they stop. Sometimes air gets into the system and they make a knocking sound.'

Some heating, I thought with an acerbity provoked by lack of sleep.

'I wondered what it was for. The hammer, I mean. No, I got used to the noise. More troublesome was having to share my quarters with Ham.'

Min laughed and scooped an egg triumphantly out of the pan and on to a plate.

'I'm awfully sorry. If we shut her in the kitchen she chews the doorjamb and howls. I'd forgotten that she's taken to sleeping in your room. She used to try and sleep with us but Robert was driven mad by her fidgeting. He had the idea of leaving a bone in your room and it got her into the habit of sleeping in there. Now I think it's just the smell of the carpet she likes.'

This explained the stains. I ate my egg and a piece of toast and drank some rather bitter instant coffee with undissolved powder floating on the surface. This, possibly the worst breakfast in my life, reminded me of the most luxurious and I told Min about the breakfast at Foxcombe and Caroline Protheroe's attempt at suicide.

'It's difficult to imagine that degree of despair,' said Min thoughtfully. 'I suppose most people, including me, would be driven to anger by that kind of betrayal. Anger and contempt. I don't know, though. Robert's never even flirted with another woman in front of me so I can't really tell how I'd feel. Sometimes I think that he doesn't like women very much. Perhaps underneath that manly exterior he's queer! It's never occurred to me before. Of course he would have to be bisexual since the children are evidence of his heterosexuality. Does he look queer to you?'

'No,' I said truthfully. 'One of my very best friends is homosexual and there's a distinct difference.'

'What? I mean, I live this ridiculous, domestic, bucolic existence and I don't know about these things. Instruct me.'

I thought about Peter. Apart from all the obvious things like an affinity with beautiful things which, after all, some heterosexual men have, and a tendency to dress and move in a feminine way, which was by no means universal among homosexuals, there was something else which was shared with women and not with heterosexual men. A sensitivity to and a cognisance of intuitive feeling and an associated vulnerability. I tried to explain this to Min.

'But what about paratroopers and men with bowler hats and moustaches? Isn't the Army supposed to be full of suppressed catamites, all terribly butch because they're hiding their own terror of sexual deviation?'

I gave it up and admitted that I just didn't know.

'I'm going to have to go and buy a cake for tea,' said Min. 'I forgot to get one yesterday and though Vivien always says that she's dieting, she's pretty greedy if there's anything going. And the children will like it. Oh, and I'd better get some vegetables to go with the beef for lunch tomorrow. Do you want to come?'

I said that I'd like to and fetched my coat from the boot room where I'd put it the night before. I'd been surprised to find a plentiful stock of coat-hangers there, not one of them with a coat on it. Also the room was warm, being, I guessed, next to the boiler. As Min hadn't got round to lighting the paraffin stove in the kitchen for breakfast, I spent five minutes in the boot room thawing out and restoring my nose and hands to a normal colour.

'Come on,' said Min when I returned to the kitchen. 'What on earth have you been doing? I've been ready for hours.'

She was wearing a khaki-coloured anorak, very large and sensible, and a red woolly hat with a pom-pom on the top. I suppose my eyebrows must have contracted involuntarily when I saw it for she grinned and pulled it further down over her ears so that it looked quite ridiculous.

'All right, Daisy, my girl. None of your *dernier cri* here. You'll have to push the Land Rover so that I can get it started. But the stables are on a slope so you won't have to get inelegantly heated.'

We got the coach-house doors open with a struggle for the snow had blown up against them. All Land Rovers have that embattled look, as though they've been driven regularly up and down no-man's land for the duration of World War I but this one had the mien of a defeated enemy. Min got in and I began to heave like mad from behind until I felt my muscles throb painfully. Suddenly it slipped forward rather easily so I knew Min had remembered to take it out of gear. She was perfectly right about the road sloping downwards. The ground inclined so steeply that the Land Rover rocketed away in a blast of exhaust and was out of sight before I had time to retrieve my gloves and bag from the disused corn-bin into which they had fallen.

I walked down the hill in the glistening tracks made by the tyres and marvelled at the astonishing beauty of the hills and woods beneath their padding of snow. I caught up Min at the cattle-grid where the Land Rover stood roaring and pulsating like a bull that had just been let out of its shed. Min drove as she lived, with a disregard for trivialities which I admired, though I could never aspire to it myself. This included 'halt' signs at road junctions and other motorists and as she drove the entire time in four-wheel drive, whatever the terrain, I quickly caught the mood of blithe insouciance and devil-take-the-hindmost as we wallowed like a balsa raft in a choppy wake.

Great Swosser was the nearest small town to Weston Hall – a large village, really, with one main street and quite a good supply of shops. I told Min that I had some shopping to do and that I would meet her back at the Land Rover in three-quarters of an hour. My first purchase was at the butcher's where I bought a couple of pounds of meat for Ham. Then I went to the chemist for flea powder, worm tablets, two rubber hot-water bottles and some soft lavatory paper. At the draper's I bought a pair of men's blue-and-white striped flannelette pyjamas and two large, pink towels. In the hardware shop I bought an electric fire. At the grocer's I bought two bottles of the only champagne they stocked (to ease my conscience about the electric fire), a bottle of cognac and some more cigarettes. In the newsagent's window I saw a small black-and-white china cat and I bought it for Eleanor, suddenly divining that she would like that much better than the book I had brought for her which, I realised now, was too grown-up.

Min's eyebrows rose when she saw me stumbling back to the Land Rover with several shopping bags on each arm.

'I remembered that I'd promised to get some things for an elderly friend. I'm going to drop in on her on my way through London,' I lied, as a paper bag burst open and the hot-water bottles fell into the snow-filled gutter.

We were just turning into the drive of Weston Hall when Min said, 'Damn! I forgot to buy some cheese. Oh, no hell! I didn't buy any tins of dog food either.'

'I just happened to pass the butcher, so I got Ham some meat,' I said, hoping that Min wouldn't take this as a criticism of her housekeeping.

'Daisy! You are good! How wonderful! If only I could have you here all the time. No one else ever thinks about things for the house. No wonder I never get any work done. I know they're going to cancel my contract and I'll never get the chance again. God, it's so frustrating!'

'Could you do some work this afternoon? I could get the tea ready if you showed me where things are.'

We spent five minutes arguing about it and expressions of willingness and guilt flew back and forth until it was agreed that I would get the tea, with the understanding that Min was eternally in my debt, an obligation on which she insisted though I was willing to waive it. Robert was lunching at St Lawrence's so Min and the children and I ate fish fingers, an innovation that Min had just discovered and was very pleased about, with baked beans, followed by the tinned peaches which had been offered at supper the night before. After lunch I gave them their presents. For Min I'd chosen the new biography of George Eliot, which had been well reviewed and which, though I was looking forward to reading it myself, seemed to delight Min out of all proportion. I supposed she was almost never given things except at Christmas and perhaps not the kind of things she really cared for.

I gave William a book about natural disasters – volcanoes, earthquakes and tidal waves, that sort of thing. He thanked me very charmingly and opened it, pretending to look at the pictures. I could see that he was thinking about something else and that he wasn't very interested. When I gave Eleanor the china cat she flushed a brilliant red and the expression in her eyes was one of horror. She mumbled a sort of thank-you and put the cat down on the table as though it had the power to scorch. I was surprised. It certainly wasn't a candidate for the Victoria and Albert but I hadn't thought it was that bad. It was the kind of thing I would have loved at her age, sentimental and pretty. Min's pleasure quite made up for the two failures and I had to remind her that she was going to spend the afternoon working or she would have begun reading the biography at once.

She went off after a little more persuasion and I began the washing-up. It took much longer than it should have done, given the rudimentary nature of the lunch, because the water took so long to drain away. So after I'd stacked the things to dry, being unable to find a clean drying-up cloth, I tried to clear the waste-pipe. I found a damp packet of caustic soda in the boot room but this, along with two kettles of boiling water, failed to do the trick. After a quarter of an hour's search in the laundry room, I found a spanner roughly the right size and I was kneeling on the floor with my head under the sink, having unscrewed the joint of the waste-pipe, when Robert came in.

'What are you doing?' He sounded both astonished and annoyed.

For some reason I felt caught out and absurdly guilty, as though I'd been stealing the sherry.

'I just thought . . . something seemed to be stuck . . . ah, there we are,' I concluded as the pipe voided itself into the bucket I had placed beneath it.

'Where is Min?' he asked, contracting his nostrils as I showed him the mass of fat, peelings and tea-leaves that the pipe had given up.

'She's gone to do some work. I said I'd get tea. Min bought a cake.'

I was gabbing, something I tend to do when feeling nervous. Robert looked so extremely cross that I found myself chattering on, inconsequentially.

'Your mother's coming to tea, as I expect you've remembered. Do you think she'd like toast? It's a ginger cake. Perhaps she'd rather have bread and butter?'

'Oh, damn and blast! I'd forgotten she was coming.' He rubbed his chin with his hand and made a face, baring his teeth. 'The last thing I need . . . oh well, I suppose I'd better be there. Oh, bloody hell!'

'What do you think . . . toast or bread-and-butter?'

'I haven't the slightest idea. What *does* it matter?'

I felt crushed and then irritated by the scorn in his voice.

'I'll just do up the screw in the pipe then and get on with making the tea,' I said rather coldly, putting down the bucket and picking up the spanner.

'You will not!' he said, with emphasis. 'Give me the spanner.'

'Well, but the thread on the bolt's almost gone. You've got to be very careful or they'll get crossed. Hadn't you better let me . . .? I've been examining it . . .'

'Thank you. I think I can manage without your help,' he said, with so much schoolmasterly irony that I was silenced.

He got down on his hands and knees and stuck his head into the greasy recess. There was the sound of energetic rasping of metal on metal and then a telling pause. When Ham wandered up and sniffed at Robert's trousers, wondering why her master was in this unusual posture, Robert brought his head swiftly out from under the sink and glared at me. I looked at Ham who wagged her tail and looked from one to the other of us. Robert went back to work and finally there was a snapping sound and he reappeared with the nut in his hand.

'Thanks to the bungling efforts of other people this screw is beyond repair,' he said, slamming down the spanner and looking white with temper. 'I suppose now I'll have to telephone for a plumber.'

The unfairness of this made me nearly lose my own temper and I had to remind myself that this was Min's husband and that we had to spend two more nights under the same roof. He went stalking out into the hall and I bent down to look under the sink. I saw at once that he'd been trying to screw the nut on to the wrong projection, which was extraneous to the joint. It didn't take me long to fasten the right parts together. The pipe was a little loose where it connected to the wall, which was the bit which Robert had broken, but that seemed unimportant. I turned the tap on. The water flowed away rapidly and there was no suggestion of a leak below.

Robert came back into the kitchen. 'The telephone lines are still down,' he said, standing with his hands in his pockets and looking moodily ahead of him. 'I suppose we'll have to manage without the sink for the time being.'

'I've mended it,' I said, turning on the tap to show him.

He looked at the sink and then at me. 'I don't suppose it'll last,' he said, with unparalleled ungraciousness, and went out again.

I picked up a tray from beside the dresser and scrubbed it clean. In a cupboard I found some tea-cups that were full of spiders but were very pretty and a lovely Georgian teapot, lead-grey, on the same shelf. There was an old, bent electrolytic plate in the boot room. I made up a bowl full of boiling water and caustic soda, dropped the plate in and sank the teapot on to it. In seconds it shone as brightly as though it had been carefully polished. A cucumber in the fridge was still reasonably firm so I made cucumber sandwiches and put the ginger cake on to a plate. I looked for napkins but there didn't seem to be any. After this I couldn't think of any more preparations I could make so I gave Ham her worm pill concealed in a plate of meat scraps and dusted her coat generously with flea powder while she was eating. I had found her brush lying on the bread bin so I gave her a vigorous grooming which she seemed to enjoy, despite the choking smell of the flea powder. I knew that Robert would be angered by my interference so I was alert, listening for his footsteps in the passage between the kitchen and the hall.

I literally jumped when a voice said behind me, 'You must be Min's schoolfriend. I'm Vivien Weston, Robert's mother.'

She had come in through the back door, past all the old pantries and cupboards that lined the servants' corridor. It was after all her house still, in a way, so there was no reason why she shouldn't have, but her silent materialisation had unnerved me.

She was shortish, about Min's height and her hair was chin-length and straight and silvery-white. She had Robert's long, sharp nose, like a wizard in a fairy tale. Her eyes were very dark, like his, but there were pouches beneath which I hadn't noticed on him. Her skin was pale and freckled, even on her hands. She looked at me with cold, unembarrassed interest, then at the brush in my hand and at Ham.

'That dog seems to be going grey. She'll have to be put down. Old dogs are a menace in the house, urinating on the carpets.'

Ham sensed that she was being talked about and wagged her tail and gave a little whine of pleasure.

'There's a very peculiar smell. Like the stuff the gardeners used to spray on the chrysanthemums. Derris, was it?'

She wandered over to the table and looked at the tray.

'That teapot's Georgian. I suppose Min's scoured it to an inch of its life with silver polish.'

'I cleaned it. Of course I used an electrolytic plate.'

'Did you, indeed.'

She looked at me with raised eyebrows and then smiled suddenly and charmingly. 'I don't know your name. Min did tell me but I've forgotten.'

'Diana Fairfax,' I said, smiling in my turn, prepared to be on good terms if at all possible.

'And you were at school together? You don't look like contemporaries. Of course, having children ages women. After I'd had Robert I told Hector that if he wanted more children he'd have to go out and father them on the female population of Dunston Abchurch. I'd done my bosom and waist quite enough damage.'

She had quite a good figure for a woman of her age, which was probably in the early seventies. She was a little stout but her legs were thin and well-shaped. I hardly knew what comment to make. Anything personal would have been impertinent but she seemed to expect praise. I smiled approvingly and said nothing.

'You're not married?'

'No.'

'Hm. Surprising. I should have thought you'd be attractive to men. You've got a good neck. Still one can't tell what appeals to the other sex. Mary Campbell, who sits on the Red Cross with me, has been married three times and she's got a face like a colicky horse.'

I began to feel annoyed, not unreasonably.

'Where do you think Min wants tea?' I asked, with a suggestion of sharpness in my voice. 'Do you have it in here or should I light a fire somewhere? She's doing some work on her book.'

'In the drawing room, I suppose. So Min is still trying to qualify as an intellectual. She's wasting her time, of course. There's no money in it and men don't like that sort of thing. But I must be careful, of course, with this underwear-burning and Women's Lib that is so popular with the middle classes. I expect you are very clever, Diana. You certainly look most intelligent.'

She gave me again her smile that was undeniably attractive and her dark eyes gleamed. But I was already on the defensive and supicious.

'If you'll show me the way, I'll carry the tray,' I said.

'Oh, good, yes, come. I long to show you the drawing room.

A girl who knows how silver should be cleaned will appreciate a Rokesmith room.'

She walked off ahead of me, her good brogues making sharp sounds on the tiles as we crossed the hall.

'There! Look!' she said, throwing a pair of double doors wide.

It was certainly a remarkable room. The walls were hung with a pale blue silk, rather dingy now. The plasterwork of the ceiling and the rocaille on the wall panels was handsome and plentiful, the chimney-piece magnificent.

'This was Rokesmith's last work, completed only months before he died in eighteeen thirty-seven. What do you think of it?'

I looked at the huge windows hung with butter-yellow silk curtains which were wearing into shreds. Around the room were small gilded sofas and chairs and card-tables and tea-tables of fruitwood and mahogany. Drawn up round the fireplace was an Edwardian set of sofas and chairs upholstered in dirty calico. In the hearth was an electric fire with two elements above a spirited modelling of fake coals. Newspapers, books and an ashtray advertising Martini lay on a black vinyl coffee-table by the sofa. A shelf of orange Penguin paperbacks shared a cabinet with some porcelain that I burned to examine. On the marble chimney-piece with its gilt bronze mounts stood a squat, imitation-oak clock and a pair of badly-painted apricot plaster poodles. I was dumbfounded by this eclectic mixture.

'The hall and dining room were done by Rokesmith's partner, after he died, and they are perfectly dreadful. But this room has something.'

'It certainly does. It's a beautiful room. Shall I put the tray here?'

I shoved at the newspapers with my knee and put the tea things on the coffee-table. The fireplace lacked even a proper grate so I switched on the coal-effect fire and at once a very visible orange light-bulb lip up and a fan began to swirl energetically. With an unpleasant smell of burning dust the elements crackled into niggardly life.

'I think I'll go and get my coat from the kitchen,' I said, as Vivien plumped herself next to the fire, took a plate and helped herself to the cucumber sandwiches. 'It's awfully cold.'

'Bang the gong in the hall as you go through,' she said, without looking up from her food.

I sounded the gong as instructed and, having fetched my coat, had just got as far as the double doors of the drawing room when I heard Robert's voice in conversation with his mother.

'At that rate there won't be any sandwiches for the children. You might wait until they come in, Mother.'

'Children hate cucumber sandwiches. They're very good. That girl seems competent. She's very good-looking.'

This tribute astonished me after the remark about my neck. It taught me that Vivien was at all times to be watched.

'I'm surprised Min isn't deeply depressed by the competition,' continued Vivien. 'You mustn't let having a pretty woman around lead you into evil ways.'

'I happen to think Min extremely pretty,' said Robert's voice, very crossly. 'And I don't personally care for painted fingernails.'

'My dear Robert, if *that's* all you've got against her, I'd say that Min's goose is well and truly cooked.'

'It isn't all. You're an appalling trouble-maker. It's really quite unforgivable.' Robert sounded at his most pompous. I heard Vivien laugh, delightedly. 'She's annoyingly managing . . . overbearing really. Got too good an opinion of herself. Conceited.'

I shall never be forgiven for the sink, I thought, and was cross with myself for feeling hurt. I rattled the door handle and then walked in. Robert was reading the titles of the paperbacks, with his head on one side, and Vivien was looking at me with a pleased smile on her face. Nearly all the sandwiches were gone. Min came in after me, followed by the two children.

'I've done a really good amount of work,' said Min. 'Hello, Vivien.' They brushed cheeks. 'It was the feeling that there was someone there who could cope whatever happened.'

'I always feel "cope" is a very middle-class word,' said Vivien, taking another sandwich.

'Middle-class or not, it expresses the sense of struggle and low attainment appropriate to my mood,' said Min, very acidly for her. 'Usually I'm distracted by thoughts of disaster but with Daisy there I knew she'd manage far better than I could so I just didn't think about anything else. Must you go on Monday?'

I looked sorrowful and remained silent.

'Ooh, sandwiches!' said Eleanor. 'What are they?'

'Cucumber, darling,' said Vivien, holding the plate towards her.

'I hate cucumber. I only like brown sugar sandwiches.'

Vivien looked triumphantly at Robert who sat down on the sofa next to her, his legs stretched out in front of him and his chin on his chest in an attitude of brooding.

'Brown sugar sandwiches? How disgusting. Where have you eaten those?' asked Min.

'Polly Saxby always has them for tea when she asks girls home. She never asks me so I haven't eaten them but the other girls talk about them. Then they play games.'

'What sort of games?' asked William, paying attention for the first time since entering the room.

'Well, forfeits for one thing. I know they play that because Katherine Brand told me she had to take her knickers down as a forfeit and . . .'

'Thank you, Ellie. That'll do,' said Robert. 'It doesn't sound as though you're missing very much by not being asked to tea.'

'I am, though,' said Eleanor, growing very pink. 'There isn't anything I'd rather do than go to tea with Polly Saxby but she never, ever asks me.'

'Why don't you ask her to tea here?' suggested Min.

'Oh, Mummy!' said Eleanor with absolute scorn. 'That shows you don't understand anything!'

'Come and sit next to me, Eleanor, and share this piece of ginger cake,' Vivien patted the sofa between herself and Robert. 'It's from a shop and consequently not very good but your mother has more important things to do than provide decent food for her family and of course your parents can't afford a cook.'

William who had seemed momentarily interested by the description of the forfeit now looked as though he were asleep on his feet. His eyes were shut and he was swaying as though to some internal music.

'My word, I think Mummy must be fattening you up for sacrifice,' said Vivien. 'Those hips are taking up a great deal of room, Eleanor. You can have your own tent at the next church fête, with a sign outside saying "See the Fattest Lady". Wouldn't that be funny?'

Eleanor hung her head and I saw that her eyes were full of tears. Robert shook his head at Vivien. Vivien pretended not to see him.

'What time must we be ready for dinner?' I asked, anxious to change the subject.

'Where are you going to dinner?' asked Vivien, her eyes sharp with interest.

'To Milecross Park,' said Min.

'Oh, the South African man. I hear he's rather good-looking. What a pity he's so vulgar.'

'He isn't vulgar.' Min looked angry. 'I think I like him better than anyone else around here. He's not nearly so dull as most of them. He's very attractive. And enormously charming.'

Vivien looked at Robert and raised her eyebrows. 'I sometimes wonder if Min is quite satisfied with her role as wife and mother. Some people, you know, are not fitted for a domestic life.'

'You weren't, I know,' said Robert, quite rudely. 'I didn't see you for days on end when I was a child. You were too busy with your boyfriends.'

'I couldn't help it, darling. They clamoured for me. What could I do? Poor little Simon Maitland. Committed suicide, you know. Because of me.'

'I could hardly help knowing, considering you tell us about it almost every time you come here. It seems to be your only achievement . . . driving a harmless boy to his death. He must have been a remarkable fool.'

'I must say, in the thirteen years that you've been married you've grown extraordinarily uncouth. I wonder why.'

'I think I'll go and lie down for an hour,' I said, deciding to leave them to bicker in private.

'Lie down? Why on earth should a healthy young woman wish to lie down at half past four in the afternoon? You're not pregnant?'

'Mother!'

'I hope not,' I replied, calmly. 'It would be inconvenient, to say the least.'

Once in my room I turned on the electric fire which I had carried upstairs with the other things and toasted myself in front of it for a while.

Then, being genuinely sleepy, I got under the bedclothes and fell into a doze.

## CHAPTER NINE

When I awoke the only light in the room was the glow from the electric fire. It had warmed the space around my bed beautifully. My watch said six thirty. I took my dress from the wardrobe. It felt damp so I hung it from the canopy of the bed to air in front of the fire while I reapplied my make-up and gave my hair a good brushing. The rising warmth, in collusion with the damp, took the creases out of my dress as effectively as any lady's maid.

It was too late for a bath and anyway one a day in that monument to English fortitude was all I could endure. I pulled on my dress and thin tights and slid my feet into a pair of high-heeled, black suede shoes. I had a debate with myself on the subject of economy versus comfort but it was very brief. I decided to leave the fire on.

In the kitchen, which was empty apart from Ham who was stretched snoring in front of the paraffin heater, I washed three glasses which I had found in the butler's pantry and took the champagne out of the fridge. I suddenly had a wild longing for an olive but as I hadn't had the foresight to buy any, if, indeed, such things were to be had in Great Swosser, I contented myself with a piece of ginger cake. It was very dull and dry but I was hungry. It occurred to me to wonder why Eleanor was so fat. Min's food was on the meagre side and it was hard to get down what there was of it.

Robert and Min came in and I repressed an impolite expression of amazement at the transformation in them both. Min was looking very charming in a dress of blue silk and Robert wore a black tie. A dinner-jacket can do something for the plainest man and Robert was, I had to admit, not plain.

'Where did this come from?' he asked suspiciously, looking at the glass I held out to him.

'It's just a small present from me to thank you for having me to stay. I bought it from Beale's this morning. It isn't bad actually.'

'I should say it isn't!' said Min, taking her glass and gulping at it noisily. 'This is heaven. We never have champagne at home. Why don't we?'

'I've always thought it an overrated drink,' said Robert. 'Suitable for tarts and racehorse owners.'

I felt like snatching his glass back but reminded myself of the sink episode and adopted an expression of cool amusement.

'Robert!' Min was indignant. 'Your mother's quite right. You have become uncouth. I suppose it must be my fault. Ignore him, Daisy. He's terribly jealous of Charles Jarrett. He's the man we're going to have dinner with. He breeds racehorses and is terrifically rich.'

I was pleased to hear it. A rich South African would be bound to have proper ideas about heating. I noticed that Robert had, despite his disdain for champagne, emptied his glass. I was about to fill it for him but he took the bottle very firmly from me and refilled all our glasses.

'What a pity we haven't any crisps,' said Min, looking about vaguely as though some might come floating down like Danae's shower of gold. 'You couldn't be an angel and do something about my dress? Robert tried to pin it but it doesn't feel quite right.'

I took out the safety pin that was holding the fabric in a tight fistful to one side of the zip.

'Do you want another pin?'

'Needle and thread, please,' I muttered while trying to see how it should go.

There was an intensive search for a needle and cotton, but, once found, the repair went quite well and by the time we'd finished the bottle of champagne no one would have known that I'd had to use bottle-green thread and a darning needle.

'You're a wonder,' said Min. 'I'd forgotten that you were always a whizz at sewing. Now where's my brush? I must just do my hair and then I'm ready.'

Before I could stop her, she had picked up the brush that I'd used on Ham and run it through her hair.

'What's that terrible smell?' asked Robert, as a cloud of flea powder drifted round her head like a nimbus. 'Min, there's something on your brush.'

Min looked at it absent-mindedly, pulled off a handful of Ham's black hairs and went on brushing.

'Probably talcum powder. I use it sometimes when I've forgotten to wash my hair.'

'I don't think so,' said Robert, his nostrils looking pinched. 'They wouldn't be able to sell anything that made people smell like that. It's vile.'

It occurred to me then that when, in later years, I looked back on this weekend, I would remember Robert as a large, delving, sniffing animal, like a bad-tempered tapir, thrusting his pointed nose distrustfully into everything and guarding his territory with angry growls.

The babysitter, a young girl called Muriel from the village, had arrived by now and had been taken off by Eleanor to watch television in the housekeeper's room. Muriel had looked very impressed by our collective glamour. She very definitely lacked anything glamorous in her own appearance, being tall and gawky, and wearing gumboots, but I was glad to see that she held Eleanor's hand and spoke kindly to her.

Min insisted that I sat in the front of the Land Rover while she drove and Robert pushed. I fell in with this plan without protest. I wanted, for the sake of my tights and shoes, to avoid a run down the hill in the dark and snow to the cattle-grid. Reminding myself of the remarks about nail polish, conceit and champagne, I refused to allow myself to feel guilty as I heard Robert heaving and groaning behind us but I did remind Min to depress the clutch, which I thought was pretty nice of me in the circumstances.

We drove the seven miles to Milecross Park in comparative silence, apart from the clamour of an overstrained engine and the heavy panting of Robert in the back, as the roads were beginning to freeze and Min had to concentrate. The house was large and well-lit. I felt cheerful as soon as I saw it. There were two Rovers, a Mercedes and a Bentley on the gravel outside the front door, beside which our Land Rover took on a rather *dégagé* air. A pretty maid let us in and took our coats. I was sorry to see, as she carried it off, that mine had a large streak of mud down the back, which had definitely not been there when we set out.

Our host came forward to greet us as we were shown into the drawing room. Charles Jarrett bent to embrace Min with just the amount of appreciation and flirtation in his manner which is acceptable both to an attractive woman and to the husband who is looking on. He must have inhaled some of the flea powder for he recoiled slightly and cleared his throat before shaking hands with Robert. Then he turned to me to be introduced.

He was dark-haired and very brown-skinned with sharp, grey eyes and an expression of amusement that predisposed me in his favour from the first, especially after twenty-four hours with Robert.

'Welcome, Diana. I may call you Diana?' he said, retaining my hand, which was as clammy and cold as a refrigerated joint, for a moment in his warm one.

There was something healthy and energetic about him, as though he'd always been fed on the right food and got in that important hour before midnight. Standing next to him, Robert looked tired and depressed.

'Of course,' I murmured, returning his smile.

'You're not at all what I expected. I see that it was worth combing the neighbourhood for an extra man to make up the table. Now I know why women make so much of a single man in the country. I shall never again feel that I'm asked out for any particular merit I may have. Only that I am a man and I can come alone.'

'It's perfectly true. If you were deaf and dumb, ate only nuts and dried fruit and had to be carried about in a litter, you would be just as socially desirable as you are now.'

Charles laughed a lot at this sally, which was nice of him, and took me over to meet the other guests. Of course I couldn't remember anyone's name nor did I get much impression of anyone except the woman standing next to me, who was drab and stooping, and asked me at once if I was a gardener. I was slightly taken aback by the directness of her approach though I realised that she wasn't asking me if I was employed nine to five to dig up someone's best plants by mistake for weeds and jam the lawn-mower with fir-cones.

'In spirit I am,' I replied, 'but unfortunately I don't have one.'

This was not quite true as I had a walled plot twenty-five feet long behind my house in Orchard Street which was crammed with all the beautiful and rare plants I could find but I didn't very much want to talk about it. She looked disappointed for a moment but then began on her own garden which, it seemed, was very large, stifled with ground elder and trussed by convolvulus, run over by hordes of deer and rabbits, blighted by icicle-forming winds from every possible direction and managed by a gardener who was dishonest, disabled and without a particle of sense.

'Oh dear. I do hope that at least you have good soil,' I said, incautiously.

She was off again at once. Her soil was the very worst anyone had ever had to garden on. It was all sand and stones in some parts without a scrap of nutrition, while in other parts it was such heavy clay that ten men could not dig a hole in it. In addition, only last week she had discovered honey fungus of the most virulent kind.

'Goodness,' I said, feeling that I must show some concern for this wretched state of affairs, 'perhaps you ought to think of moving. If you think you could possibly find a buyer?'

She looked at me with the utmost indignation and astonishment and then said, very frostily, 'Many people consider my garden to be one of the most beautiful in the North-East.'

We ended our conversation by mutual consent and I talked next to a gynaecologist, a short man, sandy in colouring, who was quite unlike any other gynaecologist I had every met in being shy, modest and diffident, to the point of speaking so quietly that I hardly heard anything he said. He was so delighted to find that I had no children and therefore no history of complicated births to recount that he began to drink more deeply and to speak up.

'You would not believe the number of women,' he said, emphatically, 'who regale me over dinner with the most intimate details. It really is most embarrassing.'

'But surely you're used to these things?' I said. 'Aren't all these matters everyday and humdrum and quite impersonal? So we're told and so we want very much to believe.'

'In my consulting rooms, yes. But I am after all an ordinary man.'

I looked at him with respect for I knew that not many gynaecologists thought that of themselves.

'I long for romance and illusion, just like anyone else. Making love is a question of imagination, not just physical responses to stimuli.'

I thought that if he had been a little taller and a little less sandy, he would have found romance and illusion more easily, regardless of his profession, but kept this idea to myself. Dinner was announced and we drifted towards the dining room. There were splendid fires banked up in both rooms and the air was balmy with warmth and the scent of hothouse lilies, of which there were two massive arrangements, one in each room. Everything at Milecross Park was bold and unashamed. The sofas were softer and deeper, the tables longer and shinier, the paintings bigger and brighter, the carpets thicker, the chandeliers more glittery.

I was reminded of Foxcombe Manor, probably because both bore the unmistakable mark of the interior decorator in the degree of finish and attention to detail. Mrs Studley-Headlam's house was much prettier and more to my taste but both houses had been put together all at once instead of acquiring furniture and objects piecemeal. Though Milecross Park was Georgian, the decoration was, on the whole, contemporary. There was a huge, granite sculpture at one end of the dining room, punctured haphazardly by large holes, like a piece of petrified sponge.

'Do you like it?' Charles asked, seeing me staring at it as we milled about the dining room looking for our places.

He leaned quickly over the middle of the table and exchanged a place-card for one that he held in his hand.

'There's been a mistake. You're sitting next to me. Beatrice,' he called to a woman in navy blue, who was noticeable for a bossy, self-important air as she found people their seats, 'you're sitting here.'

'I don't think so,' said Beatrice, coming round. 'Horace said . . . oh!'

She saw the card with 'Beatrice' written in an educated hand and the corners of her mouth dropped for a moment. She gave him an unfriendly look.

I sat down next to Charles at the far end of the table. Charles put the card with my name on in front of me. I saw Beatrice look furious and shake out her napkin as though she were swatting wasps. I turned back and saw Charles watching me.

'You know, that woman's going to hate me for ever,' I said, unable not to smile.

'I wouldn't be surprised. Beatrice has a lot of influence socially, so I'm told, but you have your own, quite different, pre-eminence so you won't mind that.'

'I shan't mind it because I'm going back to Cambridge on Monday so it won't matter a jot.'

'Are you? What a pity. You didn't answer me when I asked you what you thought of that lump of stone.'

I looked at it. It was neither beautiful nor informative nor especially interesting.

'I don't really like it at all.'

'Good. I'm glad you didn't lie out of politeness. It's pretty hideous isn't it. Its called '*Passchendaele.*'

'Really? Good heavens, I can't think why.'

'Artists imagine that if they write about or paint or depict, in some way, some very serious event . . . and you can't get much more serious than a world war . . . it gives their work probity.'

'I think that's very cynical.'

'Yes, it is. And not fair in every case. But I buy these things because when they become valuable, in twenty or thirty years' time, I'll be able to sell them without a qualm. I don't care about them . . . they're just wallpaper. But wallpaper that's accumulating value in leaps and bounds. After dinner I'll show you something that *is* worth looking at.'

'So there is something that you want to have just because it's beautiful?' I asked. I was thinking of a sculpture by Michelangelo or a painting by Raphael.

A dish containing half a dozen oysters was put down in front of me. I saw Robert, who was sitting on the other side of the table a few places up, pick up a fork and prod the glistening, grey flesh warily. I thought of the tapir and smiled to myself.

'Oh yes. Are you smiling because you're confident you know the answer to that?' Charles said, looking at me so teasingly that I suddenly caught his meaning and felt disconcerted.

It was Coleridge who said that a man's desire is for the woman but the woman's desire is rarely other than for the desire of the man and I'm ashamed to admit that I can vouch for a particle of truth in this little piece of misogyny. I was quite willing to flirt with Charles if he wanted to flirt with me, with no purpose but to make myself agreeable and indulge my vanity. I would never see him again after this evening and if his intention was to make Beatrice jealous I was happy to fall in with the plan, having disliked her from the first glance.

'Min said you bred racehorses. Is that what you did in South Africa?'

'No. We owned land on which coal was discovered in large quantities twenty years ago. I had to learn very fast how to mine. There wasn't much time for anything else. But I always wanted to come to England and breed horses. My grandfather was an Englishman who never got over his homesickness.'

'And do you like it now you're here?'

'Yes, I do. On the whole. It's small but I'm getting used to that.'

'Geographically small, you mean?'

'Yes, in that way, too. I think I'm a little homesick, myself. But I like the countryside and I like this house. I like English people like Min . . . eccentric without knowing it. She's intelligent and truthful and sweet-tempered.'

'Is Min eccentric? I've never thought of her as that.'

'To me she seems so. So frank, so entirely herself. Watch her talking to Beatrice's husband. He doesn't understand what she's talking about and is wavering between boredom and feelings of inferiority. But she isn't interested in the impression she's making, only in what she's trying to say. That's very unusual. I'd call that eccentric. Also, she's a very attractive woman . . . yet she has a tidemark around her neck like a plimsoll line and she smells of tick repellent.'

For a moment I wondered if I should confess responsibility for part of this censure of Min's grooming but I wanted to hear more.

'So I assume that you don't approve of Beatrice and women like her? Yet . . .' I paused, thinking how to put it delicately.

'Yet I was prepared to seduce her? Well, why not? Her husband would rather I slept with his wife than lose the chance of being invited to my box for the racing season. And Beatrice wants me to make love to her.'

I was slightly taken aback by this. It seemed rather conceited, to say the least. I bent my head forward to look at Beatrice. From the smugness of her expression she was talking either about her children's schools or about her voluntary work. Who would have thought that she imagined herself rolling naked over a large double bed in the arms of Charles Jarrett, some frivolous underwear, bought for the occasion and very different from her usual sensible cotton support bra, lying disregarded on the floor where he had tossed it? I turned back to Charles and realised that he was watching me again. He suddenly laughed without saying anything. I wondered if he guessed what I had been imagining. The oyster shells were removed and replaced by a tiny portion of white fish, probably turbot.

'This is very good,' I said, anxious to introduce a note of proper dinner-party persiflage into the conversation. 'It was clearly fished with the worm that ate of the king. Actually that's rather a disgusting idea. I've never liked eating lobsters since someone told me that their favourite food was decomposing sailors.'

After I'd said this, which struck me immediately as maladroit, I told myself to calm down and stop trying so hard. Charles ate his turbot in three mouthfuls, disregarded the parsley and prawns which decorated it and sat back in his chair.

'I want to know about you. Min said, when she telephoned on Friday, that you were an old friend and she hadn't seen you since Oxford. It didn't sound promising. I imagined an earnest bluestocking with a scrubbed face, broken veins and sensible shoes.'

I told him as briefly as I could about myself. As I'd been through it all with Min less than twenty-four hours ago, I was able to give a polished account. He listened very calmly, never once taking his eyes from my face or interrupting. When I'd finished, he frowned and looked thoughtful. The fish was replaced by saddle of lamb but he ignored it and continued to reflect.

'It sounds a very circumspect life,' he said, at last.

'Is that a criticism?'

I tried to speak lightly but I began to feel resentful. There are men who become aggressive when they are attracted to a woman. I've never been able to decide why . . . whether it's because the fear that the desire might not be gratified makes them feel vulnerable or if it's a more primitive, involuntary response, connected with urges to drag women about by the hair.

'Not a criticism. No, I'm puzzled. Your life is admirable . . . directed, controlled, successful, full of pleasure and beautiful things that satisfy you. Never a foot wrong. Or perhaps you're not going to tell me about the mistakes. There's no reason why you should, of course.'

'There isn't anything to hide,' I said, laughing but still feeling a trifle defensive. 'Of course I've made mistakes. But they're not very interesting to talk about.'

'Tell me about your family. If you'll forgive my curiosity?'

Of course I was flattered by so much undisguised interest. I told him about my parents and tried to make their inadequacies ridiculous (not at all difficult in my mother's case), so that he shouldn't suspect me of Freudian angst. I found myself telling him about the second, and last, meeting with my father, just before he died. It wasn't something I'd spoken of before though I'd often thought about it. I'd been terribly nervous and excited beforehand, imagining that the encounter would be the beginning of something terribly important. My father had shaken my hand, given me his solicitor's name and address and told me to get in touch with him if I got into difficulties with my allowance at Oxford. He'd expressed the hope that I would study hard and not make the mistake of getting in with a fast set. He had shaken my hand again on parting. The interview had lasted about half an hour. He died of cancer two months later and left me everything he had . . . not a huge amount, as he'd been living on capital for years, but enough to buy myself a house and live reasonably well.

'The only emotion he expressed at all was when he asked about my mother. It was like seeing the outline of a door suddenly appearing in a rock. Through the chink there was a gleam of concentrated malice that was at the core of him. He said that he supposed she was by now a *debauchée*, living with some drunken gigolo of a painter in a haze of alcohol and delusion. It was an accurate description, but I didn't tell him so. Afterwards I thought that I was probably fortunate. Most people spend their lives struggling to recover from the impact of their parents' personalities. I've probably missed all sorts of pleasures by not having a father who loved me but, on the other hand, I have nothing to recover from.'

'I suppose that's true,' said Charles. 'My own father was a hard man, selfish, even cruel. I hated him for a long time before I understood him and the hating made me pretty unhappy. But I suppose my feelings about him were also a spur. To be different . . . to be independent.'

'That's just what happened between my mother and me. She acted as a catalyst. To be unlike her in every way possible.'

'So what about men? Where are they in your life?'

I felt defensive again. 'There have been some,' I said coolly.

'I don't doubt it. More than enough to choose from, I imagine. But they seem peripheral to the story. Have you ever lived with a man?'

I didn't like the imperious way he was questioning me. The implication was that there was something wrong, something defective about me. I could have told him to mind his own business. But that would seem as though I were safeguarding myself.

'Yes, a couple of times.'

'But it didn't work?'

'No.'

'So what is it that you are afraid of?' he asked, looking at me very directly.

'You're neglecting me, Charles,' said the middle-aged woman on his left, who had overheard the last part of our conversation and was obviously curious. 'I can tell this young lady,' she cast a look at me that was rather chilly, 'is proving terribly fascinating.'

'As you say,' said Charles, unperturbed by her ill-humour.

But he turned to her and asked her about her husband who was in America, doing something dull and important, so I began to talk to the amiable young man on my right, called Jamie, who seemed pleased to have my attention. He had just become engaged to a fair, chinless girl further up the table and was clearly besotted by her. He was studying psychology, having acquired a medical degree at Edinburgh University. While he was talking about synapses and neurons, my attention wandered a little as I watched Robert who was talking to a woman with fluffy blonde hair and, as far as I could gather from the snippets of conversation, not much brain. She seemed to be finding Robert hard-going.

'Are you inferring that French food is overrated?' she asked him, with an attempt at playfulness.

'No. *I* was implying. *You* were inferring from what I said that I think so,' he said, patiently, as though he was going to ask her to write it out a hundred times. 'Anyway I wasn't implying that, exactly. I just said I didn't like all those pies and pâtés stuffed with little birds, all beak and feet and no taste.'

'It does seem a shame to kill them,' said the woman, with a trilling laugh. 'Anyway I adore my sweet birds in my garden. We had a long-tailed tit nesting last year.'

Robert was foraging among the bones of the lamb for the last scrap of meat without bothering to appear interested in this piece of information. The woman looked discouraged and I didn't blame her.

'How would you treat depression these days?' I asked Jamie, as he paused for a moment.

'Well, first you'd have to establish whether the depression is brought about by extraneous causes. To be truthful, we still aren't much good at treating it. With anxiety we're doing very much better. There are all sorts of treatments and approaches and people can be cured, sometimes permanently. I'm studying phobias at the moment. Some people have spent twenty years or more not being able to leave their own house, for example. Now they can be gradually rehabilitated and lead more or less normal lives.' He plunged his fork enthusiastically into a profiterole.

'Is agoraphobia the most common phobia?'

'I should think it is. But you'd be astonished at what frightens some people. What do you think theophobia is?'

'I suppose it must be a fear of God.'

He looked disappointed for a moment. 'Yes, you're right, but I bet you can't guess what potophobia is.'

'Fear of drugs?' suggested Charles's neighbour who, I suddenly remembered, had been introduced to me before dinner as Charmian.

'No. Drinking. What about chaetophobia?'

None of us could think what that could be. Charmian who, I think, wanted to impress Charles, entered into the game with a great display of spiritedness, guessing a fear of things with tails, a fear of things flying in the air or a fear of things on strings.

'All wildly out. It means a fear of hair. What about antlophobia?'

Jamie was delighted to find himself the centre of attention and appeared unstoppable.

'Fear of being changed into a stag?' I suggested.

Fear of being bitten by ants was Charmian's suggestion which was every bit as good as mine, I had to admit.

'Fear of suitcases,' shouted someone from further up the table.

'Fear of floods,' said Robert, after everyone had finished laughing.

'Cheat,' I said, seeing by Jamie's crestfallen face that Robert was right. 'Classicists aren't allowed to play.'

'Who knows what spermophobia is?' said Charles.

'Fear of sex!' said several people together.

Charles looked at me and narrowed his eyes slightly. His look was so concentrated that I felt that others were following his gaze. I knew that I was starting to blush and I felt furious.

'No,' he said, still looking at me but beginning to smile. 'Actually it means a fear of germs.'

'Yes, that's right,' said Jamie. 'Fear of sex is actually coitophobia or erotophobia. Jolly bad luck to suffer from that!' and his eyes swivelled to his fiancée with a look of longing.

The conversation remained general until the end of dinner and afterwards, in the drawing room, I stood with Min and Charmian by the fire.

'What do you think of that?' said Charmian, pointing to a large painting of red and blue squares on the opposite wall, which I'd just been thinking was rather ugly. 'Rather common, isn't it? The whole house is, really.'

Min looked furious. 'I think it's terribly clever,' she said. 'Of course you need an educated eye to see it.'

I felt a touch on my arm suddenly.

'Come with me,' said Charles. 'I promised to show you something beautiful.' He put his hand under my elbow and we went into the hall.

'This is Horace, my secretary and factotum,' he said, taking a coat from a young man and holding it for me to put on. Horace, who had large spectacles and short, black hair that stood up on his head, gave me the faintest of smiles.

The coat was a sheepskin, tremendously warm and smelling of cigars. I was slightly reassured by the staid nature of the garment . . . hardly the stuff of seduction. Charles led the way through several doors until we reached what must be the back of the house. We went outside into a yard that had been cleared of snow. The moon was up, appearing to swim through a swell of livid, rolling cloud. A light was on in one of the loose boxes.

'All right, Benny, I only want to look at her for two minutes,' said Charles to a short man in a flat cap who stank of horses.

Benny touched his cap to me and went away.

'Come on. Don't be afraid.'

It never occurred to me to be indignant at this imputation of cowardice for I was frankly terrified. Charles took my arm, led me firmly in and bolted the door behind me. The horse was walking up and down on the length of its rope and as we entered it began to jerk its head violently and roll its eyes and dribble fearfully. Its skin rippled and its hoof skidded on the floor. Charles spoke in a low voice and made shushing noises while I pressed my back to the door and prayed not to be trampled to death. Charles walked up to the horse and put his hand on its head-collar, moving very deliberately and speaking all the time in a soft voice. The horse grew calm beneath his touch and soon was standing so tranquilly that it might have been a beach donkey.

'This is Astarte. The best mare I've ever owned. Isn't she wonderful?'

'Wonderful! She's certainly very . . . large.'

He ran his hand over her back and her skin quivered in response but she only turned her head to look at him with moist, brown eyes. Then I began to suspect that there was some analogy being drawn between me and the mare and that Charles was showing me that he could exert his will over me in the same way. I put the notion firmly away from me, telling myself that so much unaccustomed country life was going to my head and we were not in a novel by Mary Webb.

'She's in foal again. That's why her coat looks so good. It'll be her last foal. I'm going to retire her.'

'Not . . . put her down?' I said anxiously.

As some people fear to go to India in case they see beggars, I feared to enter a farmyard in case it was pig-sticking day or some hapless bird was having its neck wrung. I couldn't understand how farmers could lean over the sty wall and tickle Percy's back and feed him his favourite turnip while planning the next day to slit his throat from ear to ear. Charles laughed.

'Good God, no! It would be like shooting my wife . . . if I had one.'

I was curious to know if he'd ever had one but I was keener still to stay on impersonal topics as we were shut in together with nothing more than the brood mare as chaperone. He gave Astarte a last stroke and then came over to me. It is odd how someone else's confidence diminishes one's own, as though there were some system of counterweights in operation. I had never met anyone as self-assured as Charles and I suddenly felt as jittery as a schoolgirl.

'You're cold,' he said, putting his hands on my shoulders.

'Absolutely freezing!'

'You're a very delicate creature, are you?' he said teasingly.

I can't explain why I suddenly felt the ridiculous desire to burst into tears. Thank goodness I didn't, but it was only by closing my eyes and imagining myself somewhere else that I retained any composure.

Suddenly he let me go and said, in a very matter-of-fact voice, 'We'd better go in. They'll be wondering where we are.'

We walked in silence across the yard to the house. Benny appeared. He'd obviously been waiting for us.

'Settle her for the night, Guv?'

Charles nodded. I gave up the sheepskin coat to Horace who was waiting in the hall. Chinese emperors could hardly have had more efficient or more discreet service than Charles commanded. Horace refused to catch my eye though I tried to smile at him. I felt as though I'd been smuggled up the stairs from a closed carriage to gratify the sexual wants of some Hapsburg prince. It was a relief to get back into the drawing room and see the usual well-bred faces and frumpish evening clothes of the English at play.

Robert drove us home. I sat next to him and Min sat in the back, talking all the way.

'I always enjoy myself when we go there. It's so lovely to be warm and eat delicious things. If only one could ask for second helpings. That Charmian woman is an absolute bitch. I adore Charles. He's too good for these people. They only want to be catty about him because he's got so much more lovely money than they have. But they wouldn't spend it half as well. What did you think of him, Daisy? I could see he was nuts about you. I knew he would be.'

There was as much complacency in her voice as if she were an Edwardian matron and I a daughter she was eager to get married off.

'He certainly likes you,' I said, cautious in my reply because of Robert.

'Good! What did he say?'

'He said you were intelligent, truthful and . . . warm-hearted, I think. Something like that. He said you were eccentric.'

'No, did he really?' Min was delighted. 'But I'm the most conventional person there is. Housewife, mother . . . and not very good at being that.'

'He was talking about something less obvious. Something about your absolute honesty . . . lack of artifice, I think he meant.'

'I'm so flattered. Dear Charles! Now tell me what else you were talking about. I could see you were both rapt. Tell me *everything*.'

I smiled to myself in the darkness. When we were children those had always been Min's first words after any separation. But I found myself unable to speak in front of Robert because I was quite certain that he was listening. And also that he was hostile. I was startled, therefore, when he said, 'He was quite right about Min. It's the thing I love about her most. He must be a more perceptive man than I thought.'

And perhaps the same is true of you, was what flashed through my mind as we turned into the back drive of Weston Hall.


CHAPTER TEN


We all got up late the following morning. After a breakfast, which none of us enjoyed very much because the whites of the boiled eggs were transparent and slimy and the toast blacker than sin, I offered to cook lunch so that Min could work but she wouldn't hear of it.

'Absolutely not. I want to make the most of having you here. And I want to hear everything that happened last night between you and Charles.'

'Let me help you peel vegetables then,' I said, finding a very dirty apron hanging from the back of a door and putting it on. 'Do you have rubber gloves?'

'Only for unblocking the loo. Shall I get them? No, all right. Well if you insist on helping, there are some parsnips. Now, tell me *everything*. I saw you slipping away together after dinner.'

'We went to look at a horse.'

While I struggled with a blunt knife and very large, woody parsnips I told Min about the visit to Astarte's box.

'Charles handled her perfectly. She was absolutely relaxed with him. But I had the oddest feeling that he was showing me what he'd do with me if I allowed him to. Probably it's my overheated imagination.'

'How Lawrentian! It's the sexiest thing I ever heard! Wasn't there a D H Lawrence story about it that we did for O-level? *St Mawr* . . . that was it. Oh no, that was the other way round. The horse was a stallion and it represented the man . . . all throbbing primeval forces, earthy, and fermenting!'

'I think you're getting carried away, Min. It wasn't as exciting as all that.'

I remembered my desire to burst into tears and thought that perhaps there had been some dark, subconscious forces at work but I couldn't begin to identify them.

'He really is *the* most attractive man,' said Min dreamily, pausing in the act of peeling a potato. 'If I hadn't got to be faithful to Robert I'd go to bed with him like a shot. I hope you're going to. Then you can tell me all about it and give me vicarious thrills.'

'I've absolutely no intention of going to bed with him. For someone who's led a virtually chaste existence apart from within the legitimate confines of the marriage bed, you're extremely promiscuous on behalf of others. Anyway I'm going home tomorrow so you'd better forget all about it.'

'He's like the heroes of those novels we used to read with Gina . . . do you remember? Saturnine, harsh-featured earls swanning about with large whips under their arms, absolutely brutal and dominating yet capable of the greatest tenderness. Are you sure he hasn't taken you by the chin, turned up your face and kissed you fiercely on the lips?'

We both laughed at this idea.

'Perhaps he was put off by my tip-tilted nose of inordinate size and the deafening noise of my gurgles of laughter.'

'Oh, to see Charles in a coat cut by Weston which needed two men to shrug him into!'

'And a pair of hessians and gleaming top-boots, polished by a valet of fearfully tender sensibility, with a compound of blacking and champagne.'

We giggled until we were weak, not so much because it was funny but because we were so happy to be together, with all the old intimacy restored.

'What's funny?' asked Robert, coming in with Eleanor. 'The telephone's working again. I've just had a call from Harrison. He wants me to go in to school straight away for a meeting with the Governors about Gerald.'

'Oh, but darling . . . the beef! There'll only be three of us to eat it now that William's gone round to the Bewicks.'

'I know. I'm sorry. But I must go. I have to stand up for Gerald. Someone's got it in for him and they don't care how many lies they tell. I've got to convince the Governors that he's entirely innocent. I'll eat the beef cold tonight. By the way, I think William's seeing too much of those Bewicks. I don't like either of them. Why can't he have friends his own age?'

'I don't know,' said Min, vaguely. 'I don't like them much either. But you can't choose other people's friends. Come to think of it, I don't think I like Gerald all that much. I hope you're not going to get in a mess over it all. Why do they have to have a meeting on Sunday of all days?'

'Because the whole thing's extremely confidential. We don't want the entire school knowing about it. I can't understand why you don't like Gerald.'

'He's so superior, so keen to display his erudition. He's affected. He's got a silly way of talking through his nose as though he can barely squeeze the word out. He's an intellectual show-off.'

'On the other hand he's extremely intelligent, cultivated and kind-hearted. All the things you'd normally approve of. I think you're prejudiced.'

'Hm. Could be,' said Min, picking the boiling kettle off the stove. 'I know we're all supposed to tolerate everything these days but I can't feel that fiddling about with other people's bottoms is what we were intended by nature to do.'

'Min! Really!'

Eleanor, who'd been sitting at the table, playing with the raffia mats, looked up, interested.

'Sorry, I forgot Ellie was here. And I know I'm being unfair. I . . .'

She broke off with a scream of pain as the handle snapped off the saucepan she had just filled from the kettle and the contents – boiling water and sprouts – poured over her right hand.

'Oh my God!' shouted Robert, as we all ran to her.

'Water!' I said, grabbing her wrist. 'Stop it cooking!'

I thrust her hand beneath the running tap though she yelled with pain.

Eleanor began to cry and Robert put his arm round her.

'Poor Mummy! It's all right. It's going to be all right. How is it, darling?'

'Okay,' said Min, though she was white and shaking and whenever she tried to take it from under the tap the pain became unbearable. 'Oh dear, what a fool I am. I meant to throw that pan away because the handle only had one screw left.'

'I'll fill a bowl of cold water and you can sit at the table with your hand in it,' I said, thinking that Min was looking rather faint.

When she was sitting down she recovered her colour a little but she still couldn't bear to take her hand out of the water.

'It needs a proper dressing.' I looked at the red, swelling fingers. 'Burns are terribly prone to infection. Have you got any bandages?'

'We've only got Elastoplast,' said Min. 'And aspirins.'

'You can have two of those anyway,' said Robert and went to the cupboard to fetch them.

'What about a clean handkerchief? We could stick it on with Elastoplast. That would do as a temporary dressing. But it'll need more than that. Is there a chemist open on Sunday?'

'No, I don't think so. Oh God, it does hurt!'

'She'd better go to the cottage hospital in Great Swosser,' said Robert.

'How can I do that? You've got to go to that meeting. Don't let's fuss.'

'All right, I'll drive you there, go on to the school and pick you up on the way home. Or what about a taxi?'

'Why don't I drive Min to the hospital and you can go to your meeting?' I suggested.

Innumerable objections had to be raised and overruled but in the end that was what we decided to do. Robert felt guilty and said so, so many times that Min got quite snappy. I sat behind the wheel of the Land Rover and Min sat next to me with Eleanor in the back. Robert got us going and I saw him, in the rear-view mirror, watching us jolt down the road before he walked round to the front of the house to where the other means of transport, an old Morris Traveller, was parked.

I hadn't driven a Land Rover before but I soon got the feel of it. The lack of responsiveness in the steering and pedals was amply made up for by the feeling of invulnerability that rapidly took possession of me and I drove as though I were in command of a tank, pointing in the general direction of ruts in the snow, with my foot flat to the floor, and using the gear lever as though it were a stick in a bucket of stones. Min was very quiet but I could see that she was in a great deal of pain. Her eyes were full of tears and she was very pale. I remembered that I'd seen an empty shopping bag lying in the back so we stopped and filled it with snow. She sat with it on the seat beside her, with her hand thrust into it, and after that she was able to talk and even make jokes.

We took the bag into Great Swosser Cottage Hospital where it held the pain at bay for five minutes until it melted very messily. By then a nurse had been found to dress the hand and give Min some stronger painkillers. While Min was being seen to, Eleanor and I waited in the corridor where there was a row of chairs and a table with magazines without their covers.

'Look, here's a comic. Would you like to look at that?'

Eleanor shook her head, her expression woeful.

'Mummy's going to be quite all right, you know. By morning she'll feel a lot better.'

'Will they . . . they won't . . . cut it off?'

'Good heavens, no! What made you think of that?'

'I saw a film on television about a man who came home from the war without any arms and he couldn't . . . he couldn't even undress himself!'

She burst into tears. Full of trepidation I put my arms round her and was relieved to feel her leaning against me as she sobbed for at least a minute.

'There's a good girl,' I said, in my most reassuring voice. 'You've had a shock and that always makes people want to cry. Mummy really is going to get perfectly well and no one's going to do anything horrible to her.'

'I hate that film.' Eleanor sniffed and wiped her spectacles on her skirt. 'I haven't been able to stop thinking about it and it makes me feel so sorry for him!'

She cried again with her face pressed to my arm while I stroked her hair.

'I know what you mean. Some things are just so terribly sad that you can't really ever get over them. But you do get used to them. They're still sad but you can bear them after a bit.'

'Really?' Eleanor looked at me through her smeary lenses. 'And what about the man? Can he bear it, too, after a bit?'

'Yes, I think so. When awful things happen most people reach down inside themselves and find things to help them go on . . . courage, humour, determination, that sort of thing.'

'Do you think I could? How could I do that?'

'But nothing awful has happened to you,' I said, touched by the eagerness of her appeal.

'School is awful. Often I think I can't bear it any more. They call me The Slug. Deirdre Wright brought slug pellets to school and made me eat some. I was sick in the loos afterwards. They say I'm slimey and leave a trail. Last week they put glue on my seat and I got a mess on the back of my skirt. I got a bad house-mark for it. Deirdre said it was my slime. They take all my books away and hide them and break my pen-nibs. On Friday they poured my inkwell into my satchel. Mummy was cross with me and wouldn't believe that the other girls had done it. She said I was careless.' Her voice trembled with feeling. 'Sometimes I pray that I won't wake up in the morning. But I always do.'

'Why do you think the other girls don't like you?' I felt full of pity for this poor, plain child.

'Because I'm fat, I suppose. I'm the ugliest girl in the class, Polly Saxby says. I don't think it's quite true. Mary Drew's got spots. I think she's uglier than I am.'

'You're not ugly,' I said with some warmth. 'I think you could be very pretty.'

I was being truthful. I did think so. Her features were blunted by excessive flesh but I had an idea that without the swollen cheeks and fat neck and those hideous spectacles, she would be a very passable-looking girl. Her eyes were porcine but her lashes were dark and long.

'Do you? Really?' Eleanor looked up at me, blinking.

'Yes, I do. People often lose weight when they grow up. When all those nasty little girls are grown up they'll be sitting round the edge of the room hoping someone's going to ask them to dance, and you'll be swirling round in the middle of the floor with all the boys wanting to dance with you.'

Eleanor looked entranced for a moment at this idea. Then her face fell. 'I can't dance,' she said, gloomily.

At that moment Min was led up to us by the nurse and I was given a bottle of painkillers and instructions to bring her back on Wednesday, much as though Min was a lunatic at large and I was her keeper. As we spluttered and coughed away in the Land Rover, I asked Min how she was feeling.

'Pretty depressed,' she admitted. 'The painkillers have made me feel dreadfully tired and my hand hurts like hell still. It's come up in the most enormous blisters. How am I going to manage? That stupid old nurse said I'd be in bandages for a fortnight and that the skin would take a month to renew itself. A month! Well, it's curtains for my book. I'd better resign myself now to a life of selling cakes for the local Conservative Party.' A tear ran down her cheek. 'I'm sorry to be so gloomy and especially when it's so lovely to have you here. It's just the unbelievable frustration. I mean, it's going to take me all day to peel a potato, one-handed.'

Another tear followed the first.

'Suppose I stayed on for a while,' I said, wondering as I spoke whether *I* was the lunatic at large. 'I could do the housekeeping while you wrote your book. You're left-handed after all. So you could write.'

'Oh, Daisy! Daisy, darling!' cried Min, flinging her arms about my neck so that I nearly drove into the tree we were passing. 'You wouldn't! You couldn't be so marvellously wonderful as to do this for me! How could I ever deserve such a friend as you are! But what about your teaching? And your research?'

I reminded her that I was on sabbatical leave for two terms so that I could write my book about Thomas Love Peacock.

'Actually I haven't got any ideas as yet so it won't hurt to do something quite different while things drift about in my mind for a while.'

'Oh, Daisy! If you'll do this wonderful thing I promise I'll work till I drop! I'll get up at five to start and only stop to have lovely chats with you. And you must get on with your work as well. But what about books? Will you have to go to Cambridge to get them?'

'I'll have a few sent and I can read them and get my ideas sorted out. Don't worry about it.'

'I can't believe it,' said Min, after a pause. 'Now I'm glad I burnt my hand. Five minutes ago it seemed catastrophic. But if you're going to stay it's the best thing that could have happened.'

I was so touched by this expression of affection that I put the Land Rover into second instead of fourth and we spun through a hundred and eighty degrees on a patch of ice. After that we drove in silence so that I could concentrate, silence which Min broke as we entered the back gates of the park for the last run up the hill to the stables, which had to be done at speed if we were to manage it at all.

'Now,' she said, 'you will be able to go to bed with Charles Jarrett.'

We went into the house and Min sat down at the table while I got on with the half-cooked lunch. The beef was put back into the oven and I dug the black bits out of the potatoes that Min had peeled and put them under the beef to roast. I opened the second bottle of champagne although it was only four o'clock in the afternoon and after two glasses, in combination with the painkillers, Min was thoroughly cheerful and said that her hand didn't hurt at all, at least, only when she thought about it. I washed the sprouts that had been all over the floor and because they looked so old, shredded them to fry in butter. I put the parsnips on to roast with the potatoes and made up some English mustard. I'd just got everything cooked and into dishes and was pouring some red wine (I'd found Robert's store in the larder) into the meat tin when Robert came back.

'How is it?' he said, going over to Min and tenderly examining the bandaged hand. 'You look extraordinarily cheerful.' He kissed her forehead and then, remembering me, said, 'How did it go at the hospital? Thank you for taking her.'

'It's fine,' said Min. 'I'm so drunk I can't feel a thing.'

Then she giggled a little. Robert smiled at me. It was a polite smile only and without warmth but I took it as a token that we might manage to be civil to each other for two or three weeks. Robert was still in happy ignorance of this development and I thought it politic not to be the one to enlighten him.

'I can see you've done a good job. Thank you.'

'Actually she's not supposed to drink alcohol with those painkillers but only, I think, because it'll knock her out.'

'Well, she's certainly not going out to operate heavy machinery this afternoon so I can't see that it matters. Something smells good.'

I put the vegetable tureens (lovely things with massive fruit-shaped finials which I'd found in the still-room), on the table and Robert lifted the lid of each one, examining the contents. I'd already sharpened the carving knife on the steel which I'd found at the back of the drawer. Robert picked it up and ran his thumb along the edge, with a critical frown on his face. I knew perfectly well what he was thinking and smiled to myself as I put a pile of hot plates down in front of him. He began to carve the beef without saying anything. William came in just then.

'Golly, I'm starving. What've you done to your hand, Mum?'

He started to giggle so convulsively that I wondered if he might be drunk. He was perfectly steady on his feet but his eyes were unfocused and his pupils enormous.

'Sit down, William, and stop giggling. Mummy's burnt her hand quite badly and it isn't very kind of you to laugh.'

'Sorry, Dad.'

'Diana cooked all this,' said Min, pouring herself a large glass of red wine.

William looked at me and began to giggle again until his face was red and his eyes were running.

'If you're going to be stupid, you'd better leave the room.' Robert looked really annoyed.

'Sorry, sorry,' William murmured and began to eat, with no more than the occasional burst of laughter.

'Did you know, Daddy,' said Eleanor as she pushed her fourth potato whole into her mouth, 'Diana's going to stay and look after us. For a long time.'

'Not really a very long time,' I said quickly, seeing Robert's expression of amazement. 'Only a couple of weeks or so. Until Min's hand gets better.'

'It's true,' said Min, her speech now slurred. 'Darling, wonderful Daisy's going to be a ministering angel . . . such a dear, lovely angel. I think it's the most noble thing I ever heard, don't you, darling?'

'I do. I certainly do.' Robert continued to look at me in astonishment. 'I'd say it was heroic. Well, children, we must all do our best to help Diana. We've probably all been rather selfish about helping your mother but that's got to stop.'

The children looked depressed.

'What does heroic mean?' asked Eleanor.

'Someone who behaves like a hero. In this case it means very brave. Like Hector and Achilles. Sometimes it just means the most important person in the story.'

'Who's that person you said?' Eleanor reached for a fifth potato. 'Dackerlees, did you say?'

'Achilles, you clot!' said William, paying attention for the first time. 'Everyone knows the story of Achilles being dipped into the River Styx. His mother held him by the heel so that bit stayed dry and he was killed by an arrow through his heel.'

'The point being that Thetis wanted to make her son invulnerable,' said Robert. 'No, Eleanor, you've had too many potatoes already. But do you know the story of Achilles and the tortoise, William? It's what's called a paradox. A sort of contradiction. Achilles and the tortoise are going to run a race. Achilles can run ten times as fast as a tortoise and so gives the tortoise a hundred yard's start. Who do you think wins the race?'

'Achilles, of course,' said William.

'Well, if you think about it, Achilles can never overtake the tortoise. Because while he is running the first hundred yards the tortoise runs ten. While Achilles runs that ten the tortoise runs one and while Achilles runs one the tortoise runs one-tenth. And so on.'

'Until they're both running tiny, tiny little bits,' said Eleanor, holding up her finger and thumb tightly squashed together.' Then she looked downcast. 'I don't understand.'

'I think I do,' said William. He began to play with the mustard jar and the bottle of tomato ketchup, moving them along at decreasing intervals.

'Can't understand it either,' said Min, her head drooping so that her hair dipped into the remains of food on her plate. 'I know what I'd do if I were that tortoise. I'd crouch down behind a lettuce leaf and as he came thundering by I'd spring out and bite his heel.'

'Min darling, you're hopelessly drunk!' said Robert, gently pushing back her head.

'Hopelessly!' she agreed.

'Oh dear! She'll have a hangover in the morning. We ought to have stopped her,' I said.

'Never have a hangover!' said Min. 'Want to go and lie down.'

While Robert took Min up to bed, I fed Ham and did the washing-up. The washing-up brush was so greasy and matted with old bits of food that I threw it away and used a torn-off bit of clean rag instead. Washing-up brush, pot scourer, rubber gloves, apron, I wrote on a piece of paper. I went on a tour of inspection of Min's broom cupboard. By the time I'd finished the shopping list went over the page. Robert came downstairs again and found me rummaging in the larder.

'I'm afraid you've taken on a tremendous job. We really are grateful.' He ran his hand through his hair and looked harassed. 'This isn't the easiest of houses to run and it's unfortunate we haven't got any help at the moment. Min doesn't seem to be able to find anyone. If the children can be fed and their uniforms washed I'm sure no one will mind everything else being rough-and-ready.' He smiled and this time there was some warmth in it. 'You mustn't tire yourself out on our behalf.'

'How did the meeting go?' I asked, accepting the glass of wine he held out to me. 'Or is it too secret to be told?'

'No. I don't see why I shouldn't tell you. It's good of you to be interested. Well, I'm delighted to say that Gerald has been entirely cleared. I mustn't brag but I do think that the argument I put before the Governors may have helped a little. I pointed out that it was Gerald's word against Dalrymple and that the record of each should be the deciding factor as to whom we believed. Of course Gerald won without contest. Dalrymple has always been a nasty piece of work, always in trouble and very much disliked by the staff. I won't go into the whole thing . . . I don't want to bore you. But the end result is that Gerald is reinstated and the matter closed. I've been so worried about him. He's been fearfully tense and depressed about the whole thing. I've felt the strain too. I may have been rather bad-tempered the last couple of days. I can only say I'm sorry.'

'I'm so glad it's turned out all right. But of course it's naïve to suppose that since mud had been thrown none of it will stick. Poor man! He's still got a lot of disagreeable moments to get through. People will be suspicious of him and even if they aren't, he'll think they are.'

'That's exactly what Gerald said. I thought he'd be much more cheerful about the outcome than he is. Perhaps when Min's hand is better we could have him to supper. Although she doesn't really like him, I know. But I'm tired. I can't worry about it any more tonight. I'll go and give William a hand with his maths homework. That boy gets more idle and disorganised every day. "Alas, regardless of their doom, the little victims play!"'

'"No sense have they of ills to come, nor care beyond today,"' I said, with the smug satisfaction one always feels when able to finish someone's quotation.

'You like Gray?'

'Yes. The *Elegy* is one of my absolute favourites.'

'"Now fades the glimmering landscape on the sight, And all the air a solemn stillness holds,"' said Robert, in declamatory tones.

'"Save where the beetle wheels his droning flight, and . . . something, something . . . drowsy tinklings lull the . . . something . . . folds –"'

'"Distant folds,"' Robert corrected. 'How beautiful! "All the air a solemn stillness holds" . . . I've so often felt that at dusk when I'm out in the orchard. Well, I must go and sort out William.'

'I'll see to Eleanor, shall I?'

'Oh, would you? That child worries me. I don't think she's very happy.' He sank back quickly into his usual gloom. 'Children are nothing but anxiety, it seems to me.'

He sighed and went away. I was tremendously pleased that I seemed to have found a way through to Robert. If quoting Gray made him happy, I knew yards of it. I went upstairs and knocked on the door next to Min's room which had ELLIE written on it in crooked red capital letters. There was no answer. I knocked again and then opened the door quietly in case she had fallen asleep. The room was empty.

Standing on the chest of drawers in pride of place on a home-made paper mat was the black-and-white china cat I'd given her. Some ten or twenty empty biscuit wrappers on the floor fluttered in the draught from the open door.

'Hello,' said Eleanor, behind me. 'I was in the lav.'

Then her eye travelled to the china cat.

'I was just admiring that rather nice mat,' I said, quickly. 'Did you make it?'

Eleanor looked pleased.

'Shall I make one for you? It's very easy. You fold a bit of paper into eights . . . or sixteenths . . . and cut bits out of it down the sides, little half-moons or V's. When you open it out it looks a bit like a doily. Mummy won't have doilies at home. She says they're genteel. I don't know what she means. They always have them at school on sports day.'

'I'd love a mat like that. I remember making them myself when I was your age.'

'The only thing is, I haven't got any nice paper left.'

'I'll get some from the newsagent's tomorrow.'

'That would be something to look forward to.' Eleanor pushed her spectacles on to the bridge of her nose with her finger. 'Monday's are dreadful because it's games. I always want to go to the lav but the girls won't let me. They look under the door and over the top while we're changing so I always have to play netball while I'm bursting to go. I hate Mondays. I try not to drink anything all day.'

'That's very bad for you. You ought to drink. It's more important than eating.'

Eleanor suddenly looked down at the floor and put her foot squarely over one of the biscuit wrappers. I didn't think that she trusted me enough for me to say anything about them but I felt that I was beginning to understand her. I began to lay plans.

'What about a bath?' I said, to change the subject.

'I've had it. When you go to bed you *may* find something that will interest you strangely.'

'Really? Goodness, that sounds exciting. Goodnight, then.'

'Goodnight.'

I went downstairs. From somewhere in the house the notes of *Lohengrin* soared and dipped. I sat in the kitchen by the stinking paraffin heater and started a new list. Things to be done tomorrow. Change wick in heater, it began, and continued until I had more things on the list than could have been completed in a month. I could hear the loud bits of the opera from the kitchen and wished that I could listen to it properly. Just as I was thinking that, Robert came in.

'I'm so sorry,' he said, yawning. 'I've neglected you. I fell asleep in the library. It's a shame to leave you on your own like this. I really am sorry.'

'Please don't worry,' I said, folding up my list and putting it beneath the pot with the dead cyclamen for safe-keeping. 'I've been perfectly happy organising myself for tomorrow. What time shall I get breakfast?'

'Well, I leave the house with the children at ten past eight. Try to, anyway. But we can get ourselves some cereal.'

'No, no, I don't in the least mind getting up. Anyway I don't think there is any cereal.'

'Oh, well, then.' He yawned again. 'If you really don't mind I think I'll go to bed.'

'I shall too. I'll see to things in here, don't worry.'

'All right. I'll bolt the front door. Goodnight. And thank you.'

He went away and I felt suddenly . . . not lonely exactly . . . but sorry to be going to bed alone. I had forgotten Ham. I let her in and she preceded me up the stairs to bed as though we were a steady married couple for whom familiarity had replaced excitement with all the comfort of custom. It was not much after ten o'clock when, lying in bed in the glow of the electric fire, listening to Ham swallowing glutinously and smacking her lips, I felt something sharp on the pillow dig into my cheek. I snapped the light on, remembering the nameless black things that lived in the bed-canopy, and saw that it was a folded piece of paper with my name on which somehow I had missed when I got into bed. I opened it and read:

Dear Diana, Will you be my friend, please. I am very glad that you are going to stay. Please be my friend, with love from Eleanor.

## CHAPTER ELEVEN

'Oh, my satchel!' wailed Eleanor, halfway through breakfast. 'I forgot to clean it out. Everything's inky!'

While she finished eating I cleaned it out as much as possible though some of the books and writing things had to be thrown away.

'You'll catch it,' said William, seeing me put a dictionary in the bin.

'I know. It's English today and Miss Pivot always makes us use them. I think I'm getting a tummy ache. Perhaps it's the eggs. We don't usually have them scrambled.'

'It isn't the eggs. It's nerves,' I said firmly. 'Now, stop worrying. I'll ask Mummy to telephone Miss Pivot and explain about the dictionary.'

I saw that Robert was looking at me in surprise and I guessed that he thought me very officious and that I was exceeding the terms of our compact.

'You can borrow mine,' said William, getting it out of his bag and handing it to Eleanor. 'The old bitch won't notice it's not quite the same. I don't need it today. But if you get mine inky I'll beat you up.'

'I don't think you should talk about Eleanor's teacher like that.' Robert looked very stern. 'Or any woman, come to that.'

'Isn't Ham a bitch?' asked Eleanor. 'What could be nicer than being like Ham?'

They went off arguing the point, at least Robert was arguing and the children weren't listening any more. I was clearing up the breakfast things when Min came down.

'Have they gone already? That's good. Robert gets in such a state if they're late. Goodness, that was a wonderful sleep! Who was that man who went to sleep for fifty-seven years and when he woke up he found he had all the wisdom of the world? I feel, if anything, much more stupid.'

'I can't remember. Some old Greek. How's the hand?'

'Robert will know. Well, it hurts a lot but not as much as when I first did it. Look! Fresh orange juice. How brilliant of you.'

'Finish it off with your painkillers,' I said, opening the bottle and taking out two.

Min's hand was a round paw of bandages and she was virtually helpless. I cut her toast into squares and chopped up the scrambled egg which had become rather solid. Min said it was perfect and she'd never enjoyed a breakfast so much. While she ate I repeated to her what Eleanor had told me.

'The poor child!' said Min, tears coming into her eyes. 'I wish I hadn't been cross with her about the ink. Why didn't she say? She told me a few weeks ago that the others were beastly to her and I did just mention it to Miss Pivot when I saw her the next week. She got frosty at once and said that all children were spiteful and everyone had to learn to stand up for themselves. She treated me as though *I* was a difficult child. She was so bristly and tetchy that I shut up.'

'Well, if she won't do something about it you must speak to the headmistress.'

'Do you think so?'

'I'm positive. Eleanor hasn't said much to you because she doesn't want to worry you. I'm certain that things are serious enough to make it urgent that the school does something.'

'Oh dear. All right.'

'Come on then. Let's find the number.'

I looked up the number in the book, dialled it for her and stood over her while she waited to be connected.

'Tell her you'll report the matter to the Governors if something isn't done at once about supervising the changing rooms. Bully her. She'll understand that.'

Min did as I suggested. I couldn't hear exactly what the woman on the other end of the telephone was saying but the tone was minatory. Min seemed to be faltering and losing ground. I shook my finger sternly at her to show that she must be firm. Min's voice suddenly grew sharper and colder and more cogent with every exchange and I could tell that she was enjoying herself. When she threatened to ring up the chairman of the Board of Governors who was a close friend of the family, the protesting voice on the other end of the line grew quieter and I knew Min had won.

'My God, I'm glad you made me do that,' said Min afterwards. 'That bloody woman said that Ellie was a natural victim for bullying! As though bullying was to be tolerated and condoned! I must have been mad to let the situation get out of hand. What can I have been thinking of? I meant it, too. I jolly well will write to that old fool Poulsen if she doesn't see to it. I know he and Vivien had an affair for years. Bless you for insisting.'

She kissed my cheek.

'Well, we'd better wait and see what results we get before we congratulate ourselves. Now let's get you dressed. Then you can start work and I can go shopping.'

'You must take the housekeeping money. Robert always leaves it on the dresser on Mondays.'

I was rather despondent when I counted up the notes Robert had left. It was a very small amount to feed five people on for a week. But I felt bound in honour to stick to the budget. Once Min was settled at her desk with everything she needed spread out around her, I put on my coat, now very much the worse for wear, and went out to find the gardener who, Min assured me, was well used to push-starting the Land Rover. I found him standing in the walled garden, sawing up logs. His name was George Pryke and I realised at once that we were not going to get on. I asked him, very politely, to get the Land Rover going.

'When I've finished these 'ere logs.' He continued to saw.

'I'm sorry but it can't wait,' I said, seeing the huge pile of uncut branches and feeling annoyed.

He made a few more cuts and then turned and walked off ahead of me to the stables with the slow deliberation of an octagenarian though he could not have been more than fifty.

'She'll not like startin' this weather,' he said, rubbing his hand raspingly along the stubble of his chin.

'Well, she started yesterday and the day before so I can't see why she won't today.'

I got in and slammed the door. I sat ready, the clutch disengaged and my hands expectantly on the wheel for a good two minutes before I realised that he was still standing there, rubbing his chin.

I slid the window open crossly. 'What are you waiting for?'

'I reckon she won't start.'

'She certainly won't if you don't push her! Please get on with it.'

We began to move forward at a pace that could have been outrun by the most languid tortoise. Feeling really furious now, I got out and began to push the Land Rover myself and from the way we suddenly bowled forward I knew he'd hardly been pushing at all. I gave a last heave as I ran alongside, jumped into the driving seat and, as the incline of the hill took over from George Pryke's pathetic efforts, managed to get the engine to fire. I was very hot and extremely angry. From the energy with which he'd been sawing those logs, there was nothing wrong with the man.

I drove into Great Swosser and went to the garage I'd noticed on Saturday morning. I told a nice young man called Bob what the problem was. He said he'd suggested to Mr Weston that the Land Rover needed a new dynamo two or three months ago. I asked Bob how much a new dynamo would cost and he named a sum that, I'm ashamed to say, seemed to me a very small price to pay for the convenience of having the tiresome thing start when you turned the key. But, of course, my income only had to stretch to one person and a small house and anyway it was supplemented by private funds. I asked Bob if he could fit it on the spot and he said three-quarters of an hour was all he'd need.

I left the Land Rover there and went to the ironmonger's shop where I bought half of the items on my list, including a pair of gumboots for myself. The scale of expenditure brought out the owner of the shop, a Mr Ransome, to serve me personally. I consulted him about the Aga and he professed to be the expert for the area. He was so much in demand that he couldn't think of coming for at least five weeks so I offered him cash on completion of the job and he said he'd come that afternoon.

I then went to the butcher and gave him a standing order of meat for Ham, to be delivered twice a week, and selected some meat for the human part of the household for the next two days. The greengrocer's was less satisfactory. Most of the vegetables had a flexible quality that told of their great age but there was nowhere else to buy them. I did the best I could and went on to Beale's where I got the rest of the things on my list, including packets of proper ground coffee. Coffee beans were apparently Apples of Sodom from the vehemence with which Mr Beale denied ever having had such a thing in his shop. I bought a case of champagne, a great extravagance but one which I easily justified to myself by recalling the bathroom at Weston Hall. This I paid for myself. Similarly, for the brooms, mops and washing-up brushes from the hardware store I paid with a cheque.

'Happen you'll want to pay th'account?' asked Mr Beale, with an air of one doomed to disappointment. I'd explained to him that I was temporary housekeeper at Weston Hall.

'Certainly I will. How much is it?'

He named a sum that seemed moderate and I got out my chequebook again.

'I'd like the itemised bill, please,' I said, thinking that Min might possibly want to check it over.

Mr Beale fetched it and I ran my eye over it to give myself some idea of the family's weekly consumption. Certainly there were a lot of baked beans and fish fingers eaten in the Weston household.

'What about all these biscuits? Are you sure there hasn't been a mistake? I'm sure your accounting is excellent but thirty-seven packets of biscuits in a month seems excessive.'

'That'll be Miss Ellie's biscuits,' said Mr Beale. 'She always comes in to see me afore catchin' the school bus 'ome.'

I went to the bank, a small branch open only Mondays, Wednesdays and Fridays, and made an arrangement for regular cash withdrawals.

By now I was so weighed down with parcels that I had to return to the Land Rover and load up the back. Bob told me that five minutes would see the job finished. I wrote out another cheque with a feeling of light-heartedness. Bob's eyebrows rose as Mr Beale's delivery boy came up with the case of champagne and heaved it into the back of the Land Rover.

At the last moment I remembered the drawing paper for

Eleanor. A sense of justice made me look for something for William but there didn't seem to be anything that might do. It occurred to me then that he was a very introverted boy and something of a mystery but my experience of children was too narrow for me to draw any conclusions.

I got back just in time for lunch. We had bacon and tomatoes and I made some real coffee. Min was in that state of euphoria of one who finds that a difficult piece of work is unexpectedly going well. After lunch I persuaded her to take more painkillers and sent her back to her desk while I went upstairs to made the beds.

William's room was as sparsely furnished as Eleanor's but he had contrived to make something almost stylish of it. There were posters on the walls of black men in sunspecs leaning over saxophones in some kind of last agony and a white female pop singer in a tremendous sulk. The room reeked of incense sticks and there were piles of ashes like wormcasts lying everywhere. I made his bed and picked up the things that were lying on the floor, including a packet of cigarette papers with a rectangular section torn from the cover. I stared at it and then a great deal that had been puzzling me about William became clear.

When I went back down to the kitchen to start preparations for supper, my attention was caught by something jiggling violently high up on the wall. It was one of the bells on the bell-board. I gathered from its mute agitations that it was missing a clapper. I could just make out the faded script beneath it which said 'Back Door' so I went to investigate. Mr Ransome had come to mend the Aga. I apologised for keeping him waiting and explained about the bell. He said if I had such a thing as a step-ladder about me, he'd wire in a bit of metal so that it would ring. I led him to the Aga and went off to look for a ladder.

George Pryke was still sawing logs in the walled garden and paused for long enough to wipe the sweat from his forehead and indicate that there was a ladder in the tool-shed. When I asked him to get it and bring it up to the kitchen he looked at me with as much astonishment as though I'd ordered him to construct a rocket and launch me to the moon. He stuck out a repulsively coated tongue and rolled his eyes a little and said he'd be up with it when he could spare the time.

'I'm afraid it can't wait,' I said sternly. 'Mr Ransome is in the kitchen, expecting it. At once, please.'

I went back to see how Mr Ransome was doing. The contents of the Aga were all over the kitchen and he was scraping away inside.

'Sooted up,' he told me. 'Can't 'ave bin serviced this many a year.'

I fetched some old newspapers, a little late for the floor which was covered in black grit. I could see that Mr Ransome was applying himself so I went to the telephone. First I rang a bookshop in Winkleigh, which was the nearest large town, about fifteen miles away. After I'd placed an order with them I rang my own Cambridge number and caught Mrs Baxter, my excellent daily help, just on the point of leaving. I explained that I was staying in Lancashire for a week or two and asked if she would go in every day, see that the plants were watered, forward the post and generally keep an eye on things. I reflected, after I put the telephone down, how much I could have done with her help at Weston Hall. The bathrooms had yet to be cleaned and I wanted to do something about tea for the children in addition to making supper, which I had been about to start when Mr Ransome arrived. I began to see that domestic life in a large house was much more arduous than I had imagined. The drawing room would have to stay dusty.

I returned to the kitchen to find George Pryke there, standing with his large boots in the most extensive pile of soot, holding the step-ladder and distracting Mr Ransome from his task with prurient gossip. My appearance put a stop to it and George shuffled slowly away, printing black foot-marks the length of the passage to the back door. Mr Ransome worked on with only the occasional remark so I was able to concentrate on supper. I fried some onions and several pieces of shin of beef and then filled up the dish with red wine, carrots, a strip of orange peel and a sprig of rosemary which I had recognised beneath its coating of snow in the walled garden. I put this in the gas oven and turned my attention to making scones, which was about all I had time for.

My repertoire didn't run to cakes and I couldn't find a cookery book but I'd once spent a weekend helping Peter's mother to make scones for a garden party at the Palace. I'd made two hundred in several batches and I was certain that if ever I was hit hard on the head and became an amnesiac, I should still be able to recite 'eight ounces of flour, three ounces of butter, one and a half ounces of caster sugar, four table-spoons of buttermilk' even if I couldn't remember my own name.

Of course the pastry cutter I found in the drawer was bent and brown with rust but a straight-sided tumbler did the trick. I had to take out the shin of beef to cook the scones and I felt, in the circumstances, quite proud of the domed, floury rounds, lightly touched with brown, that came out of the oven some fifteen minutes later.

While I was attacking the bathrooms, including cleaning out the plug-holes, a job only less disgusting than rodding drains, Mr Ransome beavered away and when I came downstairs the Aga had been reassembled and he was in the process of lighting it. My immense joy was only slightly spoiled by discovering that I had a large, sooty streak down the front of my skirt.

I pressed a very reasonable charge for two hours' work into his hand and he was so delighted that he said he'd mend the bell for free. I'd forgotten about it. He was fashioning a new clapper from a small piece of metal he'd fetched from his van, and I was peeling potatoes, when the telephone rang. Min didn't appear and it went on ringing so I answered it myself. A voice said, after a pause, 'That's Diana, isn't it? I was ringing Min to get your telephone number but there you are. I thought you were going home this morning.'

It was Charles Jarrett's voice. The South African accent was unmistakable on the telephone though I hadn't noticed it at dinner. I have to admit that my pulse did speed up on hearing him. I explained about Min's hand and he was sympathetic.

'How long will you be staying, then?'

'I don't know exactly. Two or three weeks, I suppose.'

'Damn! I've just arranged to go back to South Africa for two weeks. I can't cancel it now.' There was another slight pause, then he said, 'Will you come and have lunch with me . . . here . . . on Friday? I'm leaving that evening. I'd take you to a restaurant but there isn't anywhere in the area with decent food. Don't dress up. I'll have come straight in from the paddocks.'

Thinking that by Friday my clothes would be nothing more than dirty rags anyway, I accepted and thanked him for Saturday.

'It was an unexpected evening all in all,' he answered. 'You were something of a thunderbolt. I'm still dazed.'

I laughed. 'I can't be too long away from here on Friday. I have serious duties to attend to.'

'All right. One o'clock. Goodbye, Diana.'

I put the telephone down and went into the kitchen to find Mr Ransome clearing up his tools. He told me he'd mended the bell and gave me instructions for stoking and riddling the Aga. He'd had a look in the coal store and there was enough anthracite for three or four days. 'Order Anthracite,' I wrote on my list for tomorrow. I thanked him with genuine appreciation of all he'd done and then got out the new floor mop and filled a bucket with soapy water. I washed the flags clean and wiped up George Pryke's footprints to the back door. But all the time I was distracted by the memory of Charles's voice on the telephone. The readiness of a man to pay compliments to a woman says more about his self-confidence than the strength of his feelings for her. I knew that perfectly well yet I was flattered and spent much more time thinking about him than I wanted to.

At a quarter to five the children came in.

'Is someone grand coming to tea?' asked Eleanor. 'We don't usually have a cloth. What are these? Can I have one now?'

The table did look quite inviting. I'd found a red-and-white-checked tablecloth in a cupboard that seemed to contain more table linen than ten houses could properly use. I'd laid the table with pink-and-white ironstone plates and cups and put out bowls of raspberry and strawberry jam. I'd picked a few branches of a winter viburnum from the walled garden and put the tiny blush-coloured flowers into a blue jug. I hoped Min wouldn't think I'd been too meddlesome. When she came in and saw the table she began to laugh.

'Oh Daisy, how like you that looks! You always did know how to put things together. I'd forgotten we had this stuff.' She picked up a plate and looked at it. 'It's really pretty, isn't it? I don't know why we always use those hideous mugs that came free with petrol. They just seem to be ready to hand. Oh, home-made scones! I'm ravenous!'

'You really don't think I'm being interfering?' I asked, still anxious for reassurance.

141

'Daisy. Believe me, any changes you make will be humbly and gratefully received, I promise you! It will be like having an interior decorator free of charge.'

I began at once to make new and extensive mental lists, beginning with the relegation of those dreadful mugs to the dustbin.

'These scones are good,' said William, helping himself to two and spreading them thickly with butter and jam.

He seemed brighter than usual, not inclined to giggle or stare abstractedly at the same thing for minutes at a time. I noticed that his pupils were no longer enlarged. He asked Eleanor if she'd got into trouble about the dictionary.

'No. Miss Pivot didn't notice. But she's bound to eventually. And you'll want yours back anyway. Perhaps I might break my arm before then.'

'What on earth's that got to do with it, silly?' asked William, full of scorn.

'Harriet Anderson broke her arm and when she came back to school everyone was really nice to her because they wanted to write on her plaster and she'd only let the people she really liked do it. She didn't let me, of course.'

'What's that got to do with Miss Pivot? *She* didn't want to write on Harriet's plaster, I suppose,' asked Min, helping herself to another scone.

'Mrs Anderson came to school and said to Miss Pivot that Harriet wasn't to be made to do anything she didn't want to in case she got overtired. After that Miss Pivot didn't even say anything when Harriet lost her spelling book. Usually if you haven't got it she screams at you and her neck goes red and spots come out on her face.'

'Really?' said William, beginning to be interested.

'Yes,' said Eleanor, encouraged by his attention. 'And she gets really tall and big black wings sprout on her back.'

'Now, darling, you're making it up,' said Min, while William folded his arms and leaned back in his chair with an expression of deepest contempt.

'Anyway,' I said quickly, seeing that Eleanor was looking mortified, 'I've ordered you a new dictionary . . . same edition . . . from Brightwell's in Winkleigh. They promised me they'd put it in this afternoon's post so you should have it by Wednesday.'

The others looked at me in astonishment.

'I feel terrible,' said Min. 'It never occurred to me to do such a thing.'

'Well, you've got other work to concentrate on,' I said quickly. 'These domestic details are my job at the moment.'

'But the awful truth is that I don't think it would have occurred to me anyway. Eleanor, wasn't that kind of Daisy? Don't you think you ought to thank her?'

'Never mind,' I said, seeing that Eleanor was sitting quite still, with her mouth full of scone, not even chewing.

'It was so kind,' said Eleanor, at last, with a spray of crumbs, 'that I haven't ever heard of anything kinder. Not even when that girl made seven coats out of stinging nettles so that her brothers could stop being swans. It was kinder than that and up till now that's the kindest thing I've ever heard of.'

'Well, it was certainly much less trouble than that. And less painful,' I said, suppressing a desire to laugh, for Eleanor was absolutely serious.

'Why didn't they like being swans?' asked William. 'You could fly enormous distances wherever you liked. As soon as it rained you could fly somewhere else and always have good weather. And you wouldn't ever have to go to school. You could muck about doing nothing all the time. I think it was a cruel thing for her to do.'

'Perhaps they wanted to be with their sister,' suggested Eleanor hopefully.

William did a noisy and convincing impersonation of someone being violently sick, just as Robert came in.

'Hello, everybody. Usual witty and scintillating family conversation taking place, I see. Thank you, William, that will do. Why don't you start your homework if you've nothing better to do than pull silly faces?'

'Hello, darling. How did it go?' asked Min, and without waiting for an answer, went on, 'Look at the marvellous things Daisy's been doing. Look at the table. Isn't it lovely? And the scones are perfection! Oh, darling, what a shame they're all eaten. Eleanor, give your father that last bit. You've already had two.'

'And she's ordered me a new dictionary,' chimed in Eleanor. 'And Miss Stoppard was sent to come into the cloakroom with us at changing time so I was able to go to the lav. It's been quite a good day and I'm glad I didn't die in the night after all. I shouldn't have had the scones then.'

Robert looked around with an expression of bewilderment and shook his head as Eleanor proffered her bit of scone.

'No, thank you, darling. I had a piece of cake and a cup of tea at school. Not as good as Diana's, I'm sure.'

The words were friendly but there was a coldness about his tone.

'Goodness, a tablecloth!' he added, looking at it. 'How very respectable!'

'It was your mother's doing that Miss Stoppard went into the changing rooms,' I said hastily to Eleanor. 'She rang up the school and told your headmistress, in no uncertain terms, to jump to it. Gosh, she was fierce! I was quite frightened myself!'

'Mummy, were you really?' said Eleanor, giggling.

She put her arm through Min's and pressed her cheek against Min's arm. Min stroked Eleanor's head with her free hand and looked at me with a smile. I hoped she wouldn't say anything about my having bullied her into making the call, as I knew Robert had had as much as he could bear of my interference, and fortunately she didn't.

'Well, I've had quite a good day, too,' said Robert, making an obvious effort to relax and be genial. 'It's wonderful to have all that business about Gerald out of the way and to get on with a normal school day. Perhaps I'll just have a cup of tea before I start marking. No, don't worry, darling,' as Min made a move to get up. 'I'll do it. You've been working hard as well . . . at least, I hope so. How's it going?'

'I'm starting to feel encouraged,' Min replied. 'I've stopped panicking and allowed myself to take apart the work I've done so that I can structure the thing properly. Before, I felt that there was so little time that I just had to move forward but now I see that I was just getting into rather a tangle.'

'That's excellent,' said Robert. 'I'm sure you'll . . . Good Lord!'

His path across the kitchen floor between the table and the gas cooker had taken him near the Aga. He approached it suspiciously and laid his hand on the black enamel top. He removed it quickly.

'This thing's warm!'

'I hope you don't mind,' I said hurriedly. 'I just happened to mention it to Mr Ransome this morning and he said as he was coming this way this afternoon, he might call in and have a look at it. It was all his doing really . . .'

'Daisy! You clever, clever girl!' said Min. 'Oh how lovely! But do you mean to say he was here this afternoon and I never knew?'

'Well, it only took a couple of hours. There wasn't any point in disturbing you as you said at lunch that your work was going well.'

'You seem to have been busier than any of us,' said Robert, his nose looking more pointed and like a wizard's than ever. 'I'm sure it would be nothing to you to spin several sacks of straw into gold while we're all asleep.'

'Everyone's got fairy tales on the brain this afternoon,' said William, with disdain. 'I'm going up to my room.'

I thought I understood Robert's resentment. I hoped, anyway, that it was on behalf of Min, that he was afraid that any small improvements I might make would seem to highlight Min's domestic incapacities. I was anxious not to hurt her feelings myself.

'I think I'll go and make up my bed,' I said, deciding to take no notice of Robert's *froideur*.

I'd arranged with Min, over lunch, that I would sleep in the small white bedroom opposite the green room. Min had been astonished that I had wanted to change.

'It's only a maid's room! It's so small!'

'I'll be able to keep it clean and tidy more easily.' I omitted to mention that I'd noticed that there was neither a central heating pipe within nor a branch without. Perhaps as important, there was no canopy over the bed. It was only a matter of time before whatever lived up there would cease to see me as a threat and run down to investigate. It was childish at my age but I had an extreme dislike of spiders. Also my electric fire would be able to heat the little room up in five minutes. A final inducement to make the change was the probability that it would return me to a solitary occupancy of my bed as Ham would remain loyal to her bone-smelling patch of carpet. I made the transfer and plugged in the fire. I was not regretting my offer to stay on. Min's happiness was ample reward, if I needed one. But it was glorious to be sitting in a warm room, quite alone, in heavenly peace.

I read a little Jane Austen and allowed myself a sip or two of brandy. It occurred to me that there was no character like Charles Jarrett in Jane Austen's novels. For one thing all her men were English and were all under the sway of the early-nineteenth-century's innumerable, intricate and subtle conventions. If anyone was a little like him, it must be Henry Crawford. Good-looking, charming, self-possessed, perhaps as egocentric? Certainly there was a touch of arrogance. I was suddenly annoyed with myself. I was dwelling far too much on Charles. I returned to my book and lost myself in Elinor's difficulties with Mrs Ferrars.

Suddenly it was seven o'clock. I went downstairs to find the kitchen deserted. The Flying Dutchman was bemoaning his fate somewhere in the house and I assumed that Min had gone back to work. The tea things were washed up and there was a note on the table from Min.

Just had a good idea and have gone to write it down. Please call me to help with supper. I insist! Min.

It was hard to see what Min could do one-handed. But I fetched her as instructed and she put out knives and forks and spoons and glasses and poured out two glasses of champagne. She was tremendously impressed by my prodigality in buying a whole case.

'This is the life!' said Min. 'I feel so happy despite this stupid old hand. I've already knocked it about twenty times today. At least all the blisters must have popped with the beating it's had. Still, I don't care. It *was* good of you to get that dictionary. I know I should have thought of it. I'm going to make a real effort to organise myself better.'

'If I were you I'd concentrate on making that preface the very best bit of work you've ever done and leave the rest to me. You can worry about everything else when I've gone. And don't worry about me. I've really enjoyed today.'

And thinking about it, I really had. My reforming zeal had been allowed full rein and I had a sense of great satisfaction. Suddenly I noticed that I'd stopped hunching my shoulders with cold.

'One thing you can do as a monopaw is to turn out that heater.'

The kitchen was wonderfully peaceful without the hissing and popping of the paraffin stove.

'I spoke to Charles on the telephone today,' I said, while pounding the potatoes with butter and hot milk. 'I just happened to answer it. He's asked me to have lunch with him, at Milecross Park, on Friday. I'll leave you something to eat, don't worry.'

'Worry! I shall be in a ferment of lascivious fantasy!'

'Strictly lunch only, Min dear. The rest of the country may be growing slender on a diet of free love and its attendant unhappinesses but I'm too old for that. I've reached the age when I'm picky about that sort of thing.'

'What possible process of selection could exclude Charles Jarrett?'

The entry of Eleanor put an end to the conversation before I'd thought of an answer.

'One thing that's clear to me, Min,' I began, while getting warm plates out of the Aga, 'is that you desperately need help with the housework. Why not let me advertise locally and try to find someone?'

'If you think you could,' said Min, 'I'm all for it. We've always had someone from the estate but now they can make more money at the biscuit factory in Great Swosser. I know Robert would be glad to pay. He's not at all mean. Besides, he feels it's his fault that we haven't got enough money to run the house. Although, of course, it's Vivien's fault.'

'Why Vivien's?'

'Because Robert's father left all his money to her. He died ages ago when Robert was seven. He just didn't look ahead and see what might happen. Vivien has entire control of the money and she wanted Robert to run the estate. Robert refused to do it. They had the most awful quarrel and haven't ever made it up, really. She's so mad with rage because she can't have her own way that she won't let us have more than a pittance though there's masses of money invested in madly safe things. Vivien lives like a tzarina while we scratch in the dust.'

'Why wouldn't Robert run the estate?'

'Because he simply hates farming. He says he doesn't want to be up to his elbows in cow-dung all day when he could be reading Ovid. He says he isn't cut out for farming and I think he's perfectly right. He won't admit it but what he really hates is killing things. And that's what being a farmer is about. You couldn't be an arable farmer round here. It's too hilly. When Robert was a boy his father used to take him to markets and abattoirs and places like that. Robert just couldn't bear it. He even felt sorry for the rats when they used to take the terriers into the barns.'

Robert himself came in, followed by William, so I got on with serving supper.

'I could smell something good all the way upstairs,' said William, flicking his hands for a microsecond beneath the tap before sitting down. 'Bloody hell, it's warm in here!'

'Don't swear, William,' said Robert wearily. 'It isn't clever.'

'I wasn't meaning to be clever.' William helped himself liberally to mashed potato. 'I meant to express extreme surprise. Anyway, you say "bloody hell". Usually expressing bad temper. That's worse.'

'I came across George Pryke today,' I said conversationally. 'Does he live in Dunston Abchurch?'

'He's got a tied cottage on the estate,' answered Min. 'He's not much good at anything but his family have worked on the estate for generations.'

'He seems very good at sawing up logs. You must have an enormous stack of firewood.'

'I suppose we must,' said Robert.

'And where to you burn them?' I continued. 'Not in here. Nor in the drawing room. And the boiler takes anthracite, doesn't it?'

'Come to think of it,' said Robert lowering his fork from his mouth with its piece of carrot still speared on it, 'we don't burn logs anywhere these days. What the hell – I mean, what the blazes is he doing cutting up wood? He's supposed to be coppicing.'

'I saw him loading up his van with logs when I went to tell him he could put the step-ladder away. He tried to cover them with a tarpaulin but I could see that he'd filled nearly the whole of the back of the van up.'

'The conniving bastard!' said Robert. 'He's selling our timber on the side!'

'Language, darling,' said Min. 'Good God, that man's beyond belief! When I think of all the times I've had his wife and revolting children to tea.'

'Once, darling, to be fair.'

'Well, yes. But it seemed like a prison sentence. She kept telling me that there was a price reduction on made-up curtains at Handley's and they did a very nice three-piece suite. I could tell she thought we were living like gypsies. Then she went on and on about how well her Barry and Sharlene were doing at school. Sharlene picked her nose throughout tea and wiped her finger on her socks which were bright pink with frills round the top!'

'It isn't like you to be a snob, darling,' remonstrated Robert.

'No, you're right. I'm ashamed of myself. But it was provoking!'

I was encouraged to see that Robert didn't appear to be offended by yet another example of my meddling. But this was because it had nothing to do with Min or Min's shortcomings.

'I suppose I ought to get rid of him.' Robert's tone was depressed. 'We can't have pilfering.'

'We've probably had it for the last three hundred years,' said Min with surprising sharpness. 'If you chuck the estate people out of their houses for petty theft, they'll all be empty and fall to bits with damp in another two years. The houses, I mean.'

'Supposing I keep an eye on George Pryke,' I suggested. 'If you tell me what he's to do each day, I'll go out every couple of hours and check that he's doing it. If he's completely unco-operative, then you can sack him. But he'll have had a chance to behave.'

'That's an excellent idea!' said Robert, relieved to have the decision postponed. 'If there's any of that bottle of champagne left, which I see you two girls have been guzzling, I'd like to propose a toast. "Great is Diana" as the Ephesians said. Long may she reign over us.'

There was an undoubted element of satire in this toast but it did turn out to be the beginning of a better understanding.

# CHAPTER TWELVE

At nine o'clock the next morning I went out to the stables, taking the long way round through the walled garden. George Pryke was nowhere to be seen. I looked around. A movement caught my eye in one of the greenhouses. I walked over and peered in. I saw George's features in profile as he sat bent over a newspaper, sipping from a mug. Through the dirty panes I could see that the newspaper was open at a full-page picture of a naked girl of awesome dimensions. George was chortling and sticking out his tongue revoltingly. I opened the door. George closed the newspaper, put it on the bench and then leaned back in his chair, staring at me and thrusting out his paunch in a defiant manner.

'Just takin' me tea-break. Was you wantin' more ladders 'eaved about?'

'No, thank you.' My manner was distant. 'Mr Weston tells me you are coppicing this morning.' I looked pointedly at my watch. 'I presume you began work at half past eight.'

'A-ha.'

'It seems rather soon to take a tea-break?'

'Well, I couldn't 'ave me breakfast at 'ome as my Jessie's gone to 'ospital to 'ave 'er hexamination. She's poorly with 'er womb, like.'

'I'm sorry to hear that.'

I was perfectly sincere. I was very sorry for Mrs Pryke, regardless of the state of her womb.

'She's a martyr to 'er womb. Give 'er gyp for years ever since our first. Bleeds like a stuck pig.'

'How far have you got with the coppicing?' I interposed.

'Ent started yet. There's five acres to do. Take me best part o' three weeks.'

'You'd better get going then. Mr Weston will come down and see how you're getting on when he gets home this evening. After lunch I'd like you to bring me up some logs. Ring the back-door bell and I'll show you where to put them.'

I opened the greenhouse door very wide and stood back to allow him to pass through. George Pryke looked at me with an expression of abhorrence. Then he rolled back his lips from his gums in a grimace like a chimpanzee and got up very slowly.

He picked up his newspaper and Thermos flask and walked past me out into the cold with the bilious, wrathful humour of Coriolanus going out to face the rabble. I went over to the boiler. It was rusty but warm. I opened the plate on the top. A good fire of logs burned briskly. Nothing, not even a withered pelargonium, grew in the greenhouse. All the broken panes of glass were plugged with rags or had cardboard tacked over them. A flowerpot contained pipe dottle and cigarette ends. On the floor were crumpled pieces of greaseproof paper, beer-bottle tops and spent matches. In one corner was a pile of magazines. I picked up the top one. A pair of red, glistening lips and a dropsical bosom flaunted themselves on the first page. I dowsed the fire with the ashes that had fallen through into the grate.

I went to the stables where the Land Rover was parked and saw the bristly head of George Pryke above a pile of fencing stakes. He was crouching behind it, waiting to be called to push. I turned on the ignition and the Land Rover burst into life. I let it run for a minute or two so that George would get a taste of exhaust and then roared off down the drive with as much élan as if I had been behind the wheel of a Hispano-Suiza.

In the village stores at Dunston Abchurch, I asked if I might put a card in the window. The woman behind the counter, who had regarded me from the moment of entry with cold suspicion, took the card from me and read it.

'Tha'll be from Weston Hall then?'

I said that I was staying there for some weeks.

'Folks don't want this kind o' work, nowadays. They can earn more at t'biscuit factory.'

'Do you happen to know' (I almost said 'does tha' know' – other people's accents are very contagious) 'how much the factory pays its workers?'

'Aye. 'appen I do. Our Marilyn works at t'factory. Five shillin' an hour for watchin' machine put t'custard into biscuits. Our Marilyn's as fat as butter, sittin' there doing nowt all day long.'

I wondered if she was aware that she was quoting Shake-speare. I wrote 'six shillings' into the space I'd left at the bottom and handed it to her.

'Eh! That'll mebbe change things!' she said, putting her

spectacles on to her large, fleshy nose, the better to read it. 'And folks might like th'idea o' workin' at t'big 'ouse. From what I 'ear there's all manner o' things goin' on. 'Tis said that Mrs Weston (who ent a bit better than she should be, o' course, we all knows that) and Mr Weston 'ad sich a fallin'-out that 'e took a red-'ot poker and –' here she leaned her mauve, acrylic-covered chest on the counter-top and whispered something in my ear, which would have made Edward the Second tremble in his boots. 'If I'd 'ave conducted meself like Mrs Weston, m' father 'ld 've chucked me out of 'earth and 'ome! But we all knows there's one rule for grand folks and another for t'poor.'

I was struck speechless by this woman's spite until I realised that she meant Vivien and not Min.

'Is there a charge for displaying an advertisement?' I asked, in a lofty tone intended to quell gossip.

'Aye. Sixpence. You'll want it prominent, I daresay. Folks wi' money want it all done at once.'

I thanked her and handed over sixpence. I had intended to buy something from the shop as a return for the service, but her grudging attitude made me feel disinclined to purchase so much as a packet of chocolate finger biscuits.

I stood outside on the shop doorstep for a minute and admired my own advertisement. Next to it was a card which said, 'Bride's dress, white, unworn. Also two adult brides-maid's dresses, cerise (lovely), unworn.' It was the 'lovely' in brackets that struck me as being especially poignant. I wondered with what excitement and pleasure the bride had chosen the cerise-coloured dresses. I imagined her unpacking them when she got them home from the shop, showing them to friends, trying on the bride's dress and striking graceful attitudes before the glass. Was there, in Dunston Abchurch, a lattter-day Miss Havisham, striding about a bungalow, brood-ing on the treachery of men, letting the cake teem with ants and the prawn cocktail grow mould? In that case, I reminded myself, she would be wearing the dress, not trying to sell it.

Being in the country was having its effect. I was spending a large part of the day doing physical work, which left my mind free to wander. I detected an expansion of imagination, probably leaning towards the sentimental, but which, in its unconstrained emancipation, could only do me good.

Min and I had cheese on toast and apples for lunch. I told her

I'd put in the advertisement for domestic help. We were just discussing what sort of person would be the ideal housekeeper when the back-door bell rang. It was the post. There were bills for Min and several letters for me, readdressed by Mrs Baxter. There was one from Peter from Rome. I read it with great pleasure. Peter had modelled his style on that of Augustus Hare, immensely informative and lyrical with a liberal sprinkling of superstition. It was so good that I read it aloud to Min and we agreed that we hardly needed to take the trouble of going ourselves, enduring tedious flights and bad hotels. Peter concluded the letter by saying that a great friend of his, an American professor of Fine Arts and his wife, were about to spend three weeks in Cambridge and were desperate for somewhere to rent. Could I, Peter asked, possibly assist them in finding somewhere not too large but reasonably attractive? Money was no object. Of course I could.

I went out to the hall at once to ring the number of the London hotel which Peter had given me. I explained to Peter's friend, whose name was Herbie Finkelstein, that my house was available to rent for three weeks at the sum of . . . I drew breath, wondered how I dared . . . and named a rent which seemed steep even for my own precious home. He said that would be fine and he'd telephone me once he'd got to Cambridge and seen it. After I'd made arrangements with him, I telephoned Mrs Baxter and told her about the new tenants. She seemed quite excited by the idea and promised to let me know at once if they started making fires in the middle of the drawing-room floor or any of the things that tenants were currently rumoured to do.

Herbie Finkelstein was a fast mover for I had a telephone call at seven o'clock that evening, saying that he and his wife were so thrilled with my 'beautiful little home' with all its 'divine *objets*' that they were doubling the rent. It was no skin off their nose, he informed me, as his college was paying and even double the rent would seem quite moderate in Massachusetts.

Min and I celebrated with champagne, of which Min drank a great deal as she had had a bad night and thought it was because she had been inadequately drunk. My excuse was that I was physically exhausted, having twice walked down to the wood which George Pryke was supposed to be coppicing.

The first time I'd gone with Min, so that she could show me the way. It was staggeringly beautiful, all black, bare branches and unbroken semolina snow. We came across some sheep, which had wandered into the park from the fields, their fleeces sulphur-coloured against the whiteness of the snow, hung underneath with lumps of ice, like muddy lustres. Ham was thrilled to see them but they ran off, baaing, and refused to play. George had been sitting on a log drinking tea but had got up and made a show of working when he saw us. Ham, who disliked him as much as I did, barked and growled until we were reduced to shrieking to make ourselves heard.

The second time I arrived with Ham but without Min and found that George had lit a fire on the snow and was drying out his newspaper. He gave me the sort of look which, long ago, turned Atlas into a mountain but set to with his axe, with an air of sullen oppression like a man in chains. I heard the stroke of his axe grow more infrequent the further I walked from the wood. 'Standing pools gather filth.' An old proverb but none the less true, I thought, recalling his unwholesome complexion, mottled with dirt, and ochreous eyeballs.

He'd brought the logs up after lunch and stacked them in an outhouse near the back door. Then he followed me into the house, carrying an old grate I'd noticed in the coach-house where the Land Rover was kept. It fitted the fireplace in the drawing room perfectly. As instructed, he carried in a basket full of logs and placed it by the grate, all with the insolent mien of one who knows that rebel forces are massing in the North to quell the despotic plantation-owners of the South.

I had three telephone calls that afternoon in answer to the advertisement and I arranged with each applicant that they should come up to the house the following day for an interview. I made some more scones and baked a piece of bacon hock with leeks, sultanas and dried apricots for supper, cleaned the drawing room and put up a camp-bed in my bedroom for Ham who, contrary to all my hopes, wanted to be with me wherever I was. Plentiful food, of the kind she liked, had won her faithful heart.

I was sitting at the kitchen table, scraping tetchily at the plate of the iron which was, inevitably, scorched to a dark tobacco brown, when a voice behind me startled me so much that I dropped the iron on to the floor. I turned to see Vivien leaning over my shoulder, grinning sardonically.

'Did I give you a fright? You poor thing! I imagine your nerves are quite played out with so much travail. Oh yes, I know all about it. Mrs Pickles at the village shop showed me your card in the window. She thinks you're Robert's mistress and that poor Minerva is living permanently in her dressing-gown, smoking sixty a day and weeping disconsolately, being forced into a *ménage à trois*.'

'I hope you undeceived her?' I said, picking up the iron which was now in three pieces and quite beyond repair. I got up and wrote 'iron' on my shopping list.

'I did no such thing. It would be unkind to deprive her of the pleasure of telling it to everyone who comes into the shop. Actually I hinted that you and Robert had been engaged before he married Minerva and that I thought there was some illegitimate fruit somewhere in the background.'

'Thank you.'

'Oh, surely you don't *mind* what they think of you? I'd thought you a little more . . . superior. Of course they'll make up just anything. My!' She looked around the kitchen. 'You *have* been a busy little bee! Oh, do I see scones? I'll stay to tea.'

'I was just going to light the drawing-room fire,' I said, trying not to sound annoyed.

Vivien followed me into the drawing room.

'You've found the grate, I see. I wondered what Minerva had done with it. It's brass and steel, you know. Quite good-looking when cleaned up.'

'No, I didn't.' Brasso, I added mentally to my shopping list.

'What have you done with that perfectly ghastly Simu-cole fire?'

'I've put it in the cupboard under the stairs.'

'Good. Perhaps mice will come and gnaw out its insides while it's there and I'll never have to see it again. It isn't even as if it's convincing. I'd rather have a plain old bar-heater any day, if I can't have a proper fire.'

I perfectly agreed with Vivien but said nothing, bending instead to put a lighted match to the fire I had already laid in the grate. As the flames ran over the newspaper and the kindling began to crackle, I stood up and my eye fell on the imitation oak clock and the apricot plaster poodles. It seemed that Vivien was looking at them, too, for she stepped forward and scooped them into her arms.

'Into the cupboard with those!' she said, opening a door beneath one of the window-seats and pushing them in. 'Now, what shall we . . .? Ah, I know!'

She opened a door in one of the alcoves beside the fireplace and took out a blue-and-white double-gourd bottle.

'Pretty little thing, isn't it? There were a pair . . . oh, yes, here's the other. What date would you say?'

I took one of them in my hands. It was Japanese, painted in a vivid underglaze blue with three wise men and the pine, plum and bamboo, known as the 'three friends'.

'I'm not really sure. Late seventeenth century? Early eighteenth?'

'Yes, I would think so. Now how do they look? Just the tiniest improvement on those poodles. Come and look in this cupboard and help me chose some other pieces to go with them.'

We spent a happy quarter of an hour, trying out combinations of jars, plates, candlesticks and bowls until we felt that we'd achieved something balanced and in proportion with the scale of the chimney-piece. The fire had really got going and was warming a good three feet of the room immediately in front of it. I had visions of being able to have coffee in comfort after dinner, instead of having to sit all evening on hard kitchen chairs. Vivien looked critically around at the rest of the room.

'As you're such a domesticated girl, it might be worth while to do something with the rest. That horrible little table must go. There used to be a sofa-table there and a large stool here. Let's look in the attic.'

Half an hour later we staggered downstairs, carrying the first piece of furniture, a beautiful walnut sofa table. Then we carried up the black vinyl coffee-table with its beastly little chrome legs. We tottered downstairs again with an ottoman, which was appallingly heavy.

'If I'd known we were going to do furniture-moving I'd have arranged to have George Pryke here,' I said, a little resentfully. 'He's about as repulsive, lazy and unpleasant as anyone could be but I imagine he's strong.'

'George Pryke?' Vivien gave a sly smile. 'When he was a young man he was as strong as a bull. He had red hair and a moleskin waistcoat. He used to take me poaching sometimes when I was first married. Robert's father was always away, doing something tedious, studying mangelwurzels or something. When George had emptied his snares we used to go to his hut, right in the middle of the woods, and make love. I think it was the smell of blood. It always made me very passionate. Oh, don't look so shocked! You are a little Goody Two-Shoes!'

'I suppose it's middle-class to be discriminating,' I said caustically.

Vivien laughed and shook her head. I suddenly saw that she must have been very pretty as a girl. Even now she was attractive. The bright silver of her hair suited her. She was still flamboyant, not a whit faded.

'Now, now!' she said. 'Don't let's quarrel when we were getting on so well. Let's get this blasted thing into the drawing room. I've had a brilliant idea.'

We returned to the attic and Vivien went through the contents of several tea chests before she gave a triumphant shout and began to pull out great quantities of fabric. I went to help her and saw that they were slip-covers for chairs.

'I knew it. I was sure they must be here though I haven't seen them for years. Look at the fabric . . . quite enchanting!'

It was a heavy linen, with parrots, peonies and butterflies in coral, red, chartreuse and primrose-yellow on a pale-blue background. She was right. It was utterly charming.

'I had these made myself thirty years ago. Let's go and see if we can fit them on. Oh, I'm so excited!'

I felt excited, too, as we struggled and pulled and stretched the covers over the filthy calico of the sofa and chairs. Vivien stood back, her eyes sharp with enjoyment. The room was transformed. I forgot about being tired and banished the horrid image of Vivien and George Pryke in the poacher's hut.

'It's superb! I can hardly believe it!'

'Just a few flowers here and there . . . perhaps a large arrangement on that table. When you get your Mrs Moppit she can clean that rug. It's that disgusting dog.'

Ham, recognising the word 'dog', wagged her tail to show that she was joining in our rapture. I looked at my watch.

'Goodness! The time! I must go and get tea ready. The children will be coming home at any minute.'

It was still too cold to have tea in the drawing room so I put a clean cloth on the kitchen table. Vivien pulled her chair over to the Aga, kicked off her shoes and rested her bony, stockinged feet against the warm enamel.

'What you want in here is an armchair. Or, better, a sofa.'

Annoyingly she was quite right. The kitchen was certainly big enough and it would be just the thing for the chats that Min and I looked forward to between our work.

'Ah, Eleanor, darling. There you are. Give your grandmother a kiss. Goodness, what a cold little snout! If you put on any more weight, dear, someone will come and put a ring through it and lead you to market. William, come here! How strongly you always smell these days. Like an oriental bazaar.'

I only put out half the scones, of which Vivien ate three very quickly. She looked round for more with dark, greedy eyes but when none were forthcoming she got up, put on her coat and shoes and said she'd better go before it got absolutely dark.

'Oh, are you going?' said Min, coming in with a blue ink-stain across the bridge of her nose and her hair sticking up at the back where she'd been running her fingers through it while thinking. 'Why not wait and then Robert could drive you home.'

'No, thank you, Minerva. I've had a good tea. You'll see we've done things in the drawing room. Now, if you'll take my advice you'll go and comb your hair and wash your face. No point in positively throwing your husband at another woman's head. You don't want to concede *every* battle.'

'Half the time I don't know what Vivien's talking about,' said Min, as soon as she'd gone. 'Oh damn! There aren't any scones left. I might have known Vivien would eat them all.'

I brought out the rest of the scones from the warming oven and refilled the bowl with jam. Then I went to the larder to get a small jug that I'd noticed the day before. It had a handle of twisted ivy leaves and was very pretty. The jug was no longer there. I thought it odd. As far as I knew, no one but myself had had any need to go into the pantry since yesterday.

'It's my birthday in two weeks,' said Eleanor, picking up crumbs from her plate and leaning her head back so that she could drop them into her open mouth.

'You'll choke, darling,' said Min. 'Don't do that. What would you like for your birthday? What about a new doll?'

'Polly Saxby says she's given dolls up and that only silly babies play with dolls at nine.'

'Well, that isn't any good then. We can't have Polly Saxby sneering at us.'

Eleanor looked suspiciously at her mother, detecting a note of satire.

'What about getting George Pryke to build you a little house in the woods?' I suggested and Eleanor, who was dropping in her last crumb, immediately turned purple and began to choke.

'That's a brilliant idea,' said William, speaking for almost the first time since arriving home. 'I could use it as my headquarters.'

'No, you couldn't. It's going to be mine. I might let you share it sometimes. And what have you got to be head of anyway? You can stop hitting me now. The crumb's gone.'

'That's a marvellous idea,' said Min. 'George Pryke could surely stir himself to hammer some planks and nails together.'

'It could have two little windows,' said Eleanor dreamily, 'and a front door with a letter-box. Could it have a letter-box, do you think?'

'Easily,' I said. 'I'm going into Great Swosser tomorrow. I'll ask Mr Ransome if he's got a little brass one. He seems to have almost anything you can think of.'

'A real letter-box! I was just thinking of a hole but a real letter-box would be much better.'

'I'll make you some curtains,' I said, getting carried away with the idea.

'Ooh, lovely. Can they be pink with flowers on?'

William made his customary being sick noise and got up to go upstairs.

'We ought to call him George Prick, really, because he *is* such a prick,' he said as he picked up his satchel.

It was unfortunate that Robert should happen to come in just at that moment and overhear the remark. William was made to apologise which naturally made him very sulky and it got the evening off to a bad start. I thought it was unwise to make such a fuss about it. William was quite bright enough to judge his audience. I doubted very much if he'd be saying it to old ladies or Mrs Pickles. It was, after all, an old word quite familiar to Shakespearian audiences of every degree. Eleanor wanted to know what the fuss was about.

'In *The Sleeping Beauty*, is it rude to say that she pricked her finger on the spindle?'

'Be quiet, Eleanor, for a minute, darling,' said Min. 'Robert, why don't you ask Gerald to supper next week? It's Daisy's idea. She nobly says that one more won't make any difference.'

Robert stopped looking annoyed and looked pleased instead.

'I'll ask him. It's very kind of you, Diana. Extremely kind. The poor chap's still rather low.'

We agreed to ask Gerald for the Wednesday following. Eleanor came round to my side of the table and opened her satchel so that I could see in. Besides books and pens there was a brown paper bag of apples. She looked at me and giggled conspiratorially. I nodded approval. The day before, I'd put the coloured paper I'd bought in her bedroom with a note on her pillow saying that I should very much like to be her friend. She'd come down to me when I was alone in the kitchen preparing supper and put her arms round my waist.

'It's lovely paper. I've never had *yellow* paper before. Only blue and brown. Thank you, very, very much. I'd like to give you something in return.'

'Aren't you going to make me a lovely mat?'

'Oh, yes! A yellow mat. But it's not the same as giving you something I had to pay for, is it?'

'It's not the same but every bit as good. It's the pleasure that matters, not the paying.'

'Well, that's lucky because I haven't got any pocket money left. But what could I do that would make you pleased?'

'What would please me is that you wouldn't buy biscuits at Mr Beale's any more. You see they make you put on weight but they don't do you much good. It isn't the sort of food that a growing girl ought to be eating much of.' Eleanor went very red. 'I saw how many you'd been buying when I paid Mr Beale's account. Does Mummy know you put them on the bill?'

'I don't think she ever looks at the bill. She just pays it. It isn't stealing, is it?'

I saw that her eyes were full of tears.

'No, certainly not. I'm sure Mummy wouldn't be cross if she knew. Well, not very, anyway. And if you don't buy any more she need never know. I won't tell her if you don't want me to.'

'But poor Mr Beale! He always says I cheer him up when I come in.'

'Buy half a pound of apples instead. They'll cost just the same. And do you much more good.'

'Will I get thin?'

'Yes, provided that you eat sensibly. Perhaps just one scone at tea . . . that sort of thing. Have something of everything but not too much.'

'Will you really be pleased if I do that?'

'It would please me more than anything else I can think of.'

'All right then. Actually I don't want the biscuits so much now. I'm not so hungry in bed.'

Then she blushed again and I understood that she didn't want to be unkind about Min's cooking.

After dinner we went into the drawing room for coffee. I'd kept the fire made up and the room was almost warm. I'd lit candles because none of the wall sconces had bulbs in. Min clutched my arm when she walked in and saw what we'd done.

'Daisy! Genius! Pure bloody genius! What do you think, Robert? Isn't it miraculous?'

Robert, who was behind us with the coffee-tray, looked about in great puzzlement.

'It certainly looks different. Yes, much better. Definitely better. But I can't see what you've done, exactly. New sofa and chairs? And those ghastly poodles have gone.'

'Mrs Grudden, our last daily, gave us those. She said the room needed cheering up. It was kind of her, I suppose. Then I forgot to notice them any more so I didn't get round to chucking them out.'

'Can I have them, then?' asked Eleanor, who had come in with us. 'I've always liked them.'

'They aren't new chairs, just old covers that your mother found in the attic,' I said quickly, in case Robert thought that I'd been insanely extravagant. 'She's really responsible for all this. She knew where things were. We rather enjoyed ourselves.'

'Vivien has always had style,' said Min, throwing herself into a chair by the fire and sighing with satisfaction. 'She's not wholly a bad old bird. Of course she makes incredibly bitchy remarks but often it's just because she's bored.'

'Some people, when they're bored, model the Taj Mahal in matchsticks or make bits of pottery to give to their friends as Christmas presents. My mother tries to wound as many sensibilities as she can and makes love to the man who's come to read the meter,' said Robert acidly.

'Does Granny really make love to the meter-man?' asked Eleanor, putting her head round the door.

'I thought you'd gone up for your bath,' said Robert. 'Now run along and don't say anything to Granny about it.'

'I don't think your mother would mind if she did,' I said, when Eleanor had gone. 'She seems to glory in frankness.'

Robert looked at me speculatively but forbore to ask what I meant. I asked him if he'd managed to have a look at George Pryke's work on his way home.

'I did stop for five minutes. I can't say I was impressed. Looked like about two hours' work to me. I asked him what he'd been doing and he said he'd had to spend his time running around after a pack of women. Actually it wasn't as complimentary as that.'

Robert gave a short bark of a laugh and I felt rather annoyed.

'Running, indeed! A continent moves faster than he does.'

'What are you going to do about him, darling?' asked Min. 'We really can't afford to pay him for doing nothing.'

'I don't know,' said Robert, frowning. 'I'll have to think about it.'

'That means you won't do anything, I know, but I'm too relaxed and comfortable to quarrel. Daisy's had this very good idea for Ellie's birthday.'

We talked about building a little house in the woods until the fire burned low. Robert liked the idea very much and told us about a tree house he had made in those same woods when he was twelve. On the whole it was our most harmonious evening yet.

# Chapter Thirteen

In the morning Min and I went into Great Swosser. I dropped her at the hospital and drove on to Mr Ransome's where I bought an iron, candles, a small hand-held electric sanding machine and a letter-box for Ellie. Then I bought, for myself, two pairs of jeans, a thick, navy guernsey and a navy duffle-coat from a clothes shop called Blubb's Ladies Outfitters.

Next to Blubb's was an antique and bric-à-brac shop. As in most of these sort of shops, the greater part of the contents of the shop fell into the second category. I was just casting my eye over the chamber-pots, flat-irons and horse-brasses in the window, in case there was a door-knocker for Eleanor's house, when I saw the jug with the ivy-leaved handle that I'd been looking for yesterday. I went into the shop. The owner, an old man with very tremulous hands, got up from his chair by the stove. I asked to have a better look at the jug. I recognised the small chip beneath the spout. I asked him where he'd got it and he told me that a schoolboy had brought it in.

Apparently the boy had brought him several pieces in the last few months. The old man seemed keen to talk. I imagine he didn't have many customers. He described the boy as being a nicely-spoken, attractive boy with an eye for superior articles. I bought the jug, at a reasonable price, and left the shop.

I gave my skirt and coat to Mr Beale who said they would come back from the dry cleaner's in one week. After doing the rounds of the butcher's, the greengrocer's and the baker's I picked up Min and we drove back to Weston Hall. I put the jug back in the pantry. I still hadn't decided quite how I was going to deal with the problem of William. I felt that tact was required to avoid a row. Min and I were just finishing our mushrooms on toast when the back-door bell rang.

'It's odd how often that bell rings these days,' said Min. 'Is that your first interviewee? I'll just take a helping of rice pudding into my study and leave you to it.'

'Don't you want to see the applicants? You'll have to put up with them much longer than I.'

'I have complete faith in your ability to pick the right one. I always choose the one who looks most like a daily help. I can't help myself. If Hitler applied for the post wearing a crossover apron and his hair tied in a duster, I'd give him the job.'

I opened the back door.

'Mrs Butter. I've come in answer to your advertisement. Housework, hours to suit.'

I was somewhat taken aback by her appearance. She must have been in her sixties, short and bone-thin, wearing a navy coat that looked expensive and white kid gloves. Her hair was permed and dyed platinum blonde. She wore a thick layer of peach make-up. Her eyes were shadowed with blue and I was convinced that her long, very black eyelashes were false. Min would have closed the door on her on the spot. I asked her to come in.

'My!' she said, looking around. 'You've got a grand old place here! Romantic, isn't it? I like a good bit of romance meself. What I always say is, there's no pack of cards without a knave.'

'Do you?' I faltered, at a loss.

'What I mean to say is, you can't have a big house without a deal of dirt.' She looked at the kitchen table and clucked with dismay. 'That'll need more than a scrub, I doubt.' She looked at the curtains and closed her eyes for a moment with an expression of torment. 'Historical's one thing. I call those a disgrace. Begging your pardon, Miss. My Stan always said as how I was too outspoken. Still, fair fall truth and daylight.'

'Let me show you the rest of the house so that you can see the size of the job,' I said, beginning to feel encouraged.

Mrs Butter looked around the house in a manner that could only be described as exhaustive. She opened all the cupboards, lifted the edges of carpets and looked behind curtains, even beneath lavatory seats and down plug-holes. I felt myself growing more and more apologetic the further we went as Mrs Butter's cheerful, proverbial style of conversation was gradually stilled into clickings and tuttings of disapproval. We walked back in silence to the kitchen. I leaned against the Aga rail, waiting for her to tell me that it was too much for her to take on. She looked at me in silence for a moment. Then she began to laugh.

'The Lord knows I must be addled in my wits but I like a challenge. I'm bored at home since my Stan went to Abraham's Bosom and of course, the money'll come in handy-like. Better wear out than rust out. What do you say to me, Miss . . . what did you say your name was?'

'Fairfax. But please call me Diana.'

'Thank you, I will. When we're not at work, that is. I don't hold with too much familiarity. When money's changing hands it leads to misunderstandings.'

'I'll talk to Mrs Weston and telephone you this evening.' I'd already explained about my role as temporary chatelaine. I thought I'd better see the other contenders before making up my mind. 'You don't happen to remember the recipe for a Victoria sponge-cake?'

'Ay, I do. Three eggs, six ounces each of butter, sugar and flour, half an hour, gas mark three. Stanley always liked a nice sponge. You'll be new to cooking then?'

'Well, no. Just a certain kind of cooking.'

'I see. You're used to doing fancy things with prawns. I like dogs.'

For a moment I was confused. Then I saw that Ham had managed to get out of the boot room where I had shut her at the first ring of the doorbell. It seemed that Ham liked Mrs Butter for she ran over to her and sniffed her knees, in an ecstasy of tail-wagging and whining.

'That'll be the Prussian Leather she can smell, happen. I always put a dab behind me knees. It were Stanley's favourite. He liked a woman to look after herself. Couldn't stand slipshod ways, couldn't Stanley. Good dog.'

Mrs Butter gave Ham's head a final pat and got up to go, replacing her gloves, smoothing down each finger in turn as though she was going to partner me in a quickstep. I saw Mrs Butter out and began to make the cake, according to her instructions. While it was cooking, I did some ironing. I'd just finished my tenth shirt when the doorbell rang for the second time. I was dreadfully bored with ironing and delighted to have an excuse to stop. Mrs Brewer was morose and unfriendly. She didn't like old houses and she didn't do floors. The third applicant, Matty Pym, was equally unsuitable. She recited a long list of ailments and told me all about her health in the greatest detail. As walking up to the house from the village required that she have a good sit-down and a cup of tea to restore her to anything like her usual self, it was obvious that she wouldn't do.

Over tea, and the cake which turned out quite well, I told Min and the children about Mrs Butter.

'There is something a bit strange about her. Hard to say quite what.'

'Perhaps it's the small black toothbrush moustache?' suggested Min.

'No. I was expecting that. I think it's the false eyelashes. But I got the impression of hard-working, conscientious honesty. All the qualifications that matter. Actually, I really liked her.'

'Will she wear her false eyelashes to work?' asked Eleanor. 'Doesn't she have any real ones?'

'I don't know. She hasn't got any eyebrows, just pencilled arcs. It's the way film stars looked when she was young. I think she likes things to be under her control . . . Bright and cheerful, very positive.'

'A bit like you, Daisy,' said Min, smiling at me affectionately. 'Your tastes are no doubt very different but it's the same desire for regulation of chaos. I just muddle along, focusing on things here and there that seem important to me and only noticing the rest when I come up against it. I suppose that means I'm more selfish.'

'I don't believe it has anything to do with selfishness. Mrs Butter and I aren't doing things so much for other people as calming our own fears, I think.'

'What have you got to be frightened about?' asked William.

'Being alive, being a separate person responsible for my own actions, pain, loneliness, all those things.'

Death, I was thinking, but didn't want to put morbid ideas into the children's heads. They would find their own way there soon enough.

'Lots of things frighten me,' said Eleanor. 'I'm frightened of my voice squeaking on a high note in assembly, I'm frightened of break-time in case no one will play with me, I'm frightened in English in case Miss Pivot askes me to read aloud, I'm frightened at lunch in case I get a bit of gristle because you aren't allowed to spit it out . . .'

'Goodness, what a baby you are!' interrupted William scornfully. 'I might be frightened if I was stuck up a mountain in a blizzard and all the rest of my team were dead. Or lost underground on my own with my last match just about to go out. I say *might* be.'

'Oh, William! I hope that won't ever happen to you! How would you bear it!'

She looked at her brother, with tender, protective fearfulness. I thought of Tom and Maggie Tulliver and I could see that Eleanor would be capable of Maggie's kind of passionate, self-denying love and probably that William would, like Tom, be unable to recognise or value it.

While the children did their homework I finished the ironing and stirred, at intervals, a stew of mutton, barley and onions. We were having too many stews but I could think of no other way to cook the cheap cuts that were all we could afford. With Herbie Finkelstein's rent, I would be richer than I'd ever been before but I was certain that Robert would revert to suspicious resentment at the sight of a fillet steak. He was slowly growing more relaxed with me and at times, last night in the drawing room, for example, was actually friendly. He ate everything I cooked with an air of fastidious deliberation, as though he were a well-mannered guest, thanking me and praising with a cold courtesy. I hoped Min wouldn't mention the Land Rover. She'd been as impressed by my having it repaired as if I'd taken the engine apart and mended it myself.

After supper, Robert made coffee while Min and I went into the drawing room. Min and I talked about *The Mill on the Floss* as I'd mentioned to her my observation of Ellie, really as a prelude to talking about William.

'I've only read it once,' said Min, trying to put a log on the fire and wincing as she knocked her bandaged hand on the wood-basket. 'Good God, why can't I do anything without my hand getting in the way! It's the most frustrating thing I've ever had to endure in my entire life. But I shouldn't complain when you're being so perfectly saintly. Please don't think I'm not grateful.'

As she'd already thanked me at least twenty times that day I was in no danger of suspecting her of ingratitude.

'When I got to the end of it,' Min continued, '*The Mill on the Floss*, I mean, I was on a train. I was so shocked, so unprepared for such sadness that I began to cry buckets and all the people in the compartment sort of froze into a ghastly silence, not even liking to turn the pages of their newspapers or catch each others' eye. I suppose they were all terrified that

I might involve them in hideously embarrassing explanations about having been raped by my father or my mother having just died.'

'Who's just died?' asked Robert, coming in with the coffee.

'No one. Don't George Pryke's logs burn well? I suppose he's had to take a substantial drop in income now we're using them.'

'Talking of incomes,' I said, despairing of finding a way of introducing the subject with any subtlety, 'I found out today, quite by accident, that William's been supplementing his. He's become an antique dealer.'

If I'd said that I was really the Sugar Plum Fairy in disguise, Min and Robert couldn't have looked more astonished. I told them about the jug in the junk shop. Robert drew in his breath sharply and the firelight threw his frowning face into dramatic chiaroscuro.

'Oh dear,' Min said, looking very worried. 'Are you quite sure it was the same jug? Must it be William? There are lots of boys with fair hair who go to school in Great Swosser. It seems such a sneaky thing to do. Dishonest . . . let's face it! And why? He gets pocket money. And I buy him clothes and books and pencils and things.'

'Marijuana's very much more expensive than pencils.'

'What!'

Robert sprang from his chair.

'William's smoking pot.' I went bravely on though Robert began to stride up and down, his arms folded across his chest and his head down, every line of his body expressive of anger. 'Everything points to it. His dilated pupils, his moodiness, his giggliness. Plus the fact that his room smells of it. And there are cigarette papers in his room with bits torn off the packet. That makes a sort of filter. Masses of people smoke pot in Cambridge, dons as well as students. I've tried it myself . . .'

'I've never heard such arrant nonsense in my life!' Robert's voice was furious. 'William's twelve! He's a child! He's moody and giggly because he's an adolescent. I must say I resent very much the accusation that my son is a drug addict!'

'Which you'd be quite right to do if I were so silly as to make such an accusation,' I said, getting angry myself. 'Of course that isn't what I meant. But no doubt the other boys at school . . . you said his friends were older . . . are smoking it and William will be under a great deal of pressure to do as they do. I think . . .'

'I think you've got a very active imagination,' interrupted Robert, with a snort of furious laughter. 'Not content with running my house you want to bring up my children as well! I suppose you'll be saying next that Ellie is selling herself on the streets!'

'Robert! Shut up! You're making an idiot of yourself!' said Min. 'I think Daisy might be right. There is something the matter with William. I've been noticing how odd he is sometimes. I thought it was just growing up. Let's talk about it calmly. Getting angry and shouting won't help . . .'

'I'm damned if I will! I don't feel calm! I feel bloody upset! I'm going to talk to William!'

Robert stalked out of the room and slammed the door.

'Daisy, I'm so sorry! Oh, bugger this hand! That makes the fiftieth time I've knocked it. Don't take any notice of Robert. He gets angry and then the next minute he's sorry. It was a shock.'

'I don't think I broke it very well, did I?' I said, feeling unreasonably upset. 'I thought he'd be angry and it made me nervous. Oh dear, I think I'll wash up and go to bed. You and Robert can sort it out when he comes down. He'll hate me being here. Do you think, perhaps, I ought to leave in the morning?'

'Oh no! Daisy! Don't even suggest it! I couldn't bear you to go! Robert'll get over it. He's just terribly short-tempered and he loves the children so much. He's afraid for William. Afraid you might be right.'

Min helped me with the washing-up as much as she could and I was glad to have her company. Then Ham and I went to bed and Min went back to the drawing room to wait for Robert. Although I was physically tired, my mind was like a jam-jar full of wasps. I really hate rows. I lay in the gentle glow of the electric fire and went through it over and over again.

Should I have said nothing and minded my own business? No. They'd have found out for themselves, eventually, but by then William might have come to grief. Goodness knows what he might turn to when the disposable family goods ran out. Should I have told Min and left her to inform Robert? Perhaps that would have been better.

But I knew that husbands were often jealous of their wives' girlfriends and were alarmed by the idea of being discussed in unflattering, intimate detail. Which, of course, they frequently were. I had felt, probably wrongly, that courtesy demanded that something so serious should include Robert in the telling. Now I regretted it but it was too late.

I decided that I wouldn't give it another minute's thought. William was all that mattered. The row was unimportant. I was determined to relax and think about plants, always a soothing subject. Within less than a minute I was thinking about Robert and justifying myself all over again. I got heated and turned the fire off. Then I was cold and turned it back on. I recited poetry. Someone came up to bed. I heard the water-tank thunder and the lavatory flush. The house became quiet. Then someone else came up and the noises started all over again. I settled myself for sleep.

How dare he take his bad temper out on me? I'd spent half the afternoon ironing his blasted shirts. I felt like going downstairs and screwing them into a heap. No, I was thinking about it again. More poetry. Robert liked Gray. I hated Robert. No! Stop there. By one o'clock in the morning, I was a miserably wakeful, exhausted wreck.

I awoke to find daylight filling the room. I looked at my watch. Half past eight! I got up and ran downstairs in my dressing-gown. Min was there, struggling to fill the kettle one-handed. The breakfast table was covered with bowls and packets of cornflakes.

'I overslept, I'm afraid,' I explained rather unnecessarily.

'I've only just come down myself. My hand was hurting so I took extra painkillers and they knocked me out. I was asleep by the time Robert came up so I don't know what he and William said to one another. I do hope Robert didn't get angry with William and upset him.'

'Heavens! I just remembered. Mrs Butter will be here in half an hour. I'll go and get dressed. I'm sure she thinks people who are in their dressing-gowns at nine in the morning are children of Satan.'

'All right. I'll go and get on with some work and you can introduce us over a cup of tea later on.'

I got downstairs again, fully-clothed, just as Mrs Butter made her entrance. She wore a clean overall and had a scarf around her blonde curls. Above the false eyelashes her eyelids were shadowed with mauve to match her Crimplene trousers.

'I'll get straight down to it, like. The mill gets by grinding. Where do you want me to start?'

I had expected to spend the first few days supervising Mrs Butter and showing her what to do but five minutes working with her taught me that Mrs Butter knew exactly what she was doing. She worked with tremendous energy and with a thoroughness that would have fulfilled a hospital matron's wildest dreams. I left her to it and went back to the ironing board.

At eleven I made tea and Mrs Butter and Min were introduced to each other. Mrs Butter's eyes slowly took in Min's holey jersey and torn jeans.

'Well, there's many a good cock's come out of a tattered bag. I hope we'll suit,' said Mrs Butter. 'So far, so good. It's not what I'm used to, but a change of pasture makes fat calves. Here's a list of things I'll be needing.'

She gave me a piece of paper on which she'd written meths, wire wool, Fuller's earth, scouring powder and borax. I was encouraged to find a fellow list-maker.

'That lounge grate pays for cleaning. I like to see where I've been and you certainly can that in this house! There's only me at home now Stanley's passed over, and I'm that bored with meself. Still, yon's an ill husband that's not missed.'

'Have you any children, Mrs Butter?' asked Min.

I could see that she was having trouble keeping a straight face.

'Only the one. Roland . . . but I always call him Roly. Little children weigh on your knee, big ones on your heart. Nothing but a worry. Still, it's an ill bird that fouls its own nest, like.'

She looked narrowly at Min, who was trying to disguise a laugh with a cough. I patted Min on the back and she grew more composed.

'Ay, well, an idle person's the devil's cushion. I'll get on now.'

'Min! I think she knew you were laughing at her!' I said, when Mrs Butter had gone.

'I'm so sorry,' said Min, with a burst of laughter. 'I wouldn't hurt her feelings for anything. But she's so odd. And when she said her son was called Roland. Roland Butter.

Roll-and-butter, you see? Oh dear, I'm sorry! And I did like her.'

While Mrs Butter took the library by storm, I wired a plug to the little electric sander I'd bought from Mr Ransome. The kitchen table was stained with ink and paint, probably from when the children were small. The wood was grainy and worn and each groove was filled with something like black chewing-gum, an amalgam of food and dust which had accumulated over many years. The table was Victorian and of indifferent looks. The patina would not be mourned by the most dedicated conservationist. I approached it boldly and began to grind the surface. It was one of the most satisfactory tasks I'd ever undertaken, the results far outstripping the effort. It did my ruffled feelings a great deal of good, imagining that I was sanding Robert's pointed nose. Inch by inch the wood became pale and smooth and clean. The table was large but after three-quarters of an hour it was immaculate.

'You've made a grand job of that!' Mrs Butter was unstinting in her approval. 'Now it'll pay for a scrub.'

Min came to say goodbye to Mrs Butter and to thank her. Though I think Mrs Butter had a fairly low opinion of us both when it came to domestic matters, none the less she was pleased by our enthusiastic praise of all she had achieved. Thanks to her, I found that I had an afternoon to myself with nothing to do but get tea and supper. Some books had arrived by the morning's post but I wasn't in the mood for work. I called Ham and went out for a walk.

There had been a slight thaw, only enough to take the snow from the trees, but the effect of the yews and bare oaks against the still unsullied whiteness and the pale, ashy sky was lovely. I looked back at the house. The older part was, as Min, had said, romantic. Its asymmetry only added to its charm.

I walked down the slope that led from the back of the house and through an opening in a high box hedge. Beyond was an enormous expanse of dark lake. It was a complete surprise. No one had mentioned its existence. A few ducks swam disconsolately between the reeds in the black water just beyond the thick ice, which was frozen into grey bubbles and wrinkles at the lake's edge. Ham directed a short uninterested bark at them which they ignored, then began her search for the perfect stick. In the middle of the lake was an island and on its banks stood a swan.

The beauty of the scene stirred my heart. I remembered Robert and felt a pang. I wanted to be able to return to see this enchanting place in summer, surrounded by green beneath a blue, scintillating sky. The feeling of depression returned in full force. I felt confident that my friendship with Min was restored for good and that almost nothing could destroy it now. But Robert would be an impediment. It seemed to me that the marriage was, despite Robert's tiresomeness, a success. After thirteen years Min was still very much in love with him. I could see that he was good-looking, intelligent, cultivated, a good father, all the things that Min would want. But I knew that I could never like him.

There was a boat-house further along the bank. I walked over to have a look at it, enjoying the sensation of the sparkly surface compacting beneath my feet. Ham came too, bringing her stick. The door of the boat-house was a little stiff but responded to a kick. Its interior consisted of one room built out over the water, full of dead leaves, old newspapers and cobwebs but perfectly dry. It had pretty diamond-paned windows on three sides, with seats beneath. In the room below were two boats on wooden slipways.

I looked through one of the windows to the island across the lake. The swan launched itself on to the surface of the water and began to run, more and more furiously, until it was airborne. It was then that I had an idea. It was so good that I decided to hurry back to the house to consult Min. I hung my damp duffle-coat in the boot room and went into the kitchen. Robert was sitting at the table reading a newspaper.

I hesitated in the doorway but he'd already seen me. He got up.

'Please,' he said, waving a hand at the chair next to his. 'I came home early, specially, so that I could talk to you before the children came in.'

Then he smiled, very briefly, and lifted his eyebrows in an expression of mock alarm. 'I promise I won't shout. I very much want to talk to you.'

He continued to look at me and held the back of the chair next to his. I sat down and composed my face into what I hoped was an expression of calm neutrality but I must have looked thoroughly defensive for suddenly he laughed.

'I must have been a beast for you to look at me like that. How can I apologise for the way I behaved last night? I was rude and stupid and I deserve to be kicked.'

'Go on,' I managed a smile. 'That's a very good beginning.'

'It's not enough, I know. And when you've been so good to us, looking after the house, cooking us wonderful things to eat, helping Min. You've transformed our lives. I've behaved very badly. I felt all the time I was being a brute. I'm thoroughly ashamed of myself. Is there the smallest possibility that you might be able to forgive me?'

'Yes. I might even forego the kicking.'

I rather despised myself for the feeling of relief this proffering of the olive branch gave me.

'I was angry with you because I couldn't stand the idea of William being deceitful. It hurt me to think of him being so secretive and shutting himself away from us . . . stealing our things as though we were his enemies. It seems only moments ago that he was a little boy, a fat little thing with blond curls . . . he was a beautiful child, really . . . playing with his boat on the lake and running to me because he was afraid of a duck that was trying to steal his sandwich.'

'I do understand. It's what anyone who loves his children would feel. It was stupid of me to be upset. It's my besetting sin . . . taking things too seriously.'

Robert looked at me in surprise. 'You give such a strong impression of self-confidence. I'm so very sorry to have hurt you.'

I smiled and shook my head.

'You were right, of course, about the drugs,' Robert went on. 'William denied it at first but then he confessed. Poor little devil! Apparently the other boys in his class say he's stuck-up and a snob because he lives in a big house. The older boys use him to run errands and, I gather, like the idea of having power over a boy whom they believe to be socially superior. He feels he has to do as they do. He seems to be quite frightened of the bigger boys. I must say, I'm rather at a loss as to how to deal with it.'

Robert looked depressed and sat slumped in his chair, leaning his head against one hand while running the fingers of the other back and forth along the smooth grain of the kitchen table.

'Obviously it won't do just to speak to his form master,' I said, 'as this is something that happens mostly outside school hours.'

'And the staff are a part of the problem, I think,' said Robert. 'I distinctly got the impression during William's last Parents' Evening that the staff saw me as bourgeois filth. Great Swosser Comprehensive is something of a communist cell. Marxist interpretations of Jane Austen, you know the sort of thing. They seem more interested in indoctrination than education.'

'Perhaps it isn't the right school for William.'

'I don't think it's the right school for anyone. It's governed by envy and self-justification. Those boys are going to scoff, just like their parents, at all the things which offer the greatest inspiration and consolation . . . music, painting, literature, history . . . intimidated by their own ignorance. It makes me very sad.'

Robert threw back his head, hooked his elbows over the back of his chair, and stared at the ceiling. He was a sort of Hamlet, I decided. Intelligent, sensitive and scrupulous, and with all Hamlet's much-discussed inability to make up his mind.

'If I gave up teaching and ran the estate William could go to a decent school. That's what it comes down to. I'm pleasing myself at his expense.'

'I don't think self-sacrifice works,' I said slowly. 'It places an intolerable burden of guilt on the beneficiary. I think there must be another answer though I confess I can't quite see it yet.'

'Thank you, Diana, for your tolerance of my wretched temper. I couldn't sleep last night after talking to William. I went over it all again and again. Anxiety, fury, frustration, self-reproach. I thought about William and then I thought about you. Finally it dawned on me that what I felt was a great weight of gratitude. Thank God, you saw what we had missed. I *am* grateful. By lunch-time today I knew I had to get this off my mind and try to straighten things out with you. You've been more forgiving than I dared to hope. If I behave badly again, I'll take that kicking.'

'I'm really rather a coward and only kick people smaller than I am.'

He laughed and picked up my left hand in his right and gave it a little shake. It was a gesture of friendship, quite without sexual overtones, but when he'd let it go I remained conscious of the warmth and pressure of his fingers for some time afterwards.

'I forgot,' he said, smiling. 'An invitation for you. It's the St Lawrence's Ball next Saturday. Min and I have to go. Will you make the evening tolerable and come too? The food will be abysmal and I can't promise the band will be up to much but it'll give the younger masters something of a thrill if you'll come.'

'Yes, I'd like to. But what about a dress?'

'That thing you wore to Charles Jarrett's dinner will be fine. Most of the women look like overgrown versions of Shirley Temple. They seem to equate formality with frilliness. Even their hair goes into frills.'

'I'll look forward to it. Now, what about some tea?'

'I'll make it. It's one thing I am competent to do in the kitchen.'

While Robert made tea and I cut bread for toast we talked about Mrs Butter. He laughed at my description of her and said that he was looking forward to meeting her. Then he went off to do some marking while I prepared a chicken and some potatoes to roast and started to make a sauce with celery, apples and cider. The children and Min came in at the same time to have tea and we discussed the St Lawrence's Ball.

'Why don't we ask Charles as well?' suggested Min. 'Then you could have a lovely time, smooching sexily around the floor together, and drive the headmaster's wife into a frenzy of jealousy.'

'Is she in love with Charles?' I asked, in some surprise.

'No, you clot. She's dying to cuckold her husband. He drinks, is probably impotent and, I imagine, thumps her from time to time and they absolutely loathe one another. She's not bad looking in a tumbled sort of way but so rapacious that every man she fixes her eye on starts to tremble and make excuses.'

'What does she want to do with these men?' asked Eleanor,

refraining from a second piece of cinnamon toast by sitting on her hands.

'Stupid!' said William, and whispered something in Eleanor's ear.

'Really? No! Crikey!' Then she looked puzzled. 'What on earth for?'

'Charles, you will remember,' I said, to change the subject, 'will be in South Africa at the time of the St Lawrence's Ball. I shall have to make do with whatever partner I can get.'

'You can dance with Robert, though that won't be very exciting. But poor Miss Mingot will be dreadfully cut up. She's been in love with Robert for years. She'll be agonisingly jealous of you. I've told him he's got to be beastly to her so that she can get over him and find someone else.'

'What's this?' Robert came in at that moment. 'Did I hear my name? Is there any toast left?'

'I was telling Daisy about Miss Mingot. She goes painfully crimson whenever she sees you and when you gave her a cup of tea at last year's prize-giving I thought she was going to faint.'

'I've never given her the least encouragement,' said Robert, looking annoyed. 'I think you're making the whole thing up.'

'Darling, who ever needed encouragement to fall in love? And don't you remember your talk about Herculaneum when you fell off the platform? Miss Mingot screamed and because she was doing the slides for you everyone thought she'd electrocuted herself on the projector. Someone pulled the main switch and plunged us all into darkness.'

'Daddy! Why did you fall off the platform?' cried Eleanor with great interest. 'Were you drunk?'

'Certainly not! I was stepping back from the screen so that I could see the ground plan better. Miss Mingot is a very nervous woman. She overreacted, that was all. I wouldn't have been hurt at all if we hadn't been suddenly blacked out. As it was, someone trod on my hand and I couldn't write for a week.'

'She screamed, darling, because she was terrified that you'd hurt yourself. That's love for you.'

Min, who had been grinning throughout this recital, started to laugh.

'If that's love, why weren't you screaming, too?' said Robert, also beginning to laugh. 'I could hear you giggling throughout the rest of my lecture. It was very off-putting. My hand hurt like the blazes, my trousers were split, I'd broken my pointer and made a complete ass of myself in front of the entire school and all you could do was laugh!'

'I'm so sorry, darling, but you looked so funny. One minute you were pompously giving us all these old dates and the next minute you were doing a fine impression of a windmill over the orchestra pit!'

Min was quite helpless now and I had to laugh myself. Luckily Robert and the children were all convulsed as well.

'Anyway, that doesn't prove a thing,' said Robert, wiping tears from his eyes. 'Miss Mingot is a very unfortunate, lonely girl and we mustn't be unkind about her.'

He rather spoilt the effect of this homily by a further burst of laughter.

After supper Robert had more marking to do, so Min and I sat in the drawing room on our own and talked at great length, first about William and then about her mother. Then the talk drifted to a review of our lives and what elements we would add or subtract if we could have the remaking of them. While we talked I reflected on the difference one half-hour could make. After that conversation in the kitchen with him, not only did I no longer hate Robert but I would have been very interested to hear what excisions and additions he would have made to his own life.

# Chapter Fourteen

In honour of lunch with Charles, I washed and dried my hair and exchanged the navy guernsey for the white cashmere. I put on a clean pair of jeans and cleaned my shoes and my fingernails. These were all the improvements my depleted wardrobe permitted.

Mrs Butter was qualified in her praise.

'You look grand, dear, but for yon nasty jeans. You'll not catch a rich man looking like a navvy. Fine feathers make fine birds.'

I was astounded that Mrs Butter had put two and two together and made such a large sum. She was very gorgeous in a coat and skirt of kingfisher blue and a boater with a matching ribbon, which she removed carefully, before putting on her apron.

'If you could change the beds and shampoo the drawing-room carpet . . .'

Mrs Butter was travelling to the door to get on with it before the words were out of my mouth.

It was a beautiful day, with a weak sun shimmering on the snowy fields and the sky very pearly and full of light. Milecross Park looked handsome and prosperous. There wasn't a broken rail in the miles of fencing that led up to it, not an untidy field shelter nor a straggly bush. Horace opened the door as soon as I drove up.

He looked at me through his thick-lensed spectacles when I wished him a good morning and gave me a polite smile. He took away my duffle-coat, handling it with as much care as if it had been sable, then returned to take me through the drawing room and into the conservatory.

'This is lovely!' I said, looking at the glass-and-steel room which was filled with white lilies, hyacinths, amaryllis and other exotics which I didn't recognise. 'It's very modern . . . yet it looks just right with the house.'

'Charles designed it. He copied the proportions of the window- and door-frames of the house. It's the only bit of the house he really likes. Because it's so bright. He missed the South African light and space. A glass of Chablis? Charles asked me to look after you if he was late.'

I connected this sudden animation with a strong admiration for Charles.

'Which I am. Ten minutes,' said Charles, walking in at that moment. 'An important buyer called in without warning. Only you, Diana, could have brought me away so soon.'

He looked a little different from my memory of him. Browner and perhaps a little older. He wore riding breeches, an open-necked shirt and a black jersey. He smiled at me and at once I felt the formidable impact of his self-assurance. He took two glasses of wine from Horace and gave one to me.

'Will you be warm enough if we eat in here?'

He indicated a small table which was laid for two.

'It's perfect. Anyway, after a week at Weston Hall, I imagine I'm impervious to cold. I must hold the world speed record for bathing.'

He laughed. 'It's certainly a very English house. When I first went to dinner there I was so cold I had to sneak out to the car and get a jersey. I'd been wearing it at the stables all week so it must have smelt to high heaven. Luckily there was a very smelly dog there to provide camouflage. Min had forgotten to buy potatoes. There was a handful of very small, very green, sprouting things in an enormous dish which no one liked to risk. I had to ransack the kitchen when I got home for something to eat. The wine was good and we all got amazingly drunk.'

'One of the best things about Min is that she is well aware of her shortcomings and lives quite happily with them. I don't think she has a single complex and so there's nothing spiky about her.'

'It's as I told you before. She isn't concerned with making a good impression. I'd rather eat at Weston Hall despite the cold and awful food than almost any other house in Lancashire. Tell me how you know each other. Did you meet at Oxford?'

So, while Horace brought us a simple but excellent lunch of tender noisettes of lamb and salad and cheese, I told him all about our friendship from the very first day when I had stitched up Min's hem. As before, Charles was a good listener and seemed interested in every detail. When I told him that there had been a quarrel and that we hadn't seen or spoken to each other for fifteen years, Charles was on to this like a hawk swooping down to a vole and prised the entire story out of me.

'So this man was in fact your first lover?'

'Well, yes, he was. Though that isn't particularly relevant.'

'Not as far as your quarrel with Min is concerned, no. But it *is* relevant.'

I ignored this and described the reunion and. what had happened since.

'So now you and Robert are to be friends. Is it going to work?'

'I hope so. For Min's sake. I really think I'm beginning to understand him better.'

'Robert,' said Charles thoughtfully, swirling the remains of his chablis in his glass, 'is the cell-mate of his own conscience. He's stuck in a job which is way beneath his capability and he muddles through life in a house far too big for his income and energies. And he lacks the courage to change anything.'

'That's rather an exaggeration, I think. It's not quite as bad as that. And Min and he are happy together. Though he is a little like a twentieth-century Hamlet. Moody.'

'I haven't read Shakespeare since I left school but from what I remember, yes.'

'Don't you like reading?'

'Yes, but not fiction. I read biographies and books about travel. History, sometimes. I don't like something that's made up.'

'I think it was Carlyle who said that history was a distillation of rumour. And the art of biography is the arrangement of a biased selection of half-truths. Everything written is really fiction. And fiction . . . well, good fiction anyway . . . is made up of truths within a framework of invention.'

'Now you're going to lecture me. You've got a pedagogic glint in your eye. Of course, you're right. Let's say that I prefer to read something that means to be factual. The fact is that I find you disturbingly desirable. The second fact is that in . . .' he looked at his watch, 'four hours' time I shall be leaving for South Africa.'

'And I must go back to Weston Hall soon,' I said quickly.

He laughed. 'I wasn't suggesting that we go upstairs and make love. I've got to go back and look at some horses and make innumerable telephone calls before I leave. And I know,' he took my hand and held it in his strong, warm one, 'you're . . . shall we say . . . apprehensive?'

'You make a great many sweeping assumptions,' I said, removing my hand. 'You seem to imagine that you only have to whistle and any woman will tear off her apron and fling down her sickle and come running!'

'You mean I'm conceited?'

'Yes. I think you probably are.'

'"Probably,"' he mocked. 'How polite you English are. You don't like to say so outright because you're in my house and you've eaten my lunch. Is that it?'

'I don't like rows. And I don't enjoy hurting people's feelings.'

'And I've wounded yours by suggesting that you're frightened of sex.' He took my hand again and held it firmly. 'I'm sorry. It was unkind. I won't tease you again. I'm a conceited bastard, not fit to kiss your feet, much as I'd like to.' He looked penitent but I knew that he was still laughing at me. 'I know what will speak to your heart and convince you that I am a man of sensibility. Horace!'

Horace came, remarkably quickly. I wondered if he had been listening to our conversation.

'Have you a spare cookery book?' Charles turned to me. 'It has to be simple food, you said?' I had mentioned briefly my difficulties in the kitchen but I was surprised that he had taken notice of what had been just a passing comment. On reflection, though, Charles seemed unlike most other people, including myself, in that he concentrated on what was being said, instead of using half his mind to compose his reply. I nodded. 'Well, Horace will know the sort of thing.'

Horace went away.

'Does Horace cook, then? I hadn't realised.'

'Yes, he's an excellent cook. He provided this lunch and our dinner the other day. Horace is a man of taste and intellect. Read theology at Oxford. You should talk to him.'

'But I didn't realise . . . what's he doing, running your house and taking people's coats?'

'How conventional of you. I assure you Horace doesn't feel himself demeaned by taking your coat. His thoughts are his own even when struggling beneath a ton of upper-class English outer garments.'

'Hm. I think I detect just a touch of defensiveness there. You're finding the natives troublesome?'

Charles laughed and seemd very pleased. '*Touché*. Perhaps you're right. There is something that irritates me about the English *en masse*. Perhaps I have an inferiority complex.'

I didn't believe it for a minute.

'Tell me about Horace. Quickly before he comes back.'

'Horace has been in and out of mental hospitals since he was sixteen. He's clever and talented, one of the brightest people I've ever met. But ordinary life is an impossible strain for him. He had a major breakdown before his final exams. After he left

Oxford he spent three years in a psychiatric ward. I met him at a hunter trials. He was selling flags for the local mental hospital. It was immediately obvious that here was someone exceptionally intelligent. And extraordinarily unhappy. We talked. I offered him a job. He started here as a yard boy, sweeping up, washing cars, cleaning boots. I wanted to see what he was capable of. It wasn't long before he rose to running the place, more or less. His nerves are still shaky and he has bad days. But he knows he's safe. And that I respect him.'

I thought of Charles handling the mare, Astarte. I could imagine him handling Horace in the same way. Did Charles look for people's weaknesses so that he could exercise his skill in mastery over them? He had analysed both Min and Robert with swift accuracy. Would it be possible to have a relationship of equality with him or would he insist on having the whip hand? I had never met anyone so self-possessed. It was impossible that he was without his own Achilles heel. I wondered what it was.

'What are you thinking about? You look very serious. Are you worried about Horace being trapped in a lifetime of dependence? I promise you that the moment he can break free he will. It will be an emancipation from himself and not from me. I see him as my friend. As my equal, if you like.'

This was so close to what I had been thinking that I was startled. Horace returned with a book which he laid beside my plate. It was Elizabeth David's *French Provincial Cooking*.

'Oh, Horace! This is perfect!' I was delighted. 'May I really borrow it?'

'I don't use it very much.' Now that I knew part of his history I could feel that there was about Horace an unusual degree of tension which he covered by a very deliberate manner. 'Most of the recipes are things that are better made in quantity. There's usually only Charles to cook for. Or a dinner party, when something more elaborate is needed.'

'Yes, I see. But this will be perfect for Weston Hall. What a shame that the Great Swosser greengrocer doesn't sell garlic. Never mind, I shall enjoy using this. Thank you.'

'I wish I didn't have to go away.' Charles looked at me with something like regret when Horace had left us alone again. But his regard was wholly without speculation. 'Don't fall in love with anyone unsuitable while I'm away.'

'You're only going for two weeks. I'm not likely to fall in love with Robert's homosexual friend, Gerald, or the geography master from St Lawrence's. Our social life at Weston Hall is extremely uneventful. And oddly enough I really like it. It's my first real experience of family life and I love being able to be alone but with someone else always about. I've never felt so utterly myself with other people. I suppose it's like being a child again and staying with Lady Bart. But this time I know I'm useful and there isn't a feeling of indebtedness.'

I rose to go and Charles got up, too. He took hold of me by the shoulders as he had done in the stables. I forbade so much as a ligament to tense. I did my best to return his gaze coolly. I don't know what made him smile suddenly. He kissed first one cheek and then the other, very tenderly.

'I'll see you to the door.'

Horace was there with my duffle-coat. He handed me two heads of garlic.

I thanked him for the lunch and the garlic with real feeling. Horace gave me his curiously opaque smile. Charles saw me to the Land Rover. Once I'd started the engine further conversation was impossible and he merely lifted his hand as I drove away. I thought about him all the way back to Weston Hall. So much, in fact, that I overshot the turning. I parked the Land Rover and went up to the house. Min was waiting in the kitchen.

'I know it isn't tea-time but I had to know how the lunch went. I've been madly good today and worked all the time I was eating those excellent chicken sandwiches. Tell me *everything*. Was Charles incorrigibly sexy?'

'Min, I really think you'll have to do something to damp this passion. Cold baths, hard manual labour, yoga or something. Perhaps I'd better slip something in your tea. What was it they gave the troops? Bromide, wasn't it?'

'Something like that. And if history is even remotely accurate, it didn't do any good. Every army of occupation since man learned to sharpen a stick has left behind a multitude of bastards. It's probably what wars are for . . . the mixing of bloods.'

'All right, nothing in the tea,' I said, putting leaves in the pot. 'Perhaps you'd better satisfy your curiosity and go to bed with him yourself.'

'No chance of that. I could see he was delirious about you the moment he saw you.'

'I think Charles is more than a little fond of you. But he knows there's nothing doing as you're firmly married to Robert so he's turned his attention to me as I'm attainable. So he thinks, anyway.'

Min looked at me over the rim of her tea-cup.

'If you expect me to believe that, you must think I'm birdwitted. I may be inexperienced but I can see when a man's besotted. When I married Robert he was terrifically in love with me. It was obvious to anyone. And I could see that Charles had that same look . . . as though he'd been hit over the head with a concrete post. You've got cynical, that's the truth of it.'

'I'm not suggesting that men don't fall in love and feel tremendous passion for a particular person. I'm just saying that sex is another thing altogether.'

'Perhaps Robert and I would benefit from a little sexual experimentation. But the damage done by infidelity is permanent, from my observations of other people. They may decide that it's worth their while sticking together, but the marriage is crippled.' She helped herself to several spoonfuls of sugar. 'Has anyone ever been unfaithful to you? I mean, someone you considered yourself seriously attached to?'

I thought for a moment. 'No. I don't think so. All my relationships have come to more or less the same end.' I saw that she was looking at me with curiosity and decided to trust her with the truth. 'The trouble is, I don't like it. Sex. It makes me feel . . . attacked, invaded, beleagured . . . I don't know. The lover becomes the enemy.'

'Daisy! Darling! That's very sad. But how brave of you to admit it. I'll never tell another living soul. Not even Robert.'

I laughed. 'Do you tell Robert absolutely everything?'

'Probably everything. But of course most of the time he doesn't listen. Oh dear, so you don't like it. And do the men get angry?'

'Sometimes. Sometimes they say it doesn't matter. But I get so fed up with the recriminations, the questioning, the theorising. I just can't stand it and so I end it. Sometimes they go away of their own accord. Sometimes they want to marry me to prove that they love me so much it simply has to come right in the end. But I know that it won't.'

'So why do you sleep with men in that case?'

'Because I'm an optimist, I suppose. I live in hope.'

'Haven't you ever really loved anyone?'

'I don't think so. I love Peter. But he only likes men in bed so I don't suppose that counts. I've been in love for a few days, sometimes a few weeks, but it hasn't lasted. No matter how much I start out liking them, I come to hate their greedy insistence. I feel as though I'm a buffet table and they're wondering if they can manage three puddings on the same plate.'

'So, romantically it's all right? Kissing and so forth? It's when it gets carnal you don't like it. It isn't just a question of aesthetics? I know you're nuts about things being rarified and beautiful. You always were, even at the age of thirteen.'

'Was I? I can't remember. Doomed to disappointment then between school and my mother.'

'You haven't told me what happened with Charles.'

'Nothing happened. It was a very civilised lunch. As usual, he questioned me, I talked, he digested it all . . . for future use, I suspect. I hardly know anything about him. He turns all *my* questions quickly aside and I can't bring myself to be rudely persistent. It's all got to be the way he wants it.'

'Don't you like him?'

'Oh, yes. I like him. More than I want to, really. I don't trust him, though.'

Min giggled. 'If only I could see him drive his high-perch phaeton to the inch. I can just imagine him taking your wrist in a cruel grip and bending his saturnine face over yours. Damn it, what am I saying? Why shouldn't it be over mine? Why should you have all the fun?'

'Because you've got what everyone of sense really wants. A husband with whom you're in real sympathy. The rest is one-tenth excitement and nine-tenths disillusion and insecurity. Now let's address our minds to the mundane matter of tea. One thing's certain, I'm ready to give Charles a glimpse of my lavender kid boots and perhaps even the hem of my lutestring petticoat in return for this cookery book. Now what shall it be?' I opened the book and riffled through the pages. 'What about these little pancakes? *Crêpes dentelles*. Eggs, butter, flour, sugar, milk, we've got all that. I'll leave out the rum and put in grated lemon as she suggests. Serve with melted butter and sugar.'

'Mm. Can't wait. What are we having for supper?'

'Pork chops. I'll do them with potatoes, white wine, garlic and bacon. She says juniper berries but I don't suppose we've got any.'

'I don't think so. Who is this she?'

'Elizabeth David.' I showed her the cover of the book.

'Is she a good cook, then?'

'Oh, Min darling, where have you been? It's like asking if Dickens is a good novelist.'

This provoked an argument about what made a good novelist in the nineteenth century and as we talked, I thought for the second time that day these talks, spontaneous, serious and silly by turns, were what made the quality of family life so rich and so desirable. This particular family, anyway. Finally, by a tenuous series of leaps, we got on to Ellie's birthday and my latest idea which was to convert the boat-house for her to play in.

'Apart from anything else, I don't know if it's a good idea to have Ellie playing alone in the woods with George Pryke hanging about. He's the sort of man who might go berserk. He sits in the greenhouse, heating himself to a libidinous frenzy with magazines. Did you know that he and Vivien were lovers?'

Min hadn't known. Any ideas of serious work being done were abandoned and as I made the batter for the pancakes and peeled potatoes, we discussed Vivien as keenly as though we were gossip columnists and our livelihoods depended on meeting a deadline with a compilation of exhaustive, salacious detail.

The pancakes were a wild success with everyone. Ellie explained that she hadn't been able to eat the pudding at lunch as it was apple crumble with all the hard pieces of core left in so she was allowed two. Everyone else had three, except for me as I'd had such a good lunch. Robert came home looking tired but after the pancakes he recovered his strength and did a convincing impression of his headmaster dancing the eightsome at the St Lawrence's Burns' Night, after too many glasses of wine cup.

'What are you all laughing at?' asked Min, coming in just as he sat down exhausted. She'd been to answer the telephone. 'I could just about do with a jolly good laugh. That was Winifred Eccles on the telephone, reminding me about the Spring Bazaar, which, perversely, they always hold at the beginning of February. It never feels like anything but the profoundest pit of winter to me. Of course, I'd forgotten. Even with two hands I don't think I could rustle up any lavender bags between now and Thursday.'

'You couldn't,' I said. 'Lavender bags are made in July. What have you got to do exactly?'

'Stand behind a stall in the village hall. That's the easy bit. I've also got to produce something hideous and completely undesirable to sell to the inhabitants of all the Dunstons who are misers and skinflints to a man.'

'Last year Min forgot about it,' said Robert, in a tone of exasperation. 'She'd gone to London to see Boris and Inman, her prospective publishers, and I had to go and spend ten pounds on jars of lemon curd from Beale's.'

'We steamed all the labels off,' said Eleanor. 'Daddy steamed his hand and said a frightful word. I've forgotten what it was.'

'I remember. It was f—' William was prevented from finishing what he was going to say by Robert's hand being placed swiftly over his mouth.

'We wrote all our own labels so that the bazaar ladies would imagine Mummy had made it herself. Daddy said it was lying out of kindness to Mummy and so it was all right.'

'It was an awful pity,' said Min, 'that what Robert thought was lemon curd was in fact piccalilli.'

'I'd never heard of piccalilli. I thought it was a brand name for lemon curd,' said Robert. 'It was yellow, after all.'

'Several people bought jars before Winifred spotted bits of cauliflower and pickled onions ogling at her through the sulphurous murk. I'm surprised they've asked me to help them again. Winifred did say that it might be better to give the jams a miss this year after last year's "unfortunate episode". As though we make a regular thing of brewing up pickles to sell under misleading labels.'

'Anyway it's quite the wrong time of year to make jam,' I said. 'Supposing I made a few cakes? Would that do? Elizabeth David has a good recipe here for chocolate and almond cake. And this coffee cake sounds all right.'

'Daisy's got a new idol. She consults the oracle with every problem. I hope she's got a chapter about the correct way to brush teeth or none of us will get to bed.'

'You'll be laughing on the other side of your face, my girl, when the Westons triumph on the cake stall,' I said, calmly. 'Now you'd better go and do some work to make up for an afternoon of dissipation and idleness.'

'Really? What have you been doing?' asked Robert, sounding interested.

'Oh, Daisy's been to Milecross Park. You'd better ask her.'

However, when Min had gone back to her study, Robert took William away to do his prep in the library while he composed a Latin entrance paper. After supper, when the children had gone to bed, the talk went from the conversion of the boat-house to lakes to descriptions of water and Robert read extracts to us from *The Ancient Mariner*. He read very well, with great dramatic emphasis. I closed my eyes and saw in my imagination the great banks of emerald ice, as tall as the ship, and remembered learning those very lines at school when Min had sat next to me in a gym tunic and plaits which were endlessly coming undone.

## CHAPTER FIFTEEN

The next morning, Saturday, I took Min to the hospital. They gave her a much lighter dressing this time which left the tips of her fingers uncovered. The nurse gave me some rolls of bandaging, pills and various ointments and said that I should change it every two or three days and only to bring Min back if I was worried that it wasn't healing properly. Behind her back Min was making idiot faces, crossing her eyes and letting her tongue hang out. The nurse suddenly turned and saw her.

'Some people think they're very clever. But the really clever ones don't have accidents with hot water and end up in hospital,' she said acidly, and walked away.

'She'll be polishing that little set-down for weeks each time she tells it,' I said, leading Min away. 'But as a piece of *esprit d'escalier* it wasn't bad.'

Min was very pleased to have her fingertips restored to her and as soon as we got home, went off to her room to work, in an excellent humour. I was unpacking the shopping when I saw Ellie walking past the kitchen window. As usual she'd forgotten to put on her coat. I found it and took it out to her. She was carrying something carefully in her hand and didn't hear me when I called so I followed her into the barn.

The barn contained nothing more than some bales of straw and an ancient tractor. In the far corner were several large corn bins. Eleanor had opened the lid of one and was leaning so far over that she was in danger of falling right in. She didn't hear me until I was right behind her. She jerked upright and spun round.

'Diana! Oh help! Promise you won't tell! Cross your heart and hope to die!'

Her eyes were pleading. I crossed my heart.

'Look!'

She pointed inside the corn bin. A black-and-white cat, of scraggy proportions and disgracefully matted fur, was suckling a litter of tiny kittens. I counted two ginger, one tabby, and two black-and-white. The mother cat looked into my eyes with a blinking gaze as she gently curled and stretched her paws. Then she bent her head to lick the kitten nearest her, the strength of her tongue rolling the helpless creature on to its back where it mewed frantically, its eyes tight shut.

'You promised,' said Ellie, taking hold of my hand so fiercely that I could feel her nails digging into my palm. 'You swore a sacred oath.'

'All right. I won't say anything to anyone. But why is it such a secret?' I bent down to stroke one of the kittens but took my hand away when I saw that the mother cat became anxious.

'Because George Pryke always drowns the kittens when he finds them.' Ellie began to cry. 'Last time there was such a lovely little white one. I called her Snowy. And that horrible, *horrible* man killed her! I think it must be terrible to drown.

And they're so helpless. It's such a cruel thing to do. And poor Booty goes everywhere looking for them. She miaows like anything and gets hard lumps under her tummy.'

I gave Ellie my handkerchief and she sobbed into it for a minute while I watched the mother nudging and licking her young.

'Beauty, did you say her name was?'

A misnomer if ever there was one. The poor thing looked as though the bearing of countless progeny had wasted her frame to a skeleton beneath the dirty fur.

'Booty. Short for Puss-in-Boots. She's got white legs like skating boots. William says it's a silly name but I like it and she does too. She always comes when I call her.'

'I see you've given her some milk.'

'I buy it from Mr Beale. He's in the secret, too.'

'But she needs meat as well. She looks very thin. I'll go and chop up some of Ham's meat for her.'

'Oh, Diana! Would you really? Oh, you're my very, very best friend! And you won't tell Mummy and Daddy?'

'No, I promised. But surely they wouldn't want George Pryke to drown them? It's a vile thing to do.'

'Mr Pryke told me he'd been given strict instructions. So I thought I'd better not mention it and remind them about Booty in case she got drowned, too. Mr Pryke says she's a hopeless mouser and ought to get the chop. Oh, it does sound so horrible. Does he mean with his axe?'

'I don't know. I don't suppose he'd do anything as dreadful as that.'

Privately I thought the man was capable of anything, however terrible. I went into the kitchen and cut up plenty of fresh meat into tiny pieces, surmising that Booty's teeth were probably in need of attention. When I put the plate into the corn bin, next to her front paws, Booty started as though she'd been given an electric shock and began to eat with the intense concentration of the starving.

'We must feed her twice a day,' I said. 'And she must have fresh water as well as milk, if she's to feed the kittens properly. And fish. When the kittens are weaned she must go to the vet and have an operation to stop her having any more. We'll find good homes for these.'

'But what about Mr Pryke?' asked Ellie, looking despondent.

'He's bound to find them eventually and drown them. He always does though Booty's so clever at hiding them.'

'Leave him to me.'

The weekend passed peacefully. There was a snowstorm on Saturday afternoon. We gathered in the drawing room for tea and watched the huge clots pour down from the sky. When it got too dark to see outside, we played Consequences until supper-time. I was surprised to see how well William could draw and commented on it.

'It's my best thing but the art at school's hopeless. They make you draw from your imagination all the time but I want to learn how to draw things properly.'

It was the first time I'd heard William speak enthusiastically about anything. I realised that this was a possible ingress into the mind of this unfathomable child but couldn't see how to help him as I couldn't draw myself.

Sunday was a day of flamboyant brightness and after lunch we went for a walk around the lake. Ellie and I took some scraps for the ducks while Robert and Min walked arm-in-arm and Ham and William ran round us in circles. Ellie held my hand and we stared at the dark water and the woods, now blazingly white again, looking for the swan until our eyes ached.

On Monday I went down to the woods to speak to George Pryke. He was sitting on his usual log, reading a newspaper, but he got up when he saw me and made a mild attack on a tree bole with his axe, with the slow feebleness of an old lady doing waist-reducing exercises. Every man has his price and I knew what George Pryke's was.

'You remember that wheelbarrow you saw in Mr Ransome's?' I began. 'The big aluminium one you were telling me about?'

I had previously, in a half-hearted attempt to get on better terms, admired the old wooden barrow he was using and he'd told me it was harder to push than if Old Nick himself was sitting in it. He'd seen a barrow in the ironmonger's which had a pneumatic tyre, but Mr Weston didn't hold with replacing things that weren't worn out. He preferred to wear out the folks that worked for him. This had been said in a tone of grumbling resentment, punctuated by a disgusting clearing of the throat and a flying gobbet of spit which landed on the ground just in front of my shoes.

'I'll buy that barrow for you, Mr Pryke, on one condition.'

'Eh? What's that?'

George Pryke straightened up and looked at me closely. There came into his amber eyeballs a light of understanding and his expression changed from sullen to lascivious.

'You must not drown Booty's kittens. If you do, the barrow will go straight back to Mr Ransome. Or I shall donate it to the Great Swosser Cottage Hospital.'

'I thought that cat were hatchin' again. So, you don't want 'em drownded.'

He considered.

'All right. 'Tis a deal. Though what Mr Weston'll say with a yard 'eavin' with the brutes, I couldn't undertake to say.'

'I shall talk to Mr Weston. Now remember, even one kitten drowned and that barrow goes straight back.'

I bought the barrow that same morning and George Pryke lifted it out of the back of the Land Rover as tenderly as though it were a sleeping baby. He wheeled it away, his tongue twisting in ecstasy. I checked on the kittens. They were beginning to open their slate-blue eyes. Their coats were soft and bright in pitiful contrast to Booty's snarled fur. After two days she was beginning to know me. I picked up the tabby kitten and stroked its head with my finger. It hissed at me and struggled, its tongue rosebud pink. I gave it back to Booty and she licked it energetically, removing my scent.

I wanted to tell Min and Robert about the kittens but I couldn't break my promise to Ellie. Every time I spoke to her about it and urged her to tell them herself she became so red and tearful that I realised that the previous drownings had been a profound emotional shock for her. I was worried that Robert might be angry when he found out about the kittens, as he was more or less bound to, and consider me not only interfering but encouraging Ellie to be deceitful. It was hard to justify, looked at from Robert's point of view, having a secret with Ellie which excluded her father and mother.

On Wednesday I spent nearly all day in the kitchen. In the morning I made three cakes for the Spring Bazaar and a fourth, plain chocolate, for tea. Then I began to prepare things for supper as Vivien and Gerald were coming and I was anxious that eveything should go well.

I made a *potage bonne femme* with potatoes, carrots and leeks. That was easy, inexpensive and would suit, I hoped, all palates including the children's. I had struggled for twenty minutes to make clear to Mr Potts, the butcher, what I meant by a *contrefilet*. He rarely found takers for fillet steak and to have someone request a large piece for roasting was as startling as though I had demanded a trussed humming-bird. He obstinately refused to understand what I meant by the upper fillet so in the end I bought the whole fillet and paid for it myself, rather than use up a week's housekeeping in one go. I trimmed it and tied it with string so that it was ready for cooking and peeled some potatoes for *gratin dauphinois*. Cream was available in abundance and, thanks to Horace, I had garlic. In Cambridge I would have made a green salad but here that was an impossibility so I'd chosen celery as an accompanying vegetable. For pudding I made an apple tart.

The dining room was terribly cold and gloomy. It would have been as cheerful to eat in there as feasting at the bottom of a deep pond. So the children and Min had tea in the drawing room while I got to grips with the kitchen table. On a white linen cloth I put out the Georgian silver knives, forks and spoons which Mrs Butter had rubbed until they dazzled, and some napkins which Mrs Butter had starched. They were old and grey but of the finest linen damask. I had debated with myself whether I dared to use the wonderful dessert service that was stacked higgledy-piggledy in the pantry. It was probably Coalport, influenced by Sèvres, with borders of *bleu celeste* and birds of paradise in the centre panels. In the end I decided that I would. For the soup and the beef there was a Minton dinner service that was extremely pretty with gold-printed decoration and enamelled rose festoons. I put candles in the silver candelabras and a glass vase of viburnum, which was still the only thing out, in the centre. I'd cut some ivy earlier in the day and shaken off the snow. I trailed it around the silver candelabras and was rather pleased with the effect.

I found two table lamps in a spare bedroom and put one on the dresser and one by the Aga so that I could see to cook without the inquisitorial glare of the central light.

'Let me help, Diana, please!' said Ellie when she came in.

'It's like Christmas, it's so sparkly. What a pity we haven't got any crackers.'

'You can put out the salts. And the butter. I'll do the glasses.'

Ellie wanted to write out place-cards as she'd seen her mother do for formal dinners. She spent a long time cutting up bits of coloured paper and writing the names of everyone in her best handwriting. Then she went off to do her homework while I shaved the potatoes into the thinnest slices possible.

'Good Lord!' said Min, when she came in. 'It's like the table in *La Belle et la Bête*! I hope there's a magic arm to do the serving of the food. If only I had a dress with enormous skirts and a tiny crown. Robert had better be the Beast. Or perhaps Vivien would be best suited by nature.'

'Best suited to be what?' asked Vivien, coming in, shedding wet snow on the clean kitchen floor.

'Best suited to be at the head of the table,' I said, arranging Ellie's place-cards so that she had Gerald on her right and William on her left. 'You'll be nearest the Aga, too.'

'You've got all the old things out,' said Vivien, stroking a silver fork. 'I took the best stuff to the Dower House but this is not bad. Oh, just a minute. I brought you something.'

She threw her coat on to a chair. I took it and hung it up while she searched through a large bag.

'Here!' She handed me a bundle of something wrapped in newspaper. 'They're from the garden. I knew you'd be stuck for flowers.'

'Vivien! How marvellous!'

The paper contained five iris stylosa, just unfolding their furled delft-blue petals with a faint sweet scent. I put them in the vase with the viburnum and lit the candles. The table sprang into light and shadow.

'It's the most romantic thing I've seen in ages,' said Vivien, pleasing me very much. She came over to see what I was doing. 'What a delicious-looking sauce. Madeira is it? Robert should be completely under your spell by the end of the evening. How clever of you.'

She was obviously annoyed when Min and I laughed.

'I've so enjoyed today,' I said, bending down to put the potatoes into the Aga. 'I feel tempted to give up academic life and become a museum curator. Imagine being with beautiful things all day. And the tranquillity of all those large rooms and the hushed atmosphere.'

'I bet a museum's anything but tranquil,' said Min, idly nibbling a stalk of celery. 'I should think it's nothing but squabbles all day long between the staff over whose shards get the best showcase, why Jobbin's salary is more than Hoggins' and whose turn it is to make the tea. You could be an interior decorator.'

'I don't know why you should want to be anything at all,' said Vivien, picking a slice off the finished apple tart. 'Why not just have fun? It seems absolute madness to tie yourself down to getting up early and not being able to go away if you want to.'

'But, Vivien, someone's got to earn money and someone's got to produce all the things you enjoy,' said Min, starting on another stick.

I took the celery away from Min and put the apple tart in the pantry. When I came back, Vivien was saying, 'I never heard such nonsense. It's the height of *un*selfishness to enjoy yourself. Then you aren't a nuisance to other people, always having to be pumped out or dried out or listened to or being asked over for Christmas just because they think you might be lonely. I'm delighted to say that never in my life has anyone had to do anything for me. I've always been quite independent.'

'What about all the men and women who've worked on the estate to keep you in comfort and ease?'

'Of course they haven't done it for *me*. They've done it for money, for themselves. If I weren't paying them, do you think they'd so much as iron a handkerchief or milk a single cow?'

'All right, what about all the men who've been at your beck and call? Who've taken you to Monte Carlo and Venice, carried your things, driven you around, taken you to the theatre, and so on. What about Robert's father whose money has allowed you to do what you want?'

'Darling Minerva, you aren't thinking. Too much grubbing about in books has made you positively stupid. Those men weren't doing it for *me*! They were hoping all the time that they were going to have a lovely, lovely time with me in bed, lots of lubricious, unbridled sex until their hot little whatnots could do no more. They were wholly self-interested. I've never given a damn about them or anything else really and therefore I've never been a plague to other people's consciences or demanded their sympathy.'

'What's that noise?' I said suddenly.

'It's Ham, barking,' said Min, opening the kitchen door. 'I wonder if it's Gerald? The front-door bell doesn't work and Robert was posted to let Gerald in as soon as he arrived.'

We peeled Gerald off the front door and wheeled him in, an exhausted human cryogen. I rushed him to the drawing-room fire. I'd lit it in the morning and piled logs on all day to make sure the room was warm. I took his coat, and gave him a glass of champagne, which he could barely hold because of violent shivering.

'Gerald! God, I'm sorry!' said Robert, coming in with Min, 'I was meant to be listening for you. I went into the library to look something up and must have dozed off. Were you ringing for long?'

'No matter, dear boy.' Gerald stumbled to his feet. 'These two beautiful ladies came to my rescue.'

His teeth were still chattering but his face was beginning to lose its purple-and-white mottling and was becoming an even red. I had imagined Gerald to be something like Peter, pale and slender and effeminate, but he was fleshy, if not actually fat, and rubicund. His dark-brown hair was parted in the centre and his large brown eyes had several bags beneath. He bore a strong resemblance to Oscar Wilde. I offered him a bowl of mixed nuts and raisins, which was the most sophisticated thing Beale's could come up with, and he crammed a generous handful into his mouth. Vivien came in then and Gerald remembered that he had met her at a school play.

'Oh, did we?' said Vivien. 'I can't remember. It was the most ghastly evening. The play was something absolutely poisonous about people yelling to each other out of dustbins. I was consumed with boredom!'

'It was Samuel Beckett's *Happy Days*, Mother. Gerald directed it,' said Robert, with some firmness.

'Did you really? I thought at the time that the director must be mad. So you're the man responsible for the most terrible evening of my life!'

Gerald lifted his upper lip in a sort of smile but was clearly taken aback. Vivien gave him a provocative look through half-closed lashes. Gerald had very curved lips, of a strong brownish-purple colour. He put them together in a sort of *moue*.

'It was good of you to come to an amateur performance. Inevitably there are shortcomings but I trust the valuable experience gained by the boys makes the sufferings of the audience worth while.'

He gave a little neigh as he said this and I remembered Min's criticism of him and saw what she meant.

'Of course,' continued Gerald, his voice becoming more nasal as he warmed to the theme, 'when one has the great privilege of seeing a superbly artistic performance in one of the great theatres of the world, one's own efforts do seem paltry. Last night I saw the *Entführung* at Covent Garden. It was sublime! I had the most tiresome journey back this morning . . . every train late, nothing to eat or drink, appalling cold . . . yet the memory of the exquisite beauty of the music made my tribulations seem nothing!'

'Robert likes Wagner,' said Min, into the silence which followed Gerald's fluting pronouncement. 'It's all a bit noisy for me.'

'My dear Min! The *Entführung* is Mozart!' Gerald was almost honking in his eagerness to correct her. *Die Entführung aus dem Serail*! It is like confusing Shakespeare with Daphne du Maurier!'

Robert broke in with an energetic defence of Wagner. I saw Min's eyebrow's rise and her eyes close and I knew that she was cross. It seemed that Gerald was aware of it too, for he turned to Min.

'I apologise. It was a stupid comparison.'

Min gave him a half-smile and turned away to ask William whether he had finished his homework. William said that he had and attacked the nuts and raisins and kicked the leg of the chair he was sitting in until told to stop by Robert. There was a slight feeling of awkwardness which I was just about to attempt to fill with questions about the performance when Vivien said, 'Of course, tenors make very good lovers.' Robert sighed heavily and put his hands to his head. 'I've always found that,' continued Vivien. 'What was that man's name? Luigi Corto or Corso, something like that . . . so good in *La Bohème*. He was an astounding lover. Such stamina. It's well-known that the physical type tenors are supposed to be . . . what's it called, endomorphic, I think, anyway barrel-chested and short-legged . . . is tremendously virile and amorous.' She turned to Gerald. 'Haven't you found that, Mr Benson?'

There was the briefest of shocked silences. I saw Min bite her lip to hide a grin and then Robert and I began to speak together, and stopped.

'Sorry, go on, Diana.'

'I was only going to say . . . is there any truth in the idea that body-shape relates to personality? Ectomorphs being sensitive and introverted for example? And mesomorphs, aggressive?'

Robert and I discussed this proposition rather half-heartedly while Gerald recovered his composure and Min subdued her desire to laugh. Vivien smiled widely and listened to our efforts to make conversation.

'One might ask whether stamina is all?' said Gerald, coming in gamely. 'What about sensitivity? Tenderness? Surely,' he honked through his nose, 'durance can be vile without love?'

'Good Lord!' Vivien looked scornful. 'I hope you don't mean to suggest that love has anything to do with sexual pleasure?'

'But I do,' said Gerald, looking at her with brown eyes that were melancholy. 'I think that it has . . . should have, anyway . . . everything to do with it.'

I was rather more impressed by Gerald, then, and I understood why Robert liked him. As the evening went on I saw that the affectation was a shield for unusual sensitivity. The food was much praised by everyone. What would have been run-of-the-mill stuff in Cambridge or London, seemed rather remarkable at Weston Hall.

'Daisy is the most brilliant cook,' said Min, smiling at me.

'Actually, I'm not a very good cook,' I said. 'I'm more interested in reading about cooking than actually doing it. I see it as one of the easily accessible pleasures of life and I've learned the basic techniques in a rational, plodding sort of way.'

'Rational indeed,' said Gerald. 'Which has the great advantage of placing appetite in your control. All the pleasures of life are the better for being indulged with restraint. One should dip in one's toe rather than wallow.'

'What about love?' said Min. 'That's one of the greatest

pleasures of life. Surely that must be the exception? If it can be restrained, then is it really love?'

'I've always found that the unsatisfactory part about *Jane Eyre.*' I gave Vivien a third helping of potato. 'If she really loved Rochester, wouldn't she have given in and gone away with him after discovering about his mad wife? She didn't mind making him miserable. Or not enough, anyway. She *had* to be made respectable, which rather seems to deny that she loved him.'

'Think of the period in which the book was written,' protested Gerald. 'Jane was reared in the harshest of circumstances. Self-reliance was bred in her with the burnt porridge.'

'But plenty of lovers did run off with each other despite the social conventions of the times,' I persisted. 'Think of George Eliot in real life. It was only seven or eight years after the publication of *Jane Eyre* that she went off with Lewes.'

'We must distinguish between the experience of love and the expression of it,' said Robert. 'When the expression of love is suppressed to save inflicting pain on others, that must be a noble restraint. Most people are really much too selfish.'

'What is love?' asked Gerald. 'Do we have any idea at all what we mean by the word? It is often defined as the desire to put another's well-being before your own. To love someone more than oneself. Is that possible, excepting the love of a mother for her children? I agree with Robert that we are all too selfish. If it does happen, isn't it really a wish for self-renunciation and therefore the gratification of a selfish desire?'

'What queasy consciences you've all got.' Vivien helped herself to the last fragments of *gratin dauphinois*. 'When I was having an affair with Johnny Eames, the painter you know, his wife tried to commit suicide five times.' Robert groaned audibly. 'Each time a different method,' continued Vivien. 'Setting light to her hair outside our bedroom door was one. And I'm not talking about the hair on her head. And once she hanged herself out of the bedroom window with our bedsheets. But the knot came undone and she fell to the ground and broke both ankles. Johnny said that suicide was the only form of artistic expression in which she showed some originality. She wrote a tremendous amount of bad poetry which was published with the ambiguous title *The Wet Blanket*.'

'Are you quite without scruple?' asked Robert in disgust.

'I don't know what scruples have to do with it. Three months after I finished with Johnny, his wife left him. She went off with a man who made erotic sculptures out of playing cards. He had an exhibition called *Pokerwork*. Once the drama had gone from the relationship, you see, she was bored with it.'

'What worthless people you seem to have spent your time with,' said Robert, getting up to clear away the plates.

'I don't know. Some of them were amusing. And some were clever and some were good-looking. I don't think moral worth is a frightfully interesting quality in a friend, frankly.'

Vivien became quite entertaining as she got rather drunk, telling us about parties on the Riviera with painters and writers and the rich hangers-on who picked up the bills. I was reminded of my mother, who would so much have liked to belong to Vivien's world but who had been obliged by lack of funds, social standing and talent, to play the same game on a less exalted level.

The claret Robert had provided was good and Gerald was enthusiastic about it. But in some way he remained sober and tense and I got the impression that, despite the occasional flight of rhetoric, he was tethered by an oppression of spirit. Min was trying, I could see, to overcome her dislike of Gerald for Robert's sake but Gerald was nervous of her, which made him artificial, and this irritated her.

Eleanor and William came in to say goodnight, having had supper in front of the television as a treat. Gerald took from his pocket a bar of chocolate for each of them. Ellie put her arms around his neck and gave him a kiss. He was evidently a friend she trusted. I realised, looking at her, that there was a shade less double chin. It was a pity about the bar of chocolate, but it was unrealistic to expect her to go entirely without sweets. Just as I was thinking this, Ellie came round the table to me and gave me the bar of chocolate.

'I'm trying to get thin,' she whispered to Gerald, 'and it's very hard not to eat all of a bar of chocolate in one go. If Diana gives me a tiny bit each day it will taste even nicer.'

Ellie's dieting was something that we had kept secret, as the idea of surprising everyone seemed a spur to her determination. It hadn't occurred to her that its progress was going to be self-evident. I cast an anxious glance at Min but she was listening to Vivien and hadn't heard. I looked at Robert. He was looking at Ellie with such love that, for some reason, I felt a lump in my throat. Min got up to see them into bed though William protested that he was quite old enough to put himself to bed and that the idea of Min looking after *him* was quite ridiculous as in any dangerous situation she would double all his problems and be a bloody nuisance. Ellie wanted to know what dangers might arise in going upstairs to bed and was instantly crushed by William's saying that there was the danger that he might be provoked into pushing her down them if she continued to ask stupid questions.

Because of the weather Gerald left to go home at about half past ten. He was profuse with thanks and hoped that he might have the pleasure of dancing with all of us on Saturday at the St Lawrence's Ball.

'You'll look rather silly dancing with Robert,' said Min, with a laugh.

Gerald blushed crimson. Obviously the recent allegations of homosexuality had reduced him to a state of smarting sensitivity. Fortunately Vivien, quite unintentionally, distracted us by saying that he would not be able to dance with her as an evening at home with Foxe's *Book of Martyrs* would be bags more fun than being propelled round the assembly hall in the arms of prosy schoolmasters whose dinner-jackets smelt of mothballs.

Robert drove Vivien home after she'd invited me to lunch for the following Monday. He was back before I'd finished clearing the table and stacking plates to be washed up in the morning.

'On the whole, barring one or two unfortunate remarks from my mother, it was a good evening,' said Robert. 'Thanks are very much due to you, Diana, for a great deal of hard work. I'd better give you another pound. I can't believe that beef came out of the housekeeping. No, don't, please, refuse to take it. I must be allowed to pay for the food that's eaten in my own house.'

He frowned and his eyebrows shot up into almost vertical lines. I took it with a murmur of thanks, smiling to myself at the thought that a pound was about a quarter of what it had cost.

'I think it cheered him up,' continued Robert. 'I've a

suspicion that he's drinking rather a lot at the moment. I could smell whisky on his breath in the staff-room at lunch-time.'

'I noticed that his hands shake,' said Min. 'I don't think they did before. Poor Gerald! It's rotten for him. He's always so kind to the children. I forgive him everything for that. If only he wouldn't part his hair in the middle and wear so much scent. I'm surprised he doesn't wear a green carnation.'

'What does it matter what someone looks like?' said Robert irritably.

'Darling, you are naïve! It's incredibly important what people look like. When I think about someone, my mental picture of them is entirely coloured by their physical appearance. It's quite impossible to separate looks and character because the former has such an effect on the latter. Think of the difference it makes to someone's life if they are attractive to the opposite sex, for example.'

'I think that's a very superficial thing,' said Robert.

'The thing in itself is superficial,' I said as I put the knives into a jug of water to soak overnight. 'But its effects aren't. Men fall in love with some women and not with others. The plain ones may be better, cleverer, worthier, but men don't fall in love for those things. It's based solely on looks. Luckily it doesn't have much to do with whether people are happy or not or it would be dreadfully unfair.'

'But beauty isn't an absolute,' objected Robert.

'Well, there are unconsciously accepted models of physical beauty.' I polished the wax drips off the candelabras as I thought. 'It is possible to divide people generally into groups of attractive and unattractive with, obviously, some borderline cases. Fortunately many, perhaps most, people are seeking something other than romantic passion. In a way you might say that romantic love is only for the good-looking. The unattractive have to fall back on shared interests or something worthy like that. So it does bear Min's ideas out.'

Robert laughed. 'I don't believe a word of it. Never mind. I feel suddenly as if I don't care about anything. I suppose it's a combination of tiredness and alcohol but it's a good feeling. What did you think of Gerald? You seemed to get on all right.'

'I thought that he was intelligent, kind, truthful . . .' I paused, wondering what I did think ' . . . and that he was perhaps the unhappiest person I've ever met.'

# CHAPTER SIXTEEN

The next day was Thursday. After lunch Min and I packed three cakes and six bags of scones into the Land Rover and drove to the village hall. It was a depressing red-brick building, decorated inside with a great deal of flaking forest-green paint. Mrs Eccles separated herself from the crowd and came over to us.

'How do you do? You must be Mrs Weston's friend. I've heard all about you.'

From the wild curiosity of her glance it was clear that she'd heard Vivien's version. I sensed that she was disappointed that I wasn't wearing something flowing in scarlet chiffon. Most women were gathered around the cake stall, which in my limited experience of such goings-on was always the most popular. My cakes and scones were exclaimed over and given a prominent place. It seemed that however much Min was despaired of, she was still the resident of the biggest house in the area and therefore everything about her had a degree of importance. Min and I were put in charge of 'Pegging the Line', a sideshow in which the object was to see how many clothes-pegs you could fasten to a yard of string in one minute. The person who pegged the most won a basket of Rose du Bois talcum powder and bath-cubes.

As a game I thought it had a limited appeal. In fact it seemed to me impossible that anyone could care tuppence about it. I was quite wrong. Long after the cake stall had sold out (which happened about five minutes after the start of the bazaar) the inhabitants of Dunston Abchurch were queuing to 'peg the line' and Min and I were hoarse with yelling encouragement to our favourites. So partisan had I become, so determined that Miss Mipp, an octogenarian with knotted, arthritic hands, should win the Rose du Bois, at which she had cast such a longing look, that I added another ten pegs to her total when I wrote it down. Mrs Pickles from the village stores had the highest score but Min told Mrs Eccles that Miss Mipp had won it. At the close of the bazaar when the prize-winners were read out Mrs Pickles looked at us as a pike looks at minnows.

Min had won the 'Guess the Weight of the Fruit Cake' competition, entirely by luck. She might as well have been guessing the weight of a baby hippopotamus. I'd bought a teapot from the white elephant stall. It was Spode, absurdly cheap and, I hoped, didn't drip as badly as the one we generally used. Min had bought a salmon-pink, lace-trimmed, quilted handkerchief bag from the handiwork stall.

'I had to buy it,' she explained as we drove home. 'I asked Miss Sprockett, who was serving on the stall, what on earth it was for. She told me it was to keep handkerchiefs in. I said it looked more like something one might keep *risqué* underwear in . . . perhaps sequinned garters. Meaning it as a joke. But she got very red and sort of blew up like a frog and said that she'd made it. Of course, after that, I had to fork out ten shillings. It's a pity I haven't got any handkerchiefs. And after I'd been so generous the mean old thing said, with a nasty look at me, that she was avoiding the jams and pickles stall as she'd had such an unpleasant shock last year.'

We described the bazaar in some detail over tea and made Robert laugh. I'd bought lurid pink bath salts for Ellie from the home and beauty stall and, from the toy stall, a box of pastel chalks for William which were of professional quality, hardly used at all and worth far more than the two-and-sixpence I'd paid for them. I'd also bought, from the produce stall, pelargonium cuttings which had deliciously scented leaves.

'It's odd how enjoyable these things are,' I said musingly, meaning the bazaar. 'Full of bossy women and breathtakingly horrible things for sale, yet there is a community feeling about the whole thing that's very appealing.'

'Daisy's got her "Miss Read" look on,' said Min. 'Everything's grist to her mill, the prattle of barefoot, ragged children, old men bent over gnarled sticks, grumbling round the chestnut tree on the village green, the sparks from the smithy as Job, the handsome, muscular village blacksmith . . .' She went no further as I threatened her with a raised fruit cake.

We all slept late on Saturday. When I came down, the children had helped themselves to cereal and I could see them through the window, running about with brooms and buckets. A plan had been formulated over supper the night before that they would clean all the cobwebs, rubbish and dead leaves out of the boat-house so that we could begin to decorate it. I didn't expect that they would stick at it for long. The idea of doing things is, generally, so much more enthralling than the actual doing of them. I thought it ought to be one of the privileges of childhood to be able to indulge the excitement of these ideas without the laborious consequences, to make up in some measure for being constantly under instruction.

I was pleasantly surprised when they called me out two hours later to inspect their work. William had cleared the rafters of cobwebs and Ellie had dusted the window-seats and swept the floor. I asked them what they'd done with all the rubbish. They pointed proudly to the window. I looked out and saw a scum of leaves and shreds of newspaper on the ice-bound surface of the water, in which the ducks were wading, perhaps looking for spiders. It didn't really matter. It would all be absorbed as soon as there was a thaw. Ellie ran up to the house to get some bread for the ducks while I measured the windows. The walls would have to be painted. I would get a paint card from Mr Ransome the next time I went to Great Swosser so that Ellie could choose. It was now February. There was every chance that the weather would warm up between now and Ellie's birthday in a couple of weeks, so that we could paint in some kind of comfort. I was writing down measurements when I heard Ellie screaming.

I dropped my pencil and ran out. Ellie was running down the slope towards me, her mouth wide open and tears tumbling down her cheeks. I took her in my arms.

'He's done it! He's drowned them! Booty's kittens!' Grief overwhelmed her and she couldn't speak.

'What's up, El?' William had followed me out and was shaken out of his customary insouciance by his sister's anguish.

'Look after her,' I said. 'I'm going to speak to that man!'

I walked so fast up to the house and round to the barn that I was panting by the time I got to the cornbin. It was empty, apart from two plates with particles of Booty's breakfast adhering. I went outside. There was a bucket by the barn door. I steeled myself and looked in. There was an inch or two of water in the bottom but no bedraggled, furry bodies. Suddenly George Pryke appeared in person, round the corner, pushing the barrow I'd given him. Presumably he'd used it to take them off and bury them. The sight of the barrow was enough to fan my anger to a blaze. I stalked over to him.

'What have you done! I told you not to drown them! It was cruel! Unforgivable! How could you!'

George licked his lower lip with his tongue and began to chortle.

'I takes my orders from Mr Weston. I ain't goin' to be ordered about by a pack o' women.'

'In that case I'll have that barrow back!'

I took hold of the rim of the barrow and began to pull it away.

'Oh, no, you don't!' said George, gripping the handle tightly and pulling in his turn. 'This 'ere barrow's mine!'

'It's not your barrow any more! You broke our agreement! Let go! You pig!'

We were shouting at each other and struggling over the barrow as Ellie and William rounded the corner. Ellie ran to my side and tried to help me get the barrow away. George Pryke was obviously enjoying himself for his tongue was revolving like mad as he grinned and grunted.

'You absolute bastard!' I yelled, beside myself with fury, tears running down my face now. 'I'd like to put your fat head into a bucket and drown you like those poor . . . little . . .'

I gave a sob and felt a pair of arms close round me and heard Robert's voice saying in my ear, 'It's all right, Daisy! It's all right! No one's drowned the kittens! Come on, everyone, calm down. Ellie, let go of the barrow!'

I looked at Robert in astonishment.

'The mother cat moved them herself,' Robert went on, letting me go and stroking Ellie's head. 'I saw her, not half an hour ago, carrying them one by one into the cow-shed. Come on, look, I'll show you.'

We followed Robert into the disused cow-shed. There, in a manger of muddy hay, lay Booty, licking her kittens. She looked up at us and gave a little mew when she saw Ellie. Ellie bent down, still crying, and began to kiss her passionately. Robert picked up one of the kittens and stroked it with a finger that looked ridiculously large next to the squirming ginger body.

'Wonderful, isn't it?' he said, laughing as it spat at him. 'A mother's instinct to take care of her young.'

He put the kitten back in the manger.

'I've made an idiot of myself,' I said, feeling very embarrassed. 'I'd better go and apologise to George Pryke. Why didn't he say he hadn't drowned them?'

'Don't worry about it. I should have been very upset myself if he really had drowned them. I expect he enjoyed the drama of it.'

'But, Daddy! He always does drown them!' cried Ellie, looking up at him through wet spectacles. 'He says you told him to!'

'Do you really think I'd tell him to do such a thing? When you remember that all through your childhood I've made you return tadpoles and ladybirds and caterpillars to wherever you found them.'

'I remember you were furious with me when I killed that butterfly,' said William, with some feeling.

'Then you might have known that I'd never tell George to drown the kittens. Ellie, you should have had more faith in me. I'm going to speak to him.'

He went out into the yard while we hung around the manger and made a fuss of Booty. Later that morning I found George by the compost heap. He stuck his fork in the pile when he saw me coming and stood with his hands on his hips, grinning.

'I must apologise, Mr Pryke.' I wanted to smash his face in. 'I'm afraid I lost my temper.'

'Another time per'aps you'll make sure o' your facts afore calling folks names,' he said, narrowing his eyes in a sinister way.

'Yes, I was mistaken. I'm sorry.'

It was nearly killing me but it had to be gone through.

'There's some folks would 'and in their notice after bein' called a pig. And a bastard. Surprisin' that young ladies know these words.'

'Well, it was all said in anger. It's best forgotten,' I said, turning to go.

'Where'd Mr Weston be, then, if I'd 'anded in me notice?'

I repressed the obvious answer. No point in piling Pelion upon Ossa.

'O' course you could make it up to me, if you'd a mind. Missus is still in 'ospital. A chap gets lonely. A wench with a temper's pretty fiery all round, I've found.'

'Oh, for goodness sake!' Vivien had a great deal to answer for. 'Please keep your horrible insinuations to yourself or I shall report you to Mr Weston!'

George licked his lips very slowly, with an evil look in his eye.

'From what I've 'eard Mr Weston's been puttin' it about a bit, too. Why should 'e 'ave all the fun?'

Suddenly he put out a hand to grab me. I evaded his outstretched fingers and ran back to the house. Robert was in the kitchen, talking to Ellie. He saw that I was very angry and very out of breath.

'What's the matter? Have you had another row with him?'

'Yes. Never mind.' I didn't want to talk about it in front of Ellie. 'I'll get on with lunch if I'm not interrupting anything.'

By the time I'd cooked it and we'd all eaten it, I'd calmed down. I took the dressing off Min's hand. It was healing very well. There was plenty of new, pink skin and she said that it hardly hurt her at all now.

'I'm so glad those Americans are renting your house so you can't go yet, even though my hand is nearly better. But you must do some of your own work.'

I knew she was right. I took *Nightmare Abbey* up to my room to do a little quiet reading and after two pages fell deeply asleep.

We drove to St Lawrence's in the Morris Traveller, which was more cramped than the Land Rover, but less dirty. Muriel the baby-sitter and the children were having baked beans and fish fingers in front of the television. I didn't have high expectations of the evening but Min was actively dreading it.

The school was early nineteenth century and surprisingly handsome, though spoilt by the usual proliferation of modern outbuildings and huts in the grounds. The assembly hall was in the main school and must once have been a beautiful room before its walls were covered with wooden boards recording head boys and rugby captains. A large and ugly stage had been put in at one end. The room was spacious and there was a small dance floor in the middle of the tables. The whole building smelt strongly of floor polish, disinfectant and Brussels sprouts. We wandered about the headmaster's drawing room with glasses of wine before the gong rang for dinner.

Robert and I were on the same table but too far away to talk. I was seated between a little, fat, bald man, who taught maths, and the school Bursar. The Bursar, who asked me to call him Alastair, was a retired major, who talked without pause. He chuckled after everything he said, effectively drowning my replies, to which he never paid the slightest heed. As he drank, his face, which was round and pink, became damper and shinier until it was covered with fine drops like crystal beads. He got out his handkerchief and mopped, but that merely smoothed the drops into a glistening sheen.

He had an endless repertoire of stories from his travels with the Army which I quite enjoyed hearing. He assumed that I was middle-class, good-natured, uneducated, voted Conservative, belonged to the Church of England and was contented with my lot. It was clearly his way to assume this about everyone. It made for restful if unstimulating conversation. It was with some reluctance that I turned to the mathematician whose name was Gordon and who looked a much tougher nut to crack.

Gordon seemed depressed to find that I had no children. It was obviously the only topic of conversation he felt safe with when talking to women. I discovered that he had four children. We covered their ages, genders, schools, music lessons, temperaments, their strengths (very many), their weaknesses (hardly any), their physical progress and his anxiety as to the shortness of his two sons.

'You know,' he confided in me, his glossy pate reflecting the candlelight, 'I suffered a good deal as a boy because I was short. You wouldn't think it to look at me now but I was the shortest boy in my class and it was very painful to me.'

Of course I didn't say that I could well believe it as, standing up, I could have used his bald head to rest my chin on, if I'd been so inclined. Instead I widened my eyes and looked sympathetic.

'I'd have given up my place at the top of the class, willingly, for an extra nine inches. It's difficult for a woman to understand that, perhaps, but for a man, lack of height is a severe humiliation.'

'I can understand it,' I said. 'If you asked any woman whether she'd rather be beautiful and dim or clever and ugly, my bet is that she'll choose the former. I would myself. Shocking, isn't it?'

I smiled, remembering the conversation with Robert and Min about the importance of looks. Here was our argument neatly illustrated. Min was right. Robert was in many ways naïve.

'Anyway, the most marvellous thing happened to me,' continued Gordon. 'At Cambridge I met my future wife and I grew several inches, at the same time.'

'Is your wife here this evening?' I asked, wondering if she was the kind of woman whose admiration would add cubits to a man's stature.

'Yes. Over there. In the brown dress. She's looking this way.'

He waved to a woman on the next table, whose huge front teeth and thick-lensed spectacles flashed light at us like a beacon signalling the arrival of the French. He told me all about his wife as we grappled with breasts of a hard, dry chicken, masked by an undistinguished sauce which bore a puzzling resemblance to semolina in both texture and sweetness, and some very wet Brussels sprouts. Over pudding – brittle, yellow sponge-cake, bottled cherries and ice-cream – I talked again to Alastair, whose face by now was like the wall of a grotto, dripping with plashy rills. He told me all about the various fiascos it had been his lot to deal with while serving with the British Army in Egypt.

I began to have that feeling of strain which comes over me if not allowed to play any part in the conversational game but return of serve. It was a relief when the musicians struck up on the stage, though it was not a very good band. The Bursar grabbed me at once and we were first on to the floor. Fortunately he could dance, though in that bouncing, bobbing way that makes one's calves ache. His left hand was marshy and his right burned hotly against my back. He steered me firmly around the floor, holding tight, as though he thought I might try to make a dash for it. I suspected that he'd frequently had to dance with the inebriated wives of the top brass and wasn't taking any chances on his partner suddenly keeling over.

Gordon and his wife joined us on the dance floor and jigged around, their cheeks pressed together. The Bursar took me back to my seat and then went off to talk to a parent. Robert, at the other end of the table, was having an argument with a woman who had clearly been sinking more of the Nuits-St-Georges than was good for her. She kept putting her hand on Robert's arm and was gazing intently into his face. He looked more and more annoyed. Min was on another table and I could only just see the top of her head. I looked around the room and caught the eye of a young man. He stood out from the other diners, partly because he was the only person not wearing a dinner-jacket. Instead he was dressed in a crumpled corduroy suit with a large yellow bow-tie. He had very long straight dark hair and wore an expression of deep discontent. He wasn't talking to his neighbours but staring moodily at me. I looked away and saw Gerald threading his way through the tables towards me.

'Diana! What a dress! Gladden my heart and twirl with me around this silly little floor.'

Gerald's dancing was of the slow, shuffling variety which requires no concentration. We talked very happily about London and our favourite restaurants. From there we went on to our favourite books. It was an undemanding conversation during which we found a great many tastes in common. He was palpably more relaxed and less affected than he had been at Weston Hall. We stayed on the floor for the next dance and I was resigning myself quite cheefully to circling aimlessly about with Gerald for the rest of the evening, when a woman came up to us and struck Gerald smartly on the arm.

'Come and talk to Mrs Buchanan,' she barked, ignoring me. 'She's making noises about a contribution to the library fund.'

'Oh God! The tedium!' muttered Gerald to me, as he took me back to my table. 'I'll hope to dance with you again when I've sewn this thing up.'

Robert was still arguing with the same woman, who was almost cross-eyed with alcohol-poisoning by now. He seemed to imagine that he had a listening, comprehending audience for he was making points with great forcefulness, striking them off on his fingers. I felt a touch on my shoulder. It was the moody young man who'd been staring at me earlier.

'Care to dance?' he asked, very offhandedly.

We made a circuit of the floor, much to the detriment of my shoes for he was not a good dancer. The next time round we did better.

'Sorry,' he apologised, unconvincingly. 'I never learned to dance. I thought this sort of thing was a racial memory. I never saw so many extinct species.'

He explained that he was the new art master. It was his first job after university and he was loathing it.

'Everyone here's hopelessly out of touch with anything important. They think that life begins and ends with a public-school education. And this is a very fourth-rate public school at that. And the things they teach the boys! Crap like Shakespeare. I ask you!'

I said that I'd always thought Shakespeare rather a good writer and what fault did he have to find with him?

'He's dead, that's what's wrong with him! They've never read anything by great living poets. Ginsberg, Corso, William Burroughs. I don't suppose you've ever heard of them?'

He looked down his nose at me, his eyelids weighted with disillusion.

'Oh yes, I have, actually. What was that thing called when Ginsberg did unspeakable things to himself in a hotel bedroom with a broom handle? And I suppose everyone's read *The Naked Lunch*? It's rather dated now, surely?'

The young man, whose name, appropriately, was Storm, looked startled. I didn't tell him that I had taught hordes of young men with the same views and the same haircut, all in dreadful fits of sulking and rage. I had read the authors he mentioned in order to acquaint myself with their gods. Frankly I felt that Shakespeare had the edge. Storm clutched me a little closer as a fellow-traveller in a philistine world. He was a good-looking young man. I was only sorry that he appeared to me to be very little older than William.

'This is going to be a good evening after all,' he whispered into my ear.

I wasn't so certain. He abandoned his conventional hold on me and draped his hands on my shoulders, in a manner calculated to draw attention to us.

'What sort of painting are you doing at the moment?' I asked, twisting my face away so that his hair didn't get into my mouth.

He gave a bitter laugh and began to stroke my neck. I was sure that other members of staff would notice this before too long and that it would do him no good.

'I've given up painting. That's just uptight, élitist mythology. I'm interested in pure statement. What's the matter?'

I'd heaved a sigh, unconsciously.

'Nothing. Except . . . isn't everyone doing that at the moment?'

'All the time. Every time a tramp urinates on the roadside . . . it's a statement.' He laughed his bitter laugh again.

'Well, it sounds pretty boring and pointless to me.' I tried to discourage him from fiddling about with the top hook of my dress. 'I think I'd like to sit down now.'

'Yes, let's go up to my room. We could have a smoke. And maybe screw. Or are you too conventional?'

He looked at me in a moody, tantalising way. I reminded myself that he was wholly unsuited by age and temperament for the world in which he found himself and he was probably thoroughly miserable.

'Yes, I'm too conventional,' I said quietly. 'And boys are not to my taste.'

'You've got a pretty good idea of yourself,' he said, flushing angrily. 'There's a name for women like you.'

'Diana! Our dance, isn't it?'

I was in Robert's arms and we were quickstepping away. My mind darted back for a moment to the evening, fifteen years ago, when Hugh Anstey had rescued me from the repulsive Bunny. All the characters were different, including myself, but the sensation of enormous relief was the same.

'Was that fellow being a nuisance? He's a bit of a fool. I don't think he'll stay the course.'

'He's just a baby really. I think I was a little unkind.'

'I expect he deserved it. I saw him pawing your neck. Hardly the occasion. That woman I was sitting next to was drunk, I think. Anyway, she slipped off her chair and hit her head. I was able to make my escape while people were rushing about with sticking-plaster. What an evening! I'm sorry I got you into this. It seems worse than usual.'

'It doesn't matter,' I said, smiling and beginning to enjoy myself for Robert was a very good dancer, to my surprise.

'We mustn't make a habit of this,' said Robert, suddenly.

'Of what?'

'Oh, nothing. Sorry, I wasn't thinking.' He looked down at me and smiled kindly. 'Poor Daisy. You were upset.'

Then I knew that he had meant that it was the second time that day that he had held me in his arms. It was such an un-Robert-like remark that I was taken aback. I had always associated Robert in my mind with non-sexual male symbols like Father Christmas and Uncle Mac. It was as surprising as though Mr Pastry had given me a little floury squeeze. I had, of course, recognised that he was a good-looking man, in just the way that I might acknowledge the fine barley-sugar carving on a Caroline chair. The moment I thought this, I suspected myself of untruthfulness.

'Poor Ellie has been badly hurt by the whole business,' continued Robert. 'I thought, when I talked to her, that her feelings about George and the drowning of the kittens amounted almost to a phobia. Or do I mean a trauma?'

'I think you're right. I think it happens to children more than we realise. Impressions are so vivid and they don't have the experience or ability to detach themselves.'

'You've been very good to her.'

'I'm extremely fond of her.'

We reversed quite stylishly and I saw a woman, who was sitting at one of the tables nearby, staring at us with absorbed attention. She was thirtyish, rather pretty in a faded kind of way, with fair curly hair and a flowered dress. She caught my eye, blushed and looked away. But in less than a minute she was staring at us again, or rather at Robert. There was a yearning look in her eyes and I suddenly made the connection.

'Don't look now,' I said to Robert, 'but your Miss Mingot is looking at you as though she wants to wrap you up and take you home. Should you ask her to dance, do you think?'

'Damn!' He steered us to another part of the floor. 'Certainly not. I don't want her to think that there's the faintest possibility . . . I'm sorry, that sounds disgustingly conceited. You know what I mean.'

'I do. Poor girl! And I bet she's spent weeks having fantasies that you might ask her. You really don't think that just to give her a few minutes' happiness . . .?'

'Now, Daisy. You're off-duty, remember. The affairs of the Weston family can go to hell for one evening.'

'A just rebuke. I'm getting dreadfully bossy.'

'You're not hurt?' He looked down at me anxiously. His eyes were very dark, like Vivien's.

'Not a bit.'

And I wasn't. It was the third time he had called me Daisy. Then we stopped talking as we'd danced up to the platform where the band was and it was too noisy to hear each other. We continued to dance without speaking. He danced so well that we seemed to float about the floor together as though we were gliding on glass. It felt very comfortable to be silent. We must have danced for three or four dances, not even stopping when the music did, for suddenly they were playing 'Auld Lang Syne' and we were obliged to join hands with everyone else in a large circle and, as usual, we all looked very silly. We said goodbye to Gerald and drove back to Weston Hall.

'Poor Daisy,' said Min, from the back seat of the Morris. 'Was it absolute hell? Did you see Ginevra Yorke being carried out in a state of unconsciousness? Her dress was torn and her poor husband kept trying to cover her up with his coat. Her head was covered with sticking-plaster. She was sitting next to you, Robert. Your small-talk seems to have had a devastating effect.'

'It wasn't anything to do with me,' said Robert, with indignation. 'The wretched woman was drunk. I was doing my best to explain to her about Kennedy and the Bay of Pigs. She'd thought that Pigs referred to the Cubans. She said she thought it was rather an inflammatory way to refer to them. I ask you!'

'Darling! Poor woman! She must have been dreadfully bored. No wonder she turned to drink.'

'Not at all!' Robert's voice in the darkness sounded cross and made me smile to myself. 'She kept saying how fascinating it was. In fact that was all she said. "How fascinating. Do go on." If anyone had a right to be bored it was me. She was the dullest woman I've met for a long time.'

'Darling, you say that about all the women you sit next to!'

'Probably. Anyway this one seemed sillier than all the rest put together.'

'That was no reason to try to tear her dress off her.'

'Good God, that would be the very last thing I'd want to do! I saw a great deal more of her underwear than I cared for, as it was. Her straps kept slipping off her shoulders. She seemed not to be able to manage her clothes at all.'

Both Min and I burst into hoots of laughter.

'Are other men excited by corsetry? It sounds very Edwardian.'

We speculated about this all the way home.

## CHAPTER SEVENTEEN

The next morning, Sunday, I awoke to the sound of rain falling fast against my window. A sulky sky cast a dimness over the landscape. The trees were bare again and the snow had turned the depressing colour of mould. It was a day for books and large fires. As soon as I'd cleared away breakfast I lit the fire in the drawing-room so that it would be warm enough to sit in after lunch. I prepared vegetables, made a chocolate mousse, incorporating the juice of a Seville orange, as instructed by my mentor whose book was already beginning to split at the seams. I would send Horace a new copy as soon as I returned home. Home, as I thought of it, seemed much farther away than the other side of England. It seemed to have lost something of its usual allure. Perhaps that was as well as there were two more weeks to spend at Weston Hall. I put the leg of lamb into the oven and decided to write a letter to Peter.

After so many years of friendship, there was little we concealed from each other. I told him all about Min and how happy I was to be with her. I described Weston Hall, its beauties and its drawbacks. I told him a little about Ellie and William and gave a detailed account of my friendship with Charles as far as it had gone, as I knew Peter was incurably romantic and loved to hear details of other people's affairs. He had once accused himself of disgraceful prurience but I knew it wasn't that. It was an enjoyment of heightened emotion. I also wrote about the supper with Gerald and Vivien. I said quite a lot about Vivien, thinking that Peter would be amused by her. I described the bazaar and the St Lawrence's Ball, hoping to make him laugh. It took me over an hour. I read the letter through afterwards and was tolerably pleased with it. Then I realised that there was something missing altogether from the summary. I had said not a word about Robert. The telephone began to ring.

A woman's voice asked for Robert. She didn't say who she was, which I thought ill-mannered but it wasn't my telephone so I didn't inquire. I went into the library. For once there was no music playing. Robert was sitting in his chair behind the desk, holding a pen in his hand and staring out of the window at the rain. The room was shadowed and gloomy and the pattern of falling rain flickered on the papers in front of him. He was far away in his own thoughts and when I spoke, he started and looked quite shocked.

I went back to the kitchen and put on the vegetables. Ellie came in two minutes later.

'I've been playing with the kittens. The tabby one's getting quite friendly. Booty's getting fatter. Should I try to comb her fur, do you think?'

'I think it would be better to cut the tangles out.'

'She's getting fatter and I'm getting thinner! Look!'

She pulled out the waistband of her skirt. 'This used to be so tight it gave me a tummy ache.'

'Ellie! I admire you! That's self-discipline. Well done!'

Ellie put her arms around me. 'I started off doing it to please you but now it's me who's pleased.'

The door opened and Robert came in, looking furious. He poured himself a glass of champagne, which he usually rejected in favour of one of his own bottles of claret, so I knew he was upset.

'That bloody woman, Ginevra Yorke! You know, that ridiculous woman I was sitting next to last night. She's asked me to have lunch at her house tomorrow to discuss the Library Appeal Fund.'

'What? Who?' asked Min, coming in and only catching part of what Robert was saying.

'She's giving a lunch for the Appeal Committee. Of course I'll have to go. It will look odd if I'm the only one not there.'

'Why shouldn't you go?' asked Min, taking the glass of champagne I held out to her.

'When I accepted the lunch, she suggested that we met at the Golden Hind for a drink this evening. Her husband left for Tehran this morning. She made a point of telling me that. It was a cold-blooded assignation!'

He looked crosser than ever when Min and I began to laugh. 'It isn't funny! It's disgraceful!'

'Sorry, darling. It's your outraged virtue that's funny. Women constantly receive propositions of this kind.'

'Well, I'm sorry for them, in that case. It put me in the most embarrassing position. I was forced to be almost rude to get out of it. What's the matter?'

Min and I were helpless with laughter. At that moment the telephone began to ring.

'Oh God, if it's her again I'm out.'

I picked up the receiver.

'Person-to-person call from South Africa for Miss Fairfax.'

'Speaking.'

Then I heard Charles's voice.

'Diana. How are you?'

'Oh, Charles! Very well.'

'It's good to hear your voice. I'm not coming back for a while. There are various problems here. How much longer are you staying with the Westons?'

'Certainly another two weeks. After that I don't know. I ought to go home and do some work. I can't concentrate here.'

'Too much housework?'

'Yes, but I'm loving it.'

'I wish I was loving it here. It's terribly frustrating. There's a strike on at one of the mines.'

'How is it otherwise? How are the wide-open spaces? And the lack of tiresome Englishmen?'

He laughed. 'The wide-open spaces are tremendous. I always forget how beautiful it is. Light pours down on to the mountains like liquid from a cup. But there's one great flaw.'

'What's that?'

'You're not here.'

'I don't know what I ought to say to that.'

'All right. Don't get worried. I just wanted to hear your voice. I'll ring in another week. Goodbye, Diana.'

'Goodbye, Charles.'

Then he'd rung off. I felt cross with myself. I'd been too guarded. I might at least have said that it was nice of him to have telephoned. I went back into the kitchen.

'It's all right. It was Charles,' I said, seeing Robert looking at me with a hunted expression.

'Well, that takes the biscuit, I must say,' said Min. 'Everyone's having romantic telephone calls except for me. I feel jolly left out. What did he say?'

'Only that he isn't coming back on Friday, after all. There are problems at the mine.'

'I'm sorry. Are you very disappointed?'

'I don't know.'

The next day, I had lunch with Vivien. The Dower House was on the edge of the park, only a quarter of a mile from Weston Hall, so I walked there. The rain had stopped and the snow lay in curiously shaped mounds like meringues. Much of it had disappeared altogether and for the first time I saw grass. There was a cold, damp wind blowing but a hint of blue in the sky. Suddenly I was impatient for spring. I stopped and looked up at a cedar of Lebanon. Its great needled branches spread like horizontal fans, forming a *treillage* which reminded me of the ceiling of King's College Chapel. But it wasn't spring in Cambridge I longed for. Min had several times suggested that I stay on after the Americans had left my house. I was tempted. But I would have to get down to some proper work.

Vivien's house was, as Min had said, Queen Anne and quite lovely. Yew hedges, fifteen feet tall, ran at right angles to the house towards the iron railings in front of it, framing the façade and making a square garden which was planted with box and standard rose trees. The proportions of the house were perfect. Inside it was warm and very bright. Vivien had used bold colours to great effect. The drawing room into which I was shown by a neat and competent-looking maid was painted cantaloupe-pink. Her furniture and paintings were good. I accepted a glass of sherry and was glad that I'd bothered to put on my tweed coat and skirt, now back from the dry cleaner's. Vivien was wearing an aubergine-coloured dress bound with heavy black braid. It suited her flamboyance. Her black eyes were sharp with curiosity.

'Now, Diana, tell me how they all are at the Hall. Minerva calls you something else. Dahlia, is it?'

'Daisy.'

'How dreadfully *ingénue*. I prefer Dahlia. It suits you. There's something rather glossy yet stiff about you. No, stiff isn't the right word. Strait-laced, perhaps.'

I was annoyed as I knew she intended me to be but I took care not to show it.

'Everyone is very well. Min's hand is almost better.'

'So you're leaving soon? That's a great pity. Robert and Minerva are so bored with one another. It will be frightful for them to be stuck with each other again.'

I laughed. 'That's nonsense, Vivien. They must be about the happiest married couple I know.'

'That's a very Dahlia sort of remark. It conjures up appalling pictures of three-piece suites and bedroom slippers. Hector and I were never happy for two days together. But that stopped it being dull, thank God!'

'Hector?'

'Robert's father. At least so he thought. *I* think it was probably a man called Conrad Denzil who came to catalogue the library just after Hector and I were married.'

She sighed and looked almost wistful.

'I hope it was Conrad. He was a tremendously good lover. Hector was pretty hopeless. Awfully silent and intent, as though he was doing accounts. You know, a duty requiring concentration. Luckily he was so repressed by years at boarding school that he preferred . . . what was it called then? . . . self-abuse. But when he found out that I'd been unfaithful he got tremendously roused. It's odd how people can't give up the habit of unhappiness if their childhoods are unpleasant enough. Now Conrad was fun.'

Over lunch, served by the maid who seemed inured to Vivien's style of conversation, I heard more details of her past. She ate a very large portion of salmon and hollandaise. I had a more moderate lunch which I enjoyed very much. She was curious to know why I hadn't married, as I suppose many people were but were too polite to inquire the reason. Vivien knew no such inhibitions.

'You're not a lesbian, are you? I did wonder, seeing you and Minerva together. You seem suspiciously fond.'

'I'm not. I do like women but I don't want to go to bed with them.'

'I've only done it once. I was staying with the Pentecosts. Pamela Pentecost is a well-known sapphist. One must always fall in with one's hostess's plans, however one may dislike church, long walks or tennis. This was a good deal more interesting than all three but I couldn't get used to all that hair and softness. And of course it's nothing but a sort of endless fondling. Madly frustrating and pointless really.'

The maid, whose name was Lily, held a dish of profiteroles from which I was to help myself. Her pale blue eyes were quite blank. I managed to get Vivien off the subject of sex for twenty minutes while we talked about gardening, which she turned out to like and to be quite knowledgeable about. After she'd eaten three-quarters of the profiteroles we went back into the drawing room. We drank coffee and smoked cigarettes and I complimented her on the elegance of her house.

'It's easy to have a good house if there's money,' she said, blowing perfect smoke-rings up to the ceiling. 'Robert's a fool. Come to think of it, he's so like Hector . . . obstinate and stuffy . . . he probably is Hector's son after all. But Hector was never squeamish. He adored hunting and was an excellent shot. Robert always hid himself away with a book. He was such a nervous boy. Until he went away to school. Then he became silent and it was no longer possible to tell what he was thinking. Hector died during Robert's first term at prep school. It was bad timing. Although they were so different Robert loved his father. More than he loved me, actually.'

Vivien drew on her cigarette, reflectively. Something of her habitual, hectic gaiety was dampened and I sensed that this was a rare moment of truthfulness.

'Hector had a stroke. He was only forty-two. Robert came home for the funeral. He hardly spoke. He didn't cry. His skin looked like rice-paper . . . grey and translucent. He wouldn't talk to me at all. It was as though he blamed me.' Vivien shrugged. 'I tried to explain about the stroke but Robert wouldn't even look at me. His eyes had that sort of baffled look that I've seen in them since, when he's hurt. Dear me, I've made myself gloomy, remembering it all. Anyway,' she laughed and stubbed out her cigarette with great firmness as though finishing with unpleasant memories, 'I expect he's passionately in love with you by now and as wax in your hands. Why don't you persuade him to run the estate and then we can all be comfortable? Now, say you will, Dahlia dear?'

'I'm sorry, Vivien. Robert isn't the least bit in love with me and even if he were I shouldn't try to persuade him to do something he so clearly doesn't want to do. He feels quite badly enough about it. I certainly wouldn't want him to feel more guilty than he does.'

'Does he, do you think?' Vivien narrowed her eyes against the smoke of a fresh cigarette.

I thought for a moment. I didn't want to betray Robert's confidence but I didn't imagine that he would tell me things that were strictly not for broadcasting. I decided it wouldn't do Vivien any harm to know how her son felt. I knew that she delighted to shock and appear mischievous, even malefic, but I thought that I had glimpsed something softer during this conversation.

'He's worried about the children. William, especially. The school he goes to isn't doing him any good. It's impossible for him to fit in.'

'Because the summit of his parents' ambition lies beyond two weeks of drunkenness on the Costa del Sol?'

'Well . . .'

'Oh come on, Dahlia, let's be frank.'

'William's very good at art. He needs to go to a school where it's well-taught.'

'And I'm supposed to pay for this? I don't like not having my own way. I admit it. But if Robert will meet me halfway I might think about coughing up the school fees. Tell him that if he saves me money by doing the accounting for the estate, I'll pay a thousand a year for William's school. He can keep that silly job as a schoolmaster if he wants. I don't care.'

Vivien frowned and stared into the fire. I saw that she felt that she was being absurdly magnanimous in climbing down from her original terms.

'I can't tell Robert that. He'd be livid and say it wasn't my business. And he'd be perfectly right. Why don't you come to tea one day this week and put it to him yourself?'

Vivien wriggled in her chair. 'I don't see why I've got to do all the work. He was bloody rude about it when last we talked about money. Why should *I* come crawling? It's *his* child.'

'And your grandson.'

Vivien tossed her head and looked sullen.

'Do come, Vivien. I'll make a chocolate cake and we'll have it by the fire. If you decide you don't want to talk to Robert about it, then you needn't. I shan't mention it to anyone.'

'Well . . . all right.' Then she giggled. 'Don't think I don't know you're trying to bribe me with the cake. I'm not a child, though you're treating me like one.'

'I *was* hoping it might do the trick.'

I thoroughly enjoyed my walk back through the park. I was stuffed with good food and Vivien's company was invigorating in small quantities. The wind was warmer and a great deal more snow had melted. The beauty of the great stands of oak, ash, beech and chestnut, all growing with enough space to develop their proper shapes, filled me with delight. In a hollow a group of snowdrops bloomed, their white bells blotched with green. I thought of Wordsworth's lines, 'the meanest flower that blows can give, Thoughts that do often lie too deep for tears.'

I was happy. I thought that I could not have done harm by my talk with Vivien and might have done good. When I got back I would feed Ham and Booty and do something about supper. I would check the drawing-room fire first of all in case Min had forgotten to keep it going. I'd make those little pancakes for tea which everyone loved. I smiled to myself as I recognised a sense of profound satisfaction. I enjoyed most of my work at Cambridge and had thought I was happy. But this simple job, supplying the needs of Min's family, gave me much more pleasure.

I felt necessary to other people's lives and I loved the feeling. For the first time in my life I wanted children, to have someone other than myself to work for, worry about, plan for. I wanted to make someone else happy, to engage with every kind of experience, even the banal, boring and mindless. As I neared Weston Hall Ham dashed out to meet me. We ran the rest of the way together and reached the kitchen hot and breathless. I hung up my duffle-coat, blew up the drawing-room fire with bellows and got down to supper: chicken in a béchamel sauce with cheese and breadcrumbs. I was a little doubtful about this recipe but if Elizabeth David recommended it it *must* be all right. Just as I'd finished making the batter for the pancakes, the children came home and Min, drawn by the sound of our voices, joined us.

'Mummy, you've got your jersey on inside out,' said Ellie. 'I hope you haven't been out anywhere today. I hate the thought of people laughing.'

'Don't worry, darling. I haven't been anywhere. I've only seen Mrs Butter today. I've worked very, very hard and it's almost ready to send off to the publishers. When it's finished we must have a celebration. What shall we do?'

The usual difficulties arose that occur in any family trying to choose a holiday. Each had an entirely different idea of what might be enjoyable and everyone looked on the suggestions of the others with scornful distaste. Ellie wanted to go to Winkleigh Zoo. William wanted to go to the cinema and see the latest James Bond film. Min and I wanted to go shopping and have lunch in a decent restaurant. While we were arguing about the best plans, Robert came home. He was silent and seemed abstracted. When the children had gone up to their rooms to do their homework and Min had gone off to polish a few sentences he stayed behind in the kitchen.

'All right, spill the beans,' I said inelegantly.

He looked surprised.

'How did you know there was something to spill?'

'Not difficult. A single-cell amoeba could hardly help recognising that something has happened to annoy you.'

'Yes, it has, actually, but I thought I'd better not mention it in front of Min in case she got upset.' I lifted my eyebrows in what I hoped was an encouraging manner and Robert continued. 'When I arrived at Ginevra Yorke's house for the Appeal Committee lunch I found I was the only guest. I'd been on break duty at eleven so I hadn't been near the staff-room or I might have found out that no one else was going. Ginevra told me that they'd all had lunch-time clubs or meetings and that in the end I was the only one to accept. She simpered . . . that's the only word for it . . . and accused me of being ungallant. I asked her what gallantry had to do with it. I suggested we make another arrangement for a lunch-time when everyone could come. I'd put my coat back on and was just going to the front door when she burst into tears.'

'So you realised then that it was all a ruse to get you alone to her house?'

Robert nodded. 'Mad as it may seem, the woman was trying to . . . what's the word?'

'Compromise your virtue?' I said, with an unsuccessful attempt to repress a smile.

'Now, Daisy, this is serious. The poor woman's demented, I

think. She should be receiving some sort of psychiatric help. Well, if you're just going to roar with laughter I shan't tell you any more.'

'Sorry, sorry. I really want to hear. Go on. I'm quite serious now.'

Robert looked at me suspiciously but I maintained a solemn expression.

'Of course, I felt obliged to stay and ask her what the matter was. She told me she was terribly lonely. I pointed out that her husband had been gone scarcely twenty-four hours but she said it wasn't that kind of loneliness. It appears that her husband is a brute and drinks. She told me all about it.'

'I suppose it's a variation on "My wife doesn't understand me",' I murmured.

'Well, you can be cynical if you like but I felt dreadfully sorry for her. The fellow is obviously perverted. He likes to strap her to the bed and . . . well, perhaps I'd better not go into it. He must be some kind of sexual psychopath. And yet he seems quite a decent, straightforward man. What on earth is funny about that?'

'It didn't occur to you,' I said, laughing very much despite my best efforts, 'that she was trying to . . . turn you on?'

'No, of course not. I . . . Good God, the little trollop! You mean she was making it all up? And I fell for it! I must be the world's biggest fool!'

Robert's expression changed from amazement to anger and then he began to laugh.

'If I were you, I'd tell Min,' I said. 'I can't imagine her being upset or jealous about it. After all, you didn't take up the invitation.'

'I thought she closed the front door with unnecessary force. Good God, it's finished me for ever as far as women are concerned.'

'I'm very sorry to hear that,' said Min, coming in. 'What has?'

'Oh darling, just some ridiculous nonsense of Ginerva Yorke's. Why have you got your jersey on inside out?'

As I'd expected, Min enjoyed the tale of attempted seduction enormously and wasn't in the least put out.

'I'm impressed,' she said, eating the raw carrots out of the pan as fast as I could scrape them. 'From what Daisy tells me,

most men would have been flinging their clothes off in the hall
and getting down to it.'

Robert looked at me, inquiringly. I smiled enigmatically and
fetched another bag of carrots.

The next day it was warm enough to be able to paint. Ellie had
chosen primrose-yellow for the boat-house walls. I went
straight after breakfast to Mr Ransome and bought the paint,
some brushes, a roller, some white spirit, sugar soap and
sandpaper. Min said she'd come and help me after lunch, so I
made a start on my own. The washing-down and sandpaper-
ing was tedious and took me all morning. I went in to make
some egg sandwiches and a flask of coffee for our picnic lunch.
Mrs Butter was putting on her coat to go home.

I thought she didn't seem quite as chirpy as usual, so I asked
her how Roly, her son, was. He seemed generally to be the
fulcrum of her thoughts.

'It isn't what Stanley would have thought right. A year
Roly's been out of work. Now he says he's been offered two
jobs and he hasn't decided which to take. My Stanley were
forty year in the biscuit factory. He started as the tea boy and
ended up head clerk in bookkeeping. Steady and respectable,
that was my Stanley. Spit on a stone and it'll be wet at last.'

'Has Roly been living on the dole?'

'Eh now!' Mrs Butter's eyes flashed. Her eye-shadow was
fashionably pink which made her look as though she was
suffering from blepharitis. 'I don't hold with handouts. If
you've got your family you don't need charity. I put aside
money every week for Roly. He don't go short.'

'How old is Roly?'

'Thirty-seven come June.'

'Thirty-seven!'

I didn't say that it seemed old to be living on handouts
from his mother. I realised that Mrs Butter was scorchingly
sensitive on the subject of her son. It wasn't my business to
be critical.

'He's very lucky to have a mother like you.'

'He's a good boy to his mother. Comes to see me every
month and rings me every week, regular-like.'

'That *is* good. And pretty unusual, I imagine.'

I revised my previously wholly unfavourable impression of

227

Roly. Unless, of course, he stayed in touch only for the cash benefits.

Min and I worked hard in the boat-house all afternoon. We talked about Ellie and William and I told her that I had discovered in myself a longing to have children of my own.

'I would never have thought it! Not that you wouldn't make the most wonderful mother. Of course you would. But in my experience it's the most scatty and selfish people who have them . . . the worse they are at being parents the more they have.'

'Do you remember that poem we did at school, by R S Thomas? "We live in our own world, A world that is too small For you to stoop and enter"? I think it's called "Children's Song". Those lines that go, "You cannot find the centre Where we dance, where we play, Where life is still asleep Under the closed flower." I feel as though I've glimpsed again a world which I'd half forgotten. When we were children together at school there was a particular kind of happiness, then, that I want to feel again through my own children. A happiness unspoilt by calculation and constant self-regulation. Am I making myself at all clear?'

'Yes. I remember the poem. "Under the smooth shell Of eggs in the cupped nest That mock the faded blue Of your remoter heaven."'

'Fancy you remembering that poem!'

'I remember it chiefly because you loved it so much. You used to recite it endlessly in the back of the car when we were going home for the holidays.'

'Of course I did! Mullins used to drive us. I'd forgotten about Mullins. He liked "The Revenge". We used to shout it out the windows . . . "At Flores in the Azores Sir Richard Grenville lay, And a pinnace, like a fluttered bird, came flying from far away." I'm not happy about the scansion of that line. Not Tennyson's best.'

'"Then sware Lord Thomas Howard: ''Fore God I am no coward',"' Min declaimed. 'Heavens, it's good stuff!'

'It's strange to remember that I liked "Children's Song" because it made me feel safe and remote from grown-ups. Now I see it from the outside, an enchanted country I can no longer enter.'

'Why not have Charles's children? They'd be terrifically good-looking.'

'Now, Min. Remember you're a happily married woman.'

'Is anyone really happy married in the way you mean? So that they can't imagine being even happier with someone else?'

'Min! You're not saying that you'd rather be married to Charles?'

'No . . . o. I don't think so. No, of course not.'

But I could see that she was thinking about it.

'But Robert is so much better-read than Charles. So much better educated altogether. Don't you think that after a month or so, when the novelty of the sex had worn off, you'd feel the lack of another mind filled with the same kind of ideas as your own?'

'Would you?' asked Min, dropping a blob of primrose paint on to the Thermos flask.

I got to grips with the Thermos, with white spirit and a rag.

'Yes. I think probably I would. I find Charles's foreignness alarming, as well as exhilarating. I don't suppose he and I think about anything at all in the same way. I want affinity. I want likeness, recognition, sympathy.'

'The danger is that your wants will be quite unrealistic. You've lived the kind of life that's under your own control, more or less. Once you're married huge compromises are necessary. You can't so much shape things for happiness, you have to prise happiness out of what there is. Two people have more momentum, you've got to rely more on luck.'

'It's just that feeling of being a little out of control that I want suddenly. Something surprising and challenging. Perhaps even alarming. Something that changes me despite myself.'

'I hope you find it,' said Min very solemnly, dripping paint on to the remaining egg sandwiches.

Three days later I finished painting the boat-house. The colour was perfect. Clean and pretty and inviting. I got out Min's treadle sewing machine and made a workplace for myself in the boot room so that I didn't have to put everything away each time. I knew quite well that the merest mention of a sewing machine in connection with proper curtain-making was heresay but there were three large windows and only two days left in which to make the curtains. Also they would probably come in for rough treatment from the children and would be stronger if machine-stitched. The fabric had a background of pale green with pink and yellow roses and dark-blue convolvulus all over it. I'd found it in the attic. It had once been two pairs of much larger curtains but the linings were rotten and the edges faded.

With Robert's permission, I'd taken George Pryke off coppicing and he was luxuriating in the warmth of the greenhouse, painting white two old wicker chairs and a wooden table. After that his instructions were to repair the boats. I'd found some pink damask cushions for the chairs and a green rug for the floor. Ellie had helped me choose the things.

She'd also found two Victorian paintings of country life in the attic. One was called 'At the Smithy' and the other 'Bob's Faithful Vigil'. The second one seemed to me very sad. It depicted a sheepdog resting his head on the bed of an old man, obviously his master, who looked pretty dead. Ellie said he was having a lovely sleep and the dog was waiting for him to wake up and take him for a walk. I think it was Francis Bacon who said that art has divine qualities because it submits the shows of things to the desires of the mind, as opposed to reason which submits the mind to the nature of things. We hung them side by side on the wall that didn't have any windows. They were admirably painted and too good, in a way, for the purpose, but being unfashionable, they were valueless.

The paraffin heater from the kitchen warmed the boat-house easily. I was rather worried about the children burning themselves on it or knocking it over and causing a fire but Min pointed out that they never had, all the time it had been in the kitchen. The whole project took up nearly every minute of the time I had left from cooking and shopping even though Min was now doing the washing-up and generally helping where she could. She very sweetly ironed my one and only nightdress for me and burned a hole in the hem which she was even more sorry about than I was. Mrs Butter did everything else and did it to perfection. I'd told Min that these would probably be the last few days of my stay. She had looked woebegone.

'I know you've got to go and it's selfish of me to want you to stay but I'm going to miss you so dreadfully that I can't bear to think about it. Of course I love Robert and the children but it isn't the same as having someone really to talk to. I have to adapt myself to talk to a man or a child.

With you there's no need for adjustment. I'm my true self, whatever that is.'

I'd put my arms around her and hugged her for that.

'Do stay just one more week anyway. Couldn't you?'

'Let's see. It's worse for me than you, you know. I do love it here.'

Now that the snow had gone I walked with Ham in the park and the surrounding countryside whenever I needed a break from curtain-making. The wildness and the beauty of the hills, the woods, rivers and waterfalls transported me. I thought I must have been mad to have spent so many years in a town, however superior Cambridge was to the general run.

Vivien came to tea that Thursday. I made the cake as promised and we discussed being mummified and having our brains hooked out through our noses, a subject instigated by William, until Robert came home. He was late, it being photography-club night, and I saw at once that he was tired and not in a good mood. I hoped that Vivien would have the sense to keep quiet and wait for a better moment to put her proposition to him.

'Dahlia thinks I ought to pay for William to go to a deent school instead of that Bolshevik ghetto he attends.' I knew then that it wasn't going to be any good. It was obvious that Vivien disliked giving in, as she saw it, and wasn't going to attempt to be tactful or persuasive. Robert gave me a look of disfavour. I hoped my expression was apologetic. 'You'll have to do something in return. I don't see why I'm always expected to make sacrifices.'

'For one thing, no one is expecting you to do anything,' said Robert, with something of a snort. 'For another, there is no question of sacrifice with or without William's school fees in the question. You've got more than enough money to educate twenty grandchildren if you choose.'

Vivien looked rather smug and smiled slyly. 'Well, anyway, you can do the accounts. And save me paying that fool Willis.'

'Willis isn't a fool. He's intelligent and honest and he does the accounts far quicker than I could. And he gets them right. You know I've no head for figures.'

'So you don't want the money then?'

Robert clutched his head with his hands. 'I think this would be better discussed in private.'

'I'm not going into that freezing library.'

I got up to go.

'Now, Dahlia, sit down. This is all your scheme.'

Robert still had his head between his hands so I put out my tongue at Vivien as far as it would go. The children looked quite delighted. Vivien smiled at me, very sweetly. I put all the cups and plates on to the tray and took them out to the kitchen. Before long I heard Robert's voice very loud, then a silence, and then Isolde began her plaint. Vivien came into the kitchen.

'What a sulky creature my son is. Well, I tried.'

'No, you didn't.'

'Don't say *you're* cross with me, too.'

'I am. You know that really you want to do something for William. And when you choose to be charming you could persuade Tamburlaine to take up petit point.'

Vivien looked rather pleased by this tribute, as I intended that she should. She did a sort of twirl on one leg and tra-lahed, '"He sobbed and he sighed, and a gurgle he gave, Then he plunged himself into the billowy wave, And an echo arose from the suicide's grave – 'Oh willow, titwillow, titwillow!'"'

Ellie and William came in. Vivien took their hands and they skipped in a circle singing as much as they could remember of the words. Robert walked in in the middle of this hilarity and looked thoroughly offended. I knew he felt that we were all hand in glove against him. I offered to drive Vivien home but Robert said he would drive her. I could tell that he was in his stuffiest, crossest mood and I was pretty sure that he'd been coming in to tick me off for interfering.

When he came back I was helping Ellie with her geography homework so his gun was effectively spiked. Min helped me wash up after supper and the moment she announced she was tired, I said I was, too, and we went upstairs together, leaving Robert downstairs to lock up. He looked quite thunderous.

At breakfast his anger seemed to have abated. He was very quiet, which wasn't unusual, and ate his bacon and tomatoes with an abstracted air. He went off with the children and I relaxed. I made Ellie's birthday cake in the morning and decorated it in the afternoon. I iced it with pale-blue icing and built a little house out of chocolate finger biscuits. I used angelica for rushes and made a swan from white icing, using fuse-wire inside for the neck. It was dreadfully fiddly and several times I nearly lost my temper but in the end I was fairly pleased with it. At one point I remembered the cake Poppy had made for me, so many years ago, which also had blue icing and my eyes filled with tears. I chided myself for a fool. Poppy was long dead and beyond being hurt. I hid the cake in the still-room.

Over lunch Min and I had discussed Robert's quarrel with Vivien.

'Robert was an idiot to lose his temper,' said Min. 'It was a chance to do something about William and he threw it away. It's his ridiculous pride. Or ego. I don't know what to call it, really.'

'But Vivien was at her most provocative.'

'She's always provocative. Knowing that, surely one can make adjustments and ignore it.'

'I think it's a masculine failing to see all negotiation as latent attack. Women are, on the while, more able to admit being in the wrong or that they've made idiots of themselves. And to apologise.'

'Well, it's good of you to stand up for him after he sabotaged your attempt to help.'

'I only suggested to Vivien that there was difficulty and she took it from there. If Robert can't do maths, it wasn't much of a proposition, was it? Vivien should know that, better than anyone.'

'Robert's so quick-tempered. It's his greatest fault. He can be so stiff-necked and pontifical.'

'Ye . . . es.' I was thinking. 'But isn't it because he minds about things that many men would choose to ignore to suit their own convenience? He sticks to his principles even when they don't work in his favour. He's thin-skinned, but how much better to be that than to be insensitive and crass. Most men are indifferent to what doesn't affect them.'

'Daisy! You're really hopelessly disillusioned! Don't women behave in exactly the same way? Take Vivien as a case in point. Of course Hector died long before I knew Robert but I've got a very clear impression that she gave him hell while he was alive. And she's not alone.'

'Mm. That's true, of course. I suppose I am unfair. I just seem to see it so much more often the other way round.'

'It's a great irony that you dislike men so much when you're free to let your fancy light where it chooses and I, who like men better than women, am stuck with perpetual faithfulness.'

I was startled by this frank explication of our positions. Did I dislike men? When I thought of how for thousands of years they had grabbed all the best jobs, all the money and all the power for themselves with absolutely no notion of fair play, I thought I did. When I remembered the warmongering and the violence and the crime for which men were ninety per cent responsible, I was sure I did. But these generalisations were not really useful. Men like Peter and Robert were perhaps exceptional but they did exist. No, the word was not dislike but distrust.

'Do you really like men better than women?' I asked Min, handing her the mixing bowl and a spoon so that she wouldn't drip any more cake mixture from her finger on to the floor. 'That surprises me.'

'I've never been in any doubt about it. I don't have much in common with most women. They seem to want to talk about things I know hardly anything about. The rearing of children, cooking, gardening, charity work, the iniquities of their husbands. And with an intensity I simply can't match. My jokes disconcert.'

'Well, in the country, perhaps. In Cambridge, I almost never have that kind of conversation. We're all too intent on our own careers, on courting success and winning respect. Very laudable. But selfish.'

'I'm just a frustrated academic,' said Min, looking rather depressed. 'And, by your definition, selfish, too.' I hadn't meant to imply that. But if I hadn't loved Min it might have been what I thought. 'You're really the only girlfriend I've ever had,' Min went on. 'Don't you remember at school? There were plenty of girls I was friendly with but no one who I really cared tuppence about apart from you. But you always had other friends. You and Ma and Gina are the only women I've actually wholeheartedly loved. And although I know plenty of women around here and there's a fair amount of socialising, which I enjoy, there isn't anyone who really matters. I haven't the art of imparting the sympathy and solidarity that other women want.'

'But if we seem to want what the other has . . . would we change places with each other if we could?'

'No,' said Min, giving the idea some thought. 'I couldn't not have the children. And Robert. No.'

I thought of the struggles and inconveniences of Min's life, its constant trivial demands, its comparative isolation.

'No,' I said, 'I wouldn't either.'

But I knew one of us, at least, was lying.


## CHAPTER EIGHTEEN


At breakfast the next day Ellie opened her presents. Min had given her a book about horses and a new Mason Pearson hairbrush. From Robert she had a cat basket with a red cushion for Booty. William gave her a paint-box which he said he hoped she'd let him use, as he'd had to spend all his pocket money on it and his own was nearly used up. I, with some anxiety that she would think it dull, had given her a cabaret, that is, a round tray fitted with a small teapot, two cups, a milk jug, sugar basin and toast rack. Everything, including the tray, was made of hard-paste porcelain and decorated with blue rosebuds on a white ground. It was halfway in size between ordinary and a doll's tea service. I'd seen it in the shop where William had sold the ivy-handled jug. I had fallen in love with it at once and because it was of late manufacture, no older than the twenties, it had been affordable.

Ellie unwrapped it very carefully and stood each piece in the specially shaped indentation on the tray.

'It's absolutely lovely!' said Min. 'Where did you find it? Look, Ellie, at this dear little toast rack. It isn't a child's piece, is it, really? It looks too good for that.'

'No,' I said, still feeling anxious for Ellie hadn't said anything, 'it's for grown-ups' tea or chocolate. They were very popular at the end of the eighteenth century and then came into vogue again in the early part of this century.'

'Is it *really* for me?' said Ellie finally in a tight little voice, and then I knew she liked it.

I got up to put the kettle on for more tea. I felt Ellie's arms wind tightly round my waist and I turned round to give her a kiss.

'I'll take very good care of it,' she whispered, 'and use it every year on my birthday for the rest of my life starting with tea this afternoon.'

Robert had been instructed by Ellie to ask Gerald to the tea, which we were having in the boat-house, but Gerald had been away for the last two days. Robert said he had to go into school anyway as he wanted to get some books and catch up on some lesson preparation. He'd call in on Gerald, who had a flat over the school library. We were not to bother to get lunch for him. Vivien was also invited though Ellie had been less keen on this idea.

'I don't know that I specially want to be told how fat I am on my birthday of all days. But I suppose she's got to come.'

'There isn't a friend from school you want to ask?'

'Oh no! I want to be able to enjoy myself. I don't want to worry whether they're having a nice time or whether Granny's going to say something awful. Families are horribly embarrassing. But you feel so hurt for them if people don't like them. Sometimes I think I'd prefer to be an orphan.'

We tried to tempt Booty to come and sit in the new cat basket by the Aga but, though she was much tamer now, she wouldn't stay indoors so we put the basket into the manger. Robert said that Ellie could keep one of the kittens and train it to live in the house as soon as Booty was fed up with looking after it. Ellie was both delighted by the idea of having one of the kittens and horribly anguished by the necessity of rejecting four.

'Don't be late, darling,' said Min. 'Tea's at four o'clock. You could pick up Vivien and save her the walk.'

Robert said he would and gave Ellie a special birthday kiss and hug.

'Hello? What's this? My incredibly aged daughter is much thinner than she used to be. It suits you, darling. Have you been banting?'

'No. I'm just trying not to eat so much. It's a present for Daisy. I don't suppose anyone ever had such a funny present before, do you?'

Robert looked at me. I felt myself blush. His eyebrows went up. I began to carve a cold chicken and refused to catch his eye. I heard him go out and close the door quietly. Min and I made some egg sandwiches or at least I did while Min ate the crusts.

Then I made some orange jelly and set it in the hollowed-out orange-skins. I gave Min some cream to whip to fill the meringues I'd made a few days ago. Ellie was given the job of piping, in pink icing, the initials of each guest on to some biscuits I'd made the day before. William speared cubes of cheddar and squares of tinned pineapple on to cocktail sticks. He'd said he wouldn't come to the tea party unless there was this particular culinary treat. We packed everything into baskets and put the baskets by the back door, an area which was cold enough to serve as a refrigerator. Then, incredibly, by the time everything was washed up and the icing washed off the table, chairs and floor, it was time for lunch. I was immensely grateful for fish fingers and baked beans and remembered, with derision, my former snobbery about this kind of food.

By the time Robert came back at four, with Vivien, we were all starving again and longing to start tea. I brought out the birthday cake and was gratified by the general praise, particularly Ellie's rapture. Only Robert didn't admire it. Whatever he'd eaten for lunch didn't seem to have agreed with him. He looked dyspeptic and tired, his face grey and his nose very sharp. I'd made Thermoses of hot chocolate and tea and put them into a basket with two bottles of champagne. We walked down to the boat-house, carrying extra chairs, baskets, and cushions. Ellie carried her present from me, very slowly and carefully. I followed with the cake. I'd lit the paraffin heater after lunch so the room was warm. Ham immediately stretched herself in front of it and went to sleep, with heavy snores.

'Dahlia!' said Vivien, when she saw it. 'It's perfectly charming!'

'Min and the children helped, too.'

'I dare say. But I recognise the Dahlia style.'

'Don't call her Dahlia, Granny,' said Ellie. 'It's Daisy.'

'It doesn't matter,' I said. 'It's just your grandmother's joke. I don't mind a bit.'

Vivien looked rather put out. She gave Ellie her birthday present. It was a dressing-gown, dark blue with a red tasselled belt.

'Though it may be a little large for you, my dear. You seem to be losing weight.' She looked speculatively at Ellie. 'Perhaps you've begun puberty early. That makes for so many interesting little changes. Why, I remember when I first got the curse . . .'

'Mother!'

Robert sounded so fierce that for once Vivien shut up.

'What a prudish little boy you always were,' was all she said.

'Can anyone see the swan?' I said, going to the window. 'It'll be dark in a minute.'

The lake was a silver bowl beneath the purpling, gloom-gathering clouds. Among the black rushes on the farther bank two white shapes stretched their necks to each other.

'He's got a mate,' I said. 'I'm sure that's lucky for your birthday, Ellie.'

'Isn't Gerald coming?' asked Ellie, suddenly remembering.

'No, darling,' Robert helped himself to a sandwich. 'He must be away for the weekend. We ought to have thought of asking him sooner. Isn't the light wonderful, fading over the water? Now you can't see the far bank. It's very cosy in here.'

'We used to come here sometimes, Hector and I,' said Vivien. 'There was a chaise longue against that wall and . . .'

'What colour were the walls?' I asked, quickly. 'They were a dingy grey before we painted them.'

'Let me see,' Vivien looked thoughtful. 'No, I can't remember. Once we had a party on the lake. There was a picnic set out for us on the island. Some of the men stripped off and swam over without waiting for a boat. Of course they had to eat their food with no clothes on. It was just like the painting of *Le Déjeuner sur l'Herbe*. Perhaps not quite so decorous. We took it in turns to tell the most salacious stories we could think of. We had to hand out napkins to all the naked men.'

'I suppose it would have been uncomfortable to get crumbs in one's bare lap,' said Ellie thoughtfully.

'Let's each of us tell a story now,' said Robert. 'Perhaps it will shut Mother up for a while.'

So Robert began, as it was his idea, and told the story of Orpheus and Euridyce. He told it very well, so that I heard it as though for the first time. Ellie thought it very mean of the Thracian women to tear the sorrowing Orpheus into pieces but William said he thoroughly approved as Orpheus was nothing but a dope from beginning to end.

'I mean, fancy looking back when you've been told it's the *one* thing you *mustn't* do. I ask you!'

Min told the story of Ivanhoe. It was a good story but complicated, the way Min told it, and as she obviously favoured the intelligent, resourceful, beautiful Rebecca over the beautiful, milk-and-water Rowena, we could only feel that the ending, when Ivanhoe goes off with the wrong girl, was something of a let-down. However, it had enough of romance for Ellie and fighting for William to satisfy each of them.

Ellie told the story of the Princess and the Pea. Naturally William persisted in misunderstanding pee for pea and he and Vivien sabotaged the telling with ribald remarks about incontinence and the number of mackintosh sheets required with twenty mattresses until Ellie got quite cross and Robert had to tell them to be quiet.

William told the story of Tantalus which he'd just read the day before. He told it very graphically and we all felt rather sickened by Tantalus's plight, having eaten and drunk so much ourselves within the last hour.

I told the story of Tobermory, the cat who is taught to speak during a house party and who then exposes the hypocrisies of the hostess and guests, by telling what he has overheard. Everyone laughed very much though I was conscious that my storytelling powers fell short of Saki's.

Then Vivien told the story of her namesake, the Lady of the Lake, who was Merlin's mistress. She gave a very adulterated version and had them smoking cigarettes and drinking cocktails until we were all in fits of laughter. Robert laughed more than anyone, having apparently abandoned his prejudice against champagne and drunk nearly a bottle on his own.

When we'd sung happy birthday and eaten some of the cake we blew out the candles, put out the heater and carried the baskets back to the house by torchlight.

'My best birthday ever,' said Ellie.

Min and I exchanged glances of satisfaction. William recited what seemed like every single minute of his best birthday which, as it had consisted of a day's motor-racing, left us less than enthralled. In the end we had to beg him to shut up. Robert, whose bonhomie had suddenly deserted him, said he had a headache and would spend half an hour in the library. He looked very tired and again his face was drawn and grey.

'Do, darling,' said Min. 'We won't inquire the reason for the headache. I'd sleep it off if I were you.'

Robert gave a wan smile and went away. When Ellie was sent to get him at supper-time she found him fast asleep on the sofa in the library, so we went ahead without him. He appeared again just before the children went to bed and we had a last round of Pit, which was Ellie's favourite game and was satisfyingly noisy. Robert shouted as loudly as any of us so I assumed that his headache had gone. He offered to see the children to bed and declined any supper, saying he was still full of a very good tea. Min, Vivien and I sat for a while around the kitchen table gossiping and drinking coffee. Vivien had eaten heartily at both tea and supper and Min remarked on this, asking how she managed not to put on weight.

'Laxatives, Minerva. Flush it through the system fast and it doesn't have time to cling.' Vivien took my last cigarette without asking.

'But surely that must be dreadfully bad for you?' I said, lighting it for her.

'Possibly.' She shrugged her shoulders. 'What do I care? I'm seventy this year. I don't want to go on for ever. I like my life but it isn't as amusing as it was. So many of the people I really liked are dead already. And some have become tedious in old age, telling one about their colons as though they were *objets de vertu*. Food is one of the few great pleasures of old age. I'm bored with sex. Oh, I know I talk about it but I can't be bothered to get undressed any more. I like gardening, but not when it's blazingly hot or freezing cold. I should guess that there are about thirty perfect gardening days out of the three hundred and sixty-five.'

'Vivien, you sound almost depressed,' exclaimed Min.

'No. I'm not. But I don't want to be. If I find I am, I shall take steps.'

'Like what?'

'You'd be the last person I'd tell, Minerva. I can just imagine you mishandling the whole thing on my behalf. You mind your business and I'll mind mine.'

Min laughed. 'I'll take you home, shall I? I'm ready for bed.'

While they were gone, I washed up for the final time that day. I marvelled at Min's good humour under provocation. Of course she could be furiously angry but she didn't bristle or take umbrage at small offences. I couldn't think when I had seen her be petty. It was a tremendously attractive quality. It was the obverse side of her incompetence in domestic matters. She was detached from trivial issues. I knew that the same could not be said of myself.

The following morning I woke early. I got out of bed to look at the dawn . . . grey and pink curds like the flank of a skinned salmon. Ham and I had breakfast alone together and then I took some out to Booty. I had intended to go back and do some reading in the warmth of the kitchen but the hint of sun and blue sky was seductive and I fetched my duffle-coat to take Ham for a walk around the lake before getting out my books. It was a perfect spring morning, exceptional for February. The light was clear, the wind fresh, the water sparkling. I was tempted to take a second stroll round but I was firm with myself. I came back the long way, past George Pryke's greenhouse.

On an impulse I opened the greenhouse door and went in. It felt remarkably warm. I opened the stove. A few sly gleams of scarlet winked among the ashes. George obviously stoked it well on Saturday afternoons before leaving for home so that it would be warm for Monday. I looked at my watch. Still only eight o'clock. I sat on George's chair and looked around me. Really, with a dozen new panes of glass the greenhouse would be perfectly serviceable. It was a handsome old building and a shame to let it fall to pieces. I longed to put the greenhouse to better use than as a repository for George's erotic magazines.

Suddenly, through the green and white smudges of algae and shading paint which obscured the light, I saw a face peering in. It was Robert.

'Hello,' he said, opening the door. 'I thought I saw movement. I supposed it was George. Silly of me. It was pretty unlikely that he'd come in on Sunday.'

'I was just thinking how good it would be to repair this and use it again. I love the smell of greenhouses . . . damp earth, tomato plants, heliotrope. And think of the pleasure of working in them, pricking out seedlings while the rain patters on the glass outside.'

'I can remember, as a boy, helping Harrington, the head gardener, to string onions. I think it was raining. Yes, I'm sure it was.'

'How lucky you were to grow up here.'

'I suppose . . . yes, in some ways.'

'We never stayed anywhere more than a couple of years. Just as I'd arranged things to my liking we were off again, usually to somewhere less agreeable. As one might expect, Mother's boyfriends got plainer and poorer as she got older.'

'But it made you what you are. We none of us can regret that.'

'*Merci du compliment.*'

'I want to thank you for everything you did for Ellie's birthday. The cake and the food and organising the boat-house. She was so happy.'

'I loved doing it. It gave me quite as much pleasure as Ellie.'

There was a pause. Robert idly picked up a dibber from the bench and turned it around between his fingers, frowning. He looked dreadfully tired and his expression was so severe that if I had known him less well I should have been alarmed. I was on the point of making a joke about Ginevra Yorke but by a providential spark of intuition, I perceived that something was wrong. His hands, turning the dibber, looked very white. They were beautiful hands, long and fine with well-shaped nails. I smelt the sharp, sweet smell of burning applewood from the stove. I felt suddenly as though I myself were outside the scene, looking on to a coloured, moving image . . . as though it was an image projected by a camera obscura. I heard him breathing. For a moment I thought I could hear the beating of his heart. But that must have been my imagination.

Suddenly, to my astonishment, a spasm shook his mouth so that he was forced to bite his lips together and tears began to run down his face. No man had ever cried in front of me except for Poppy. I felt a moment of panic.

'I'm sorry. I'm so sorry!' he said, fumbling in his pocket for a handkerchief.

Not finding one, he wiped his face on his sleeve. If he'd been a woman my natural impulse would have been to put my arms around him but shyness prevented me.

'Won't you tell me what's wrong?' I spoke timidly. I was terrified of stemming the confidence by an inappropriate word. Robert looked sharply at me. I had no clue to his thoughts. Then he looked away and began to speak.

'When I went into school yesterday I found this letter. On my desk. Of course, he thought I wouldn't find it until tomorrow.'

He pulled a sheet of blue writing-paper from his pocket and gave it to me. I began to read it.

Dear Robert,

By the time you find this, I suppose the pack will be baying and everything will be discovered. I'll be out of it all but you, my poor friend, will have to live with the knowledge that the man you thought was decent and civilised and self-controlled was in fact a self-besotted, degraded monster. I lied to you. I can't express my sorrow for this. In fact, my sorrow for everything that has happened since the afternoon I got back to my flat and found Dalrymple sitting naked on my sofa, reading Proust.

I hope you will manage to laugh when you read this. I didn't laugh then nor have I been able to laugh since, but there is something ridiculous in all our loves, I think. I thought I loved Dalrymple. He has since proved to be cunning, devious and manipulative. Yet . . . I'll be truthful since it hardly matters now . . . I still love him. By comparison with myself he is an angel. I am, I know, a loathly brute. Perhaps you will be able to think more kindly of me when I tell you that I haven't had a moment's happiness since the moment when I let Dalrymple take my hand.

I don't matter any more. It is a long time since I believed in Heaven or Hell. But my poor mother doesn't deserve this. If you find no pity for me . . . and I admit I deserve none . . . do what you can for her. I know I can trust you to do that.

The final penalty I ask you to pay for believing in me is to make the truth known. I have no right to blight a young life and I'm ashamed of myself, bitterly ashamed, that I was willing to have Dalrymple branded a liar.

Everything I want to say sounds as though I'm sorry for myself so I'll finish and get on with the job. Thank you, Robert. Your friendship was one of the greatest blessings of my life,

Gerald.

When I'd finished reading this I sat with my hands on my knees, holding the letter, feeling the shock prickling over my skin.

'I went straight to his flat.' Robert spoke in a low, strained voice. 'He was lying on his bed, unconscious but still breathing. There were bottles of pills and whisky... empty... beside him. My first thought was to ring for a doctor, an ambulance. I lifted the receiver, dialled the emergency code... and then put the receiver back before I could ring. Nothing could undo what Gerald had done. Or prevent its consequences. The remorse, the humiliation, the revilement, the loss of everything he valued... his job, his friends. He'd chosen death. I stood by his bed, looking down at his face. I wiped away a trickle of saliva from the corner of his mouth. I sat on the bed and held his head in my arms. There was a volume of Shakespeare open on his bed. He must have been reading it while he was waiting for the pills and whisky to work. I read aloud the last act of Hamlet, holding him, until he stopped breathing.'

I saw a tear roll down Robert's cheek. He wiped it angrily away. I folded up Gerald's letter with hands that were shaking.

'He was a nice man,' I said, inadequately. I thought again of Poppy. I remembered his funeral and Min saying just that to me. 'You did exactly what I should have done in your place. It was the right thing to do.'

Robert looked at me.

'Oh, Daisy!' He sighed so violently that it was like an expulsion of pain. 'Was it? I've asked myself that question over and over again. It's been torturing me until I've wondered if I was going mad. I couldn't sleep last night. I felt a weight in my arms. It made me sit up in a state of... I don't know... grief, horror, fear. Now I'm sounding self-pitying. But I suppose I'm going to wonder what I should have done for the rest of my life.'

'It *was* the right thing! Gerald was the last man to be able to live with that kind of disgrace. Some people might shrug it off, justify themselves, forget about it. Gerald would have felt it through to the bone. I didn't know him well but my guess is that he would never have found life worth living again.'

I saw that Robert was breathing more calmly now and his face looked a better colour.

'What you did was courageous and . . . loving,' I went on. 'I used to feel very guilty about a woman who tried to kill herself. But I think I've accepted it. Isn't that what it means to be grown up? Accepting responsibility for one's own actions?'

I told him briefly about Caroline Protheroe. There were few parallels as far as our guilty feelings were concerned. But we had both seen unbearable suffering. Robert didn't say much but as I talked I felt his sympathy because the intensity of his feelings had worked contagiously upon my own.

'The odd thing is that it hasn't changed my affection for him,' said Robert. 'I ought to despise him, I suppose . . . feel disgust . . . outrage. But all I'm left with is dreadful . . . sadness.'

'If I found that Min had done something really dreadful, I shouldn't love her less,' I said. 'Pity would increase my affection, if anything.'

'And would it be the same the other way around?'

I thought about it. Of course, I remembered the quarrel. But we had not been discussing crimes committed against ourselves.

'I think it would.'

'I haven't told Min,' said Robert. 'About Gerald. She didn't like him. And she'll be angry on Dalrymple's behalf. Quite properly. The police may want to interview me again tomorrow. I called them as soon as Gerald was dead. I'll tell her after breakfast.'

'Yes.' There was a pause. 'I'd better go and make breakfast for the children.'

'That's very good of you.'

'No. I like looking after them. I think I'll pile coals of fire on to my enemy's head,' I said, to change the conversation, 'I'll put a log of wood in George's stove.'

'Let me.' Robert put in several pieces of applewood. 'Disgraceful reprobate that he is.'

We both smiled and he opened the door for me to go out ahead of him. The air was cool after the warmth of the greenhouse. We walked back to the house together. Robert made some remark about the wetness of the ground after the thaw. I countered with a remark about the snowdrops in the park. We entered the kitchen to find William and Ellie sitting at the table, arguing about who was to use Ellie's paint-box first.

Robert settled the argument in favour of Ellie and I began to fry bacon and eggs and to boil the kettle for coffee. William was in a sulk so I asked him if he'd used the pastels that I'd bought him at the Spring Bazaar. He swung off his chair and went away. Min came in, yawning, with her hair in a tangle, looking for her hairbrush.

Halfway through breakfast, William came back and placed beside my plate three pieces of paper.

'William! I can hardly believe someone of twelve has done these. But they're not only competent. They're beautiful!'

There were two drawings of the house and one of the lake. The execution was impressionistic, the colours stunning.

'I copied that picture of the Drowning Cathedral in that book in the library,' said William, looking pleased. 'I mean the way I drew it. Not the subject, obviously.'

I showed them to Robert and Min, who were impressed by them though they'd obviously seen plenty of William's work and were inclined to take his ability for granted. I felt, more strongly than ever, that William should have proper teaching and encouragement but I couldn't think how this was to come about.

We spent a day of peaceful activity. Except for Robert who must have spent the morning sleeping in the library for he looked much less tired at lunch. He joined in a very opinionated and noisy conversation about the existence of ghosts . . . Min and I holding that they existed only in fiction, Ellie and William being convinced that they'd seen lots and Robert saying that he was prepared to believe in them if only they'd condescend to manifest themselves.

'Let's watch for ghosts tonight,' suggested William. 'Let's sit up until midnight, with the lights off. I'll take the drawing room, Ellie the stairs, Dad can have the library, Mum can sit in the morning room and Daisy the dining room.'

There were general cries of protest at this plan, Min and I saying that we'd be too cold, Robert that he'd be too tired and Ellie that she'd be too frightened. William was disgusted by this unsporting attitude and throughout the afternoon approached each of us privately to gain support for his plan . . . needless to say with complete unsuccess.

By the evening Ellie had sunk into her usual Sunday-night mood about school, a state of depression interspersed with bursts of anxiety. Robert tried to cheer her up by reading us 'The Canterville Ghost'. It made us all laugh. I've always liked Min's laugh, more like a man's than a woman's, rather loud and low. She was wearing her old scarlet jersey. She put up her hand to push her hair out of her eyes with the same gesture she'd had as a girl of thirteen.

'I'd forgotten that Oscar Wilde could be funny,' said Min, when Robert paused in the reading to open another bottle of wine. 'I remember him as going on and on in the most precious way about beauty . . . and conveying only a feeling of stuffiness and artificiality.'

'And he can affect one's feelings, too,' I said. 'Think of "The Selfish Giant". I always get a terrific lump in my throat at the end. And "The Nightingale and the Rose" is unbearably sad. I can't bring myself to read it any more.'

'Gerald really is like Oscar Wilde,' went on Min. 'All that posturing but underneath strong feelings. What a pity he doesn't have the talent as well.'

I knew then that Robert hadn't found the opportunity or the courage to tell Min about Gerald. I saw him flush as he lifted his glass to drink.

'I gave Gerald's biscuit to the ducks this morning,' said Ellie. 'It was a pity because the "G" was the best icing I did. I think he would have liked having someone do a biscuit specially for him.'

'I think he would, darling,' said Robert.

He looked so terribly sad, suddenly, that I wanted to reach out and touch his hand. Oh my love, I thought to myself. The words were so clearly articulated in my mind that I jumped with the shock and imagined that I had spoken aloud. I felt my heart race.

'Time you children were in bed,' said Min, getting up to begin the washing-up.

After they'd gone I dared to steal a glance at Robert. I felt that my guilt was written in enormous accusing letters over every inch of my face. He was reading the label on a jar of French mustard. Then he sighed and put it down.

'I'm going to dry up,' he said, getting up and going over to the sink. 'Daisy, I forbid you to help. Finish the bottle and supervise our labours from your chair. Darling, I'm afraid this isn't clean,' he said to Min, handing her a plate and kissing her cheek.

Robert was of the old-fashioned school which held that public displays of affection are ill-mannered and in the three weeks I'd been at Weston Hall I'd never seen them be more affectionate than briefly and discreetly holding hands. I took the kiss as a sign that I was accepted as part of the family. I accepted, for my part, that the sensation of acute pain that lodged, quivering, somewhere in my midriff, was my due reward for the biggest, most staggering piece of folly in my life to date.

'My dears, I've made up my mind,' I said, waving my glass at them. 'Here's a toast to a weekend visit that turned out to be three wonderful weeks. I'm going home tomorrow.'

## CHAPTER NINETEEN

It poured heavily with rain for the entire journey home. All day a sheet of water fell steadily from the dark sky. Cataracts of condensation shrouded the carriage windows, separating me from the watery world outside.

From Dunston Abchurch to Carnforth, I relived the departure from Weston Hall. Ellie had cried on and off throughout breakfast. Even William permitted himself to look a little sorry that I was going. Ham lay by my suitcase in the hall, her brown eyes twitching from side to side, her expression despondent. I told her that the butcher would continue regular deliveries of her meat but of course she didn't understand. Robert, late for school, had come running out of the house at the last minute, kissed me briefly on the cheek, got into the Morris Traveller and had driven away, the children waving through the open windows. Then Min had taken me to the station in the Land Rover.

We'd stood on the platform, talking cheerfully and inanely about anything we could think of and then the train had come in.

'Come back soon, darling, darling Daisy,' she'd said, throwing her arms about me. 'Thank you for everything. I've loved every minute of having you.'

'Goodbye. I'm so sorry . . .' The porter was standing next to us and the whistle shrieked in our ears.

'What?' yelled Min, as the doors were slammed and clouds of steam were exhaled along the platform.

' . . . to be going! Say goodbye to Vivien and Mrs Butter for me.'

Then the train had drawn away from the platform and we'd waved to each other like sweethearts being separated from each other by a world war until the platform wound away out of sight behind a bend. I sat down in my seat and took my book from my bag.

I stared at the page but couldn't understand a word of it, though there is scarcely a line of Jane Austen with which I am not respectfully familiar. 'After sitting with them a few minutes, the Miss Steeles returned to the Park, and Elinor was then at liberty to think and be wretched.' She couldn't have been much more wretched than I was.

At once I ticked myself off for this self-indulgence. Lachesis was busy spinning my thread into the kind of marlinespike hitches that Min's knitted kettle-holders had got into at school, but I was still in charge of my own actions. Of course, I had been attracted to Robert almost from the moment of our first meeting. I'd deceived myself into thinking myself immune from danger because he was so cross and suspicious and unfriendly towards me. If only the power of physical attraction would operate in an orderly fashion, attaching men and women to eligible partners. If our sole purpose was to reproduce ourselves it hardly made sense to have these muddles of unrequited, faithless, scanty loves. How could I have grown to love Min's husband . . . of all men in the world, the very last I should have chosen? I sighed heavily.

This was sapless stuff. I must pull myself together. I'd known the man three weeks. A few weeks without seeing him and I'd be over it. It was all romantic nonsense, not worth another thought. I settled myself to *Sense and Sensibility*.

How Elinor could love Edward Ferrars was beyond me. He was inarticulate, gauche and spineless, a flimsy creature worked on by strong women. But who can explain the phenomenon? Why, when I thought of Robert, did I feel an electrification of my insides? The idea of him filled me with a violent excitement, until I remembered Min.

At Carnforth I boarded the train for London. The compartment was cleaner and warmer, occupied only by me and an elderly woman reading *The Lady* with frowning effort as though its contents were intellectually abstruse. I began to cheer up. I'd go straight back to Cambridge, unpack my things and have a bath. I'd light the fire and sit by it in my dressing-gown for a while, reading, before going into Hall and catching up on the gossip. I didn't often go into Hall because the food was so terrible but the last few weeks had hardened me off a little, like a tender plant exposed to life in the cold frame. I would never be a candidate for the full rigours of the open garden but I could manage one evening of haddock mornay and piped mashed potatoes, reheated to the crispness of meringue.

It was unpleasant splashing my way in and out of taxis with heavy luggage but by the time I'd got to King's Cross and into the train for Cambridge, my mind was settled and tranquil and I was looking forward to getting home. It was half past four before I turned my key in the lock at Orchard Street. A delicious smell of wood-smoke mingled with the scent of flowers. There was a note from Mrs Baxter on the console table in the hall, beside a bowl of blue hyacinths. It said that she'd lit the fire as Mrs Weston had telephoned just before three, hoping to find me already home. She, Mrs B, would call in every hour to check on the fire until I returned. There was a postscript to the effect that all the flowers were from the Americans.

I sniffed at the hyacinths and then opened the door into the drawing room. I'd grown used to the gloom of Weston Hall and I was astonished by the brilliance of the light even on this wet, dull day. I'd forgotten what a lovely room it was. On a small circular table by the French windows stood a vase of white and pink orchids. There was a dish of yellow primroses and bright green moss on the faux bamboo table by the sofa. I blessed the Finkelsteins.

I made myself some tea and unpacked. Mrs Baxter, who was as good as her word and had come to look at the fire, helped me and filled me in on my tenants. It was clear that they'd been as open-handed with her as with me and she was full of approval. On the little walnut chest of drawers by my bed was a pot of purple-and-white scented violas.

I ran a deep, hot bath. Getting into it was one of the most sensual experiences of my life. I lay in it for half an hour, trickling in more hot water from time to time and wondering if I could ever bring myself to leave it, when the telephone rang. It was Min.

'I've been desperate to talk to you all day. Not only am I missing you frightfully and the house seems like a deserted wartime airfield . . . just ghostly echoes and sad little mementoes of you, mud-splashed goggles, frayed white silk scarves . . . no, actually, empty champagne bottles in the rubbish and your bedroom smells of your scent . . . but something absolutely dreadful's happened. It's Gerald.'

'Hold on. I'm dripping everywhere. Let me put something on.'

I lay on the bed, wrapped in a towelling robe and listened as Min talked.

'Robert actually found Gerald on Saturday, but didn't say anything because he didn't want to spoil Ellie's birthday. That was rather noble, don't you think? I don't think I could have kept something like that to myself. He was interviewed by the police again today . . . apparently they spoke to him on Saturday. Poor darling! He was very calm telling me about it but of course he must be awfully upset. They were such good friends. And to find him dead! It must have been the most ghastly shock. You don't seem as surprised as I'd thought you would be. Did you suspect that he might be suicidally depressed? I remember you said that he was the unhappiest person you'd ever met.'

'If you'd just let me get a word in edgeways,' I said. 'Poor Gerald! I'm so very sorry.'

We talked about it for a long time. Min was inclined to be dismissive of the idea that Gerald had been seduced by Dalrymple and that this made him in any way less culpable.

'Gerald was thirty years older than the boy. He ought to have been especially on his guard. He should never have taken a job in a boys' school anyway, knowing himself as he did. He wasn't a fool. Unless it's rape, both people are always responsible in any sexual liaison, even if one of them is passive. You can always choose to go away.'

I wasn't quite as convinced as Min, though strictly speaking, of course, she was right. But I knew from my own experience how bullying persistence could confuse one's own ideas of what one actually wanted and if there had been a strong inclination towards the seducer I could imagine that moral considerations might disappear briefly from view.

'We shan't ever know the truth of it all. People make mistakes when they think they're in love. Who hasn't?'

There was a pause.

'I haven't,' said Min. 'But I haven't really had the opportunity. I suppose it's quite possible that I might meet someone, fall in love and make a cake of myself. Robert is a bit of a father-figure. I quite realise that. And he treats me with a kind of paternal, amused tolerance. If I met a man who thought I was wonderful, who was dazzled by me, I'm quite vain enough to commit all the worst sins, I imagine.'

'Dear Min, somehow I doubt it. You're too honest and straightforward. Adulterers have to be able to tell themselves that the feeling they have is something more important than ties of loyalty. They have to kid themselves that what they feel is not vanity and lust but a force too potent to be withstood, a destiny irresistible and sacrosanct. Or else that they're getting a rotten deal in the marriage, which entitles them to seek comfort elsewhere. Whatever the circumstances, it means that they're taking what they want regardless of anyone else's feelings.'

'All right, all right. I haven't done it yet. If I'm ever tempted I'll be sure to ring you up and get myself put back on the straight and narrow.'

I laughed. 'I didn't mean to sound hectoring. Poor Ellie. She'll be so upset about Gerald.'

'Yes. I shan't tell her he killed himself, do you think?'

'No. I don't think I would. You can say he took too many pills by mistake, I suppose.'

'I'll let her get over you not being here first. I'd better go and make tea. Goodbye, darling. Telephone me soon.'

I promised I would. Of course I knew that the little lecture I'd given about adultery had been intended not for Min but for myself.

I spent almost all of the following week in the University Library, mapping out the plan of my book. I began to see how I could pull my ideas together to make an interesting theory.

These hours were my happiest. The keen pleasure I felt in being home, in soft sheets and a comfortable bed, having everything around me for a tranquil civilised existence, was soon overlaid by other, deeper feelings. The first days of recognising my love for Robert were filled with the excitement of discovery.

So this, then, was love. There wasn't a particle of my anatomy that remained unresponsive to the idea of him. I physically ached to feel him in my arms. The thought of his eyebrows was enough to make my heart beat faster and a sick thrill run from my head to my knees. At first the drowning absorption in someone else was revelatory and every experience was touched by it. Music was more moving, nature more exquisite and books, especially, were revealed to me with a new clarity.

I began to read again *The Mill on the Floss*, choosing it for no better reason than that it had come several times into my mind at Weston Hall. Now, more than ever, George Eliot's subtle analysis of reason and feeling was deeply engrossing and I was in that state of self-consciousness and egoism which propelled me into a complete synthesis with Maggie as she falls in love with Stephen Guest. But this first reckless excitement that was a kind of happiness, could not last. After I'd been back in Cambridge for a week my mood changed and began to descend and the tatters and remnants of intoxication sank inexorably, like the wreckage of a great ship drifting down to the ocean bed.

I was lonely. I could have companionship whenever I wanted it but the loneliness was not the kind that could be assuaged by meetings in common rooms and dining halls. They were distractions but they did nothing to cure the miserable sensation of being apart from everyone who mattered to me. I went to a few drinks parties where I knew quantities of people and came home early because I felt more isolated there than at home on my own where I could feed my love with memories, uninterrupted. I found the old photograph of Min and Robert on their wedding day. I kept it by my bed and several times a day examined it to feel again the gripping pains of love. I went to a couple of dinner parties. I watched people shoving dull food into faces that were indifferent to me and the effort of making conversation was wearisome almost beyond endurance. I went to the theatre with a girlfriend, of whom I was fond, but her insentient cheerfulness was an irritant and I couldn't stop myself being caustic and almost snappy. I lay awake at night, thinking of Robert, and my desire was like a hateful incubus astride my body, forever exciting, never satisfying.

Min and I telephoned each other every day and my heart always leapt when I heard her voice because one of us, before long, would mention Robert and I could indulge my need to talk about him. My affection for Min, when I was talking to her, was unaltered, undiminished. But when I thought about her afterwards it was as though there was an increase of distance between us. I saw myself as a miser, greedily examining my hoard of gold, wretched lest it be discovered, unable to derive any happiness from it or convert it to benefit. I could only capitulate repeatedly to a longing for secret contemplation of it. At first my conscience was soothed, even flattered, by a consciousness of unimpeachable conduct. None should know of my desires. None but myself would be made miserable. I would suffer in silence until the thing went away for lack of fuelling. But as my exultation waned and gave way to depression, so my guilt grew.

My mother telephoned me one cold, wet evening about two weeks after leaving Weston Hall. I was writing a postcard to William and Ellie and was dreadfully depressed.

'Diana? I've been trying to get you all day.'

She sounded tearful and accusing, though months would go by when she would neglect to get in touch with me at all. I had long ago given up initiating any communication myself as she hated Ezra to speak to me, even on the telephone.

'I've been working. I've only just got home.'

'Oh. I see.'

She never expressed any interest in my work. I don't think she had any idea of what I did.

'What's up?'

'Ezra's left me.' She began to cry in earnest and I had a job to hear exactly what she was saying, between gulps. 'The bastard didn't even say goodbye. Just a ghastly little note, all platitudes and excuses. The truth is he's gone off with Barbara Buchan. She's got a private income and huge breasts. I've caught Ezra staring at them when he didn't know I was looking at him.'

'Oh, Mother. I'm sorry.'

I was sorry. My mother, between men, was an intolerable nuisance, telephoning at all hours, demanding that I spend aeons of time listening to the tale of her wretchedness, smoking and drinking and not eating until she made herself ill. Once I'd had to fetch her from a police station when she was charged with being drunk and disorderly. The last time Ezra had left her I'd had to pay for her to go into an expensive private nursing home for two weeks to be put back on her feet. After that she'd convalesced with me. Anyone who has had an alcoholic to stay will understand the nightmare of lighted cigarettes left everywhere in the house. There were still burns on almost every flat surface and I'd had to get up several times in the night to check that her room wasn't on fire as she always smoked in bed. A year had passed since that time during which she had telephoned me once, in order to ask me for a loan.

'I'm so lonely. I think I'm going mad. And there isn't any hot water. Something's happened to the boiler. I'm too miserable to find a man to come and fix it. One certainly finds out who one's friends are. Not a soul's been near me for two days. I think I'll kill myself. Who is there to care?'

Despite myself, I was touched by the quavering unhappiness that flowed from the receiver. I had a degree of fellow feeling.

'Would you like to come and stay for a bit?'

'You don't want me. You're always so cold and superior. I'd be better off dead.'

'Don't be silly. Just turn everything off in the flat and come here. Make sure you've unplugged the iron and turned off the gas.'

'All right. I'll come tomorrow then.'

'I'll get a timetable and give you the trains.'

We settled that my mother would catch the two forty-five, arriving in Cambridge at four. The next morning I asked Mrs Baxter to make up the guest-room bed and went out to shop before going to the library. I bought plenty of vodka . . . I knew it was useless to attempt to discourage her from drinking . . . and a chicken and some pears. I bought some scented narcissi and arranged them in her room. I made the pears into a pear and almond tart, which she adored, and the chicken into *coq au vin*. I went straight from the library to the station. The train came in but my mother wasn't on it. I waited twenty minutes for the next one as my mother was predictably hopeless about catching trains. Still no appearance. I went home and rang her flat. No answer. I ate what I could of the *coq au vin* and the pear tart and went to bed, picturing her smeared on the rails, cut to pieces or lying, unidentified, in some hospital.

I worked at home that morning, too anxious to leave the telephone. At two o'clock in the afternoon the telephone rang.

'Diana?'

'Where the hell have you been? I've been going mad with worry!'

'Have you?' She sounded pleased. 'No need, silly girl. I'm ringing from Dover. I'm going down to Roquebrune for a few days with Teddy Hodgson-Gore. He dropped in just after I called you and took me out to dinner and we suddenly sort of . . . you know . . . the whole thing fell into place and . . . darling, I'm trying to talk on the telephone . . .' There was much giggling and I heard a man's voice in the background. 'Must go, sweetie, don't want to miss the ferry. I'll send you a postcard. Byeee!'

The postcard never materialised. I moved the narcissi into my own room and went to the library. I sat in a sunless bay, by myself, and stared at the rows of books. Things had come to such a pass with me that I actually regretted my mother's failure to come and stay. The spines of the books blurred and wobbled. I closed my eyes and felt a warm tear on my lower lid. What was it Milton had said? 'In solitude What happiness? Who can enjoy alone, Or all enjoying, what contentment find?' I thought of Robert and in that quiet bay I gave myself up to sorrow.

Five minutes later, I wiped my eyes, closed my books and walked briskly home. This wallowing in self-pity was going to stop. I'd shed my last tear. The moment I got home I would destroy the photograph of Min and Robert and tear the man out of my heart and mind. I thought of Charlotte Bronte. I had sometimes suspected her of indulging her misery, especially when I'd visited the Parsonage at Haworth and found a pleasant comfortable house, neither dark nor sordid and very superior to all others of the period surrounding it. I compared my loneliness with hers after she had witnessed the harrowing deaths of a brother and two beloved sisters. How big were one's own sorrows and how little those of others! I felt a self-contempt which was wholly beneficial.

I opened the door of Orchard Street. An unfamiliar suitcase stood in the hall. There was a note from Mrs Baxter on the console table.

Dear Miss Fairfax,
A gentleman called just after you left. I took the liberty of letting him in to wait for you as he seemed to know you. Hope this is all right,
Hilda Baxter

I went into the drawing room. Standing by the French windows, looking out into the garden, was my visitor. He turned as I came in. It was Charles Jarrett.

## CHAPTER TWENTY

'Charles! How wonderful to see you!'

I didn't bother to conceal my pleasure. He came over and kissed me on the cheek. He smelt delicious, of cologne and hot, dry, male skin. He wore an elegant, slightly crumpled, cream linen suit and looked very dashing. He gave me a sharp look and then let me go.

'I came straight here from Heathrow. Have you a drink? I'm exhausted.'

He didn't look it. I got a bottle of champagne from the fridge and he opened it and filled two glasses.

'I like your house,' he said, stretching himself on the sofa and looking about. 'I had a good look while you were out. Downstairs only. It's very much as I imagined it. Orchestrated.'

I smiled but said nothing. I was amused by my delight in seeing him. A moment before discovering him in my house I'd been as miserable as I ever remembered being in my life. Now I felt that, after all, life had infinite possibilities. It crossed my mind that I might, through Charles's agency, rid myself of my incubus.

'What makes you smile?' he asked. Then when I didn't answer, he went on, 'Is there somewhere reasonable to eat? I want to unwind. It was touch-and-go until the last second whether the strike would end. It's made me very tense. Not helped by a delayed flight.'

He looked as relaxed as a tom-cat rolling on grass in the sunlight.

'Not really. Cambridge is notoriously bad for food unless you like moussaka and chips. There's the White Horse at Whittlesford. It's just a pub but the food's good and the atmosphere's not abrasive.'

That was where we went. I drove us in my Lotus Elan which still seemed astonishingly responsive and refined after the Land Rover. Charles was very amused by it, saying that it was like a prototype for a coffin, 'cabin'd, cribb'd, confin'd'. He asked me where the quotation came from. I said, *Macbeth*, and we went on to discuss my work. We ate stuffed peppers and drank an excellent bottle of Château Margaux to a Schubert string quartet. The pub was candlelit and very dark and it was possible to ignore the other diners.

'And did your new-found friendship with Robert survive the French cookery?' asked Charles.

'Thanks to you, it flourished. He was unable to resist the garlic.'

'And why did you leave?'

'I felt I must be stinking stronger than the stalest fish after three weeks.'

Charles looked up, surprised, 'Eozoic plumbing?'

I laughed and told him the adage about guests and fish stinking after three days.

'Also Min's hand was better. And I needed to get some proper work done. But it was a wrench.'

'Tell me in detail what you did after I left.'

So I told him everything that I could remember. The St Lawrence's Ball, the Spring Bazaar, Ellie's birthday in the boat-house, Vivien, Gerald. He was very interested in Gerald and before I was really aware of it he had prised the whole story of Gerald's suicide out of me, except for the fact that he had not been dead when Robert found him.

'So Robert's great friend was homosexual. Is Robert bisexual, do you think?'

'I doubt it.'

'Why does the suggestion that he might be annoy you?'

'I'm not annoyed.'

'You are. In South Africa we're not as tolerant of these things as you are here. Truthfully, I don't think I could relax with a man whom I knew to be homosexual. I wouldn't be able to understand a very fundamental part of his nature.'

'We aren't really very tolerant here, either. Only the cultivated minority are tolerant, and not even all of those. The vast majority of English people think it's disgusting or something to be joked about.'

'Have you ever been in love with a woman?' Charles asked me, pushing away his plate and lighting a cigarette.

'No. I just can't imagine it as a possibility even. I've never had the smallest desire to go to bed with even the most beautiful woman.'

'Or man, either?'

Charles handed me the lit cigarette. I wondered why he did that. It would have been more natural to offer me the packet. I suspected it was some kind of assertion of the fact that he knew what I wanted. I was being broken in, gradually.

'Wouldn't you like to know?' I said, mockingly, taking the cigarette.

'Very much.'

He lit a cigarette for himself and we smoked in silence for a while. The music changed and became more tempestuous. I thought it was probably Beethoven.

'So, tell me about Min and Robert. Why did you freeze for a moment when I asked whether Robert was queer?'

I did my best to satisfy his curiosity with the truth as far as I knew it, excepting, of course, my own feelings for Robert. He didn't seem quite satisfied. I already knew that Charles had a diviner's intuition for tracking the course of human relationships and I was very much on my guard. After a while he gave up the subject and told me what he'd been doing in South Africa. He didn't boast or put on airs but it sounded difficult and even dangerous.

'And what about when you weren't working?' I thought I'd try some of his own technique myself. 'What did you do?'

'I renewed some old acquaintances. It was interesting.'

I looked at him encouragingly. He smiled and filled my glass but said no more.

'Well, I like that! You dissect my life with your sharp little scalpel and expose every section to open view but you're as secretive yourself as the *arcanum arcanorum*. Tell me about these old aquaintances.'

'All right, I saw, among others, a woman with whom I once lived for ten years. I hadn't seen her for two. She hadn't changed, either physically or in any way that I could discover. She is still beautiful, in a bold, black-eyed, blatant way. Her name is Susannah. How am I doing?'

'Not bad. I'm hampered by an English notion that one shouldn't ask personal questions but I'm curious. I presume you were in love with her?'

'At the beginning, terrifically. She is very seductive. She was married to an important and powerful man. I was beginning to make a success of things but I hadn't the time or, really, the inclination, to acquire any trappings of money or power. I was flattered by her open declaration of interest. She was entirely without inhibitions, sexually as well as in every other way. Being with her was like drowning in honeydew.'

'So she left her husband for you?'

'Yes. That was my first mistake. Allowing her to do it. I tried to dissuade her. You see, after a time the honeydew began to feel like gum. She had no decent reticence. Nothing but desires . . . sexual, material, emotional. I never heard her make a witty or a tender remark. In an odd way, she was quite unfeminine. No softness, no subtlety, just a ruthless pursuit of what she wanted. She read the latest books, went to the newest exhibitions, attended the most fashionable concerts but nothing of what she saw or heard made the slightest impression. She wasn't stupid, exactly. She was patent. Flagrant.'

'Ten years is a long time to spend with someone you appear not to have wholly liked.'

'I felt under some obligation because she'd left her husband, though I'd advised her not to. I wasn't faithful to her and I never tried to disguise the fact. I didn't want to hurt her but she wasn't enough to give up the society of other women for.'

I began to feel rather sorry for Susannah.

'I suppose you think I'm a bastard?'

'I feel sorry for her. It isn't the same thing.'

'We became habituated to each other. It was a waste of time for both of us. It ended when I came to England.'

'What's she doing now?'

'She lives in a stunning house overlooking the sea, goes to parties, has taken up politics. Has, she told me, a politician lover.'

I wondered whether Charles had slept with her during this visit. For all he said about her, I sensed that the association had been much more important than he was ready to admit.

'You're wondering whether we slept together this time but you don't like to ask,' Charles said. 'Yes, I made love to her.'

He obviously wasn't going to say anything more though I was full of the most shameful curiosity. The waiter brought the bill and while Charles was signing it, I suddenly remembered that his suitcase was standing in my hall, like an augury. I felt a tremor of apprehension. We left the restaurant and walked out to the car park. I offered him the keys and asked him if he'd like to drive. He handled the car skilfully, with no attempt to drive fast or to show off. I stole a glance at his profile in the darkness. The lights from cars coming the other way made his eyes glitter. He was incredibly good-looking. I could quite see why Min was fixated. He was frowning slightly, concentrating.

'Well?' he said, not taking his eyes from the road. 'What's the result of the scrutiny? Do I go to the Porter's Arms for the night, where Horace has booked me a room? Or may I spend the night with you?'

My heart-rate leaped into *allegro con fuoco* at that and I tried to think calmly. I'd been free from thoughts of Robert all evening. It wasn't possible to be with Charles and think of other men. For two weeks I'd imagined, in a wholly unprecedented way, making love. I hadn't been able to separate thoughts of Robert from desire.

'You can stay with me, if you like.'

He didn't say anything. The words lingered on in the darkness. I felt a further stir of trepidation but I didn't think of taking them back. I unlocked the front door and switched on the drawing-room lights.

'Brandy?' I asked, my voice sounding strange to myself.

'I suppose that's how you look when going to the dentist,' said Charles.

This made me laugh.

'It's a pity this house is so small,' continued Charles, standing before the unlit fireplace and looking at me with some amusement. 'It means you have to stand within ten feet of me.'

'I was just getting myself a drink,' I said, crouching down to take a bottle of Hine from the cupboard.

With four strides he was beside me and pulling me to my feet.

'You don't need it.'

He put his arms round me and looked at me, I thought, mockingly. Then he began to kiss my face, very slowly and firmly, finally reaching my mouth. While I have always found the act of love-making ugly and alienating, kissing has always seemed to me ridiculous. However hard I try not to think of it, the idea of a snail's foot always comes into my mind. Charles's mouth was dry, thank God, and hard, in the proper romantic tradition. He knew what he was doing and didn't quiver and quake as some men did, which made me feel as though the pilot of my aircraft, now cruising at tens of thousands of feet, had admitted some bewilderment over the instrument panel. None-the-less, because I so very much didn't want to laugh, I couldn't help giggling. Charles stopped kissing me.

'Stop laughing, you hopeless girl.'

He was smiling at me, not put out at all. Other men would have been annoyed, sulky or angry. He even began to laugh himself as he continued to kiss me. After a minute a part of me wanted him to go on. The telephone bell was an unwelcome interruption.

'Don't answer it,' said Charles, holding me tightly.

'I must. It's late. It might be important. My mother.'

He let me go and I picked up the receiver.

'I want to speak to Charles Jarrett, please.'

It was an unfamiliar female voice, low, strongly South African. I gave the receiver to Charles.

'Yes? Susannah! What game are you playing at, calling me here?' Charles's voice was freezing. 'How did you get the number?'

The voice buzzed, but the words were indistinct. Charles listened and then sighed. He didn't bother to conceal his impatience.

'All right, it was very clever. But I don't think Horace is fair game.' There was a pause while the voice at the other end buzzed on. 'I'm sorry, Susannah, but I'm busy. Ring me at Milecross Park tomorrow. After six o'clock, English-time.'

The voice at the other end became voluble, hysterical. I walked out and closed the door. I went upstairs, took off my clothes, washed and brushed my teeth. I put on a dressing-gown. I felt rather foolish, in a state of nervous expectancy, like a Victorian bride waiting to have the fearsome mysteries of married life revealed to her. I lay on the bed and took up the volume of Anthony Trollope which lay on the bedside table. I was just reading about the courtship of the guileless Emily Wharton when I felt a hand on my shoulder.

'Unfinished business?' I said.

'Very much finished. Let me get my clothes off. I'll take a shower.'

I went back to Emily Wharton's travails. Anyone with a particle of sense would have seen through Ferdinand Lopez. Except, suddenly, he reminded me of Charles.

'Put that book away.' Charles was standing by the bed, smiling in what seemed to me an imperious, Ferdinand Lopez manner. 'Nothing can save you now.'

'What's the matter with Susannah?' I asked, keeping my eyes politely on Charles's face as he removed his towel. 'She's still in love with you.'

'Be quiet.'

He began to kiss me again, not only my face but my neck and shoulders, while his hands stroked my body. I felt obliged to do some polite reciprocal stroking. His body was admirable, smooth and firm. I thought of Min and how she would have approved of the naked Charles. I remembered the conversation in which we'd compared him with the heroes of romantic novels. He was certainly masterful. Despite every good intention, I felt again a compulsion to laugh. I suppose it was anxiety. Charles stopped kissing me.

'Just for once, stop thinking, will you? This is one situation in which you don't need to be in control. Forget about being Diana, forget about your work, your house, your friends, your mother. Let go. You're a remarkably beautiful woman. I'm desperate to make love to you. Forget everything else. Close your eyes.'

I did as I was told and tried to still my thoughts.

'You're quite safe,' I heard Charles say, as he kissed my ear. 'I'm not going to take advantage of you. This is for you just as much as for me. Let go.'

I relaxed, as conscientiously as though obeying the instructions of my physiotherapist.

'Good girl. Now, don't tense up again. Listen to what I'm telling you. Unclench your hand. Keep your eyes closed.'

His voice murmured on and I listened and obeyed. I thought of Min and . . . no, no, not that way. I breathed calmly and willed my muscles to relax. He began to hold me tighter and I saw the mare, Astarte, in my mind's eye and recognised the tone of Charles's voice. It was a kind of hypnotism. Gradually, after a few minutes, I began to think that this was, after all, very pleasant, to lie comfortably, dreaming, on a bed with a handsome man kissing my eyes and ears and breasts and . . . I began to feel a contraction of my skin which ran over my entire body and involuntarily my breathing quickened.

'You're quite safe. Let go, let go,' he said and with the most tremendous sensation of wonder, the world began to dissolve as a feeling of ecstasy, bright, fierce, exigent, made me tremble with astonished joy. I felt as though I were climbing faster and faster to a frantic paradise. I was seized by an intense, unstoppable desire to progress to the farthest point. I said to myself, scarcely recognisable, so this is love. Nothing mattered except to go on, until my mind and body liquefied into consummate rapture and I cried out, or thought I did, for Robert.

Afterwards, as my heart began to slow and I felt the hot tears on my eyelids, I was filled with love for Charles. I felt his arms around me and wanted nothing more. Every molecule of my body was metabolised into effervescent weightlessness. I opened my eyes. His face was close to mine. I recognised him with a sense of surprise.

'My darling girl,' was all he said, sighing and closing his eyes.

I was tempted to tell him of my love. I was exultant, I was free from . . . no, no, I mustn't even think of it. That was a stupid mistake . . . in the past. Charles had given me the greatest pleasure I'd ever known. No wonder everyone went on about it so much. Now I was astonished that everyone wasn't spending every available minute in bed, making love.

People sacrificed wives, husbands, children, careers, conscience, peace of mind for it and I could quite see why. I moved a little in sheer sensuous pleasure and Charles opened his eyes. He looked at my face and smiled.

'I was right, wasn't I?' he said.

'You triumphant bastard.'

He didn't answer and I heard his breathing lengthen and felt his arm grow heavy across my body. I was happy. I didn't want to sleep. I wanted to lie in his arms and recapture the pleasure, to celebrate my return to sanity. My thoughts tangled and drifted. Reluctantly I abandoned consciousness.

The telephone woke me with a start. I looked at the clock. It was eight o'clock. I picked up the receiver.

'Miss Fairfax? It's Horace speaking. I'm sorry to disturb you so early but could I speak to Charles, if he's there?'

'Hello, Horace. Yes, just a minute.'

Charles took the receiver from me. He seemed to be instantly awake.

'Yes? No it's all right. Yes, I know. Don't worry. I know. She told me. I'm not annoyed with *you*. Really, it's all right.'

Then Charles was silent for some time, listening.

'Damn!' he said, at last. 'It means I'll have to leave Cambridge this morning. Ring Evans and get him to bring the car round as soon as possible.' He gave Horace my address. 'It's a bloody nuisance. Keep Aziz happy until I get there. Give him lunch and show him the new yard. Right. Good. I'm relying on you.'

He handed me the receiver and I put it back.

'You heard? A potential buyer's coming to look at Milecross Park. I've decided to sell it. He's one of the few people who can afford the price I'm asking. I've got to get back and make him see what a bargain it is. He's flying back to the Middle East tonight so I can't make any other arrangements. I'm sorry. I wanted to have the morning with you.'

'I'm sorry, too.'

I was. He took me in his arms and began to kiss me. Then he pulled himself away.

'No. It would be a mistake to rush it. There'll be other times.'

He only had time to shower and drink a cup of coffee before the car was at the door. I wanted to ask him why he was selling

Milecross Park and where he was intending to live. Most of all, when he was coming back. But he was preoccupied and withdrawn and I didn't want to be tiresome like Susannah.

'Goodbye, my darling,' he said, kissing me briefly, and then he was gone.

I ate a slice of toast, slowly, and thought about him. I was still in a state of excitement from last night and couldn't order my thoughts to reach any sensible conclusion. I decided to do some work at home. I wasn't in the mood for other people. I'd just succeeded in some proper concentration on the effects of Peacock's friendship with Shelley on *The Misfortunes of Elphin* when the telephone rang again. I looked at my watch. Ten thirty. It couldn't be Charles.

'Hello. Is Charles there?'

I recognised the voice of Susannah.

'He's already left. He's on his way back to Milecross Park.'

I tried to sound friendly and noncommittal. There was a pause.

'I suppose he fucked you last night.'

I was tempted to put the telephone down but the woman's unhappiness was evident and I was, to be truthful, curious.

'Is that any of your business?'

'Don't think it means anything. Charles fucks every woman he meets, just about. He's good at it, isn't he?' I remained silent and she went on. 'I know you're still there. Listen, let me do you a favour. He's a selfish bastard. Once he's been to bed with a woman he loses interest. He'll already be looking for the next one, right now. He probably won't even remember your name in a few weeks' time. Don't make my mistake. I've had to see him work through every good-looking woman, single and married, in the Cape.'

Her voice was hard and angry, but there was a catch in it as though she was near to tears.

'Why don't you forget about him, then?' I asked. 'He's obviously made you unhappy.'

'Because there isn't any other man for me. I've tried, don't think I haven't. I love the son-of-a-bitch and I'll still love him when he's old and can't fuck any more. And my children need their father.'

'Charles's children?'

I felt a sensation of shock.

'Sure. Of course he didn't tell you about them. A boy and a girl. Seven and five.' Her voice became softer and more confidential. 'This trip he was taken with them. I could see that. He doesn't like babies. But I could see that he minded leaving them, this time.'

'Is he . . . are you married to Charles?'

'No. I'm being honest with you. I don't know why I should be. I'm jealous as hell. But I've got nothing to lose. Charles won't be faithful to any woman. There's a chance he might stay with me because of the children. As I say, he can't go on screwing for ever.'

'I'm so sorry.'

'Sorry for what?'

'You sound so unhappy.'

'Yeah. Well. I'm a bloody fool. That's the truth of it. Do yourself a good turn and get stuck on some nice guy who comes home every night and wants you to take up golf with him.'

The telephone suddenly clicked and we were cut off. I put my head in my hands. I felt almost as badly depressed as this time yesterday. I wondered if I was having some sort of breakdown. I stared at what I'd written that morning about Shelley and Peacock. As far as I was concerned I wouldn't have cared if the whole boiling lot of them had never written so much as a postcard.

The discipline of years got me through. I worked on and managed in the end to write what felt like several good pages. I stopped for lunch and had a chat with Mrs Baxter whose serene common sense was reassuring. She was a tactful woman and I didn't realise that Charles had left his shaver until after she'd gone. It was neatly put away in the bathroom cupboard. I looked at it with a sensation of desire so strong that my knees weakened. I must have gone mad, I said to myself. Suddenly, I'd become a nymphomaniac, inflamed to unslakeable lusts by the sight of an electric razor. The telephone rang. I threw myself on to the bed and grabbed it. It was Min.

'Hello, Daisy. You sound rather breathless.'

'Oh God. I thought you might be Charles. Not that I'm not delighted to hear you. In fact, you're just the person I want to talk to.'

'Has Charles telephoned? Is he back from South Africa?'

'Better than that. He was here.'

'Daisy! Do you mean . . .? *When* was he there . . .? oh, help, I'm going to have a fit! Tell me *everything*!'

'He was here when I got back from the library last night. He came straight from the airport.' I remembered him standing in the drawing room and experienced further sensations in my knees.

'Go on! Tell me every single little thing! Hurry up!'

'We went out to dinner. We talked. I can't remember what about. Oh yes, how he'd seen this woman in South Africa he used to live with. For ten years.'

'Why was he telling you about her? That sounds rather maladroit. Not like Charles.'

'I asked him. He always makes me talk about myself. I felt I didn't know anything about him.'

'Go on. What about this woman?'

'At first, I thought it was over. He said that he'd slept with her on this trip but that he'd fallen out of love with her ages ago.'

'Nothing wrong with that,' said Min staunchly, in defence of her favourite. 'He was probably doing her a favour.'

The expression jarred on me, having heard it so recently on someone else's lips.

'Well, anyway, when we were driving home after dinner he told me that he had a room booked in a hotel.' I remembered his dark, handsome face. I sighed. 'He asked me if he could spend the night with me.'

'And you said? I'm going to collapse if you don't get on with it. Vicarious lust is punishing stuff.'

'I said he could stay with me.' I smiled as I heard Min's hoot of joy. 'Just as he was starting to kiss me the telephone rang.'

'That thunk you heard was me falling to my knees. Go on. Who was the Person from Porlock?'

'It was this woman he'd told me about. She seemed in something of a stew. I felt I shouldn't be listening. I went upstairs and undressed and half got into bed in my dressing-gown. Then Charles came up.'

'Where is the sal-volatile? I'm gripping the telephone with beads of perspiration dripping from my brow. I'm going to faint, I think. *Go on.*'

'Well, we made love.'

'I'm so envious I could scream! *Don't* tell me you didn't enjoy it.'

'Actually . . . it was, I suppose, the greatest moment of physical pleasure in my entire life.' I couldn't help laughing, both at the memory and at the sounds coming from the mouthpiece. 'My God, I feel better, talking to you!'

'I don't understand. Why aren't you in a state of beatification?'

'He had to go away very early. He's selling Milecross Park. He had to go back to meet a buyer. After he'd gone the woman . . . she's called Susannah . . . rang again, wanting to speak to him. We talked for a bit. It seems he's got two children by her. She says he's selfish and that he sleeps with every woman he comes across.'

'Not true,' said Min. 'I can vouch for that. Unfortunately.'

'Yes, but I think it *is* true, barring happily married women. She said that he was incapable of being faithful to any woman and I believe her. He's only interested in making people do what he wants. I knew that from the beginning. It doesn't matter. Only . . .'

I stopped because I felt a prickle of tears.

'You confused sexual gratification with love? You wouldn't be the first person to do that.'

'Oh, Min. I suppose I did. I've been rather depressed, actually, since getting back to Cambridge.'

'Why didn't you tell me?'

'Didn't want to be a bore.'

This was a lie but it would do.

'Darling Daisy, why won't you come and stay here? If you knew how we miss you! Ellie talks about you every day. And it would cheer Robert up. He's so depressed by poor Gerald's death. He's gone very silent. Couldn't you bring all the books you need?'

'I suppose I could. But it's only putting off the fact that my life has become unsatisfactory. I feel it's time to change but I simply don't know in what direction. Hang on . . . there's someone at the door.'

I ran downstairs. A spotty boy was standing on the doorstep holding an enormous bouquet of white roses. The card said *With love from Charles*. I left them in the hall and ran back up to the telephone.

'Doesn't that make you feel better?' asked Min.

'Yes. Quite a bit. Though I expect he just asked Horace to send them.'

Actually, they made me feel quite a lot better. After Min and I had finished talking I arranged them in the drawing room where they looked stunning, and waited for a telephone call. That didn't come. By the time the roses had turned brown and shed their petals over the table and he still hadn't rung, I had turned Charles out of my heart.

I was old enough to know the difference between desire and love. I wasn't in love with Charles. I knew that what Susannah had said was more or less true. I went on working at my book and seeing people when I had to. I began to listen to Wagner in the evenings, in a way I'd never done before . . . with intense concentration, until the flood of feeling the music always induced became something like a drug, which I felt I had to have when I came back from the library.

I wasn't quite a hermit during this time. I refused most of the invitations I had from men because I was afraid of ending up in bed with them and being unable to repeat the experience I'd had with Charles. But I went to dinner parties and lunches and to Covent Garden with an elderly man who'd been a friend for years and who was long past making love to me. We saw *Tristan and Isolde* and the experience was electrifying. I knew I was courting danger and that it wouldn't make me happy but I had to have that tenuous link with Robert.

Min and I spoke as much as ever on the telephone. She'd sent off her preface to her editor who'd been rapturous about it. I'd never heard Min so excited about anything. It made me understand how much of a struggle the years of domestic life had been for her . . . endless effort to do the right thing with so little reassurance that the sacrifice was doing anyone any good.

I got on with my work and began to enjoy it. I ordered a new carpet for the bathroom and spent a couple of days in London buying clothes. I sowed some sweet peas and dead-headed the herbaceous plants in the garden. I gave a couple of dinner parties. I went out four or five times with a man called Sebastian. He was very affected and wore a hat and cloak like Carlyle, which had the same mesmerising effect on the general public as the late historian's had done. I liked him because he was witty and wasn't dull. But of course before long he felt he'd served his unofficial apprenticeship with dinners and flattery and wanted to get articled. I couldn't bring myself even to kiss him and he went off, rather bitter and dramatic.

Then Peter telephoned to say that he was about to leave Rome and come back to England. Could he come and stay for a few days? He arrived in a flow of high spirits, quite brown and a little fatter, talking amusingly and endlessly. He gave me the most beautiful, extravagant presents . . . a silk shirt, a tiny marble statue of Pallas Athene and a wonderful pair of shoes. After supper we sat by the fire and finished a second bottle of wine and ate the chocolates he'd brought. I told him about Robert. It was bliss to be able to talk about him. I emphasised the hopelessness of it. Peter was very interested and enormously sympathetic. I felt relaxed and almost happy. I began to wonder whether Peter and I might live together on a more or less permanent basis. We were the best of friends. I wanted to banish the feeling of loneliness which had trotted after me, like a hungry stray, since my return from Weston Hall.

'It's glorious to see you, you darling girl,' said Peter. 'I'd almost forgotten what a chum you are. It's been a long time and so much has happened. But old friends have a special charm, *n'est-ce pas*? Now, I've got something to tell you. I've met Mr Right. I'm madly in love . . . and he with me . . . and he's coming to England in two days' time. I'm dying to show him off to you. But no flashing those heavenly eyes at him. He was married briefly and so is not a stranger to the charms of the fair sex.'

'Peter! How exciting! Tell me all about it.'

'His name is Giorgio and he's writing a book on Correggio. He's sick-makingly dark and handsome. His English isn't too good but he'll pick it up quickly once he's here. He's fearfully bright. And just the teeniest bit jealous of my other friends so you mustn't mind if he seems chilly at first.'

Giorgio came and stayed with Peter in the spare bedroom. I didn't mind the fact that they hardly seemed to sleep at night and that the walls of the house were rather thin. Nor did I really mind that they spoke constantly in Italian and so rapidly that I could understand nothing more than the string of endearments that linked every sentence. I did rather mind the fact that Giorgio's body was clothed in thick black hair and that he seemed to be permanently in moult, especially in the bath, which he never cleaned himself. Peter ran round after him, cooking him special dishes. As he explained apologetically to me, Giorgio's stomach was terribly sensitive and he could only eat very well-cooked meat and vegetables or he had indigestion. He had been horrified by the rare fillet I'd served on the evening of his arrival and had made Peter put the carrots back into the pan to boil until they were pulpy.

Poor Peter! It was sad to see him so infatuated by this hirsute vulgarian who took every opportunity to make body contact with me when we met on the stairs or in the kitchen and who, when Peter's eyes were turned away, which was not often, sent me smouldering and suggestive looks. Giorgio never opened a book during the week he stayed with me, and when Peter put on a record of Mozart or Haydn, fell into resounding snoring within minutes. He seemed to be suffering from writer's block on the subject of Correggio. Instead he stalked about the house, examining everything in it with an interest that made me think he might be going to steal it. He never addressed a remark to me during the entire visit, apart from the morning when Peter was out, scouring Cambridge for fresh pasta for Giorgio's lunch. I was working at my desk and had my back to the door. Suddenly I felt a hand on my neck and spun round to find myself staring into Giorgio's big brown eyes.

'Ti piace fottere con me?'

'Non, grazie. Mi fa nauseare.'

I wasn't sure whether my Italian was quite correct but he got the message and when Peter returned, he talked very loud and very fast, flinging his hands into the air and grimacing in my direction, until Peter was nearly in tears.

'Darling,' Peter said to me a little later. 'You've been too sweet to have us for so long. Now we must go and leave you in peace. Giorgio has a wish to see Oxford and it's time I got down to a little work. *Grazie mille, carissima*, for all your tolerance.'

I saw them off with enormous relief, though I was touched to see that Peter kept his eyes on me until the last possible moment when the taxi went out of sight, almost as though begging to be saved. I was sure it wouldn't be long before I heard more of this liaison. I went in and scrubbed the bath and put the sheets from their bed into the dustbin. I looked forward to a night of peace without groans and squeaking bed-springs.

But my own experience had taught me that one couldn't fasten one's affections where one chose.

Despite the repulsive Giorgio I missed Peter. I decided to telephone Min to find out how the children were. Ellie had got chickenpox and there was every likelihood that William would get it too. I'd already sent Ellie a letter and a copy of *Winter Holiday* by Arthur Ransome. Min sounded more miserable than I'd every heard her.

'Daisy! God, I was just about to ring you! You'll never believe what a state we're in.'

'Is Ellie worse? Has William got it?'

'Yes and no. Ellie's more spot than space and is feeling ghastly. Poor little thing, we counted fifty spots on her hands alone. But there's worse. I've just got back from the hospital. William fell off a wall at school and broke his leg. He's in plaster from ankle to thigh. He's coming home in two days but he won't be able to do anything for a bit. Poor darling, he's being very brave. And just as the children need me most, my editor rang this morning to say that they want me to do another preface . . . for Madame de Staël's *De la littérature considérée dans ses rapports avec les institutions sociales* . . . she and Sisimondi were friends, you know . . . for the same series. But the deadline's June! And there's so much to read before I can begin to write! And Vivien's got shingles. Obviously she caught it from Ellie's chickenpox. I feel rather responsible. Of course Lily will look after her but I ought to visit her. I'm in despair. They'll never ask me to write anything again if I say I can't because of the children.' I could hear that Min was close to tears. 'Daisy, you couldn't . . . could you . . . just consider the possibility of coming back? You did say your book was going well now? We could take it in turns to write and be with the invalids. Do you think I'm the most selfish person alive for asking you?'

I thought, rapidly. There was only one thing stopping me from accepting the invitation. Robert. But I was getting over it. I'd got myself back to a normal routine existence. I realised that the whole thing had been a delusion and a piece of folly. I was calmer now than I'd been for weeks. I was out of danger.

'Daisy?'

'I'll come on Wednesday.'

\*

Six weeks had passed since I'd left Weston Hall. Wednesday was the first of April and the sky was very bright, with a few high hurrying clouds and a very cold wind. I took *Our Mutual Friend* with me to read on the journey, a novel I've always loved and think more highly of each time I read it. I've always liked trains. I could have stayed on that train for ever, speeding through the countryside in a state of happy anticipation about seeing Min and the children again. I'd packed myself rather a good picnic of crab sandwiches, cherries and bitter chocolate with a half-bottle of Pouilly-Fuissé. From time to time I stared out of the window and lost myself in day-dreaming. I was very glad to be able to think about Robert quite calmly, with no discernible increase of adrenalin. I was cured.

When we reached Dunston Abchurch, I leaned from the open window and called to Vokins and my three cases were unloaded with a great deal of trouble to everyone before the train drew away with a wild scream of its whistle. Vokins was looking doubtfully at me.

'The taxis is all gone 'ome, Miss, it bein' so late. And the telephone lines is down on account o' gale last week.'

It was just after six. Though the wind was cold, there was plenty of light still and I was warmly dressed.

'I'll leave the cases here and walk to Weston Hall. I shall enjoy it. I'm stiff from sitting in the train. I'll drive back in the Land Rover and fetch them. It's a wonderful evening for a walk.'

Vokins touched the peak of his cap and said he'd stand guard over my luggage until I returned.

It was two miles to Weston Hall. After leaving the station the lane grew narrow and passed through empty fields and woods. Now the trees were starting into leaf and in the soft, blue gloom of evening there was a wonderful feeling of peace. Apart from the wind in the trees and the sound of my own footfalls, there was quiet. No cars, planes, talk, not even birdsong, just a slurred, susurrant shaking of leaves.

'Now fades the glimmering landscape on the sight, And all the air a solemn stillness holds.' I repeated the words as I walked slowly, enjoying myself. I might have been absolutely alone in the world. A ghostly white patch hovered beneath the hedge. It was a clump of wild white violets. I bent to pick one. Its faint, delicious scent was almost like a sedative. It was a moment of the most perfect security and dreaming tranquillity.

A sheep bleated from the other side of the hedge and made me start. Then I heard a click of claws and, bounding round the corner of the lane, came a large black dog who threw herself ecstatically at me, uttering strange sounds, like a mixture of singing and barking from between her grinning teeth.

'Ham! Hello, you dear, silly dog!' I bent to stroke her as she rolled over and sprang up several times in quick succession to demonstrate the depth of her feelings.

I was absurdly pleased to see her. No lost Alpine wayfarer buried to his eyebrows in a drift could have felt as happy to see a St Bernard as I did to see Ham. But she was a mile from home by herself. That was unusual. No. Someone was coming down the lane. I stood still and strained to see beneath the canopy of trees that shaded the lane just at the bend. A man came in sight. He was looking down as he walked slowly, his hands in his pockets. He stopped for a moment and bent to pick something up from the road. I waited. He still hadn't seen me. I felt the oddest sensation of something tightening slowly round my heart. He walked forward again, examining whatever it was that he had picked up. When he was less than a few feet from me, he started and looked up.

It seemed to grow dark before my eyes and the scent of the violets rose up around me like a supernatural portent. I meant to say, 'Hello, Robert,' in a calm voice, but I couldn't speak. He held, on the palm of his hand, a small blue egg. I knew that every second of silence was a betrayal of my feelings. I thought, stupidly, that he meant me to take the egg and I held out my hand. With his other hand he took hold of mine and I was unable to draw it away. His dark eyes, usually so sharp, were soft with love. It was done. The suppression of my feelings, the secret enclosure of my love which I had planned with such confidence in my own powers of deception, was dispelled with the first glance. I closed my eyes for they were hot and spilling with tears. Then I felt his cheek against mine and the intoxicating sensation of his arms around me.

Ham jumped and whined around our legs. Finally a sudden, sharp gust of wind brought us to our senses and we began to walk, arm-in-arm, along the lane and up the hill to Weston

Hall, not speaking, not even looking at each other. We knew quite well that we were both dreadfully, appallingly happy.

I saw the Hall at last with a few lights winking as the trees tossed before them. I knew that no possible good could come of this and that in a minute or two I would be stricken with remorse for what I had done. This was our last moment of happiness together. I think Robert felt that too for he stopped and turned me towards him. We were both trembling with love and shame and fear. He bent his head and kissed me. The warmth of his mouth made me feel faint with longing. I could feel his heart beating. Then we let go of each other and walked side by side up the drive with Ham running back and forth ahead of us.

## CHAPTER TWENTY-ONE

In the hall, I stood quite bewildered. Then Min came running out and threw her arms round my neck. I felt her face pressed briefly to my own treacherous cheek.

'Daisy! how wonderful of you to come early! Darling, you didn't walk! Why didn't you telephone?'

It was so like my former arrival, and yet, in one particular, so unlike.

'I met Daisy in the lane while I was taking Ham for a walk,' said Robert. 'Is your luggage at the station?'

We didn't look at each other.

'Yes.' I paused and gathered my thoughts. 'There weren't any taxis so I decided to walk and then drive back in the Land Rover to fetch it.'

'Oh, Robert will go, won't you, darling? There's so much to say. At least I suppose there isn't really because we've talked on the telephone, but still I haven't *seen* you. And Ellie's going to be so thrilled. She's been miserable all after-noon. Come on.'

I allowed myself to be taken into the kitchen. Ellie was sitting at the table, her head buried in her arms.

'Look who's here,' said Min.

Ellie looked up, gave a squawk and flung herself at me. Her face and arms were disfigured with a mottling of red spots smeared with pink calamine lotion and she was much thinner.

'You poor thing! I remember having chickenpox when I was your age,' I said, kissing the tip of her nose which was the only place without a spot on it. 'I was at school. That was before your mother came. It was the summer holidays. I was supposed to be going somewhere with my mother. Italy, I think. I was so pleased not to be going with her that it made every horrible itch worth while. But I don't think I had it as badly as you.'

'Dr Turnbull says I'm the worst case he can remember,' Ellie said, with pride. 'But I feel horrible . . . as though I've got scales all over me. I want to climb out of my coat like a hatching dragonfly. Why didn't you want to go to Italy?'

'Because it wasn't much fun going on holiday with my mother. She'd be nice to me for the first two days and then she'd get tired of having me around and I'd end up on my own in the hotel bedroom. Once, in Florence, I made friends with the laundry-maids and we used to play cards with the porters and bellboys. That was quite good.'

I remembered the hot little room, stacked with linen smelling of soap, and the warning glances of the women, indicating me, when the men tried to get amorous with them. It was another humiliating experience of being in the way but the women were kind. They discussed my mother in words I couldn't understand but I divined their disapproval.

'Don't you like your mother?' Ellie was puzzled.

'Not really, no. But I feel sorry for her and I don't like her to be unhappy.'

'Daisy always spent the holidays with us after we became friends,' said Min. 'Ma couldn't afford to take us to hotels but we used to go and stay with friends who had big houses. Do you remember staying at Ticknor Castle?'

She looked at me with a smile.

'Yes. We had to change for dinner every evening and we'd only got one dress each. That girl . . . what was her name? . . . Marianne, was very sneering about our clothes.'

'She hated having to have us to stay and moaned all the time to her mother about sharing her bathroom with us. Little brat.' Min began to giggle.

'The day we left we tied her up and gagged her and left her in the bath, do you remember? I wonder how long it was before someone found her?'

Ellie was impressed by our youthful daring.

'It wasn't difficult,' Min said. 'Marianne was a soft little thing. She'd only ever had governesses. We used our dressing-gown cords as ropes and gagged her with her own knickers. It was rather bad of us but she was such a little beast. She asked for it. Ma was surprisingly mild in her ticking-off about it, though the Ticknor people rang up and made an awful fuss.'

'What interesting childhoods you've both had,' said Ellie, looking depressed again. 'I've never done anything I can tell my future children about.'

'When you're better we must think of something you can do that will make good telling,' I said, taking off my coat and going to hang it in the boot room. 'When daddy comes back with my luggage you can have the present I brought for you.'

I had brought her a little red morocco case which had compartments for sewing and writing things. There was a pair of scissors shaped like a stork, a plait of different-coloured cottons, a packet of needles, a thimble, a pincushion of yellow velvet shaped like a pear, some writing-paper with cats on and a small leather purse marked *Stamps*. The case had come equipped with these useful items and I had added a needle-point canvas painted with a black-and-white cat and the wools to sew it with, and some little pots of Windsor & Newton ink.

Ellie was just as pleased and excited as I'd hoped she'd be and went through everything several times, getting them out and putting them away again. William's present had to be put on one side as he wasn't due to return home from the hospital until tomorrow. For Min I'd bought a leather-bound edition of *Felix Holt*. We had shared a love of George Eliot ever since we'd been old enough to read her books and though I knew she didn't care for the appearance of things generally, I hoped that books were an exception. For Robert I'd bought, from the same shop, a beautifully bound set of the scores of all Wagner's operas. The covers were board, not leather, but marbled inside and out and the paper and printing were of high quality.

It had given me immense pleasure to buy the set and I'd taken it home and dusted each volume and gloated over them, getting them out of their wrapping several times to feel the pleasure of them under my hand, like Silas Marner and his iron pot of guineas. Now I felt that it was too extravagant and too particular and I wished that I'd brought him a bottle opener or the usual things one gives a man for whom one feels no particular affection. While Robert was unwrapping them I felt that my cheeks were burning. He looked at each one carefully as though they held a difficult code that he was trying to puzzle out.

'How lovely! said Min. 'You always give the most marvellous presents. Aren't you pleased, Robert?'

He hadn't spoken but continued to turn them over in his hands.

'Yes, I'm very pleased. Thank you, Daisy.'

He looked in my direction without really looking at me and gave me the briefest of smiles.

'He *is* pleased. I know he is,' said Min, hurt on my behalf. 'It's the most wonderful present. Now let's have some champagne. I got some specially for you. This is just like old times. Open a bottle, darling. You see what I mean,' she said, in an undertone to me, when Robert had gone out of the room, carrying the Wagner scores, and Ellie was getting Booty's supper ready, 'Robert hasn't got over Gerald's death. He goes for hours without saying anything. I'm not surprised poor Ellie's been miserable. I've been preoccupied, I know, though I've tried to put aside time to be with her. William's been moodier than ever. Altogether it hasn't been the happiest of times. Except for the publishers liking my work.'

A different look came into Min's eye even as she mentioned it and I recognised the old Min of school and the first year of university, very determined and single-minded.

'Your work must take priority,' I said. 'Mine hasn't really got a deadline. I'll do what I can to cheer the children up. I'll cook and Mrs Butter will clean and you'll be able to work non-stop, more or less.'

All this was a sop to my conscience. I felt that I could not do enough for Min, that I might redeem myself by helping her to achieve the one thing that really mattered to her.

'Oh, it would be good if you could do the cooking. You know how hopeless I am. It's shepherd's pie for supper, by the way.'

'Delicious,' I said staunchly.

Everything was more or less as I had left it. There were no flowers but there was generally an air of greater comfort than on the evening of my first arrival. Min got out the candlesticks in honour of my return. Robert talked about how William had been when he'd visited him in the afternoon.

'He's fed up because the nurses treat him like a little boy. They call him "poppet" and "duck" and things like that, meaning to be kind, but he hates it. He's in a bed next to an old man who sings all the time. I think he must be senile. I heard him this afternoon. Just one song, "Ol' Man River", over and over again. William says he sings in the middle of the night, too, and wakes him up.'

'Give Daisy the tomato sauce.' Min helped me to an alarmingly large portion of shepherd's pie, dropping some of it on to the table. 'Oh, blast!'

She went to the sink to get a cloth. Robert lifted his eyebrows and handed me the bottle. My stomach somersaulted and my hands trembled so much at the look in his eyes that I had great difficulty in getting the cap off.

'Let me,' said Robert.

His hand brushed mine briefly as he took the bottle from me and it was as though the accidental touch grazed my skin for I felt it on the back of my hand for minutes afterwards. I watched the granular scarlet stream run on to my plate with a pulse in my throat which hurt.

'Old man who?' asked Ellie.

'River. It's about a river in the Deep South. Supposed to be sung by slaves. It's a very good song.'

Robert began to hum it and Min and I joined in when we could remember the words. Robert had a bass voice, rather good, and was able to get a good deal of passion into it. 'Tired o' livin' and scared o' dyin' but Ol' Man River, he jus' keeps rollin along,' we sang. For a moment I thought that it was going to be all right, that we were going to be able to slip back into the old relaxed and affectionate ways.

Robert and I avoided speaking to each other at all that evening. We addressed all our words and smiles to Min and Ellie but though the omission was strikingly obvious to me, the other two appeared not to notice it. Later, I thought, when we had got used to each other we would be able to behave normally. All the time, while we were sitting at the kitchen table, I thought of what had happened and a terrifying feeling of gladness would smother the acknowledgement of treacherous weakness which I tried constantly to instil into my mind.

We all drank more than usual and when I went to bed, the room seemed to spin a little as I closed my eyes in the darkness. I heard Ham creaking on her camp-bed, smacking her lips and sighing. Everything would be as though the walk from the station had not taken place. I would never again lose control of myself. As long as nothing of the kind occurred again, no one would be hurt. I wanted nothing more. Just to be in the same room was a profound, absorbing joy which transfigured every commonplace experience. I was satisfied. Robert loved me. It was not very laudable but it was human to wish one's love requited. There *was*, there *could* be nothing more. Yet less than a minute after I thought this I found myself wondering whether it was the suddenness and unexpectedness of that meeting which had precipitated Robert's response. Had he merely reacted to my silence and perhaps the look on my face? Had he thought of me at all while I'd been away those six long weeks? I sighed heavily and Ham gave a little whine in response. Really my vanity was insatiable, I thought disgustedly, and it was another hour before I could go to sleep.

After breakfast, which we had late because it was the school holidays, Ellie took me to see Booty and her kittens. In six weeks their feebleness and dependence had been replaced by fighting fervour. They kicked their striped legs and bit everything with sham fury, their yellow eyes glaring with savage excitement. Then, suddenly, they would give up the attack and lie with their heads and limbs lolling, with shrill purrs, to have their chins and chests tickled. Booty had a resigned look about her. Clearly the maternal sentiment was wearing thin and before long she would abandon them for the next philandering, seductive tom-cat.

'I've made them tame, haven't I?' said Ellie with pride. 'I've spent a lot of time since I've been ill playing with the kittens. At least having chickenpox meant that I missed the last two days of term. I hate the last assembly. Everyone seems to win something except me. Once I got a deportment prize. As though anyone wants to have good deportment. It's like getting a prize for having the biggest nose or the fattest bottom.

It was a stupid old badge. I threw it away as soon as I got home.'

Mrs Butter was in the kitchen when we went back. She seemed very pleased to see me. I was surprised by the change in her appearance. Mrs Butter's hair had turned a very determined shade of auburn and the orange T-shirt and striped pedal-pushers she was wearing were more suitable for someone of Ellie's age. Her false eyelashes quivered above eyes that looked, I thought, a little strained and anxious. I complimented her on the way the house was looking.

'Ay well, it isn't so bad though there never were a family like yon for muck and mess. They're all of them helpless as babies! There's more than brass between them that works and them that plays. I were in service before I wed and I've seen it all.'

'What do you mean?' I asked, smiling.

'Why, I couldn't hold up me head for shame if I were to go about like Mrs Weston,' she nodded kindly to Min, who was filling the kettle to make coffee for us all. 'All holes and dirt and me hair fit for a sparrow to bide in. But, bless her, it don't worry her one jot. And them cupboards! When I die me kin can go through me drawers and happen I'll not blush to see them do it.'

'Will you be able to see them when you're dead?' inquired Ellie, very much interested.

'Ask no questions and you'll get told no lies,' replied Mrs Butter obscurely.

'Anyway Robert does work,' said Min, spilling instant coffee powder into an open drawer. 'He works hard. And so do I. And the children go to school.'

'Tch! Slumped in a chair, with a book. Stanley never held with reading. He'd have his own ideas, ta very much, and not let other folks go filling his head with history and useless stuff he didn't need. He couldn't abide books. Packed with lies, he used to say. I don't mind a magazine myself. I made a grand cake for Roly out of one of them, yesterday.'

I asked her how Roly was. She shook her head and looked gloomy.

'Still out of work. Wouldn't take either of them two jobs what he were offered. Says he's free-wheeling.'

'Free-lancing?' I suggested. 'At what?'

'Happen I can't remember, dear, yon's the truth of it. The other day I went into Ransome's and I couldn't think like what I'd gone in for. Had to come home without it.'

'Everybody does that,' said Min.

'Ay, but I found when I got home I'd the list in me hand all the time. Roly said I were to take better care of myself. He's a good lad, though he's shy of work. He's well pleased I've got myself this little job. He said, I hope they appreciates you, Mother, and I said Mrs Weston, for all her ramshackle ways, is as good-hearted as you could hope for.'

'Thank you,' said Min, putting a mug down in front of Mrs Butter and spilling some coffee on the table.

'I haven't offended you, I do hope,' said Mrs Butter, taking a sip and shuddering dramatically. Min shook her head and grinned. 'I speak as I find but I hope I says the good as well as the bad. Happen the milk's turned, dear.'

She went on in this manner for five minutes or so, while Min went through the whole process again of making coffee. I was struck by how much more talkative Mrs Butter had become. She was almost garrulous. And when I passed her in the hall later that morning she was rubbing the brass stair-rods as though feverish, her red curls shaking and her face scarlet. Her legs stuck out from the pedal-pushers like little white bones.

I went into Great Swosser and was warmly welcomed back to Messrs Ransome, Beale and Potts. I bought a large pork pie for lunch, a boned leg of lamb for supper, some carrots and potatoes and a white cabbage to shred for a salad. I'd brought several cookery books with me this time but there was still the problem of the severely limited variety of vegetables.

'You've got to have your eyes tested on Monday, Ellie,' said Min, at lunch. 'Will you feel well enough to go to Winkleigh, do you think?'

'I suppose so. I *am* better today. Just so-o itchy. And I hate the feeling on my skin all the time of this horrible stuff. Like wet towels.'

'Have a bath,' I suggested. 'We'll put witch-hazel on the spots for a change. Shall I take you to the optician's? I'd very much like to find a good greengrocer.'

'Oh, yes please! That is . . . you won't be hurt, Mummy?'

She looked anxiously at Min.

'Not the smallest bit. I shall be very pleased not to go. You ought to have gone several months ago and Dr Woods is always so disapproving. He can hardly tell Daisy off for not taking you sooner.'

Robert came in for lunch. He had bits of twig in his hair and a healthy flush. I thought he looked wonderful and I longed to have the right to put my arms around him and tell him so. Min didn't even look at him. She had no doubt seen him look like that hundreds of times. I put the pork pie on the table. It had a superb hot-water crust, the colour of light mahogany, and had been decorated by Mr Potts with pastry flowers. I placed next to it a bowl of salad – shredded cabbage, onion, apple and slices of orange in a French dressing. The bread was, as usual, excellent. If man could have lived by bread alone we would have done exceedingly well in that part of Lancashire.

'The orchard looks nearly at its best. Spring's at least three weeks early this year. It won't be long before the apple blossom comes,' Robert said, helping himself to a large slice of pie.

The pinkish-brown mottled meat was surrounded by a delicate jelly like chopped ice. We drank cider, dry and deceptively alcoholic.

'We ought really to do something with the walled garden,' Robert continued and though he didn't look in my direction, I felt that the remark was addressed to me.

'We could make a vegetable garden there which had flowers in it as well,' I said. 'Like a French *potager*. It needs a pergola along the two main axes for roses. Perhaps wisteria. Then we could replant fruit trees on the walls. Apricots, peaches and cherries. Goblet-trained apple trees in each quarter, surrounded by beans, peas, carrots and potatoes. Perhaps beetroot and turnips. Rhubarb and celery? Certainly cabbages and lettuces. Tomatoes in the greenhouse. An asparagus bed would be lovely. And some lavender hedges dividing it up. Oh, and pear trees. We must have those. And quince trees for those exquisitely scented, golden fruit. They have the most beautiful blossom and leaves.'

'Hold on, hold on,' said Min. 'How could we afford all that?'

'Well, it would almost be a saving to get some proper work out of George Pryke. And we could grow everything from seed. Apart from the roses and fruit trees. The roses can be a present from me. For having me to stay. We want lots of manure first. And a rotavator. And we must have the greenhouse repaired. I'll get the glass cut tomorrow.'

I felt excited. I'd always wanted a large piece of ground to garden. At once I began to make plans. White and pink roses for the pergola. Perhaps New Dawn and Sombreuil. Wisteria would be expensive. Perhaps just two plants in the middle, weeping over a wooden bower. There was a pile of wood by the stable in which the Land Rover was kept. I'd get George started on that straight away. I'd go into Great Swosser in the morning and buy wood preservative, as well as panes of glass.

'I'd recognise that brooding look anywhere,' said Min. 'Daisy's hatching an egg.'

'Can I help? Please?' asked Ellie.

'I'm counting on you helping me. Even William will be able to help if he wants to. This afternoon we'll look for useful things like seed trays. I think I've seen some about somewhere. We'll save every penny we can.'

'I'll organise the rotavator,' said Robert, looking directly at me for the first time since he had held me in his arms in sight of the house. 'I propose a toast.' He lifted his glass of cider. 'To Daisy's garden.'

The blood rushed to my face but I covered it by a pretended fit of coughing. There can be no more inconvenient reflex than blushing. Because my skin is so pale it's immediately obvious and consciousness of it makes me blush so much harder that my eyes water and my face actually seems to flame.

After lunch Min and I went to the hospital to collect William. Robert and Ellie were sent out to make a bonfire of the dead trees and plants in the walled garden. There were a few apple trees that could be saved but everything else was moribund except for waving plantations of weeds. These we were going to rotavate into the soil to act as a green manure. Then we would mulch the ground with farmyard manure and hoe off what came up again. I expected that a great number would make a reappearance and I was not above employing a swift blast of poison to deal with them but I thought Robert might be averse to such baneful horticulture.

At the hospital we came face to face with the nurse who had so effectively squashed Min before. She remembered us at once and her face took on a minatory expression. She conducted us to William's bedside.

'Your mother is here,' she said to William, as though he'd been blinded as well as broken his leg. He looked thoroughly miserable. 'Are your things packed and have you been to the lavatory?'

'Yes, I have,' said William. 'Hello, Daisy. I hope you've been to the lavatory. Nurse will tick you off if you haven't. She's very, very interested in other people going to the lavatory. When I was at St Bede's, our school chaplain always told us that it was the sign of an impure mind.'

'My, we are getting better.' The nurse looked annoyed. 'Impudence is always a sign of recovery.'

'And what's your excuse?'

I could only applaud William's sharpness. Nurse pretended she hadn't heard and hoicked William to his feet with unnecessary force.

'Ow! If you break it again, I'll tell everyone.'

'Get into this chair,' she said, with uncivil emphasis.

Min wheeled William out of the ward behind the stalking figure of the nurse who could have won dozens of deportment badges.

'You can put the boy in the car and then bring back the chair,' she barked, folding her arms and standing by the door.

'Oh, but can't we borrow the chair while his leg is in plaster?' I said, in what I hoped was a propitiatory tone.

'No. There is a shortage of wheelchairs in this hospital.'

I looked around. There were at least twenty dusty, folded wheelchairs in the vestibule.

'Are you expecting a national disaster in Great Swosser?' I felt very cross.

'A national disaster could happen anywhere,' she said tartly. 'There is no reason to exclude Great Swosser.'

This woman was altogether too quick.

'I should like to speak to matron.'

'Matron is in a meeting.'

'Very well. I'll speak to the Deputy Matron, or whatever she's called.'

'You mean Staff Nurse Boyle. She is in the same meeting. If

you care to wait for one hour, I will ask Matron if she will see you.'

The woman's tone was triumphant. I slunk out to the Land Rover, beaten.

'Get in,' said Min. 'I was beginning to think that you were arranging to go on holiday with that woman. A cosy bungalow for two weeks in Torquay with the secret, black and midnight hag.'

'I wanted her to let us have the wheelchair on loan. But she was adamant.'

'No matter. It's in the back. I got it in while you were haggling.'

'That's good,' said William. 'Haggling with the hag.'

By the time we'd got him home and into the wheelchair, he was much more cheerful. We took him to the walled garden. I brought out mugs of tea and bacon sandwiches which tasted very good when mingled with the smoke of the bonfire. William said they were the best thing he'd ever eaten. We took it in turns to feed the bonfire and sat on tree-stumps and upturned buckets, singing 'Ol' Man River' and other songs while ash, driven by capricious breezes, snaked lazily down and powdered our hair and knees and William's gleaming plaster cast, until the sky was dusky and the wind bitter. Then we went into the kitchen and I gave William his present. It was a box of water-colours, grown-up ones in a black tin box with little pans of paint, in forty colours. Also there were two proper brushes and a tube of Chinese white. He thanked me with the light of real gratitude in his eyes and then suddenly looked rather grey and said that he was very tired. Despite his protests Robert carried him upstairs and put him to bed.

For supper we had the leg of lamb stuffed with almonds and herbs and lemon peel. Ellie said it was the best day of the holidays so far and she'd quite forgotten to scratch. All the blisters had dried to scabs and she was clearly getting better. When she'd gone to bed, we went into the drawing room, and talked about the garden. The fire threw a soft light over the room. We sprawled in its capering shadows, with coffee and the last of the bottle of champagne, and made glorious plans. To be with Robert, to be able to watch him as he talked about nails and wire and peach-leaf curl, was bewitching, a constant bathing of the senses, like swimming in a warm current. I asked for nothing more.

# CHAPTER TWENTY-TWO

The weather continued to favour our enterprise. Though it was chilly it was very bright and, more importantly, dry. The next day Robert and I replaced the broken glass in the greenhouse while Ellie washed the seed trays and William filled them from a large bag of seed compost on the bench. I'd bought a book called *Vegetable Growing for Beginners* from Mr Ransome. He'd only charged me half-price because it had been lying around in his shop for years but it was exactly what I needed. We were going to sow celery, French beans, runner beans, tomatoes and sweetcorn in the greenhouse. As soon as the ground was rotavated and manured we would sow broad beans, broccoli, cabbage, carrots, cauliflowers, lettuce, peas, radishes and turnips out of doors. And, of course, potatoes. I'd bought a bag of Pentland Crown seed potatoes and they were already lying in a neat row on the bench to sprout. The smell of compost and putty and dust was delicious.

'What were you doing on the wall, William, when you fell off it?' asked Robert, rolling a piece of putty between the palms of his hands.

'It was a dare. We had to walk along it blindfolded while the others threw socks filled with sand at us.'

'Which wall was it?'

'The boundary wall.'

Robert stopped rolling the putty for an instant. 'Good God, it's fifteen feet high! You might have broken your neck!'

William looked rather sulky.

'Were you stoned?' I asked.

I tried to put as much unconcern into my voice as possible. William looked at me in some surprise. I smiled and hoped Robert wasn't going to get cross.

'Yes, I was,' he admitted, looking at his father furtively. 'It was a stupid thing to do. You needn't tell me.'

'Well, we won't then.' I went on scraping out the old putty from one of the glazing bars. 'You probably had a lot of pressure on you to do it. You must have realised it was dangerous.'

'Yes. I know I promised,' he said, looking angrily at Robert. 'But you don't know how hard it is to refuse. I knew they'd give me a hard time if I didn't. There isn't really any choice. You have to do what the others do. And at the time it seemed important to do it.'

Robert sighed. 'Are you going to spend your whole life doing what other people want you to?'

'That's rich!' said William. 'Ever since I was born you've been telling me what to do. You're telling me now. Because you're my father it's all right. Suppose Hitler had had a son? Or Jack the Ripper?'

'I see your point,' said Robert, exercising unusual self-control. And when you're older you'll be able to judge for yourself. Right now you haven't the experience. You're not going back to that school anyway. That's certain.'

William didn't say anything but went on filling seed trays with elaborate care. I thought he looked relieved if anything.

'Let's sow some sweet peas,' I said to Ellie. 'Put two in each of these little pots on top of the compost, like this, and then we'll cover them with half an inch more compost and give them a good watering. Then we'll do the same with these catmint seeds. We'll line the paths with the catmint. Booty will come and roll on them and nibble them. Will you do a tray, William?'

William said he would. Robert went outside and began to press putty around the new glass. His face, through the filthy panes, was thoughtful.

'Have you ever tried it, Daisy?' asked William as he placed the seeds carefully on the damp compost.

'Smoking pot, you mean? Yes. Quite a few times. It's a very good feeling, isn't it? Ordinary things seem very interesting. And sometimes very funny. And often I felt really excited and elated. But I decided to stop smoking it and I haven't for a long time.'

'Why?'

'For one thing it interfered with my work. I thought I was seeing things in a new way but when I tried to write down what I felt, I realised that it was the drug making me think it was new and interesting and that I wasn't really being more perceptive. I realised that the perceptions I had when *not* stoned were just as interesting. And more likely to be accurate and therefore useful. And I felt cut off from people who weren't stoned. I don't think it's a good idea to isolate oneself from the rest of society. And I got very giggly. It was a nice feeling but I thought I'd rather have more control.'

'But you drink champagne. Lots.'

'Yes. I can't justify thinking that that's any better. Apart from the fact that it's legal. It's just a more social thing. But of course there are people drinking themselves to death in solitude and going out and killing people by driving when they're drunk. It isn't much better . . . if at all. But I didn't do either when I was at school. When you're my age, or even not so old, you've a chance of doing these things in such a way so as not to muck up your life. A broken leg is just the beginning of the unhappiness you can inflict on yourself.'

William was silent for a while, wiping the edges of the seed tray clean. A shout of pain made us all look at Robert. He was holding his hand and cursing, while blood poured from his finger. Ellie gave a scream and rushed outside to bring him in.

'You told Daisy not to forget to wear gloves,' said Ellie, shepherding him anxiously through the door. 'And now you've gone and done it yourself.'

'I took them off to pick up the tacks and then I forgot to put them on again.'

Robert sat on the stool while I dabbed at his finger and examined it for glass. Ellie ran into the house to ask her mother for sticking-plasters. I wrapped the finger up in my handkerchief and held it above his head, applying pressure to the wound, as I'd been taught at school when we'd done first aid. For some reason this made us both smile. There was something ridiculous about my bossiness and Robert's helplessness. Also we were touching each other quite legitimately and we were made happy by this small contact.

'Why are you smiling?' asked William.

'I don't know. Oh good, here's Ellie with the plasters.'

It was quite a deep cut but after a minute or two it stopped bleeding, more or less. I put on a large plaster.

'There! It's probably a clean cut but perhaps we ought to bathe it when we go in.' I was suddenly conscious that Robert was looking at me.

I lifted my eyes to his and though our mutual gaze could not have lasted longer than five seconds, it was enough to fire up my skin and make my knees feel weak. We averted our eyes from each other with an effort and he went out to put on his gloves and continue with the work while I covered the seeds with compost and helped Ellie to write the labels.

That look had fed my longing. It was all we could allow ourselves and for the moment it was enough. I knew even that was disgraceful and a betrayal of my friendship with Min.

When we went in for tea there was a note from Mrs Butter on the kitchen table.

Gentleman telephoned. Says he's bringing Golden Boy to lunch tomorrow. Also bringing his banjo. And aunt.

While I buttered some gingerbread and made tea we puzzled over the note.

'Golden boy sounds like a horse,' said Robert.

Immediately I thought of Charles and I realised that Robert did as well, by the contraction of his mouth and lowered eyelids. A dark flush ran quickly over his face. At once I knew that Min had told Robert about my night with Charles. What could be more natural than that this kind of intimate gossip should take place between husbands and wives? Min had imagined that this was the beginning of something thrilling and had at first refused to accept my characterisation of Charles as a hunter with no desire for husbandry of any kind. Because I loved Robert I could understand everything that he had thought.

'I don't think it could be Charles,' I said, not choosing to prevaricate. 'As far as I know he isn't musical. And I don't think a banjo is quite his style.'

Robert smiled at this and then we both began to laugh. Min came in and wanted to know why we were laughing. Ellie showed her the note.

'I don't know what's so funny about this man bringing a banjo,' Ellie said, her eyes on the gingerbread. 'I've never even seen one, let alone heard one played. I'm looking forward to it. I hope the aunt isn't very old. Granny is my only relation. I don't know anything about aunts.'

'I don't think my mother is much of a guide to relatives in general. That reminds me, I'd better go and see her.'

'Oh yes, do,' said Min. 'I meant to go today but I forgot. And I've got to an important bit in a letter to Sisimondi. Anyway she'd rather see you than me.'

'I'm not at all sure that's true but, as she's my mother, it falls to me to pay the call.'

'Would she like me to go on Saturday, do you think?' I asked.

'That's kind of you. I'll ask her.'

'I'll make a cake and take it. That might cheer her up. I must think about lunch tomorrow. I suppose the horse will have its own special feed but what shall I give the banjo-player and his aunt? She might be dyspeptic, if she's old.'

We continued to speculate about the mysterious visit. Mrs Butter was unable to shed further light on the matter when questioned the next morning. At first she denied ever having taken a message but on being shown her handwriting, she recalled that the line was bad and the man's voice hard to understand.

'Foreign?' I suggested.

Mrs Butter couldn't quite remember but was pretty sure the caller had been English. La-di-da. I really began to feel rather anxious about Mrs Butter. She was immaculate as ever in a red skirt, very fully gathered, and a matching bolero top over a yellow jersey and her plum-coloured hair was fastened back, neatly, by two green plastic hair-slides. But her lipstick was rather askew and one eyelash was insecurely fixed and was curling up like a devil's coach-horse at bay.

She worked as well as ever but in a frenzied way, scouring everything almost to bare wood. She was obsessed by tidiness and Robert had to speak to her kindly but sternly about closing all the books he was reading and putting them back anywhere on the shelves in the library so that he couldn't find them. He had only just caught her on her way out to the dustbins with a pile of marked essays. Whenever I attempted to ask her tactfully how she was feeling, she would always reply, 'Very well, thank you' as though it was a lesson she'd learned and I could get no further.

I expressed my disquiet about Mrs Butter to Min, who thought she seemed much as usual and that I was worrying about nothing.

'She's always seemed odd to me and I know I seem completely lunatic to her. But she's the answer to a prayer and we're very tolerant of each other. When I drove her home one day because there was a fearful rainstorm I was quite amazed by her house. Bungalow, I suppose it is, but quite big and every luxury you can think of. She insisted on my coming in so she could show me. Gold-plated taps, monster television set, cocktail cabinet, fluffy covers on everything. I can't believe she's hard up.'

'I think she comes here because of loneliness more than anything. And to put aside money for that awful Roly. Oh, well, if you think I'm imagining there's something wrong . . .'

I was sitting at the kitchen table after Min had gone back to work, waiting for some potatoes to boil and trying to design the central part of the pergola, which wouldn't come right, when I heard a well-loved voice through the kitchen door, which was open.

'Darlings! The hall! These columns! It's absolutely *Sleeping Beauty*.'

'Peter!' I cried and hurried out.

'Diana! Darling! Always so thrilling to see an old friend in a new context! You look quite ravishing in this fairy-tale setting!'

Peter took me in his arms and waltzed me around between the scagliola columns until I was giddy. I saw Giorgio standing in the doorway, picking invisible specks of fluff from a very new-looking suit. Then I noticed that Robert had come in and was standing behind Giorgio, watching us all with a frown. Peter saw him too, and let me go.

'You must be Robert,' he said, going up to him with his most Siegfried tread and offering a graceful hand. 'Divine of you to have us. You got my message, I hope. I telephoned yesterday and spoke to a delightful woman who seemed just a little confused. Not Mrs Weston, I do hope.'

'That was Mrs Butter,' said Robert, rather depressingly. 'Is it possible that you are Golden Boy?'

'Of course! Peter's name is Holdenby. Why didn't I think of that?' I said. 'And it wasn't banjo but Giorgio.'

Robert looked at Giorgio and showed clearly by his expression that even a comb and paper would have been preferable to Giorgio.

'But what about your aunt?' I asked, torn between giggles and anxiety. 'Where is she?'

'My aunt?' Peter looked puzzled. 'I never take my aunt

about with me. She is a woman of torpid habits and has a beard exactly like George Bernard Shaw's.'

'Mrs Butter said you were bringing a banjo and an aunt.'

'Ah! Light creeps with rosy fingers across the dark of night! What I said was not aunt but lunch. Giorgio, could you be a darling and bring in the hamper. I fear my muscles are *un peu faible*.' He opened his eyes very wide and then closed them and I saw that he was wearing eye-shadow . . . a new departure. 'But Giorgio has a stunning set and the hamper will be nothing to him.'

Peter's behaviour seemed more extreme than usual, unless it was merely highlighted by rural surroundings. I wondered if he had begun to be unhappy with Giorgio. Giorgio strode into the kitchen bearing a wicker basket while Robert, his face set into unforgiving lines, and I (looking, I'm sure, immensely apologetic) followed with Peter, who gave my arm a squeeze and said, in a stage whisper which I'm certain he intended should be heard:

'Diana, the delectable Robert is as you described him! So deliciously acerbic! One might say *Weltschmerz*! It means romantic discontent, darling. One longs to see him angry! That nose!'

I thought Robert's profile was beginning to soften. I was certain of it when Peter took from the hamper three bottles of Dom Perignon and four of Puligny-Montrachet. Peter lifted the wine bottles out carefully and stood them slowly upright.

'Not single vineyard, darlings, but all this divagation prohibits anything grander.'

Robert's severity of expression softened still further when Peter brought from the basket several parcels wrapped in greaseproof paper. They contained cooked, boned, stuffed chickens, some heads of endive, a wonderfully squashy camembert and a dozen tender, scented peaches.

'Where did you get this wonderful food?' I exclaimed.

'We've been ripening the peaches all the way up from London on the back window shelf of the car. We're on our way to stay with Jerry Daubeney. His family have a castle somewhere outlandish. Giorgio has a fancy to see something English and posh. Jerry is a great friend of mine though I fear sadly disconnected from reality. And as we were going almost past your door, it seemed a shame not to stop and say "what ho".'

'It's very good of you to bring all this,' said Robert.

'My dear, springing ourselves uninvited upon you, we could do nothing less. I speak merely of luncheon, you understand.'

Peter giggled and then frowned and said something very rapidly in Italian to Giorgio, who was wandering around the kitchen, looking into saucepans and examining the knives and forks which I'd left lying in heaps, preparatory to laying the table. Giorgio left off the scrutiny and came to offer me a flaccid handshake.

'*Ciao*,' he said, with a small smirk.

Min came in just then and I introduced them. Giorgio stared at her, his eyes roving over her jeans and grubby jersey and fixing at last on her bosom where they stayed for some minutes.

'Wonderful of you to have us,' said Peter, 'and the house is heaven! Might I see some more of it? Ah! What an adorable dog!'

Ham came up to Peter, who had a genuine liking for animals, and allowed herself to be scratched and petted. She then examined Giorgio's knees, decided that she didn't like their smell and began to bark. Giorgio said something uncomplimentary in Italian to Ham which made her bark more determinedly. We all went on a tour of the house, leaving Ham shut in the kitchen. Peter was ecstatic about the drawing room and the library. Even the dining room he described as marvellously *rayonnant* Gothic.

'What a party one could have here! Fancy dress! The Lagoon party . . . everyone dressed as undersea creatures! Diana, you could come as a mermaid and I could wheel you about in a giant papier-mâché shell as your delicate little feet would be encased in a silver sequinned tail. Giorgio could be Neptune with silver fishes in his hair and a cloak and seaweed. Now Min, you are to be Thetis, a darling little sea-goddess . . . something flowing in shades of palest green with pearls in your hair.'

'What would you be?' I was amused by Robert's expression as he watched Giorgio opening the lid of the wine cooler.

'I should be a sea breeze of course, so that I could wheel you about. I should be dressed in grey chiffon with a cap of cotton wool. To represent a cloud, you know. Perhaps the smallest of fans concealed about my person. Ah, this must be the beautiful Miss Weston!'

Ellie came in, timidly, and giggled to hear herself thus apostrophised. She certainly didn't look very beautiful at that moment, being covered with scabs and with her spectacles held together across the bridge of her nose by a grubby piece of sticky tape but Peter came forward, took her by her hand and led her into the circle.

'Now, you would look quite wonderful in pink. At our party you could be a beautiful piece of coral and attach yourself to the person you love best.'

Ellie was too shy to say anything but she giggled again and looked pleased.

'And what about me?' said Robert, entering into the spirit of the thing, charmed by Peter's sweetness to Ellie.

'As host, you are the only person entitled not to dress up. You are the ringmaster, dramatically *soigné* in black tie, commanding the players in our little masquerade. I wonder if cotton-wool buskins might be rather me.'

'Very you, I should say,' said Robert kindly. 'Now what about a drink?'

Lunch was, on the whole, a success. It had the improvisational charm of a picnic, without a picnic's discomfort. Ham had to be shut in the boot room as her aversion to Giorgio deepened on receipt of a sharp kick. William and Ellie from then on cast looks of loathing towards Giorgio, who took no notice but shovelled in food and gulped down wine as though he doubted that the rations would hold out. He finished well before the rest of us, got up from the table and left the room without a word to anyone.

Peter more than made up for his lover's shortcomings as a guest and discussed Madame de Staël with Min, Cicero with Robert, vegetable gardening with me and, seeing a half-finished water-colour on the dresser, painting with William. He showed William how to draw the legs of horses convincingly, explaining the bone structure and musculature. I'd forgotten that Peter could draw. He could do almost anything well, on reflection, except choose lovers who had the smallest chance of making him happy.

After lunch we went out to view the walled garden. Peter's

raptures were encouraging. He saw at once how the gazebo, where the two paths crossed, should be and did me a detailed sketch. He had a very good suggestion for an arbour at the far end where there was no doorway and was very keen that we should put in something watery, perhaps a wall fountain, at each end of the shorter axis. He was very disappointed when I explained that we were doing the whole thing as cheaply as possible.

'So sad, these decaying families,' he said to me in a low voice. Robert was at a distance wheeling William in his chair and Min was in the greenhouse with Giorgio. Ellie was in the boat-house with Ham, who had tried repeatedly to launch herself at Giorgio from the end of her lead and finally succeeded in getting near enough to take a piece out of his silken trouser-leg. Ham had been bundled away as much for her own protection as Giorgio's. 'I thought so from the state of Min's clothing.'

'Well, Min would always look like that however much money she had. She doesn't care about that sort of thing.'

'Ah! Now I can put my finger on what is unusual about her. She doesn't want approval. Now you and I, Diana, will barter our souls for approval and it makes us vulnerable.'

'I don't care much for that idea of myself. I don't like to see myself as weak.'

'Not weak, darling. Rather, sensitive and insecure. And seeking approval is a driving force and therefore useful.' He lowered his voice still further. 'How is the heart? Is the fair name of Robert still scratched upon it?'

I sighed and had braced myself to tell Peter the truth, that if anything it was more deeply engraved than ever, when Min shot out of the greenhouse and came stalking over to us. Seeing Peter she checked herself and masked her fury with a smile. I could just see Giorgio's black curls bobbing about in the greenhouse and my imagination supplied the rest. We discussed Peter's suggestions and then began to walk down to the boat-house, leaving Giorgio sitting in the greenhouse, flicking through George Pryke's magazines.

'Do you think, Peter, that Giorgio is really the right man for you?' I asked later, as we strolled in a leisurely manner round the lake. 'He seems rather . . . rather fickle.'

Peter looked very sad and was silent for a moment. Then he said, very gently, 'Is Robert the right man for you, darling? He seems rather . . . married.'

We linked arms and walked slowly and thoughtfully back to the house.

A sudden rainstorm brought us all into the kitchen where we had tea and the remains of yesterday's gingerbread. Pretty soon Peter said that they must be on their way. We all went to the door to see him off. I put my arms around him, sorry to see him go. Min gave him a kiss on each cheek and said that she had absolutely loved having him to lunch. He clung to Min as to me. Even Robert expressed a hope that he would call in on his way back.

'I hope, my darlings, but who can tell? I will telephone from Daubeney Chase,' he said, getting into the passenger seat next to Giorgio.

Without a word of farewell to any of us, Giorgio let in the clutch and they roared down the drive with spurts of muddy gravel. Peter turned in his seat and gazed at me until they disappeared beneath the trees.

'I don't know that I ever met a man I disliked as much,' I said, as we went back into the house.

'You mean Giorgio, of course,' said Min. 'When we were in the greenhouse he suddenly grabbed my breast and shoved his tongue down my throat. I was so startled that I could only gag and yell to be let go.'

'So I should think!' said Robert. 'By God, if I'd known the bastard was mucking about with you I'd have thrown him out!'

Min looked at Robert with amusement. 'Darling, how sweet of you to mind so much!'

I felt a despicable pang of jealousy, listening to this exchange, and all evening, while we discussed Peter and Giorgio, I had to struggle to conceal feelings of misery. Robert seemed, on the other hand, to be curiously elated. How could I play the role I had assigned myself if the smallest thing was going to make me wretched?

'Robert is so much more cheerful,' Min said to me the next day. 'He liked Peter enormously. And of course, doing the garden with you is just what he needed. Ellie's nearly better and even William is happy. I knew everything would be all right again if only you would come back. And you are happy here, aren't you?'

'Yes.'

It was partly true. And anyway I was happier at Weston Hall than anywhere else. Peter had telephoned after breakfast to say that he would call in for lunch in two weeks' time, on his way back to London.

'That'll be a Saturday. Why don't we have a party then?' suggested Min. 'I don't mean fancy dress. That would seem odd in the middle of the day. But we could ask all the people we've been owing for years. It would do us good. I think Robert is lonely without Gerald.'

Min made a list of people she ought to ask and then added the names of those she wanted to ask. It came to forty-two.

'We can't seat forty-two,' I said. 'It will have to be a buffet. I don't like them much usually. I think people have better conversations if they're sitting down. You don't want to divide them in half and have two lunches?'

'Too much work. No, let's just have something informal. Something cold. Coronation chicken.'

Over my dead body, I thought, but didn't say anything. I began to warm to the idea and think that it might be rather fun. While I was making a chocolate and almond cake for Vivien, I began to turn ideas about in my mind. Several ribs of beef roasted and allowed to cool. A salmon. Suppose the weather was cool? A daube, perhaps.

After lunch William, Ellie and I went out to watch Robert at work with the rotavator. George Pryke was put to the task of double-digging the rotavated bits where the potatoes were to go. When the spectating palled as an amusement, which was quite soon, the children and I began to make a large wigwam out of hazel branches from George's coppicing, for the sweet peas. The long branches, eight feet or so in length, I pushed upright into the ground in a circle six feet in diameter. I bent their tops inwards to make a kind of roof. Then the children and I wove the thinner, whippier branches in and out horizontally between the uprights in bands at eighteen-inch intervals all the way up so that the structure was firm. It looked marvellous when we'd finished, both pretty and practical, and had the additional merit of costing nothing. William, particularly, seemed to enjoy it, working with great neatness and precision. We decided to make another one the next day on the other side of the garden to match it, for runner beans.

The children went off to play with the kittens. I went into the greenhouse to check on the seed trays. I turned the potatoes on the windowsill and prepared a box of compost to sow hollyhocks which would fill the spaces by the walls between the new fruit trees. I heard George come in. I knew it was George because I could hear the rotavator still throbbing away outside.

'I'll arrange about the manure this afternoon,' I said, not looking up as I tore the packet of hollyhock seeds across the top. 'As soon as it comes you can fork it in to the top spit. The potatoes are chitting well.'

George didn't answer. I felt two hands steal round my waist. The seeds spilled over the bench.

'I know this is wrong,' said Robert's voice in my ear. 'I've told myself that this is just what I must not do.'

I trembled and closed my eyes. I meant to tell him that he must stop but I was sick with longing. I hung my head, eyes still closed. We stood thus, in a silence broken only by the whine of the rotavator, in the dim and freckled light, breathing the sweet suffusion of our love.

'Robert,' I said, as soon as I was able to speak. 'This musn't happen again. I don't want to struggle. Please let me go.'

I felt him draw away and it was all I could do not to beg him to take me in his arms again. I didn't lift my head. I heard the door open and close. I burst into tears.

## CHAPTER TWENTY-THREE

Vivien was delighted to see me and particularly pleased to see the cake. Lily was told to bring tea at once. One side of Vivien's forehead and eyelid was covered with yellowish, crusting blisters.

'Come and sit down, Dahlia, and tell me everything. I'm so bored and fretful I could die. Look what that idiot Lawrence has given me!'

She pointed to an enormous television set in the middle of the room.

'Isn't it perfectly hideous? I've sent for men from the farm to take it away and put it in Lily's room. She and Grig can watch it instead of fornicating. It'll be as good as a contraceptive.'

'Grig?'

'Lily's husband. So she *says*. I don't believe a word of it but who cares? I've told her that there are to be no babies. She's always coming in with her cap over her ear.'

I thought of the cool, insipid Lily. It was difficult to imagine her heated with passion.

'Who is Lawrence?'

'A retired colonel who lives in Dunston Abchurch. He thinks he's in love with me. Silly old fool.' Vivien looked pleased and then winced. 'These shingles are perfect agony. He wanted to come and see me but I told him I look a fright. He may not be much but he's useful to play cards with and take me out to dinner. He thought the television might distract me. It certainly does that! I've tried watching it. There are dreadful shows where people are asked imbecile questions that a baby could answer and then they get given a stuffed lion or a dreadful thing which wakes you up in the morning and pours boiling water into your ear. Then there is this appalling programme called *Sovereign Street* where people with the vilest accents complain about each other all the time. They live in this perfectly hideous street and just go drivelling up and down it all day, grumbling about their neighbours. I should think they're all raving with claustrophobia. You never saw such unattractiveness! Can this really be what the working classes want to watch? Wearying repetitions of their own dreary lives?'

'I believe it's very popular.'

'Well, if that's what they enjoy it explains a good deal. I suppose it keeps them in a useful state of mental inertia. We must have somebody willing to clean lavatories.'

'Min's sorry she hasn't been to see you. She's working tremendously hard at the moment.'

'Such misplaced ambition. No one gives a damn about these obscure academic studies. Other than other academics, who are simply riven with jealousy anyway. Perfectly pointless.'

I didn't bother to defend my profession. I couldn't think on what grounds, other than pleasurable self-indulgence, I might assert its claims. I certainly hadn't become an academic to serve society but only because it was something I enjoyed doing more than anything else I could think of at the time.

'Before Min knows where she is, Robert will have left her for some young floozie who knows how to paint her face and satisfy him in bed.'

'Robert is the very last man to behave like that, I should have thought,' I said, with a fraction more emphasis than was wise.

Vivien paused, in the act of raising a cigarette to her lips and regarded me with slightly narrowed eyes. Then she gave a slow smile and drew deeply on her cigarette as though satisfied.

'Shall I pour the tea?' I asked. 'We're replanting the walled garden, you know. Did Robert mention it?'

'Hector had one man full-time to look after it. It was my favourite bit of the garden. It used to get very hot in summer and there were so many bees. Is the greenhouse still there?'

'Yes, we've just repaired the glass.'

'Robert didn't tell me that. He only said that you were ploughing up the ground.'

'Why don't you come and help us? The fresh air would do you good. And you're so knowledgeable.'

'I don't think I will.' Vivien stubbed out her cigarette slowly. 'I remember it all too well. I'm afraid I might fall into regretting things. Besides,' she smiled, maliciously, 'I see now. You and Robert are making your own little Paradise . . . a prelapsarian Eden . . . aren't you? I should only be in the way.'

She began to chuckle.

'What are you talking about, Vivien? You're getting fanciful. You've been too long on your own, brooding. Why not come up to the Hall and have supper with us?'

'I think I will,' Vivien chuckled again. 'Of course, Robert's been walking about like a man whose boat has sprung a leak several miles from shore, ever since you left. Yesterday I could tell something had happened to caulk the hole. You don't need me to play serpent in your garden.' Vivien laughed until her eyes were bright with tears. 'So! Righteous, captious, disapproving Robert. Those are the sort of men who fall hardest in the end.'

When I got back to the Hall, no one was in the kitchen but William who was lying on the sofa we'd brought in specially for him. He was still struggling to perfect the art of drawing horses and he had a photograph of Van Dyck's painting of Charles I on a horse in front of him. While I peeled potatoes for supper, we chatted in a desultory way about painting and its purposes.

'Isn't it like writing?' I suggested. 'There are many purposes but one of the most important must be to capture the ideas and manners of the age.'

'He looks a very small man. Because the horse and the canvas are so big. Did Van Dyck want to show him as a small man, do you think? I mean, not big enough for the job of king?'

'I hadn't thought of that. He *was* small. Something like five foot three, I think.'

'He looks very sad.'

'Who does?' said Robert, coming in.

'Charles the First.'

'My favourite king,' said Robert.

'Because you're sorry for him?' asked William.

'Mm. Perhaps. He was less of a brute than most English kings. And he did love beautiful things. He had a wonderful collection of paintings.'

I listened to them talking, as I rolled a large piece of gammon in mustard and brown sugar. Presently Robert said to me in a low voice, 'I can't let him go back to that awful place. I shall have to take a course in bookkeeping.'

'The other possibility is that you sell something. Everything in this house will be yours when your mother dies, won't it?'

'Yes.'

'So it wouldn't be stealing to sell something now. Those bits of Japanese porcelain in the cupboard in the drawing room are very old and very valuable, I think.'

'Valuable enough to pay for six years of William's schooling?'

'I'm not an expert but some of those pieces look like early Ming . . . that's pre-seventeenth century. You could justify selling them on the grounds that they ought to be in a museum. If they are Ming, one piece a year would keep William at public school.'

'I'm so sorry about what happened this afternoon.'

I looked at William with alarm but he had fallen asleep on

the sofa, his head pillowed on his arm, his fair hair spread out in separated locks like Mr Therm's.

'Don't. You needn't be.'

'It's a mess, isn't it?'

'Yes.'

'Most of the time I wonder how I'm going to stand it. But there are times when I pretend that it might be possible that we could be together and then I'm wickedly happy.'

'It won't be possible. Ever.'

'And you can bear that? Quite calmly?' asked Robert with some bitterness, slowly turning his face, which looked dreadfully sad, from mine.

'No. I don't think I can bear it.'

I felt Robert's hand on my arm and then he withdrew it as the door opened and Ellie came in.

'Will someone take me out in the boat? You promised you would.'

'So I did,' said Robert, smiling at her as she slipped her arm through his. 'Go and tell Mummy where we're going and that William is asleep on the kitchen sofa on his own.'

Ellie ran off.

'Come with us,' said Robert, looking down at me with tender pleading. 'I just want to be near you. I've got to behave with Ellie in the boat with us.'

'All right. Just let me put the ham in the oven.'

The boat, repaired by George Pryke, was a lovely old-fashioned skiff with a wooden bench for the oarsman and a seat with a wrought-iron back and buttoned cushions for the passengers. Robert took the oars and we glided out to the middle of the lake.

'There are the swans,' said Ellie. 'Let's go up to them.'

Robert rowed towards them, looking back over his shoulder. I stared at the little island. I didn't want Ellie to see me watching him. I was afraid my face might give something away.

'The next fine day let's have tea on the island,' I suggested.

'We won't go any nearer,' said Robert. 'Look!'

'Oh, Daddy!' Ellie shouted with excitement.

Paddling along behind the swans were four small grey cygnets. Robert leaned on the oars and let the boat drift while we watched them.

'There's another . . . riding on its mother's back!' cried Ellie. 'I wish William could have seen it. I'm so sorry for him with that horrible cast. I suppose if he fell out of the boat he'd sink immediately to the bottom and have to be dug out of the mud. Do you think we could tame them?'

'We could feed them every day and I expect they'd get used to coming for food. I don't think they would become friendly like cats and dogs.'

'Do let's. Can I have a go at rowing?'

'Come and sit next to me and take an oar.'

Of course we went round in circles and Ellie caught a great many crabs and giggled until she was helpless.

'Come on, you're not pulling even a little,' said Robert. 'Let Daisy have a go.'

Ellie and I changed places. I felt guilty. It was a pretext to be close to each other. I felt his body pressed against mine and saw his beautiful hands gripping the oars as we pulled slowly in unison, he stroking the water more gently to keep pace with me. We rowed without speaking. Ellie lay back against the cushions and let her hand trail in the water with her eyes closed. The sun was disappearing behind the trees in stabs of scarlet fire. The rays dazzled on the water like cracks of sizzling lava in the seabed. I remembered the St Lawrence's Ball when we had danced together. We had been in love already then, I think, but too terrified to admit it to ourselves. It was like that now, circling, drifting, dreaming, willing it to go on for ever.

'I'm cold,' said Ellie, at last.

We rowed to the boat-house and I felt Robert's warm hand round mine as he helped me on to the bank. We fastened the boat to its summer mooring, on the little jetty by the boat-house, and walked slowly back up to the Hall. Ham ran to meet us. I remembered the lane which led from the railway station and I wanted so desperately for him to kiss me again that my lips were trembling.

'Ellie,' said Robert. 'Run in and check that Mummy's keeping an eye on William.'

Ellie ran off. Robert pulled me into the shadows of the box hedge which lay between us and the back of the house.

'Daisy. I'm so sorry . . .' he said and then I put my arms around him and stopped whatever he might have said by lifting my face to his.

I don't know how long we stood there. It was an experience of love which superseded all my former imagining. Then I heard Min's voice calling into the swiftly falling dusk.

'Ham! Ham! Supper! Come along, you silly girl, supper's ready.'

Ham, who had been lying on the grass beside us, ran through the opening in the hedge and I heard Min say, 'There you are! Come on, Poppet . . . there's a good girl,' in the sort of cajoling, babyish tones in which people address animals if they think no one is listening.

She sounded so cheerful, so light-hearted, that my happiness shrivelled as though subjected to sudden intense heat.

'Oh, this is dreadful!' I exclaimed in a whisper, my eyes filling with tears. 'This is so hard!'

I walked quickly up to the house and through the back door without looking back.

Sunday was a dull day, cloudy and chilly. Reminding myself that work was the best antidote for unhappiness I sat at the kitchen table until lunch-time making notes on Peacock. Ellie sat on the other side sewing while William lay reading on the sofa. Robert was working in the garden. All was, on the surface, a model of domestic harmony. At twelve Min came to have a drink with me as I was putting potatoes into the oven under a piece of beef.

'How's it going?' I asked her, as I began to chop cabbage.

'Really well. I thought this section would be the hardest and suddenly my brain is teeming with ideas and I can hardly write them down fast enough.'

'Will you come and feed the cygnets with me, Mummy?' asked Ellie. 'They're so pretty. You ought to see them before they get big.'

'Mm,' Min said, not really listening. 'I think I'll send off what I've done and see what my editor thinks. I have the feeling that there's a whole book there and not just a preface.'

'What school am I going to next term?' asked William. 'Dad says I'm not to go back to the Comp.'

'Oh, goodness! It's all the wrong time to change,' Min frowned. 'I think it would be better for you to stay where you are for a bit. Robert's got a bee in his bonnet about that place. Besides we haven't got any money, so that's it, really.'

I saw that William was upset. I told Min about my idea of selling the porcelain in the drawing room.

'That would be stealing.' Min's voice was decisive. 'Of course it will be Robert's one day but at the moment it's Vivien's. No. It's no good making a fuss. No school is perfect. I'm sorry if you don't like it, William, but hardly anyone does like their school. Remember what we used to say about ours, Daisy?'

William rubbed his eyes with the back of his hand but Min didn't seem to notice.

'There are degrees, though.' I intended to be pacific without conceding what seemed to me important. 'There's a difference between grumbling about little annoyances and the kind of unhappiness you feel when you're forced to change your behaviour radically, to be something you don't want to be.'

'What do you mean?'

'Well,' I struggled on, inarticulately, wishing that William wasn't within earshot, but not wanting to lose the opportunity. 'William has to obey the dictates of the other boys because he's isolated. He has no support from friends because he's too different from the other boys. It's just what intellectuals experienced doing National Service in the army. And, being a child, William has little or no idea what makes him different or any reason to feel that it's worth *being* different.'

Robert came in then and stood at the sink, washing his hands. I gave him the towel. Min was lighting a cigarette and didn't see the expression in his eyes as he handed it back to me. I certainly hoped not, anyway. I don't think Robert knew what his face was giving away.

'Dad, Mum says I'm to stay at the Comp.' William's voice was anxious.

'What? Absolutely not. I'd rather teach you myself in the evenings than let you go back to that place.'

'I never heard anything so ridiculous!' said Min, really cross. 'You must be mad to think of such a thing! What a piece of work you're making of a broken leg. Boys are always breaking legs.'

'He might have been killed! That, I suppose, you'd consider worth taking notice of. I think this is a warning. It's completely the wrong place for William. I don't like anything about the school and it was wrong of me to let him stay there as long as he has.'

'*You*'ve let him stay there. I've nothing to say in the matter, I suppose?'

'Don't be silly, Min.' Robert's nose was white with annoyance. 'Of course it's a joint decision. But you've been preoccupied lately. I don't think you realise how bad things have got.'

'I suppose this is what every woman has to face when she tries to do something besides looking after the family. You're jealous and resentful. I suppose you want me to give up my work and settle down to making marrow jam.'

'Don't be stupid, Min . . .'

'I'm *not* being stupid! How dare you insult me because I don't agree with you.'

'You said I must be mad. That's equally insulting, I should have thought. Oh God, this is ridiculous! I don't want to quarrel with you. My mind's made up.'

'Well, so is mine! I'm going back to work! You can go to hell!'

Min rushed out and banged the door. The children looked at Robert with pale faces.

'Don't worry,' I said. 'Mummy'll be over it before you can count a hundred. She's tired and excited about her book.'

As I took the potatoes out of the oven and turned them over I identified a disgraceful feeling of satisfaction that they had quarrelled. I thought Min was entirely in the wrong and I was actually pleased that her selfishness was evident. Perhaps this was the beginning of a rift that wouldn't heal. Most important, they wouldn't make love while they were angry with each other. I let the full spate of jealousy rush through me like a corrosive tide and the heat from the oven dyed my face even redder than it had flushed at the recognition of my own heartlessness and egoism.

Robert helped me get lunch ready. We didn't talk. I chose sympathetic silence. I despised myself for it. The children began an argument about something silly and forgot about Min's loss of temper. I took a perfectly browned and risen queen of puddings out of the oven and left it on the warming plate of the Aga. It was a token of my superior competence. I sent Ellie to tell her mother that lunch was ready.

'I'm so ashamed of myself,' said Min, coming in and embracing Robert and me in turn. Her eyes were rather red and swollen. 'I was completely in the wrong.'

I felt a horrible confusion of disappointment and sympathy. Sympathy won but it was a close contest.

On Monday Min and I had breakfast alone. Robert had got up early and gone out to wire the walls ready for the fruit trees. The children were still in bed.

'I feel very guilty about the children,' said Min, having a second slice of toast and a cigarette at the same time. 'I don't think I'm a very good mother. I don't focus on them. I love them, of course, but I live far too much in my own world.'

'Plenty of people's lives have been ruined by dominating mothers who've concentrated entirely on them.'

'Well, of course that's the other extreme. But it's no excuse. I couldn't sleep last night. I thought about everything that you and William had said. I had a little talk with him last night while you were getting supper. He told me that he'd sometimes thought of running away. But he knew he'd be caught and brought back and then it would be worse. Daisy, I had simply no idea! Why are my children so unable to flourish at school? Ellie is bullied and has no friends. What have I failed to give them?'

'For one thing, at a rough guess, at least a quarter of schoolchildren are thoroughly unhappy. Strengths like sensitivity, imagination, modesty and self-awareness are incompatible with success in a closed society. Think of the girls at our school who were head girls and very popular. They were conventional, unquestioning, steady, middle-of-the-road girls who sang the school song with no idea of irony or scepticism, though the school was run by the kind of women we would all have given everything we had not to end up like.'

'That's perfectly true. I remember meeting Marjorie Finlay in Selfridge's once. Do you remember her? Head girl when we were in the fifth form, I think. She looked exactly the same ... little burnished, button eyes and short hair in an Alice band. She told me she was doing occupational therapy and living in a flat with two other girls from school. And this was five years after we'd all left. She was the dullest creature you've ever met. I'm no fashion plate but even I could see how provincial and unexciting she was. Yet at school she was all-powerful.'

'Her finest hour, I'm afraid. As far as Ellie's concerned, I think that half her problem was her weight. Fat girls are conspicuously vulnerable, aren't they?'

'Well, thanks to you, that seems to be a problem she won't have any more. I'm so grateful to you, you can't imagine.'

I smiled at her, hypocrite, false friend, Iago that I was. She didn't return the smile.

'Robert is critical of my maternal failings. Recently, since Gerald died, he's been . . . more remote.' Min seemed to be struggling to define her thoughts. She didn't look at me. 'He's always tired, never wants to make love.'

'Do you mind?'

'Not particularly. As long as it *is* only tiredness and not that he's gone off me. Or fallen in love with someone else.'

My eyes didn't flicker but it wouldn't have mattered if they had for Min was lighting another cigarette. She was smoking more heavily than usual. I noticed that the middle finger of her right hand was stained yellow with nicotine.

'Of course he hasn't gone off you.'

'To tell the truth, when I get into bed I think about the next bit of my work and how I can improve the bit I've just done. I've begun the conclusion. It's gone brilliantly well and it's thanks to you. But I suppose I ought to make it up to the children and Robert as soon as it's finished. I suppose we all take each other too much for granted.'

Ellie's arrival at the breakfast table put an end to the conversation. She was wearing a jersey and skirt in a horrible shade of mustard, both much too big for her.

'Are those really yours?' said Min, with astonishment.

'Yes, they're my best. We bought them just before Christmas.' She saw my face, which must have expressed disapproval. 'They don't suit me a bit, I know, but there wasn't anything else big enough. I was at my fattest. It's the worst colour in the world. Like old sick.'

'Shall we buy something in Winkleigh?' I asked. 'That skirt looks as though it's about to fall down. I hope you've got clean knickers on in case it does.'

Ellie giggled. Mrs Butter arrived wearing a boiler suit of

green and white spots and a white chiffon scarf over her curls which were vermilion and glowed like a bonfire.

'Morning, ladies. Late for breakfast a tidy bit, isn't it? Still, better late ripe and bear than early blossom and blast, they do say. You going out, Miss Fairfax? *You* look smart, I will say.'

'Thank you. Ellie and I are going to Winkleigh to shop and get her eyes tested. Can I get you anything?'

'No, ta, dear. I went to the shop before I come and got a bit of ham for me supper. I'd have asked you if I'd known you were going, though. That Mrs Pickles is as bad as bad can be.'

'Really? I can't say I like her but I didn't know she was anything more than small-minded and uncharitable,' said Min, making a mug of instant coffee for Mrs Butter.

'That poor boy was in there, the one they call Daft Harry, and Mrs Pickles was that rude to him, it made me blood boil. Nay then, I says, you've no call to insult him just because he's nicked in the head. He talks funny out the side of his mouth and jerks all the time. Arm and leg all withered up. Plastic is it they call it?'

'Spastic, I think,' Min suggested, putting the mug in front of Mrs Butter.

'Thank you, duck, that's it, likely. Well, she were telling him not to touch anything, called him a clumsy idiot. And serving everyone else first. No, I says, I'll wait me turn. You serve Harry first. He understood, you know, for he turned to me and thanked me. A shame, I call it. It's never seemed to me right that the sins of the father should be visited on the children.'

'What do you mean?' asked Min. 'What did his father do?'

'I've said enough, dear. There's little to choose between bad tongues and wicked ears.'

'Oh go on. You've made me curious. We won't tell.'

'Just fetch me yon duster, there's a good lass,' said Mrs Butter to Ellie and as soon as she'd gone, lowered her voice. 'It's always said as Daft Harry is your ma-in-law's son by that artist chap as used to live in yon gypsy camp. Eh, you know . . . can't remember his name. His pictures go for thousands, they do say. Nasty, liverish things.'

'Johnny Eames, you mean?'

'That's right. Harry were born crooked and they all said it were a visitation. Mrs Hind, as good a woman as you'll find, adopted him and brought him up as her own.'

'What! I don't believe it!' said Min. 'That would mean that Harry Hind is Robert's half-brother!'

'Ay well, dear, it's only talk. If Mr Weston don't know, there's no sense in telling him, I say. What's done is done.'

'We'd better go if we're to be back by tea-time,' I said, anxious to get away before Mrs Butter started on something else. 'Isn't it time for William to be brought downstairs?'

'Oh, help, I forgot!' said Min, and she and Mrs Butter went off to get him, the latter talking non-stop.

We reached Winkleigh with an hour to spare before the appointment with the optician. Next door to it was a small department store. We went up to the children's department and bought a pair of trousers for Ellie.

'I've never been able to buy something that was right for my age before,' said Ellie, grinning all over her spotty little face. 'I've always had to have things for much older people and have them shortened. I can't believe that's me.'

She stared at herself in the shop mirror in awe.

'You look terrific. Now, what do you think of this dress? You must have something that fits for the party.'

'Oh, but won't it be too expensive?' asked Ellie, looking at the sleeveless navy shift dress I was holding out. It would, I thought, suit her very well. 'I don't think Mummy would approve.'

'Put it on,' I urged.

Ellie pulled it over her head. It fitted her perfectly and made her look at least twelve. It was fashionably short and now that her knees were slender the effect was charming.

'Don't you like it? You needn't have it if it's not what you want.'

'I *love* it. But Mummy says I should wear bright colours. And there's no hem to be let down. She'll say it's too grown-up.'

'Mothers always say that. None of us would get out of ankle socks if we listened to our mothers. I'll buy it for you and then you'll have to wear it.'

'Oh, Daisy! I don't think I shall ever be unhappy again.'

We bought the dress, a pair of navy tights to wear with it, and a jersey to go with the trousers. Then we went to the optician's.

Dr Woods, the ophthalmologist, looked at me rather severely and said that Ellie was long overdue for an eye-test. He showed me where the skin behind her ears was red and raw.

'This has happened because Eleanor's spectacles are too small for her face, due to too long a gap between appointments.' His tone was reproving. 'It may also be that she is wearing them for too long a period. She only needs them for prolonged sessions of reading. The defect is very mild.'

'But Eleanor wears them all the time!' I was horrified.

'The spectacles are for reading only,' Dr Woods explained patiently.

'Did you know that, Ellie?'

'Yes, but I kept losing them so Mummy said to keep them on. Of course I can see most things better without them. Except close up.'

Oh Min, I thought with real anger.

'Well, anyway, you must have some new ones. Must she have these dreadful pink frames?'

Dr Woods looked offended.

'Certainly she may have other frames. But I would suggest that it is a waste of money for a child who will grow out of them.'

I ignored him and we chose a pair of dark-green frames of an oval shape that suited Ellie's face.

'From now on you only put them on to read,' I said firmly.

'It feels very odd to be walking around without them. Sort of light. I'm not used to the wind blowing in my eyes. Usually I put them on the minute I wake up.'

'I've got an idea,' I said, putting the old spectacles into my bag. 'What do you think about having a haircut?'

No metamorphosis of serving-girl into princess or drab secretary into society beauty could have given the satisfaction I felt on seeing Ellie's transformation. Her hair was washed and cut to chin-length. The old pony-tail with its dry split ends lay in snips on the floor. Ellie's ears, which had stuck out slightly, were hidden by a brown, shining fall of hair exactly like Min's. The stylist entered into the thing with kind enthusiasm.

'She looks ever so much prettier, doesn't she? What d'you think to a fringe?'

The fringe made Ellie's blue eyes look larger.

'I never realised how much like your mother you are. When those spots have gone you'll be something of a beauty.'

Ellie blushed. We went to buy vegetables and she looked into every shop window and tossed her hair and stared at herself. I bought some lettuces, French beans, a pineapple, a bunch of parsley, and three red peppers. There was a delicatessen nearby which sold olives, good French cheese, pâté, and vanilla pods. From the market I bought pink tulips and white narcissi. We had a late lunch, in a little café, of poached eggs on toast and ice-cream afterwards for Ellie. Then we went to an art shop and bought a paperback for William called *Drawing from Life*. We drove home in a state of excitement and satisfaction. When we got near Dunston Abchurch I suggested that Ellie put on the trousers and the jersey we'd bought to astound her family with her new look. We walked self-consciously into the kitchen and the response was everything we hoped.

'Wow!' said William, the first to look up.

'Do my eyes deceive me?' said Robert. 'Who is this beautiful young creature? It can't be Miss Eleanor Weston!'

'Ellie! You look wonderful,' cried Min. 'Your hair! Oh Daisy, you've worked a miracle.'

'Ellie did it herself by being self-disciplined. Getting thinner was the most important thing.'

'You'd make a good "before and after" ad,' said William. 'No one would think that you used to be really ugly.'

Sitting down at the table in what everyone, including myself, had come to think of as my place, I was surprised to see a small parcel.

'Is this for me?' I said, looking round the table.

Ellie was hanging her head and blushing. I opened it. It was a very pretty china egg-cup shaped like a swan.

'I bought it from a stall in the market while you were buying the flowers. It's a thank-you present.'

I glanced across the table and caught Robert's eye. He was gazing at me with such love that my heart turned over. I looked quickly, guiltily, at Min. She was looking at Ellie with delight. I felt a rat.

After the children had gone up to bed that night and we'd gone into the drawing room, Min said she had a surprise for us. I quite thought she was going to tell us that she'd finished her writing but instead she went to the desk and took out a cheque made out for one thousand pounds and signed by Vivien.

'You see, I felt so bad about my behaviour yesterday that I had to make up for it. And, as I was telling Daisy this morning, I think in some ways I've neglected the children. This will pay for William's schooling, a year of it anyway, and Vivien said she'd see him right through to A-levels. I went to see her this afternoon and had a long talk with her.'

'Darling it's a tremendous achievement!' said Robert. 'How did you manage to persuade her?'

I was despicable enough to feel jealous of Min's triumph, even while I rejoiced for William.

'That'll be a secret between her and me,' said Min, very mysterious. 'No, honestly, darling. Don't ask me. Just accept it. One day I'll tell you. Now don't be cross and spoil my moment of glory.'

Robert clearly felt that it would be unfair to insist on knowing and went off to make coffee, with an air of disquiet.

'I blackmailed her,' said Min, in low voice, as soon as he'd gone out. 'I told her I'd tell Robert if she didn't give me the money. And that Robert would insist on recognising Harry Hind as his half-brother if he knew about it.'

'Heavens, how did she take it? Was she furious?'

'Like a lamb. You know Vivien. The oddest things strike her as amusing. She just laughed and said it was a fair cop and she'd give me the money.'

Robert came back in and that put an end to the conversation. Min was thoroughly happy that night and drank at least two glasses more than she usually did.

'I feel that at last I've been of some use to someone. All my life I've been looked after by other people. First Ma and then Robert. And of course, you, Daisy, when we were at school. And now,' she began to sound rather drunk. 'I hope you protectors get something out of it . . . boosted self-esteem or something. Otherwise it's a pretty one-way thing.'

'Aren't you forgetting that without you my entire childhood would have been pretty much a disaster?'

'Ah! That was Ma. Of course, I wanted you there. I didn't get jealous of you until much later when men came on the scene. 'Oh dear,' she began to laugh helplessly. 'I was such a beast to you when I found you in bed with Hugh. I really thought I was in love with him. Only because he was so good-looking. I've always been a sucker for a pretty face.'

'Thank you, I'll take that as a compliment,' said Robert. 'Now do drink your coffee and don't have any more champagne. You won't be able to work properly tomorow.'

'I know. And I'm so near finishing. I'm so excited and happy. That stupid quarrel, Daisy, I must have been mad. The whole thing was utterly trivial. Now if you and Robert fell in love . . . that would be something quite different and might justify fifteen years of . . .' she hiccupped loudly ' . . . sending you to Coventry.'

She laughed very much at the idea and I looked down at my cup, thankful for the darkness which hid my flaming face. Suddenly, abruptly, Min stopped laughing. I looked up in alarm.

'I need some more cigarettes,' she said and walked, slightly unsteadily, out of the room.

It was the first time Robert and I had been alone for three days and even in that moment, when my guilt was foremost in my mind, I thought how much I loved him. He sat smoking a cigarette and looking at me. Then he said softly,

'I have no right to say it but I love you.'

We sat looking at each other until Min came back with her favourite brand of French cigarettes, very tarry and rolled in khaki-coloured *papier mais*, which I'd brought her from Cambridge. She seemed perfectly sober and very calm.

Later, in bed, I asked myself which was more immoral . . . to blackmail Vivien or to sell her porcelain behind her back? I couldn't come to any conclusion except that at least with Min's method they still had the porcelain. I surveyed my own situation. My position was indefensible. I was coming to hate myself and before long I thought there was every probability that I would hate Min. Already my tolerance had been replaced by secret observations, marking up her failures with glee. I would leave the day after the party. It was quite impossible that Robert and I could ever be happy together in the graveyard of Min's love for us both.

# CHAPTER TWENTY-FOUR

I kept myself tremendously busy during the twelve days before the party. I took Booty to the vet and had her spayed. She was back home the same evening, none the worse, with only a bare patch of fur to show for it. I advertised the kittens in the village shop. Three people came, on different days, to look at them. They all seemed kind, responsible people and we let them choose which one they wanted. Ellie cried at each departure. There remained the tabby kitten which Ellie had chosen as her own and the smallest ginger kitten, which was shyer than the others and had shrunk from the strangers' prodding fingers.

'Oh, heavens! I'll probably regret it but I'll take him myself,' I found myself saying. 'Mrs Baxter likes cats and can look after him if I have to go away. He's always been my favourite of the litter.'

'Will you bring him with you whenever you come to stay?' asked Ellie.

'I expect so,' I said, while the ginger kitten lay on his back and chewed my finger with sharp teeth. 'What shall I call him?'

'What about Eggy, as he's the only one that likes cold scrambled egg to eat?'

'I had thought of something more distinguished. Bertram, perhaps, or Hugo. No, I shall call him Lord Frederick Verisopht. He was a character in a novel called *Nicholas Nickleby*. He can be Freddie for short.'

The children had only one week of the Easter holidays left so I took Ellie to the second-hand shop at her school to buy a set of uniform to fit her. We went into Winkleigh a second time and bought new school shoes and a pair of plain navy pumps to go with her new dress. The day after, Ellie and I took William back to the hospital to have his cast changed for a lighter weight-bearing cast.

'I thought I refused permission for a wheelchair to be removed from this hospital,' said our nurse as we wheeled William into reception.

'Sorry. Did you say something?' asked William, politely.

'I told you not to take a chair!'

'I can't quite hear. Daisy, can you hear what this person is saying?'

'You were not supposed to take a chair from this hospital!' yelled the nurse.

From the door opposite a small round person bounced out, her wrathful expression framed by the impressive, frilled cap of Matron.

'Was that your voice I heard, Nurse Groper? Have you taken leave of your senses? This is a hospital not a parade ground!'

'It was my fault, Matron,' William gave a sad little sigh. 'You see I am a little deaf and Nurse Groper was angry because I couldn't hear what she was saying.'

Matron cast a look of incredulous fury at Nurse Groper.

'See me at once in my office, Groper.' Then she bent her head close to William's so that he could see her face and said, moving her lips very exaggeratedly, 'Don't take any notice of the nurse being cross. You're a brave little boy.' Then she straightened up and said to me, 'I hope your son is progressing well?'

'Oh yes, quite well, thanks,' I murmured.

We walked and wheeled our way swiftly down the corridor to X-ray and Surgical and the minute we were out of sight and earshot we giggled helplessly, to the great annoyance of the nurse who was trying to cut off William's cast with a lethal-looking spinning saw. He was very pleased with his new light cast which incorporated a wooden block under the foot to walk on. An X-ray showed that the fracture was healing well.

'Though I don't want it to get better too quickly,' he said, swinging energetically on his crutches as we walked along the corridor. 'It's only fair as I've been laid up all holidays that I should have some time off school.'

We got home in time for tea. We told Robert, who'd come in from the garden, all about our hostilities with Nurse Groper.

'I feel a little guilty,' I said, while Robert laughed. 'I expect she got into tremendous hot water with Matron. There probably *is* a rule about taking wheelchairs.'

'There's an axiom about wars . . . that they determine not who is right but who is left,' said Robert.

It took Ellie a little while to grasp this and William had to explain it to her, which he did quite patiently. I guessed that he had been touched by Ellie's efforts to look after him during his period of enforced immobility and he was inclined, temporarily, to think younger sisters not so bad.

'Well, I've got good news,' said Robert, helping himself to a third slice of cake. (I looked affectionately at the slight suggestion of *embonpoint*. I loved everything about him, that was the trouble.) 'I telephoned the headmaster of Chaldicotts this morning. One of their boys has gone back to Singapore unexpectedly so they've got a spare place in the third form. You're to go on Friday and sit their entrance exam. If you pass you can start at once. As a weekly boarder.'

'Oh, no! I shall miss you dreadfully,' said Ellie with tears in her eyes but William, who had turned red then white, was too busy thinking what this would mean to him to take any notice of her.

'William ought to sit for an art scholarship,' I said, taking the cake from Ellie and putting it back into the tin.

'Really? Is he good enough?'

'I'm sure he's good enough to make it worthwhile trying. Of course, it all depends on the examiners. You must find out when they hold them and make sure his name is down.'

Privately I thought William would walk away with it. The children went outside, Ellie to feed Booty and the two remaining kittens and William to practise with his crutches. Min appeared then. She said she wasn't hungry and didn't want anything to eat. She looked tired.

'Yes, I've nearly finished,' she said when I asked her how her writing was going. 'Tomorrow, I think. God, my head hurts.'

I fetched some aspirin while Robert told her about William's place at Chaldicotts. Naturally she was extremely pleased but she looked rather pale.

'Don't go back to work now. Come out and do some gardening,' I suggested. 'It will make you feel so much better. You can help me dig the cow-parsley out of the shrubbery. And I can show you how to water the greenhouse so you can look after it when I go.'

'You're going?' Both Robert and Min looked at me as though they had received a shock.

'Of course. The day after the party. Well, don't look so surprised. I only came to help you get your work finished. Well, now it is . . . or will be . . . so I shall go home.'

I braced myself to resist pleadings to stay but none came.

'Of course, you will,' said Min. 'It's silly of me but somehow I never thought you'd go. So soon.'

Robert looked thoughtfully into his tea-cup but didn't say anything.

'Come on, then. Let's go out before the light fails,' I said, getting up and clearing the table.

Min, armed with a fork, was something of a menace. Several times she narrowly missed forking her own foot and she couldn't distinguish between cow-parsley, which was to be dug up, and shuttlecock ferns which were to be left. But she looked much better, less strained and tired, after the exercise. I would get her to help us in the garden every day until I left, to counteract the dowager's hump she was acquiring from too much writing. I was also determined that Robert and I should not be alone together even for a minute as I knew that my resolution was weakening with every moment that brought me closer to separation from him.

We sent Min's manuscript off the next day. In the evening, as it happened, Mr Liddell, the rector, had asked us for drinks. Min had received the invitation by telephone and had been very vague about the terms. Not only did we arrive late but found that we were not to be the only guests. There were ten or twelve cars parked outside.

'Wow! Look at that swanky Aston Martin,' said Min, as we drew up outside. 'I wonder who that belongs to?'

Of course it belonged to Charles. I saw him at once, standing in the centre of the Rectory drawing room, looking very relaxed in jeans and an open-necked shirt beneath a tweed jacket. A tall black-haired girl with eyes like chips of coal, hung on his arm. She was good-looking, almost beautiful, except that her mouth and nose were fractionally too large. It was ignoble of me but I was glad that I'd put on a well-cut, pale yellow silk suit. Susannah (I knew at once it was she) wore a loud red-and-white striped dress, halter-necked and rather short. In the context of an English country drawing room the effect was vulgar.

I avoided them and struck up a conversation with our host, Harold Liddell. It was hard work but we talked about growing chrysanthemums (his choice) and roses (mine). I thought I was doing rather well as I went on to infant schooling, crèches during matins, speed limits and Vietnam. I was talking away, in complete ignorance, on the last of these subjects when I became aware that someone was standing at my side.

'Hello, Charles,' I said, abandoning the Rector, I'm afraid, quite callously.

He kissed me on the cheek, which I thought was brave of him as I could see Susannah's eyes, as sharp as screwdrivers, upon us. She was in conversation with Robert on the other side of the room.

'You look perfectly beautiful,' Charles said, his eyes admiring. I'd forgotten how attractive those eyes were. Dark grey, with a very direct gaze. He was smiling and I thought I knew what he was thinking about.

'You're not angry with me then?' he said calmly.

'I? Why should I be angry?'

'Because I didn't telephone you.'

'You sent roses. They were lovely.'

'You know what I mean.'

'Yes, I know what you mean. I wasn't angry. Disappointed at first. Then . . . grateful.'

'Ouch! You *are* angry.'

'No. Really not.'

It was true. I'd scarcely thought about him for weeks.

'I've been very tied up.'

'So I see,' I said, looking at Susannah.

Charles followed my gaze. Susannah was leaning languorously against the wall, gazing up at Robert from beneath her fringe. I thought it was probably all for Charles's benefit.

'That's Susannah. You remember I told you about her. She arrived unexpectedly in England the morning after I got back to Milecross Park.'

'Did she bring the children?'

That got him. I'd never seen Charles disconcerted and I enjoyed it very much. He looked angry.

'How do you know about them?'

'Susannah telephoned me after you'd left.'

'Oh God!' He rubbed his hand over his face and grimaced. 'That woman is a ball and chain. England is not far enough away.'

'You shouldn't have started it up again when you went back to South Africa. Not that it's any of my business.'

'I didn't mean to. Someone else told her that I was back. She came to see me. She was seductive. I couldn't resist her.'

I laughed. 'Tell me, Charles, can you ever resist a woman?'

He laughed, too, relieved, I think, that I was so calm and friendly.

'Yes, of course. If she's ugly.'

'But supposing she's not ugly. Supposing you're very attracted to her but . . . say . . . she's married to your best friend. Could you resist her then?'

He looked at me with that familiar air of calculation. 'Is that a trick question? Well, the truth is, I suppose, no. Not if she wanted me. I refuse to tell lies about it. What would be the point of denying ourselves something we both wanted for the sake of a third person? It makes better sense that two of the three should be happy.'

'Very logical, certainly. But what about honour? And trust?'

'They're not things that genuinely shape people's lives. They're concepts used to justify failure, fear, laziness. Decisions are made on the basis of self-interest and then motives are shaped to put a good face on them.'

Suddenly Susannah was walking over to us. She entwined her arm with Charles's and looked at me with undisguised enmity. Close to, her skin was tanned and large-pored, not good. Her mascara was very smudged. I thought she was a little drunk.

'Hello. I'm Diana Fairfax,' I said, seeing that Charles was reluctant to introduce us.

Her face froze for a second in disbelief. 'I thought you lived in Cambridge.'

Her voice was very low and surprisingly soft, really very attractive, a surprising contrast to the boldness of her appearance.

'I do. I'm just staying with friends.'

'Jesus! Everywhere I go I meet Charles's fucks.'

'Hello, Charles. What a lovely surprise!' It was Min. 'I didn't know you were here. I can't see a thing without my specs and I never wear them except for work. It's my only vanity.'

'Hello, Min.' Charles kissed her. 'How's the writing?'

It was typical of Charles and a large part of his charm that he remembered what was important to other people.

322

'Finished. Sent off today. I'm like a cat whose kittens have been given away. I can't settle to anything.'

'Are you another of Charles's fucks?' asked Susannah, her sweet, soft voice slurred.

'Um, no. Sadly not,' said Min, only momentarily thrown. 'Is it a club? Can I apply for membership? Daisy, you must come and meet one of my favourite men.'

'What a woman!' Min whispered, as we walked away. 'I thought she was going to sink her teeth into you and tear you into bloody ribbons! So that's the ghastly mistress! Charles certainly deserves better than that.'

'I'm not so sure.'

Min took me over to a man with grey hair and stooping shoulders, whom she introduced as Martin Doyce, the village doctor.

'I saw you when you came in,' he said to me. 'I'm old enough now to admire women without anyone being upset by it.'

'Is that good or bad?' I asked.

'On the whole very good. I like being old. I know what makes me unhappy and I can avoid it. It's a blessed relief.'

'I'm often rather miserable and I'm afraid I'm going to be again,' I said, surprised at myself for this was not my usual style. Min had drifted off to talk to someone else so I was free to be truthful.

'The great troubles are few.' Dr Doyce sipped his orange juice. 'Fear of dying, fear of loved ones dying, pain, loneliness. What do you think?'

'I suppose that sums it up more or less. Perhaps one should add poverty.'

'Some of the happiest people I've known . . . country people, agricultural workers . . . were desperately poor. But that was years ago. Perhaps there's no longer any such thing as honest poverty. You look quite healthy. Either someone you love is dying or you're in love with the wrong man. I'd guess the latter.'

'Yes.'

'You're not married?'

'No.'

'But he is?'

'Yes.'

'Happily?'

'Yes. Really. I suppose so.'

'But he likes the shape of your nose better? And your jokes?'

I laughed. 'Perhaps it comes down to something as trivial as that.'

'You bet it does. Take my advice. Give him up. The other way you not only have to fool yourself that you're happy despite the mess, you have to fool each other. All the time. It simply isn't worth it.'

'Who is that black-eyed woman with the striped dress?' asked Robert, coming to talk to us. 'Hello, Martin. Why do all drunk girls make a beeline for me?'

Min joined us.

'Because you're irresistible to women, darling, but the sober ones are shyer, and therefore slower, about approaching you.'

'That's Susannah, who's Charles's mistress,' I explained, wanting, though I knew it was base, to correct any false impression Robert might have got from my tête-à-tête with Charles. 'She has two children by him.'

'Like a racehorse put out to stud,' said Min.

Martin Doyce looked at Susannah.

'Someone else who's in love with the wrong man,' he said, at last.

'Someone else?' said Min inquiringly.

I held my breath but Martin Doyce had learned tact.

'Martin is coming to our party,' said Min, as we drove home. 'And I asked Charles, as well. I hope he won't have to bring that girl.'

'So do I,' said Robert, with something like a shudder. 'She was leaning against the wall while talking to me and when she moved away, there was a brown streak left on the paper.'

'Suntan oil, I expect,' I said, from the back seat. 'You can tell from her skin that she sunbathes constantly.'

'I noticed it was very coarse,' said Min.

Robert, for some reason, was very amused by this exchange.

William was tense and very tired when he came back from sitting the examination for Chaldicotts but Robert was enthusiastic.

'You should see the library! And the art department! Studios for painting, drawing, pottery, sculpture. I liked the head-master. Sense of humour.'

'The exams were very difficult,' said William gloomily. 'I couldn't do the physics at all. It was stuff I hadn't been taught. I'm obviously far behind.'

'Well, there are other schools,' said Robert cheerfully. 'It doesn't have to be Chaldicotts.'

'Promise you won't be disappointed if I don't get in,' said William, anxiously.

'Cut my throat if I tell a lie. I promise I won't be disappointed.'

He spoke with absolute conviction, which was kind of him as I knew that it was quite untrue. As it turned out, the headmaster telephoned the next morning to say that on the strength of William's classics, history and English papers, they'd decided to offer him the place.

'They want you to have maths and science coaching in the summer holidays,' said Robert. 'You won't mind that?'

'I'll probably mind it. But it'll be worth it,' William said. Then he took up his crutches and hobbled outside.

Robert looked rather disappointed. 'He doesn't seem as pleased as I thought he would be.'

'Of course he's pleased,' I said. 'Much more pleased than you can probably imagine. He was very desperate, you know. He just doesn't want to show how much. He wants to get his feelings under control.'

'How much better you seem to know our children than we do,' he said, sighing and fiddling about with my fountain pen that was lying on the kitchen table.

I was ashamed to recognise that the 'our' and 'we' of this remark made me wince.

'It's because they aren't mine that I can see them more clearly in some ways.'

'You must have your own children,' said Robert. 'You will be the most wonderful mother.'

I actually felt my lower lip tremble, as though I were a child. The serenity with which he said it seemed to push me away to the point of invisibility.

'Darling!' His hand was on mine. 'Of course, I didn't mean . . . what have I said? . . . I'm an idiot . . . I love you. Oh, this is torture! If only I knew what I ought to do!'

I heard the door open and I got up and fiddled with the lid of the kettle, blinking away stupid tears.

'William's got a place at Chaldicotts,' I heard him say.

'Oh, marvellous! What a relief! Oh, good boy!' Min said. 'Where is he?'

'Gone outside.'

'I'll go and find him.'

She went out.

'I've made you unhappy,' said Robert. 'I feel very guilty. Is it any comfort to you to know that I'm very unhappy, too?'

'Yes,' I said, going to the door and whistling to Ham, 'Yes, it is. The only comfort possible in the circumstances. I'm going for a walk. On my own.'

The next few days were very busy in a satisfying practical way. I didn't have much time to be miserable. First Min and I drove with the children to the school shop at Chaldicotts and spent a staggering sum of money on school uniform. That evening and all the next day Min and I stitched on name-tapes until we were seeing William R. Weston in red on the inside of our eyelids. Then we went into Winkleigh for a sponge bag, dressing-gown, pyjamas, slippers, towels, underpants and socks. The name-taping began again that night until our fingers, especially Min's, were pricked and bleeding. Ellie and Robert had brought down Robert's old trunk and tuck box from the attic and as each pile of clothes was finished it was taken up and put in the trunk. William wouldn't be going to Chaldicotts until after I'd left but I was determined that he would go with every article on the school inventory marked and in good order. I remembered with sharp clarity the tattered, ill-fitting things my mother had sent me off with before I was old enough to organise it myself, and how I'd been constantly scolded for having unmarked possessions.

When that was done I began to shop for the party, which was to take place in two days' time. I tried to consult Min but she said I was bound to know far better than she what would be suitable. Robert was equally vague. So I went alone to Winkleigh in the morning and bought boxes of fresh vegetables and fruit. That afternoon I made a *jambon persillé*, poached a salmon, and cooked the huge piece of beef. I made three pear and almond tarts, three *tartes tatins* and plenty of meringues. Min scrubbed scores of potatoes and counted plates and knives and forks. Mrs Butter washed glasses and coffee-cups and saucers and ironed napkins. Ellie came home from school on the first day of term and found Min and me having a glass of champagne at four in the afternoon.

'This is decadent,' said Min, 'but we're too tired to carry so much as a teaspoon through to the dining room without the stimulus of alcohol. Did you have a reasonable day, darling?'

'Actually . . . yes.' Ellie sounded as though she hadn't got over the surprise herself. 'Everyone said how thin I was and how much they liked my hair. And Polly Saxby asked me where I'd got my shoes as she wanted some like them. And best of all, Patricia Wigan asked Annette Drew to change places with her so that she could sit next to me. Patricia's got fair curly hair and a brace. She's really pretty.'

The telephone rang. I went to answer it.

'This is Frances Benson speaking.' There was a short pause. 'Gerald's mother.'

'Oh, Mrs Benson,' I struggled to think of the right thing to say. 'I'm Diana Fairfax. I'm a guest in the house. I knew Gerald slightly. I liked him very much.' Another pause. 'I do wish I'd had the chance to know him better.'

I wasn't doing very well.

'Thank you. I believe he mentioned you in his last telephone call. Aren't you an old schoolfriend of Robert's wife?'

'Yes. I expect you want to speak to Robert?'

I went to fetch Robert. He was a long time on the telephone. Eventually he came into the kitchen, yawning and looking very tired. He told us he had agreed to spend Saturday night at Hampstoke, staying with Gerald's mother.

'Oh, but it's the night of our party,' said Min.

And my last night at Weston Hall, I thought. But said nothing.

'I can't help it. I can't take time off during the week. She's distraught. Gerald was her whole life. She says she's afraid of going mad as it gets worse every day. She wept. Poor woman. I'll be back on Sunday. I shan't have to leave until about five. The party'll be over by then, surely.'

The next day, the day before the party, I began to decorate the house. A white cloth, polished glasses and masses of flowers lifted the gloom in the dining room a little. The next thing was to wire big branches of leaves and ivy on to the pillars in the hall. My plan was to encourage people to have

327

their first drinks there as it was just about the largest room in the house. I wanted to exaggerate the idea of a fairy-tale forest by creating a canopy of greenery. If it had been Christmas I would have entwined tiny white lights among the leaves but as it was May I had to deny myself the indulgence and stick with bowers of hawthorn, hazel and beech. I was standing at the top of a ladder tucking stems into loops of wire, with Robert holding the ladder below me and handing up branches, when I heard a voice I knew very well.

'Good Lord! What *is* going on? Some sort of pagan festival? Perhaps it'll be worth the walk after all.'

I looked down to see Robert's head turning towards the front door and I descended a rung or two to see for myself. Standing dramatically framed against the sunlight, a twist of smoke curling from the end of her long cigarette holder, was my mother.

I don't suppose anyone, since man first wrapped himself in a bearskin, has been more unsuitably dressed for the country than she. I wondered what passing local traffic must have made of her. Despite the fact that it was fairly warm she wore a cape of snow leopard over a brilliant tangerine-coloured dress. The dress was very short and very tight and revealed a figure that was still good though she was over sixty. There was a large amount of brown cleavage and brown leg at opposite ends of the dress and on her feet were peep-toe shoes with five-inch heels. Her hair was streaked quite darkly, like tortoiseshell, and hung round her face to her shoulders. The face was the difficulty. It had been pinched and tucked and treated to expensive pharmaceuticals, like the rest of her, but here alone the imitation of youth had refused to take. Even from the top of the ladder I could see that it was wizened. With her eyes set a little too close together and her long upper lip, I was reminded of a monkey. Her round brown eyes even had the same simian expression, of mournful intelligence. Well, they were mournful, anyway.

I came quickly down the ladder.

'Ah, Diana, I thought that was you. I've had to walk from the station. There weren't any taxis. I'm perfectly exhausted. You'll have to send someone for my luggage.'

'Mother, this is Robert Weston, Min's husband. Robert, this is my mother, Bambi . . . er . . .'

I paused because her surname changed so often, according to her men, that I couldn't keep up with it.

'Wadhurst. How do you do?'

She stretched out a languorous brown paw, treating him to a flash of expensively-capped teeth. She had ignored Robert until this point, thinking him to be a minion, I imagine, because of the holes in his jersey. Robert looked at her and masked admirably whatever he was thinking.

'So you're Diana's mother,' he said, rather superfluously. 'Did you say . . . Bambi?'

'Yes. Just a silly pet name everyone calls me.'

My mother's real name was Brenda which she'd stopped using a long time ago.

'I see.' Robert hadn't quite recovered from the surprise. He ran his fingers through his hair and pulled down his jersey in the way he always did when nonplussed.

'You didn't let us know you were coming,' I said, with something strongly resembling disapproval.

'Darling, I know. I came on a whim. I know I'm dreadfully impulsive. I just can't help it.' She looked sexily at Robert out of the corner of her eye.

'I hope you won't let my daughter scold me, Robert. I may call you Robert? She's such a dreadful little bosser. You'd never think I was her mother.' She gave a trill of laughter. 'She's always trying to reform me but as I tell her repeatedly, I'm happy as I am.'

Oh you liar, I thought to myself, thinking of the swollen, smudged face and the claw-like grasp of the vodka bottle. However, I said nothing but smiled patiently. Min came into the hall carrying a tray of spoons. She stopped dead when she saw my mother and looked aghast.

'Mother, you remember Min, don't you? My mother has just called in to say hello. You didn't say where you were going?'

'Min, how lovely, lovely, lovely to see you! Why, it must be twenty years! You clever little things were just going up to . . . Oxford, wasn't it?'

Min disappeared for a moment beneath the snow leopard as my mother embraced her as vigorously as though she was trying to swallow her whole.

'Gosh, what a surprise! Hello, Bimbo, how brown you

look and what a delicious scent you're wearing. Won't you stay to lunch?'

'Bambi, darling,' Mother trilled again and kept up a show of enthusiasm though it must have received a check. I saw Robert bite his lip to hide a smile. 'You always were the sweetest thing. And you're looking . . . umm . . .' her eye travelled over Min's face which was dirty from rummaging in the attic. There were cobwebs in her hair and her jersey was unravelling from the hem. ' . . . terribly fit. I've already met your dishy husband.' Robert squared his shoulders unconsciously. 'I'd adore to stay for lunch. Actually I hoped you'd have me for a teeny bit longer as I've been frightfully let down by friends and you see me homeless, roofless, a weary traveller. Of course, I'm like a gypsy. I can pitch my tent anywhere with no fuss. Not like Diana who practically has to have her bedroom redecorated by Colefax and Fowler before she can lay her head upon anyone else's pillow.'

'I know,' Min laughed. 'She's had to walk over red-hot ploughshares every day since staying with us.'

'Really?'

My mother, whose education was slender and patchy, looked suddenly doubtful. I thought Robert was looking dangerously red from suppressed laughter, just the sort of thing that brings on strokes in middle-aged men.

'I'm afraid Min and Robert are giving a party tomorrow and there won't be . . .' I began.

'Of course you can stay, Bambi,' interrupted Min. 'We'd love to have you. If you won't mind us being rather chaotic because of the party?'

Robert was sent to the station for my mother's luggage and to fetch William from Vivien's house, where they were playing card games and enjoying being rude to one another. I went into the kitchen and laid a sixth place for lunch with a sensation of profound misgiving.

## CHAPTER TWENTY-FIVE

The morning of the party dawned bright and unnaturally warm. Mrs Butter warned of thunderstorms.

'It's always said May flood never did good. Mark my words.'

Mrs Butter shook her tight blue-black curls. I'd seen blue rinses often enough but Mrs Butter's hair was the colour of ink, metallic and stiff like metal shavings. She was staying to help with the party and I'd quite expected her to come looking very dressy but instead she was wearing an all-encompassing overall.

'What good do floods in other months do?' asked Ellie, but Mrs Butter only shook her head and said, in a prophetic monotone like an oracle, 'Beware the oak, it draws a stroke, avoid an ash, it counts the flash, creep under the thorn, it saves you from harm.'

I began to feel quite certain that there was something wrong with her. She worked very hard all morning, cleaning all the places where guests might be expected to go, while I made a large bowl of hollandaise sauce and another of mayonnaise. I set Min to work chopping vegetables for salads while I whipped cream and sandwiched meringues together. Ellie carefully chopped parsley and peeled tomatoes. She wanted to mandolin the cucumbers but Min said *she* would do it in case Ellie sliced her fingers. Of course Min sliced her thumb within a minute of beginning the task. We had to throw away the slices she'd already cut because they were unpleasantly roseate. Ellie finished the other three-and-a-half-cucumbers without mishap.

Robert could be heard in the still-room, cursing and hammering away at the block of ice the fish-man had delivered that morning. He had to fill several buckets with chips of ice for the champagne and he emerged very cross afterwards, his hands red and wet like peeled prawns. We told him it was all worth while and he went off grumpily to open bottles of red wine. I decorated the poached salmon with cucumber and piped mayonnaise. When I'd asked the greengrocer for dill he'd looked as perplexed as though I'd asked for frankincense. The beef looked wonderful and needed no adornment. I crossed my fingers and turned out the *jambon persillé*. It just held together with a delicious tremble and I was very proud of its pink, green and fawn beauty, forgetful now of what it had cost in terms of strength of mind to tangle with the pig's trotters.

An hour before the first guests were due to arrive, the potatoes were baking on trays in the Aga and everything was ready. William and Ellie kept going to look at the food in the dining room and having little tastes. Min had changed into something yellow which was essentially pretty but had more crumples in it than a dress by Fortuny. She refused to take it off and let me iron it for her. Robert had put on a blue shirt and a newish pair of corduroy trousers and looked very handsome. I was just going up to change when my mother appeared, wearing a white cotton piqué dress, short enough for a game of lawn tennis. Her hair was smooth and her make-up skilful, if rather too emphatic, but there was no disguising the dark circles beneath her eyes.

'Have I missed breakfast?'

'By about three hours,' I said. 'You might as well hang on for lunch now.'

'Oh. Well, if I slept at all last night it must have been since breakfast. Frightful screaming and banging all night long. You haven't got a mad relation locked up?' She peered accusingly at Min through bloodshot eyes. 'In addition I broke one nail trying to open the wardrobe door and another trying to get into the chest of drawers.'

Her rouged mouth drooped sulkily.

'So much for your Romany proclivities,' I said. 'Not so much as a clay-baked hedgehog or a smoking campfire and you're grumbling already.'

Mother turned her head so that the others couldn't see and stuck her tongue out at me.

'I do hate it when you get sarcastic and superior. What I need is a teeny-weeny drink.'

I went to the pantry and poured her a double vodka and orange juice. She took it from me with a pout but after one sip she was restored to good humour and went off with William to look at the food in the dining room.

I took Ellie upstairs with me so that we could change. She'd wanted to keep her new dress a secret, so I'd hung it in my wardrobe. She wriggled into her tights and I dropped the dress over her head. It had the sort of spare elegance that suited Eleanor's looks. I smoothed a little foundation over the remaining red scars on her face. She looked in the cracked mirror on the cupboard door and stared as though she was seeing herself for the first time. I remembered when, as a small child, it had occurred to me to climb on the stool of my mother's dressing-table to see whether I was pretty or not. It was the birth of egoism, the idea of myself as separate from my surroundings. I had looked in the mirror for a long time but I hadn't been able to tell whether I had whatever it was that other people approved of.

I put on a plain dark-red dress, with short sleeves and a low neck. I fastened my hair into a single plait and looked into the mirror above Ellie to darken my lips and mascara my lashes. The red suited my paleness and my dark hair.

We went downstairs together. Robert was standing in the hall, holding a glass of wine. My mother was talking to him, with tremendous animation, and he was listening politely. When he saw us, he stopped paying her attention and stared at me with a sort of desperate hunger.

My mother looked sharply from Robert to me and back again and, I could tell, was rapidly coming to the very conclusion that I had so much feared she might. Though essentially a stupid woman, she had a knack for seeing the wood, mostly because the specific significance of the trees was wasted on her.

'What do you think of your beautiful daughter?' I said, pushing Ellie a little before me.

'I'm stunned!' said Robert. 'Isn't this a new dress? It is very becoming . . . very elegant.'

He twirled her round and her expression, so happy and innocent, brought a lump to my throat. I dreadfully wished she was mine. Mine and Robert's. Mrs Butter appeared in a startling concoction of Schiaparelli-pink taffeta. She looked very unsteady.

'I know you asked me to keep an eye on something, Miss Fairfax, but I'm blessed if I can think what it were.'

'The potatoes in the gas oven.' I put my arm through hers and led her into the kitchen. She felt very tottery and shivery. 'Let's have a look at them. Are you sure you're feeling quite well?' Mrs Butter nodded, the diamanté bow in her hair bobbing up and down. 'Anyway now I'm here I'll have a look.' I prodded the potatoes. 'I think they're done. We'll put them in bowls in the cool oven of the Aga.'

Mrs Butter dropped one or two which disintegrated on the floor. It didn't matter but she was very upset. By the time I'd calmed her down and we'd drunk a glass of champagne together in the quiet of the kitchen, the party had begun.

It was warm enough to leave the front door open. Everyone admired the boskage above their heads before beginning earnest drinking and talking. Very quickly there was a swell of conversation. I enjoyed being an outsider, able to stand and observe from within the dining room where I'd gone to dress the salads. I saw Vivien, her face either healed or well-made-up, talking to Martin Doyce, the doctor. Harold Liddell was also there, talking to my mother. I couldn't imagine what they could find in common. I was thankful that, unlike Elizabeth Bennet, the periods of my life spent being horribly embarrassed and ashamed of my relations were few and brief. Min was talking to the perspiring Bursar from St Lawrence's and I saw him get out his handkerchief and press it to his forehead though the hall was shady and cool. Robert was laughing and talking to two women I didn't know. I was glad to see him enjoying himelf. William was leaning on his crutches with an expression of weariness, listening to his father. Ellie was carrying round a bottle of champagne, longing to fill someone's glass. We'd shown her how to do it without creating too much fizz and she wanted to put her new skill into practice.

'Are you responsible for Eleanor's emergence as a butterfly?' said a voice in my ear.

Martin Doyce was standing beside me.

'She looks beautiful, doesn't she?'

'Utterly charming. And very much happier. You didn't answer my question.'

'Well, I had something to do with it.'

'I thought as much. It struck me at once that there had been changes here. Even the dog.' He gave Ham, who was lying down next to me, a friendly prod in the ribs with his toe. 'I notice that the dog is sleeker and fitter. William looks a little battered but Min tells me he's going to Chaldicotts. It'll be just what he needs. And Robert. He's something of a mystery. Rather jittery. Are you responsible for that, too?'

'I'm amazed that anyone can be so observant,' I laughed, not choosing to answer.

'I've known Robert and Vivien for forty years and Min for thirteen. I delivered William and Eleanor. What disturbs me is that Min alone of all of you looks wretched. She's making a game attempt to hide it. Of course I can't ask you to tell me what's wrong. I'm very fond of her and I hope she'll tell me herself.'

I looked at Min. Was it possible that Martin Doyce was right? She was standing in a group with some others, talking and waving her hands, describing something. I could see nothing amiss. I said so.

'Mm. I don't think I'm wrong.' He drained his glass. 'Vivien of course is inimitable. Shockingly badly behaved but there's no one like her.' He laughed suddenly. 'Someone asked me today if it was true that she was the mother of Harry Hind. Apparently Vivien has been dropping hints to that effect. I wonder what her game is?'

'You mean it isn't true?'

'Absolutely not. I delivered Harry Hind myself. I should know if anyone does. What's she up to, do you know? Is it just a ploy to gain attention?'

I looked at Vivien, who was listening to a tall man of military bearing, with an expression of complete boredom on her sharp, witch's face.

'I really can't imagine,' I replied.

Some instinct that she was being looked at made Vivien turn her head towards me, her silver bob of short, straight hair distinctive among the long, drooping, heavily fringed Juliette Greco styles almost everyone under forty was trying to imitate. She walked away from her companion, leaving him in mid-sentence.

'Hello, Dahlia. Hello, Martin.'

'Hello, Viv.'

They kissed, briefly. I had a sudden intimation from something in their manner that these two had once been lovers.

'Don't call me that. You know I hate it.'

Martin smiled. He spoke softly. 'I hadn't forgotten.'

'Lawrence is such a bore. I can't stand him a minute longer. Light me a cigarette, Martin.'

'He's looking at us. I think he feels humiliated.' Martin lit her cigarette. 'You don't deserve the friends you've got. Soon you won't have any. I'm going to talk to him.'

Vivien shrugged, looking up at the greenery with a critical eye.

'That was a touch of inspiration, Dahlia. It's a very good party. Quite out of Min's class. It was a sad day for Min when she renewed this little friendship, wasn't it?'

It was a sad day for both of us, in one way, I thought. But I had no intention of discussing it with Vivien. The old adage about attack being the best method of defence came to my aid.

'Why did you let Min think that Harry Hind was your son?'

'It suited me,' Vivien smiled. 'To tell you the truth, I wanted an excuse to fall in with Robert's plans about William. Of all of them William is most like me. I think he's worth spending money on.'

'Why didn't you just give Robert the money then?'

'Oh, you are a nosy parker! Because I didn't choose. Robert's always so disapproving. He's never liked me very much. Since he married Min he's behaved like an elder statesman, pompous and cold. I like my power. Now I suppose,' she raised her voice slightly, 'since he's in love with you, he's going to . . . what do they call it these days . . . fall out?'

'Vivien! I forbid you to talk rubbish!' I felt really angry. 'Anyway it isn't "fall out" but "drop out".'

'Who is that extraordinary-looking woman with the teenage clothes and the face like Methuselah? She might well be the Great Swosser prostitute. Except that she looks a little too drunk to stand for long on a street corner.'

'That is my mother.'

Vivien's eyebrows rose and I saw again a strong resemblance to Robert.

'Really? *Quelle horreur!* My God, Dahlia, I feel for you!'

'Thank you.'

As we watched, my mother made one of her characteristic gestures, a rotation of each shoulder in turn, which brought her large brown bust into billowy prominence beneath the fascinated eyes of the man she was listening to. Vivien gave a snort which drew the attention of all those standing near us.

'I can't help it,' Vivien gasped. 'It's so *piquant*. You and she! It's too marvellous!'

Everyone standing nearby looked at us uncertainly with vague, wandering smiles, longing to know what was so funny.

'Diana!'

Peter undulated towards me, arms spread wide, toes pointed, beaming.

'How wonderful to see you, dear heart.' In my ear, as he enfolded me in his arms, he muttered, 'It's been all too frightful. You can't think what a relief it is to be with someone sane! Giorgio stole some trinkets from Jerry Daubeney and the police are looking for him. Darling, we're on the run!'

'Oh, Peter! What? This is Robert's mother, by the way. Vivien Weston . . . Peter Holdenby.'

'Wonderful name, darling,' said Peter, kissing Vivien's hand. 'Just like a film star. How it suits you!' He turned to me. 'What did he steal? Just a few baubles like cuff-links and cigarette cases. And a Goya etching.'

Vivien was dragged away, rather reluctantly I thought, by a large, imperious woman in purple who demanded that she be shown the drawing room.

'Oh heavens, Peter!' I said, quite horrified. 'You can't go on with it. He'll ruin you. You'll end up in gaol because of him. And he's wildly unfaithful. You must know that.'

'Oh yes. I'm quite over him. Truth to tell, he's really rather a bore apart from the bed thing. I don't believe a word about this book on Correggio.'

'Of course not. I shouldn't think he's read a book in his life. What's he doing here then?'

Giorgio had followed Peter into the hall and was leaning up against a pillar, surveying the company with an air of calculation.

'He's got a very nasty temper, I've discovered, and he says he'll beat me up if I attempt to leave him. You know how I *abhor* violence!'

'Yes, well, you needn't make it sound so very idiosyncratic. Most rational people do. What are you going to do?'

'I thought if we could get back to London, I'd be able to give him the slip. Lose him in the crowd, you know. I've got lots of friends I can stay with, whom he's never met. As soon as he finds someone else with enough money to keep him, I'm safe.'

'Oh Peter! It sounds so dreadful. So sordid and unhappy. Next time you'll be more careful, won't you? This ought to be a lesson to you.'

'Sweet girl to care,' he said, squeezing my arm, affectionately. 'And you, my love,' seeing Robert coming over to welcome him, 'you're going to be a little bit more careful next time, too?'

'I think it's time to have something to eat,' I said, seeing Mrs Butter tottering erratically towards the dining room, bearing a tray loaded with potatoes. 'Robert, will you get everyone to come in?'

The next half-hour demanded concentration and passed swiftly. Robert carved the beef and I cut up the salmon and the *jambon persillé*, a task that called for dexterity if people were to get something that looked appetising on their plates. As I bent over the last of the salmon, struggling with the backbone, someone kissed my neck.

'Hello, Charles,' I said, without looking up.

'How did you know it was me?'

'Most of the people here are strangers and those I do know would be extremely unlikely to kiss me on the neck. It had to be you.'

'How fortunate I am to be singled out in this way. Let me do that.'

I was glad to hand him the implements.

'I think I'll allow myself a drink,' I said, watching him deal with the soft, pink flesh of the salmon in a superior, masculine way. 'The puddings will be easy to serve.'

'You're rather behind most of the guests. Some appear to be completely drunk already. One woman came up and tried to kiss *my* neck when I arrived. A total stranger as far as I know. I had to stand her up against one of the pillars or she'd have been on the floor at my feet. Very little clothing and very much make-up.'

'Oh dear. That's my mother. I hope she won't be sick and put everyone off their food. I'd better go and see.'

'No, don't go.'

Charles caught hold of me as I was about to go into the hall. He pushed the door half closed with his foot so that we were hidden from the other guests and took me in his arms.

'Charles! What are you doing? This is a civilised lunch party not the back row of the cinema!'

'You've forgotten everything I taught you. But I shall enjoy reminding you.'

He kissed me on the mouth.

'You've got a cheek! I don't just stand idly around waiting for you to come and make love to me when you choose.'

'I know you're angry. And you're quite right to be. But it wasn't just Susannah.'

'What wasn't?' I tried to free myself.

Part of the difficulty was that I did find Charles very attractive. But I knew perfectly well that he would make me or any other woman he had anything to do with miserable, and I didn't intend to be a victim, even to free myself from loving Robert.

'Stop struggling. Susannah wasn't the only reason why I didn't telephone you. I found I liked you too much and I didn't want to. I'm still fighting to get away from Susannah. I didn't want to fall in love with you.'

'Well, it's an old line but still worth a try, I suppose.'

He tried to kiss me again but I turned my head away.

'Don't be an idiot. I mean it. When I saw you at Liddell's house the other day, I knew that I had to take the risk. Damn it, Diana. I *am* in love with you.'

Robert was halfway through the door with a bottle of champagne in his hand. He must have heard Charles. He looked at us as we stood enfolded against the wall behind the door.

'Good God, I . . .' he stopped and turned very white. A tremor ran over his face. 'Daisy . . .'

He couldn't speak. He looked at us with an expression of disbelief. I shook my head, stupidly. We stared at each other in despair. We remained in this state of stupefaction for what felt like ages but could only have been seconds. Then Charles let go of me and took a step back.

'Well. So that's it.' His voice was cool but I felt instinctively that it cost him something. He laughed. 'Well, well. I see it all. Poor Min.'

He waited for us to deny it but Robert and I still stood in silence, looking at each other. I loved Robert with such intensity then, seeing the real agony of jealousy on his face, that any fool could have seen it written on mine. Charles was certainly not a fool.

'You idiots!' he said, and walked out of the room.

I never saw him again.

'Are we allowed any of those delicious puddings?' A fat woman with greedy eyes and a coy expression put her head round the door.

'Of course.' I went to the table and began to cut up a pear and almond tart. 'Which would you like?'

'I'll have something of everything, please.'

All the other guests began to come in, waving plates and demanding puddings. I drank a glass of champagne very quickly and felt better. Everyone was getting affectionate with one another. I went into the drawing room and saw Vivien reclining on a sofa next to a young man, of dark good looks. He looked more and more astonished as Vivien continued to talk. My mother, who had picked up quite a bit of Italian from living in Tuscany for six months with an impoverished potter, was talking to Giorgio who was trying to put his hand down her dress. I averted my eyes.

'Where's Robert?' asked Min, coming up to me. 'I think he ought to take Mrs Butter home. She's in a state of collapse. Do you think she's had too much to drink?'

'Probably. Everyone else seems plastered.'

'You seem quite sober, anyway. I'm not sure I am. It's a good party. What a pity . . .'

'What?'

'Nothing. I feel like Ophelia. Floating. "You must wear your rue with a difference. There's a daisy." That's good. A Daisy. And then it goes on about violets but I can't quite remember it. We did *Hamlet* for 'O'-level, didn't we?'

'Darling, you *are* drunk. Do you feel all right?'

'Oh, don't be such a bloody prig! Of course, I'm all right!'

She walked away, leaving me surprised and hurt. I saw Robert, who was filling glasses with Sauternes.

'Will you take Mrs Butter home? Min says she's had too much to drink. I'll finish pouring these.'

'Where will you be when I get back? I want to talk to you.'

'I don't know. I don't think we ought to . . . God what was that?'

'Only thunder. Mrs Butter predicted a storm, didn't she? I

340

think she's frightened of them. I'd better take her home so that she can put her head under the bedclothes.'

'I don't like them much myself. I know it's ridiculous.'

'Darling, don't look so sad. I'll be back soon. I must talk to you.'

I went upstairs to close my bedroom window as the rain was beginning to fall fast. The sill was already wet and the curtains splashed with dark spots.

'It's not bedtime, silly girl,' I said to Ham who had followed me upstairs. 'Let's go down and see if there's a little piece of beef for you.'

I was on my way past the green room where my mother was sleeping, when I heard a moan. I sighed. She *was* being sick. I'd expected it. I tapped on the door and, when there was no answer, pushed the door open. My mother lay on the bed, with her legs practically over her head, and a naked Giorgio, black hair over every visible inch, was doing unspeakable things to her. I shut the door quickly and walked downstairs.

The constant, restless pursuit of the ruination of happiness by almost the entire human race, including myself, depressed me. I went into the kitchen and began to wash up.

'There you are, playing Cinderella,' said Peter, coming in. 'It's a marvellous party. I'm having a *lovely* time. You're looking a little glum. Now let me help you. Uncle Peter will wash and you can dry and put away.'

This is what we did and very soothing I found it. Peter was in excellent spirits and soon I cheered up myself.

'I'm so thrilled your mother's taken a shine to Giorgio. They were looking at each other in quite a sexy way half an hour ago. I have hopes.'

'They're in bed right now. I accidentally disturbed them. But they didn't notice. They were too absorbed in carnal exploration.'

'Oh joy! When they cry unto the Lord in their trouble, he delivereth them out of their distress. I don't think my father had quite my predicament in mind when he used to take that text for his sermon. The solution shows how very practical and broad-minded God is.'

'What strategem will He have for my mother who will shortly be in just the same spot that you are? I think it's a very short-sighted solution.'

'Well, dear girl, as a humanist you will believe with Novalis that character is destiny. While I see it all shrouded in a lovely, flossy, ineffable mist. Either way it means your mother must be left to get on with it.'

Peter had been received into the Roman Catholic Church some years ago but I was never sure whether he believed any of it. Certainly I'd never heard him be serious on the subject.

'What have you done with the things Giorgio stole?'

'I found a delectable boy on a motor-bike outside a pub on our way here. I gave him fifty pounds to take them back to Jerry and promised him another fifty if he could bring me a note of receipt in Jerry's own hand.'

'Isn't that rather risky?'

'The whole thing sends shivers of terror down my spine. I can't tell you what I felt when we passed two large black police cars full of burly policemen, going up Jerry's drive when we were coming down it. I knew at once that Giorgio had been up to something, he was so cock-a-hoop.'

'How did you get him to give them up?

'Sleight of hand. I suggested that we stop at a pub to fortify ourselves for this party. While he was ogling the barmaid I slipped out and found the booty, wrapped it in one of Giorgio's shirts and commissioned my Paul Revere.'

'So Giorgio doesn't know you sent them back?'

'No. And that's how it must stay until we get to London.'

'In that case, reluctant though I am to see you go, you ought to leave as soon as possible. If you want to hand him on to my mother you'll have to persude her to go, too. And her *liaisons* are of extremely short duration, these days.'

Peter helped me make coffee and we carried it in two large jugs into the dining room. Then he went upstairs to find Giorgio and my mother. The party was clearly going to last until late afternoon. I was delighted to see people enjoying themselves but my own mood was solitary. I'd done everything that was needed and I'd finish the washing-up later.

'We're bored,' said William, hobbling over. 'If anyone wants us we'll be in the boat-house.'

Ellie followed behind carrying his painting and drawing things.

'Everyone admired my dress,' she whispered. 'I feel really

happy. Oh, I didn't tell you. Polly Saxby rang up this morning and asked me to go to her party tomorrow!'

'How lovely,' I said. 'You'll have to write and tell me all about it. You know I'm going home tomorrow?'

'I know. That's the only thing that makes me sad. But you'll come back soon?'

'I expect so.'

I could hear Min's voice, rather loud and rather drunk, coming from the drawing room. Peter came downstairs, carrying my mother's suitcase, followed by Giorgio, who looked tired. My mother appeared a moment later.

'Diana, there you are! I'm going back to London. Charming though this place is, rather as I imagine the House of Usher, I fancy a wink of sleep wouldn't come amiss. You're looking very po-faced. You must lighten up and stop being such a killjoy.'

'You haven't combed the back of your hair and your hem is down.'

'Oh, bugger! Who cares? Thank Min for having me, won't you. Peter seems in a mad hurry so I can't stop. I'll send a postcard. Byeee!'

I put on a mac and gumboots, called Ham and went out to wave Peter off. Thunder rumbled continuously not far off and a yellow, lowering sky threw down a steady rain. Mother sat next to Giorgio in the front. They were too busy talking to notice me. Peter, sitting in the back, waved and blew kisses until they were out of sight. Immediately, a police car came into view. They must have passed with difficulty just before the gates. I slipped away with Ham round the side of the house and walked down to the lake. I wanted to say a proper goodbye to the garden.

The light was brassy and livid, the surface of the lake pocked by rain and ruffled by wind. I waved to the children, who were sitting on the window-seat of the boat-house. Soon my hair was soaking but I didn't care. The swans were drifting in the eddies at the edge of the lake where the tall reeds were whipped by the sharp gusts. I wished we'd had a party on the island. It obviously wasn't going to happen now. I didn't think I'd be coming back for a long time. I walked for half an hour round the lake and down to the woods. Ham was the best companion I could possibly have had. Above all I didn't want to see

Robert. I hoped he'd go without coming to say goodbye. The moment I hoped it, I felt that if he didn't say goodbye I should be broken-hearted.

The walled garden looked orderly and promising. George Pryke had nearly finished the pergola. All the uprights were in. I would have given anything to see it with the cross-beams up and smothered with wisteria and roses. We'd put new pea-gravel on the old paths, I wanted to see them edged with catmint and lavender. The hazel wigwams for sweet peas and runner beans looked charming unclothed but I longed to see them covered with flowers.

I went into the greenhouse and sat by the stove in George's wicker chair. I put my head in my hands and sobbed. Then I stopped abruptly, sickened by my own self-pity. I was becoming a compulsive crier, soon to rival Florence Dombey . . . not so much a watering-pot as a watering-cart. I heard a scuffling in the corner. I hoped that George wouldn't put traps or poison down for the mice. They were a nuisance in greenhouses but I hated to think of their bright eyes, like beads of black blood, clouded with poison or their delicate necks cracked by springs. I would send Ellie a humane trap. She would enjoy catching them and putting them out somewhere safe.

I got up to check the seedlings. There was no sign of depredation. I picked up the can and began to water them. I heard the door open and I stood quite still, not looking round. I felt his hands go round my waist. He pulled me to him and I turned my face to press it against Robert's cheek.

'I'm leaving in a few minutes,' he said. 'I promised Frances Benson to be at Hampstoke in time for dinner. I've already packed a bag and put it in the car.'

I nodded my head. I felt exhausted.

'From there I'll go on to Cambridge. I'll be there when you get home. We'll have a drink.' His voice was very tender. 'Perhaps something to eat. You might be tired after the journey. Then we'll make love.'

I turned round to face him. 'What? Are you mad?'

I was angry. To place temptation before me when I was struggling so hard with my own selfishness and desire seemed like cruelty. Robert was temperamentally indecisive. I knew it was up to me.

'Probably.' Robert spoke with great emphasis, as though trying to convince himself. 'But for once in my life I'm going to act without thinking. I'm going to follow my instinct. Everyone else seems to do as they please. I've been too cowardly, perhaps even too lazy, to resist the pressures to conform.'

'No, you haven't, you idiot! You've tried to behave decently. Not hurting other people. And so have I! What else *is* there but an idea of human decency? Whether you call it God or good behaviour, what's more important than that? Not sexual gratification.'

'It isn't just a question of sexual gratification. I've grown to love everything about you. I've tried not to. I've tried to tell myself that you were a managing woman, selfishly independent and dictatorial. And that I had everything a man could resonably want to make him happy. That to ask for more was absolute greed. I've tarnished your image and blackened your name in conversation with myself. I've done my best to dislike you very much.'

I couldn't help smiling. 'I remember. You were so angry and resentful.'

'It was pride. I'd always seen myself as a man unlike others. I was ascetic, self-controlled, judicious. The moment I saw you my self-esteem was under attack. While it remained sexual desire I had some chance of denial. But, despite my best efforts, the feelings grew more intense . . . deeper. When we danced together at that dreadful ball at St Lawrence's I admitted to myself that there was a powerful attraction. I had to admit, too, that you were much more than a beautiful woman. But I was already, even then, far gone in love as well as self-deception. When I held you in my arms, in the lane on the way to the station, it was blindingly clear to me. I'd been dragging myself around like an animal with a broken back. I tried to tell myself I was depressed because of Gerald. But it was you I thought of. Your face, your body, your voice. Everywhere I looked I saw you. I lay in bed and conjured you up. You were with me at school, in the car, in the library.'

He held me tighter and I knew my resolution was weakening. I closed my eyes and listened as he told me everything I had so badly wanted to hear.

'I was thinking of you then, when I was walking down the road with Ham. Min had told me you were coming back. I was terrified, wondering how I was going to hide my feelings. I was going to be very distant with you and spend all my time in the library and the garden. Then I looked up and you were there. What I saw then, on your face, convinced me that everything I'd thought before that moment was meagre, illusory. I don't know any more what I can or should believe in. I shall be absolutely lost without you.'

'Don't make it harder. If you knew how I . . .' I stopped, feeling a violent inclination to out-do Florence.

'Go on. Say it. Tell me you love me. I want to give you everything I have.'

His arms were still around me. I opened my eyes and looked into his face which was very near mine.

'But, darling Robert, you've already promised to give it to Min.'

'Oh, shut up! Shut up!'

We kissed as passionately as though the word Min was on our lips and we were crushing it out of existence.

Could these feelings, perhaps the best of me, be wrong . . . inadmissible? It was too late for self-sacrifice. We probably wouldn't be happy but I didn't care. I couldn't give him up.

A tremendous crash made us jump apart. A pile of seed trays, which had been stacked beneath the bench, spilled onto the floor and Ellie followed after them.

'I didn't mean to listen,' she said, her face crimson as she rose from her hands and knees. 'I know it's wrong to eavesdrop. I came in to water the seeds. Then I saw Daisy and I hid under the bench to surprise her. When I heard her crying, I didn't like to come out. Then you came in and it got worse and worse.' Tears were pouring down her face now. 'You're going to leave Mummy and William and me and go away with her. I'm going to tell Mummy right now what you've planned because I can't *bear* her not knowing what you . . . you two murderers are going to do!'

'Ellie! Darling! No, we won't . . .' I put out my hand to stop her.

'Don't talk! Don't talk . . . you! I thought you were my friend! I want you to die!'

She ran out into the rain and the door banged after her. Robert and I looked at each other. His eyes were filled with tears.

'You see, darling,' I said, slowly. 'It can't be.'

'She's young. She doesn't understand. She'll get over it.' But I knew he didn't believe it.

I didn't say anything. I didn't need to. Of what use was love if it failed to reveal us to each other?

'Go now. Go and see Gerald's mother. Let me talk to Min. Don't let her see you unresolved . . . hesitating. When you come back tomorrow I'll be gone and you'll be stronger. We'll get over it in time. You'll repair things with Min. She'll forgive you sooner than she forgives me. I've finished myself with her. How stupid of me. I've shut myself off from the two people I love best in the world. But you'll have each other.'

As I said it I felt the aching chill of intense loneliness. I shivered.

'My darling,' he put his arms round me again. 'Don't look like that. What have I done?'

The words were like a door closing and I felt myself to be already alone, on the outside.


# CHAPTER TWENTY-SIX


When Robert had left me I finished watering the seed trays and filled the can with fresh water so that it would be at room temperature for the next sprinkling. I envied the hands that would do it. I closed the door of the greenhouse behind me for the last time. The rain was still streaming down and the path swirled with olive-coloured water up to my ankles. I ought to face Min and get it over as soon as possible. My mouth was dry with anxiety. What could I possibly say in my own defence? I couldn't think of anything. Except perhaps that most people in our situation would have found the occasion to betray her more completely by making love. How absurd that so much hinged on that act. Our hands had touched (not good but not really bad), our mouths had touched (that was much worse). But something was saved because the most intimate parts of our bodies had not conjoined. It was ridiculous. The betrayal had taken place in our minds, in our desires, in the fact that

Min was not a part of those thoughts, something more passive even than exclusion.

I told myself firmly not to be such a bloody coward. Min would have every right to be furious and there must be no retreating from her rage into self-protecting remoteness. She would want to hurt me and I must be hurt.

But the house was deserted. All the guests had gone. Dirty plates, glasses, knives and forks stood in piles about the kitchen. There was a note from William to say he'd gone back with Vivien and would we collect him after supper. Of Min and Ellie there was no sign. I ran upstairs and searched all the bedrooms. Then I went through the downstairs rooms again. I opened the front door and saw Robert getting into the Morris Traveller. For a moment, when he saw my face through the streaming rain outside the car window, his expression changed from sorrow to hope. It was obvious that he thought I'd changed my mind. He opened the door.

'I can't find Min and Ellie. I'm worried. Help me look for them.'

He turned off the car engine, got out and ran back with me to the house. We searched it again but without result.

'Where could they be?' I couldn't think clearly.

'Let's try the boat-house. We'll see if the Land Rover is there first.'

It was. We ran down to the lake through rain that sluiced in sheets down our backs and over our bent heads. The thunder had returned and was much nearer.

'Robert! The boat!'

In the middle of the lake was the rowing-boat, revolving and see-sawing on the choppy water. Empty.

'Could they have gone out? Not in this weather, surely!' I raised my voice to make myself heard.

'It couldn't have broken free by itself. The doors were locked. Someone has been out in it. But where are they now?'

We looked at each other. A sickening fear, which was almost a certainty, seized me and would not be reasoned with. We slid down the bank to get out the other boat. It was an older, heavier craft but watertight.

'I'll go. You stay on the bank,' shouted Robert.

I ignored him and got into the boat, pushing my streaming hair out of my eyes. The plait had long ago come undone and I tried to tuck the heavy strands down inside my mackintosh so that I could see. I wondered what had happened to the band that had fastened it and then thought how odd it was that trivial things always spring to the forefront of one's brain whenever events become dramatic or dangerous.

Robert took the oars and I sat in the stern. He pushed us away from the bank with one oar and began to row steadily out towards the other boat. The wind was blowing against us and with every stroke chill water spurted over us. Lightning trickled into the ground continuously, and the sky flashed from grey to violet. I had quite lost my fear of the storm. I imagined Maggie Tulliver and Tom on the flooded Floss. For them the drowned embrace is something of a solution and a deliverance. But George Eliot glides over the last struggle, the suffocation, the agony. Suppose Min had drowned? Robert would be mine. I bit my lip with shame and tasted blood.

As we neared the other boat I leaned over one side, staring into the tawny, churning water. We reached it and I grabbed the painter which was trailing loose. I suppose we'd both thought that someone might be lying in the bottom of it, unconscious or terrified, but it was empty. I fastened the painter to the tiller housing. Robert rowed on and I continued to gaze into the water, bent like Gaffer Hexam to the same task but unlike him, reluctant, shrinking, fearful of finding the terrible prey. Fragments of branches and strings of black weed bobbed like apparitions beneath my eyes and bubbles from the oars, like migraine-induced peripheral images, shivered and burst before I could focus on them.

Suddenly I saw a hand twelve inches or so beneath the surface of the water. A child's hand. I reached down until the side of the boat pressed through my mac and dress and bruised my rib-cage painfully. Oh God, don't let this be! God help me! I think I said it aloud. I stretched down again. Robert was beside me. With his weight the boat leaned over and I caught the hand only to feel it slip away from me. I screamed aloud and reached down until my chest and heart were tearing with the strain. Up it came, a hand and arm, and lay in the bottom of the boat where I had flung it in horror. I looked. It was a piece of white, plastic piping, two or three inches in diameter with one end frayed, which looked like fingers.

For a few minutes we sat still and let the wind blow us in circles. I was crying. I don't know what Robert was doing. For the time being our love was not enough. We were each alone with our shock and relief. Then I felt the motion of the boat change and I knew that Robert was rowing for the shore. The boat bumped against the bank and I lifted my head. Robert jumped ashore and then held out his hand to me. The next minute I was in his arms. We were too exhausted, too chastened, to kiss. The struggle on the water, goaded by fear and guilt, had killed desire. I knew that the passion had begun to die from that moment as though it were a fire on to which stifling dust had been thrown.

Ham ran to greet us as we walked back to the house. The telephone was ringing. I was first to reach it.

'Hello?' I was surprised to hear my own voice.

'It's Min. Hello? Daisy? Are you still there?'

'Min! Yes!' I paused. 'Is Ellie with you?'

'Yes. What's the matter? You sound odd.' A pause. Then more sharply, 'Has Robert gone?'

'Yes.'

Robert and I looked at each other in the gloom of the hall.

'Where are you?' I said.

'I'm at Mrs Butter's. Didn't William leave a note?'

'Yes. But it didn't mention you. He asked to be picked up from Vivien's house after supper.'

'Typical. Well, I hope you weren't worried. Mrs Butter's GP rang up and asked if anyone could go and sit with her. She's had some sort of nervous collapse. Her neighbour found her and rang for a doctor. But the neighbour couldn't stay and Mrs Butter asked for you. I couldn't find you anywhere so I thought I'd better go. It got rid of the last of the guests, anyway.'

'But the Land Rover's here.'

'I got Lawrence to give me a lift. I was pretty plastered. I thought I'd better not drive.'

'I see.'

My wits had deserted me.

'You do sound peculiar.' There was a note of annoyance in Min's voice.

'Sorry. A bit tired.'

'Can you come and pick Ellie up? I couldn't leave her alone

in the house. Vivien had already gone with William. Ellie seems rather upset. I don't know why.'

'I'll come straight away. Give me the directions.'

After I'd put the telephone down, Robert and I walked out to the car together.

'I'd better get a move on,' he said. 'I shall be late as it is.'

'Yes. Goodbye.'

'Goodbye, darling.'

He hesitated and then kissed me. He got into the car and I watched him drive away.

I noticed that the rain had slowed to an intermittent drizzle. I went upstairs and put on dry clothes, towelled my hair and in five minutes was starting the Land Rover. I found Mrs Butter's bungalow easily. Mrs Butter was sitting upright in a chair, as stiff as a doll, her mouth moving constantly as she engaged herself in conversation. Min looked relieved to see me. I told her to take Ellie and the Land Rover and go home. I would stay with Mrs Butter. Min protested but I insisted. For one thing, I knew Ellie would hate to be alone with me. She hadn't looked at me once and her face was set in an expression of sullen resentment.

'Well, you won't have to stay too long,' said Min, getting up and putting on her coat. 'The district nurse is coming round and they've sent for Roly.'

'Fat lot of good he'll be,' I said.

This conversation took place in a whisper but Mrs Butter caught the world 'Roly'.

'Is Roly coming? Have they sent for him? I doubt he'll be cross.'

Min and Ellie said goodbye and left. Mrs Butter didn't seem aware of their going.

'Are you afraid of Roly?' I asked, imagining that he might be something of a bully as well as greedy and unprincipled.

'Nay! Nay, my duck! But he's always telling me to be sure to take me pills. Only I could make such a lot of brass selling them, like.'

'Selling them?'

I was confused.

'Selling them at the comp. Yon friends of William's. They sold them to the other children as purple hearts. They weren't, of course. I knew they wouldn't do the children any harm.'

'So you've been selling your pills to boys at William's school. And obviously you haven't been taking them yourself.'

'I'll say this for them, though they're a nasty colour, I feel better with them pills than without them. I haven't felt so good these last few weeks. Sort of troubled and bothered-like. But I wanted the money for Roly.'

'You told me the other day he was thirty-six. Surely he can take care of himself by now.'

Mrs Butter said, in a confidential whisper, 'he were always delicate as a lad. Couldn't play games. His chest.'

My idea of Roly changed from a large, oily spiv to someone shorter and altogether weedier.

'Mrs Butter . . .'

'Rosa. You can call me Rosa, seeing it's out of hours.'

'Rosa. You mustn't sell them any more. I'm sure that Roly and the doctor would agree with me. You need them. And they may not be very harmful to the children but they certainly won't do them any good. Some children might get sick on them. You wouldn't want that.'

'No, I wouldn't want that, no ways.' She seemed to be wandering again and pulled herself together with an effort. 'Children are nothing but worry. And when I don't take yon pills I worry until I'm half-crazed. I shouldn't have wed the first time. But I wanted to be respectable. Ma always said, "Rosa, my girl," she said, "you keep yourself respectable and no bad'll come to you." I loved my ma. She had six of us and hands never out of water.'

Mrs Butter talked and I encouraged her by asking questions about her family. I was glad to be distracted. When the district nurse came with a new supply of pills, together with the neighbour, who said she'd stay for a while, I was reluctant to leave. The district nurse gave me a lift back to Weston Hall.

'She'll be all right again with the medicine. I'll call every day to see that she takes them and the doctor will give her a good talking-to. She told me she'd been selling them. She doesn't seem short of money to me.'

'No. But she sends money to her son who's always out of work.'

The nurse made a sound of disgust with her tongue against her teeth but said nothing more. The gates were closed as usual so I walked up the drive. I remembered walking up the drive with Robert. Ham came running up, wagging her tail and jumping up as though she hadn't seen me for days. I was terribly tired. I hoped that Ellie hadn't spoken to her mother on the journey home from Mrs Butter's. I didn't feel strong enough to stand up for myself.

I let myself in through the back door. Min was lying on William's sofa asleep. There was no sign of the children. I looked at Min's face for a long while. I'd forgotten how familiar it was to me. I seemed, in loving Robert, to have forgotten her. I reached for the blanket, which lay on the arm, to cover her but she opened her eyes.

'Daisy.' We looked at each other. 'I was waiting for you,' she said eventually. 'We ought to talk.' My heart began to beat faster. It was coming . . . that which I had so dreaded from the moment of realising that I loved Robert. Min got up and stretched. 'I'm dreadfully sleepy. I've got to the age when I can't drink without being terribly tired later on. God, how middle-aged!'

'I'll make some tea,' I said, reassured by the friendliness of this.

We sat at the table while Min yawned and stretched and combed her hair with her fingers.

'I had a telephone call yesterday. From my editor. She's thrilled with what I've done on Madam de Staël. They want me to do the rest of the series.'

'Min! I'm so pleased! You deserve it, you've worked so hard. I hope they're going to pay you lots of money. Why didn't you tell me?'

'I didn't even tell Robert. I wanted to think about it. The money's quite good, actually. Jessamy Foster, that's my editor, says I ought to go to some of the relevant libraries in France. Especially Paris and Geneva. I told her I couldn't leave the family for more than a week. She seemed to think we were living in the dark ages and that now women just went and did what they needed to do for their soul's salvation. Of course if you'd come and look after everyone, I could go. Perhaps for a couple of months.'

She looked across the table at me, her blue eyes dark. I couldn't tell what she was thinking. I imagined living at Weston Hall for weeks, without Min. Robert and I would be lovers, of course. It wouldn't be possible for us to resist. For a few seconds I imagined being in his arms. William and Ellie would become accustomed to seeing us as a couple. When Min came back the alteration in all our circumstances would be completed, perhaps relatively painlessly. It was a perfect solution. Robert and I would be happy. Min would have the work which meant so much to her. And the children . . . I remembered the moment on the lake when I had thought that my selfishness and weakness had brought about Ellie's death. I had prayed to a God I hadn't known I believed in not to let it be true. And it hadn't been.

'I'm so sorry, Min, but I really can't do it. I'm afraid I must spend the next six months in Cambridge and get my book finished.'

'Really?'

'Really.'

To my amazement Min suddenly put her head on her arms and sobbed.

'Min, darling! I'm so sorry! Look, don't be so upset! There's always a way round. You could advertise for a housekeeper, perhaps. Or you could go for a shorter time. It would still be useful. Perhaps two shorter trips?'

'Shut up, you fool!' said Min, lifting her face, down which the mascara ran like trickles of ink. 'I'm crying because I'm so bloody relieved!'

'I don't understand.' I got up and fetched a handkerchief from my coat pocket. 'Here you are. It's clean.'

'Oh, for God's sake! We don't all have your obsession with things being clean. Bugger this mascara! I wear it so seldom that I always forget I've got it on. Do I look ridiculous?'

'Spit!' I said, holding the handkerchief under her mouth. She spat dutifully and I wiped her face.

'You're just a frustrated mother, aren't you?' said Min, with a laugh. 'You don't want all these men. It's babies you want.'

'Have you been drinking?' I asked, quite tenderly, and couldn't understand what there was in that remark to make Min laugh and cry at the same time.

'No, I haven't but I will. Open a bottle.'

I did so and when Min had taken a sip or two she said, 'I was just being noble, you see. Getting out of the way so that you and Robert could be happy together and screw the living daylights out of each other.'

Every hair on my body stood on end and prickles ran up and down my skin. I lifted my glass to my lips with a hand that trembled, and took a sip.

'What did Ellie say?'

'Ellie? What has Ellie to do with it?'

'She . . . oh, nothing. I don't know what I'm talking about . . . I'm so tired.'

'If you mean did Ellie tell me you and Robert were in love with each other . . . no, she didn't. Does she know?'

'Yes.' I thought I'd better be truthful. 'She overheard us saying . . . that we mustn't . . .' I couldn't finish.

'Ellie didn't need to tell me anything. I've known for weeks. Ever since the day when I blackmailed Vivien into paying William's school fees. Don't you remember? I said as a joke that if you and Robert had fallen in love with each other, it might justify a severance of fifteen years. Something stupid like that. I was rather drunk. You must remember!'

'Vaguely.'

'The expression on your faces was enough. You both looked so sad and so frightened . . . so guilty . . . that I knew at once what had happened. I was terrified. I came out here, to get cigarettes or something, and was sick.'

'Oh, Min, I . . .'

I put out my hand but she sat back in her chair and took a gulp of champagne.

'I was sick with fear. Suddenly Robert didn't belong to me. I thought I couldn't survive without him. But I told myself not to panic. I needed time to think. So I went back into the drawing room and pretended that I hadn't noticed anything. I went on pretending. It was quite easy. Once I knew, I could see that you were so besotted with each other that you were both dreaming, wool-gathering, lost to the world.'

'I didn't realise,' I said slowly. 'But I suppose it's true.'

'Of course it's true. I made a study of it. I'm an authority on living with two people who are crazily in love with each other but who, for reasons no doubt highly laudable, aren't allowing themselves to give it physical expression. You couldn't hand each other the butter dish without going into a fantasy of longing. I saw it all. I saw how you made that garden a substitute for making love. It sounds mad, but that's what it was. I've been in an agony of jealousy and insecurity but, like most suffering, it sharpened my perceptions. The garden was a kind of love-making, as was your loyalty to me. You denied yourselves the thing you most wanted and because your object was the same . . . to save hurting me . . . you fell in love all the more. I'm right in thinking you haven't actually . . .'

'No! No, we haven't!' I was pathetically eager to reassure her.

'Well, it *almost* wouldn't matter if you had. I mean, what's so particularly dire about the friction of two bodies when the act of love has been performed in every other way, in the imagination and in every single transaction between the two of you? It's the acknowledgement of love, perhaps even just the recognition, which is the betrayal.'

'I thought exactly that today. Though I've clung to the idea that without going to bed I was still behaving properly, I knew it was a lie.'

'Well, it's good to know we're thinking along the same lines.'

The bitterness in Min's voice made me shrink but I told myself I had earned every drop of acrimony.

'I'm so . . .'

'Don't tell me you're sorry! I couldn't bear that! Knowing that you *were* sorry made me feel even more humiliated and excluded. I was consumed again by jealousy but this time I thought it would finish me off. Daisy. So beautiful, so vulnerable . . .'

'Vulnerable?'

Despite myself I was offended.

'You may know how to make puff pastry but you know nothing about yourself. Of course it's that combination of proud beauty and pathetic vulnerability that wins the day. I can see it. I can even find it touching myself.'

'Oh Min! You hate me. I can't blame you.'

'Let me finish. I was being disembowelled by jealousy. I couldn't sleep at night because of it. Work was my only refuge. I worked my head off to escape the misery. But I remembered last time. The quarrel about Hugh, I mean. The jealousy that made me so ashamed, so sick of myself, that was so self-destructive. I was determined not to let it happen again. So I used my brain. I know that you didn't, either of you, want this to happen.'

'Oh no . . .'

'All right! Let me finish. And I knew . . . really . . . that there was no hostility in it . . . against me. That you were the best friends I had. And that you were denying yourselves what you wanted more than anything in the world out of love for me.' I longed to confirm this, to assure her of our unchanged affection, but Min wanted to talk and it was the least I could do to let her. 'I knew that because five years ago I fell in love with someone myself. He taught English at Robert's school. I was mad about him. I used to pretend, when I was making love with Robert, that it was David. He begged me to go to bed with him. I said I couldn't. But every time I saw him I felt myself weakening. Just when I decided that everything else could go to hell and I would, he suddenly chickened out. His wife had got suspicious. He was afraid of her. I was furious and relieved, at the same time. It didn't matter. I got over it. But I know that what I felt about David had nothing to do with Robert and that it's quite possible to be in love with two people at once. Or six or seven probably.'

'Yes, I think that's true.'

'Well, once I'd got that far, though it still hurt like having teeth pulled, I thought I was getting to grips with you and Robert being in love with each other. And I could see that you were rather well-suited. You're very alike in many ways. So I thought my self-esteem might feel better if I got out of the way. It's not very amusing to play gooseberry. Jessamy's suggestion about going abroad seemed heaven-sent. But if you'd said yes to it, I think I might have stabbed you with the bread-knife. It's impossible not to mind one's husband being in love with someone else.'

'If I'd said yes, I think you *should* have stabbed me with the bread-knife. But nothing will happen between Robert and me. I do love him. This hasn't just been a piece of idle, capricious vanity. But . . . I don't suppose you'll believe this . . . you're just as important to me. You're such an enormous part of my life. I can't stand the thought that I've wrecked it all again. Even if there's no chance that you'll ever forgive me, I still have to go on trying.' I paused for a moment. 'I'm in awe of what you did just now. I could never have risen to such heights.'

'Well, I'm not sure that we don't both come rather well out

of it,' said Min. 'We've managed to cling to the vestiges of reasonable behaviour. It says something for education, perhaps.'

'Or perhaps just age and experience.' I finished my glass of champagne and poured another. 'It will be a long time, I know, before we can see each other again. But perhaps, do you think . . . one day, you might be able to forgive me?'

'Oh, have another glass of champagne and stop looking so miserable! Yes, I don't know why but I can. I do. You're still the best friend I ever had. I just wish you weren't a loose cannon as far as men are concerned.'

I laughed as I knew Min meant me to, though I could have cried as easily.

'So do I. I don't like being alone. I used to like it but I don't any more. I dread going back to Cambridge. I ought to move. Go back to Oxford, perhaps.'

'Well,' said Min slowly, prompted, it must have been, by sheer kindness, 'I suppose you have to go tomorrow . . .?'

'Oh yes,' I said before she could finish. 'I must do that. Don't worry. I'll pick up all the old contacts. It isn't that I don't know lots of people.'

'I know what it is,' said Min. 'Montaigne said about his friend Etienne de la Boétie . . . "si l'on me presse de dire pourquoi je l'aimais, je sens que cela ne se peut exprimer qu'en répondant, parce que c'était lui; parce que c'etait moi.' Love . . . including friendship . . . is involuntary, irrational, spontaneous. You can't analyse it.'

'I suppose it is that very quality of inward instinct about friendship which makes it so precious. How often I've struggled for it and failed. And yet the candidate, male or female, has had every qualification. But it hasn't been enough.'

'And so we shouldn't chuck out all those years for something we none of us wanted to happen and couldn't help.'

'Do you think we can really go on being friends? Of course it couldn't be just as before . . . you're bound to mistrust me.'

'I don't see why. You didn't make love with Robert when you might have. I ought to trust you, perhaps more than any other woman I know.'

I remembered Florence Dombey, the watering-cart, and controlled myself.

'God, I'm exhausted!' I said.

'Me, too. We ought to go to bed.'

'Where are the children?'

'William rang up just before you got back. He's staying the night with Vivien. I sent Ellie to bed. She was tired out.'

I didn't say anything. I would try and put things right with Ellie before I left. The pain of parting, of separation, threaded all my dreams that night.

## CHAPTER TWENTY-SEVEN

I packed my clothes before breakfast. Ham watched with the despondency that comes over all domesticated cats and dogs when they see suitcases. I took my luggage downstairs and left it in the hall. I made some porridge and fried some mushrooms and bacon. I couldn't eat anything myself. I felt sick with the misery of leaving Weston Hall.

'That smells good,' said Min, just as she always did when she came in. 'God, how I'm going to miss my cook!'

Then she came up and put her hand on my shoulder and pressed her face against mine briefly. When I turned round with the pan of porridge Ellie was there, standing in the doorway. She looked anxiously at her mother and then at me.

'Ellie.' I decided to risk frankness. 'Your mother and I have had a long talk. She knows all about everything.'

Ellie sat down at the table, glanced, very frightened, at Min and then down at her porridge which I'd just put in front of her.

'There's nothing to worry about,' I continued. 'I'm going away today and I shan't come back for quite a time.'

Ellie looked at me as though she didn't understand.

'You'll be in charge of Booty and Tabitha but I expect Mummy and Daddy will help you.'

'I will,' said Min. 'You must help us to remember, darling.'

Ellie put her head on her arms and broke into loud, heart-rending crying.

'Isn't Daddy going away then? I thought he was.'

'No, darling.' Min put her arm round Ellie. 'Daddy's staying with us.'

'I'm so very sorry to have hurt you,' I said.

Ellie continued to press her face into her arms. The telephone rang. I went to answer it. It was Vivien.

'Hello, Dahlia. William tells me you're leaving today. What time?'

'I don't know. I'll have to ring the station.'

'I'll come to lunch. You can catch an afternoon train. I'd like to say goodbye. I suppose this means it's Paradise Lost?'

'You're being mischievous, Vivien.'

Really, I thought, she was too bloody accurate.

'Chicken, eh?'

'Is that a request for lunch?'

Vivien laughed, delightedly. 'I'm going to miss you very much, Dahlia. You're a girl after my own heart. If only you weren't quite so goody-goody.'

'Thank you. I'll miss you, too.'

'Poor darling! You're not to pine. Shall I come and stay and bring you delicious details about Robert?'

'I should enjoy that very much.'

'All right. See you around twelve. Nothing too fatty. I'm on a diet.'

The line went dead. I went back into the kitchen.

'Vivien's coming to lunch. We'd better get on with the washing-up. I'll make a tomato tart.'

'I'll start on the glasses. Poor Vivien. She knows it'll be her last decent meal here.'

For some reason this struck us both as funny and we giggled like idiots. I made some pastry and reduced two tins of tomatoes with onions and garlic and a splash of red wine. I stirred in some eggs and chopped rosemary, then I filled the pastry with the mixture and made a lattice of anchovies on the top.

'That looked simple enough. I ought to be able to do that,' said Min, who had watched the procedure, while washing and drying glasses.

'Of course you can. I'll leave you my cookery books. I hope Ellie's all right.'

'We had a little talk. I explained everything as much as I could. But she's too young to understand, really. These glasses

360

seem to be multiplying as fast as I wash them. If only Mrs Butter were here.'

'Morning, ladies,' said Mrs Butter, appearing in the kitchen as swiftly and unexpectedly as though summoned by magic.

'Rosa! I mean . . . Mrs Butter. Are you well enough to come in today? Shouldn't you be resting?'

'I said I'd come up and do a couple of hours to help clear after the party. I'm feeling right as rain. Laugh and grow fat, I say.'

She looked thinner than Ham's collection of favourite sticks but her hair was miraculously back to blonde and she was dressed quite soberly. She took the drying-up cloth away from Min and replaced it with a clean one.

'You wash, dear, and I'll dry. Happen a glass needs a good rub . . . not that dabbing I see you doing.'

With Mrs Butter's help we managed to finish all the washing-up by a quarter to twelve. While she washed the floor, Min laid the table and I made a salad of things left over from yesterday's party. As I was taking the tart out of the oven Vivien and William arrived. Vivien looked hungrily at the tart.

'I won't bother with an aperitif, Minerva. We'll eat straight away, shall we?'

'But Vivien, it's only twelve o'clock,' Min protested.

The back-door bell rang.

'That'll be Roly,' said Mrs Butter. 'He's come to fetch me home. He's early. He'd better come in and wait while I finish up, if that's all right.'

I went to let him in, preceded by Ham who threw herself in a senseless frenzy against the door, barking. With one hand on her collar, I manged to get the door open. I'd expected a man wearing either a T-shirt with an amusing slogan on it and a crew-cut, or a very broad-striped suit, with slicked-back hair. I was so surprised by his actual appearance that I let Ham go.

'Be quiet! Lie down! Roly said authoritatively, in a voice of impeccable refinement.

Ham wagged her tail at once and tried to ingratiate herself by whining and dribbling. I might well have dribbled a little myself. Roly was tweedy, well-shod and elegant, with straight, dark-brown hair flopping slightly over a high forehead and a pair of blue eyes, intelligent and friendly.

'Mrs Weston? I've come to pick up my mother.'

'No, Diana Fairfax. I'm staying with Min ... Mrs Weston ... that is ... I was ... I'm leaving today ... Do come in.'

He politely ignored my confusion and followed me into the kitchen.

'Oh, Vivien, this is Roland Butter ... Mrs Weston Senior ...'

'No, actually it's Roland Milne. Stanley Butter was my stepfather. Luckily,' he added, looking at Min, whose eyes were perfectly round with astonishment. 'It would have been a ridiculous name. My friends call me Rollo.'

'There you are, my duck,' said Mrs Butter, coming in with her coat on. She beamed adoringly up into his face and he bent to put his arm round her.

'It was good of you both to sit with my mother last night. I'm grateful to you for looking after her.'

Min nodded, still too much in shock to speak. It was as though Prince Charming had claimed kinship with Mother Goose.

'Unfortunately,' continued Rollo, 'I can't stay and keep an eye on her and make sure she takes her pills. But the district nurse is going to call every day. I'm so glad she has this job, anyway.'

'Your mother is wonderful. I honestly couldn't manage without her,' said Min, gathering her wits.

'No more you could, dear, and that's a fact. Mrs Weston's like you, Roly. Head in a book, life in a muddle.'

Rollo looked at Min with amusement, but didn't contradict his mother.

'Are you staying to lunch?' said Vivien to Rollo, whom she'd been eyeing with something like approval. 'I'm very hungry and I'd like to begin my last edible meal at Weston Hall.' She sighed dramatically and Rollo, as he was bound to do, looked rather surprised. 'Diana's going back to Cambridge this afternoon and Min's taking over the cooking again. If you can call it cooking. *C'est effroyable!*'

'Yes, do both stay,' said Min.

Rollo considered the proposition.

'No, I'm sorry. I would have liked to but I must be in Cambridge myself by this evening. Do you have a car?' he turned to me, 'or can I offer you a lift?'

'You're going to Cambridge? Oh, but what an amazing coincidence!' said Min.

Rollo looked at me.

'Really?' I murmured. 'Good heavens, that would be marvellous! I was rather dreading the train. All those changes with so much luggage. Do you have room for several suitcases? Oh, I'd forgotten! There's Freddie.'

'Well, he can come, too, if his legs aren't too long. He'll have to squash up in the back.'

'He's a kitten. His legs are only four inches long at present. Are you sure you don't mind cats?'

'Not a bit. But would you mind very much leaving more or less straight away? We can drop my mother off and then get a spot of lunch as we go. I've got to stop somewhere briefly on the way.'

'No. Certainly. I'll get my luggage. His basket is in the hall. Has anyone seen my coat?'

'You two get on the road,' said Min. 'I'll take Mrs Butter home. It'll only take five minutes and it'll do Vivien good to work up an appetite.'

I went out to fetch Freddie. Of course he hated being put in the basket and mewed with ineffectual pugnacity. Beyond the front door Rollo was loading my suitcases into the boot of a shining, dark-blue Jensen. Had he bought this from the hard-earned savings of his mother? I asked myself, disapprovingly. My suitcases, the cat basket, shuddering with bellicose protests from Freddie, and the cat litter tray (about which I felt more than apologetic), filled every available space that was not taken up by Rollo's own luggage.

'I do hope you won't regret having me as a passenger,' I said, surveying with some dismay the aforementioned articles plus a bottle of milk, a cat dish and a saucer of foil-wrapped cooked meat.

'I'm quite certain that I won't,' Rollo said, opening the passenger door for me.

Min, Vivien, Mrs Butter and William were standing in the drive to say goodbye. I was dreadfully sad that Ellie wasn't there. Vivien embraced me and said that she would come and stay shortly as the place would be horribly dull without the scandalous intrigues that seemed to follow me about. This was for Rollo, I knew, but he was bending down to fiddle with his windscreen wipers and seemed not to have heard. William said he'd send me a drawing of the walled garden as soon as it looked at all interesting. Mrs Butter shook my hand and gave Rollo a hearty kiss. Min suddenly threw her arms around me. Neither of us could speak. I got into the car and we drove away, Freddie pummelling the door of the cage with frantic paws and Ham running after the car, barking.

For some way we drove without speaking. Then Rollo said, 'Would you like to borrow my handkerchief?'

'Thank you. I've stupidly packed all mine.' After a minute or so's dabbing I said, 'I feel a perfect fool.'

'"Her salt tears fell from her, and soften'd the stones" . . . now that's *Othello*, I think.'

'Yes.'

This man was certainly full of surprises. I puzzled over the disparity between the man and his mother's idea of him. Suddenly I said, 'I've heard that name before. Roland Milne. You didn't write that very good book on Spenser?'

'Yes. If you thought it good, I'm flattered.'

'I can hardly believe it! Then you were the lecturer who had flu. Because that lecture was cancelled, I went to the reunion at St Hilary's and met Min!'

'I did have to cancel a few lectures in January . . . yes.'

I was silent for a few minutes taking this in. Then I said, 'But if you're a lecturer why are you always . . . oh dear, how rude of me. Of course it's none of my business.'

He probably had a wife and ten children to keep. Though Mrs Butter hadn't said anything about him being married.

'Why am I always what?'

'Well, don't be offended. But your mother is always worried about your . . . financial status.'

Rollo sighed. 'She doesn't think what I do is a proper job. My father was something of a bibliophile . . . purely as a hobby. He never did a day's work but lived off the estate. He sold off more and more land to pay for the keep of his horses, his cellar and his library and when he died every-thing had to be sold to pay his debts. The shock of being in debt almost finished my poor mother off. She'd been brought up to consider respectability everything. She had a nervous *crise* and literally went bald. Alopecia. It was the end of a very unhappy, mistaken marriage. There was enough salvaged for Mother to live comfortably. And when she married Stanley Butter there was more than enough to spare. But she couldn't get over it. She's always considered books the tools of the devil.'

'Poor Mrs Butter. And she works so very hard to get money for you.'

'Which I put straight back into her account. She never notices. She doesn't understand sums. She never could add up even before she became ill. She left school at thirteen and went into service. My father was the son of the house. My grandfather was killed in the First World War. By the time my mother was seventeen and had risen from scullery-maid to being my grandmother's maid she was terribly pretty and my father was just down from Oxford. He fell madly in love with her. I've seen photographs of her. She really was bewitching. I'm not boring you?'

'I'm as bored as a woman with her foot stuck in a railway track who sees an express train rushing towards her.'

Rollo laughed. I admired his blue-and-white striped shirt. He was certainly what Min would have called a dish.

'My father tried to seduce her but she was firm. It was marriage or nothing. He was an impetuous, obstinate man. So he married her. The shock killed my grandmother. My father came into the estate and expected my mother to be its chatelaine. Of course, she had neither the education nor the experience. You can imagine how difficult it was for her. By the time I was born, the great love was over and my father had begun to live his life as though he were a bachelor again. He had mistresses and brought them to the house while my mother and I lived a backstairs life. He didn't bother to divorce her. He had a legitimate son and that was all that he wanted from any marriage. He liked variety and my mother was much too afraid of him to protest.'

I glanced sideways at Rollo. He looked rather bitter.

'You didn't like your father?'

'I hated him.'

'How old were you when he died?'

'Seventeen. I was in my last year at Eton. Luckily there was a trust to provide for my education so he couldn't spend that. My father never allowed my mother to visit me there. And I'm afraid I would have been very ashamed of her if she had. I wasn't a very good son when I was younger. I used to make her cry, I know. I hope I've made up for it since. If one ever can make up for those kind of injuries.'

'She adores you. She just wishes you'd settle down to a steady job.'

Rollo laughed. I liked his laugh . . . it was very whole-hearted.

'I know she's been upset because I've been undecided about my future plans. I've been offered a fellowship at Balliol. But there's also a chance to go to Harvard. I couldn't make up my mind. Also I've wondered whether I really wanted to go on being an academic. I wouldn't mind writing thrillers or doing something quite different.'

'I suppose everyone has fantasies of breaking out, breaking free. I do myself. But I don't expect I ever will.'

'Tell me about yourself.'

It didn't take long to tell. I gave a brief recapitulation of the facts. He looked as though he thought that there might be more but was too polite to press for details.

'It sounds a perfect existence,' he said, at last. 'Intellectual stimulation, living in a beautiful city, freedom to indulge pleasures and tastes.'

'Very much like yours,' I pointed out.

'Yes, I suppose so.'

'Do look at those hills.' Ahead of us was the Ribblesdale Valley and rising to our left was the great bulk of Whernside. A shifting beam of light played across its gaunt shoulders, lifting muted colours to Pre-Raphaelite brilliance. 'What a crime to be miserable when there is this!'

'Are you miserable?'

'No.'

We drove south, our speed increasing as the roads broadened and straightened. Rollo was relaxing to be with. I liked him. I told him quite a lot about the weeks at Weston Hall. He was very amused by my description of my mother and her departure with Peter and Giorgio.

'I hope they won't all descend on you. It sounds as though they're in for some hair-raising episodes. Odd, isn't it, how some people never protect themselves? They run from disaster to disaster.'

'I think it's because they're afraid to be alone. So they have to have someone . . . anyone. They can't stop to analyse what made the last disaster.'

'I think I'm the opposite,' said Rollo, putting his foot down as we came at last to some motorway. 'I'm too circumspect. It isn't often I follow an impulse. In fact I can't remember when I last did, before today.'

'What did you do today that was impulsive?'

'Tell you later. You don't strike me as impulsive either. You seem pretty much in control.'

'You'd think so, wouldn't you?' I laughed. 'But my worst fault, so I'm always being told, is that I take myself too seriously. I lack detachment. I'm quite capable of behaving like an absolute idiot.'

Rollo gave a mock-shudder. 'Good Lord! You're on your own there. Can that really be your worst fault? You must be an angel. I'm full of faults. I've got something of a temper. And I'm not at all forgiving. I give up on people too quickly if they offend my sense of what is right or good or beautiful. I'm impatient. Often a bit arrogant. Certainly selfish. The list is endless.'

I began to think that Rollo must be homosexual. It was scarcely possible that so much self-awareness could be found in a heterosexual male. And then he was so easy to be with and talk to. Companionable like Peter. Nor was he flirtatious. I stole a sideways glance. His hair was well-cut, as were his clothes, his nails were clean and his general appearance elegant without being affected. The thought was gloomy. The moment I registered the gloom I was amazed at myself.

'Are you forgiving?' he asked, unconscious of my examination.

'"Reason to rule, but mercy to forgive: The first is law, the last prerogative."'

'Pope?'

'No. Sounds like him, doesn't it? But it's Dryden. I don't think there's been much for me to forgive other people.'

'Except your parents, from the sound of it.'

'Curiously, I forgave them a long time ago. My father was so obviously an unhappy man, so inept, so repressed by his own fears that I could only feel sorry for him. And anyway, he's dead. My mother is so blatantly frightened and vulnerable, it would be like not forgiving a baby. No, I think it's been more the other way round. I've just had an unparalleled lesson in forgiveness and very humbling it's been.'

'What was it?'

'Tell you later.'

I thought about Min. Our friendship had certainly taken a hammering. Was friendship like steel, all the stronger for tempering? I should have liked to consult Rollo but I didn't want to appear in an unfavourable light. I was surprised at myself again. It was hardly possible that in the first grief of parting from Robert I should be attracted to someone else. But then as Min had said, desire, passion, love were not exclusive emotions. I reminded myself that Rollo was almost certainly homosexual.

'I read somewhere recently,' said Rollo, 'that John Stuart Mill was looking over the manuscript of the first volume of Carlyle's *French Revolution*, of which there was no copy. He went out, leaving it lying on a table. His maid, thinking it was scrap paper, burned it. So violent was JSM's remorse that Carlyle had to spend hours consoling him because he was afraid that JSM might do away with himself. Now that's a pretty good lesson in forgiveness. What about some lunch at that pub?'

We sat at a table by the window and shared a bottle of wine and ate bread, cheese and tomatoes while we continued discussing Carlyle, about whom Rollo had reservations. I admire Carlyle so we had a very satisfying argument and I forgot entirely about Weston Hall and everything I was leaving behind. Then while Rollo paid the bill, which he insisted on doing, I went out to attend to Freddie. We'd given him the run of the car to stretch his legs and I'd covered the back seat with newspaper for his food and tray. He was very pleased to see me and I felt treacherous, returning him to the basket he so hated. I hoped that now he was full of meat and milk he would sleep.

When Rollo came out I suggested driving part of the way myself and he accepted the offer at once.

'To tell you the truth, I'm exhausted. I drove all the way up to Dunston Abchurch without a break last night and then I didn't get to bed until two, as Mother was still rather manic.'

This willingness to let me drive seemed to be depressingly conclusive as far as Rollo's sexual inclinations went. I took the wheel with a pleasure that was some small compensation. I've always liked driving and this car leapt like a tiger. Rollo closed his eyes but insisted he wouldn't sleep in case I got tired myself. Within minutes he was breathing steadily and gently and didn't stir for two hours, after which he woke with a start.

'Oh Lord, I'm sorry! Was I snoring? Are you exhausted?'

I reassured him on both points but as soon as we changed over and I got back into the passenger seat I fell asleep myself. At least, it was like a long dreaming doze from which I was powerless to rouse myself but during which I dipped in and out of consciousness, hearing the sound of the engine, knowing I was in a car and that Rollo was beside me.

When I finally climbed to the surface, opened my eyes and sat up, the afternoon light was fading. I looked at my watch. It was six o'clock.

'Where are we? Shall I take over?'

'We're fifteen miles north of Oxford.'

'Oxford?'

'Yes. I did say I had to stop off on the way. The house is just along here. I hope you don't mind?'

'Not at all. But I must let poor Freddie out soon.'

'You can bring him in. We can make sure all the doors and windows are closed.'

'Are you sure they won't mind?'

'They?'

'The people whose house it is?'

'Quite sure.'

The road narrowed and then became a lane. We turned off between two stone pillars and followed a drive, weedy and overgrown. Then a sharp bend brought us up before the house. The cool, dim light revealed a handsome stone front. The porch was supported by two corbels on which sat griffins or chimerae, I couldn't quite see which. Ivy and an old, neglected wisteria grew across the mullioned and transomed windows.

'What a wonderful house! It's very old, isn't it?'

'Yes. The undercroft is fourteenth century. It was built originally as a priory. Then it became the manor for Shinlake. The same family have lived here for hundreds of years but the last of them died a few months ago.'

'Who owns it now?' I asked and immediately, before he'd spoken, I knew the answer.

'I do. Let's go in.'

Carrying Lord Frederick and his equipment, we let ourselves in and closed the door. It was very dark. With the aid of a torch, Rollo found a light switch. A naked bulb revealed the mouldering beauty of the ancient house with all the theatricality of a stage-set.

'This is the biggest room downstairs. The drawing room, I suppose,' said Rollo, opening the shutters. 'The ceiling is coming down a bit in that corner.'

'Oh, but the plasterwork is wonderful. Look at those bosses! And the frieze! This chimney-piece is quite beautiful. What's under these dust covers? Can I look?'

Rollo lifted a sheet and revealed a stuffed sofa, covered in rotting, cobwebbed silk. A smell of dust and decay combined with the general all-over smell of damp.

'I expect a lot of the furniture will be too far gone to be restored. This looks rather good, though.'

He had pulled off a dust-sheet which concealed a square piano. He played a few notes.

'It'll have to be restrung. I think some of the hammers are broken,' he said, running up and down a scale and producing something resembling a tone row. 'The house can't have had anything done to it for years. I used to come and have tea with Miss Raybrock, the last owner. She loved Spenser and liked to talk about him. I used to read *The Faerie Queen* to her and bring her chocolate cake. I was absolutely astounded when her solicitor wrote to tell me she'd left me everything. There are no relatives apparently. Let's let Freddie out and feed him. I want to show you the rest of the house before it's too dark.'

Freddie was ecstatic to be out of the cage and threw himself on to the saucer of food with loud purrs. I put down his tray and some water.

'I suppose he'll be all right. There's glass in all the windows?'

'I don't know. You're the first person I've brought here. I only got the key a couple of days ago.'

After satisfying ourselves that there was no possible exit for Freddie we closed the door on him and went on a tour. Rollo showed me the room where he and Miss Raybrock used to have tea. It was a small room, green with the last rays of the leaf-filtered light, charmingly panelled but spoiled by an electric fire and a television. On the footstool in front of the only comfortable chair was a folded rug. On the arm of the chair was a pair of spectacles. A book lay open on the seat. Rollo picked it up.

'*Venus and Adonis*. She was a remarkable woman.'

He replaced the book and we went through the rest of the house. The kitchen was large, stone-walled and stone-flagged. It had an iron range running almost the whole length of one wall and a huge dresser stacked with china on another. Everything was covered in dust and plaster-thickened cobwebs. In one corner of the kitchen was a single electric ring and an electric kettle. In the sink were a cup and saucer and a plate with a fragment of toast crust.

'An arachnologist would love this house,' I said. 'Well, anyone would love it, really. It must be the most beautiful house I've ever seen.'

The dining room was under shrouds but had a fine stucco ceiling similar to that of the drawing room. After looking into a small square book-room whose contents were swollen with damp and tumbling on to the floor, we went upstairs. Rollo opened the shutters in one of the larger bedrooms.

'Come and look,' he said.

Below us, in the garden, were huge shapes billowing like giant green waves on a swelling sea.

'I think it was all clipped once,' said Rollo, leaning on the sill beside me. 'Is it possible to cut yew hard back?'

'Oh, yes. You can cut it right back to the main trunk, if necessary. You'd have to have trestles and planks. Those hedges must be twelve or fourteen feet high. I wonder how old they are.' I glanced at Rollo. He was looking at me with a suggestion of inquiry which seemed unrelated to the yew hedges. Then he gave me a brief, enigmatic smile. He continued to look thoughtful while I pointed out to him what had probably been the original plan of the garden below. I had the impression that he was only giving me half his attention.

There was no sign of Freddie in the drawing room. We looked under the covers, up the chimney, beneath the sofa, inside the piano. Then, just as I was starting to get really anxious, I heard a mew above my head. There was a wriggling bulge between the top of the lining and the curtain heading.

'He's inside the curtain,' I shrank from the idea of venturing into that entomological vivarium.

'Stand back,' said Rollo. 'An academic's life offers few

opportunities for heroism. I've always fancied myself as the Red Cross Knight.'

He emerged a moment later with Freddie.

'You take him. I need a drink.'

He returned from the car with a bucket. Inside were two glasses, a bag of cold water and a bottle of Bollinger.

'This was ice a few hours ago,' said Rollo, laying aside the plastic bag of water. 'I persuaded the landlord of the pub where we had lunch to make me an extemporary fridge. It seems to have worked. Not perfectly cold but cold enough.'

He opened the bottle and gave me a glass. Coming at the close of an exhausting day, tinctured with every kind of emotion, it tasted delicious. Freddie, perhaps seeing Rollo as a saviour, curled on to his knee to sleep.

> 'Is this small ball of fur a noedipus,
> Or just a budding feline Oedipus?
> Will he with lavish milk by you supplied,
> Quickly forget his new-left mother's side?
> Or complex-fixed, become a groedipus?'

'Don't tell me you made that up on the spur of the moment,' I said, laughing.

'No, I'm afraid not. It's a long time since I wrote any poetry. But I've got a very good memory and other people's does me fine.' He stroked the small curved spine with one finger.

'Won't this house be rather expensive to restore?' I asked.

'I should imagine so. I inherit twelve thousand pounds with the house but I don't suppose that'll go very far. I feel slightly daunted by the size of the operation. I've wondered whether to put the house on the market and go to America and forget the whole thing.'

'Oh, but . . . how sad, when Miss Raybrock wanted you to live here! At least . . . oh, I suppose that's a hopelessly sentimental attitude.'

'It is. But I feel the same. Of course, I could accept the fellowship here and restore the house gradually. Do you think that's what I ought to do?'

I didn't answer at once. He wasn't looking at me. He had one long elegant leg crossed over the other. One hand cradled Lord Frederick. The other held the champagne. He looked very relaxed. I wished that he was less ambiguous, less inscrutable. No doubt he was just being polite in seeking my advice.

'It would be what I would do in your place. But that isn't the same thing. I don't know you well enough to answer your question.'

Rollo looked at his glass intently. Then he smiled and turned his head to look at me.

'A very fair answer. Now we must drink up and get going. It'll take two hours to get to Cambridge.'

It was almost dark as we joined the road to Buckingham. Freddie was asleep on my knee, having made a disgraceful fuss about the basket. The lights of the car threw our surroundings into obscurity. We were enclosed, alone. For the time being I was happy.

'What are you going to do in Cambridge?' I asked.

'I'm going to stay with an old friend of mine. I haven't seen him for a long time. He's nearly eighty. It was time to look him up. I'm delighted to have the excuse.'

'Excuse?'

'I told you I'd been uncharacteristically impulsive today. When I heard you were going to Cambridge I decided to take you. I *was* going to a dinner in Oxford. I cancelled it from the pub at lunch-time and arranged the visit to Theo Lang instead.'

'I don't know what to say.'

I stopped myself from grinning ear-to-ear.

'You needn't say anything. Don't feel pursued or harassed. I intend to be strictly cautious from now on. I don't understand it . . . but, standing in the kitchen at Weston Hall, something prompted me to consider an immediate decision as exigent. I knew it was the tide in my affairs, anyway, which taken at the flood might lead on to fortune. Or something even better. Nothing that has happened today has made me regret my impulsiveness. Don't be alarmed. You can tell me to get lost.'

'I won't do that.'

'Good.'

We drove on in silence for a while. Then Rollo said, 'Shall we have dinner tomorrow? I've arranged to stay for two nights.'

'Yes. I'd like to.'

We fell back into companionable silence. Then Rollo asked me if I was cold. I found I was but hadn't noticed it, being so absorbed in my own thoughts. He put the radio on. The Third Programme was playing Mozart's Flute and Harp Concerto. Freddie stirred slightly and settled again. I thought about Robert, Min, and the children. Then about Shinlake Manor, my book, my mother, very briefly, and Peter and Giorgio. Then I thought about Rollo and there my thoughts rested.

Too soon, we reached Cambridge. Rollo helped me with my luggage.

'Lovely house. Like you. Goodbye, Freddie.'

I was holding Freddie so that he wouldn't rush out into the street. Rollo stroked Freddie's head, then held my hand briefly.

'Goodbye, Diana. Eight o'clock tomorrow?'

I nodded. Just as the door closed behind him, the telephone began to ring.

'Daisy?' said Min's voice. 'You have all the luck! Tell me *everything*.'